Praise for the award-winning master of suspense
ROCHELLE KRICH

"One of America's finest suspense novelists."
Carolyn Hart

"The Mystery Woman who can do it all . . .
Krich knows how to make conflicts
between good and evil juicy."
Los Angeles Times

"Krich takes on dysfunctional families, child abuse,
domestic violence, mismatched relationships, emotional
battering . . . The author sees a bigger picture and uses
her craft to select and showcase the best ways to
illustrate her observations about society."
Houston Chronicle

"A funny, savvy, dedicated detective . . . With Jessie
Drake, Krich presents an appealing, believable sleuth."
Virginian-Pilot and Ledger-Star

"Admirers of mystery at its most provocative
will thank this author."
Publishers Weekly

"Her touch is deft and skillful. All successful
mystery writers lend a certain flavor to their stories,
and that's what creates a devoted following. Krich
has simply found a fresh path."
Charleston Post and Courier

Books by Rochelle Krich

WHERE'S MOMMY NOW?
TILL DEATH DO US PART
NOWHERE TO RUN
SPEAK NO EVIL
FERTILE GROUND

In the Jessie Drake Series

FAIR GAME
ANGEL OF DEATH
BLOOD MONEY
DEAD AIR

Short Stories

"A GOLDEN OPPORTUNITY" (SISTERS IN CRIME 5)
"CAT IN THE ACT" (FELINE AND FAMOUS)
"REGRETS ONLY" (MALICE DOMESTIC 4)
"WIDOW'S PEAK" (UNHOLY ORDERS)
"YOU WIN SOME . . ." (WOMEN BEFORE THE BENCH)
"BITTER WATERS" (CRIMINAL KABBALLAH)

ROCHELLE KRICH

A JESSIE DRAKE MYSTERY

SHADOWS OF SIN

Rochelle Krich

AVON BOOKS
An Imprint of HarperCollinsPublishers

AVON BOOKS
An Imprint of HarperCollins*Publishers*
10 East 53rd Street
New York, New York 10022-5299

First Avon Books paperback printing: July 2002
First William Morrow hardcover printing: October 2001

Avon Trademark Reg. U.S. Pat. Off. and in Other Countries, Marca Registrada, Hecho en U.S.A.
HarperCollins ® is a trademark of HarperCollins Publishers Inc.

Printed in the U.S.A.

10 9 8 7 6 5 4 3 2 1

For Hershie—
So fine.

If a man will have a wayward and rebellious son, who does not hearken to the voice of his father and the voice of his mother, and they discipline him, but he does not hearken to them; then his father and mother shall grasp him and take him out to the elders of his city and the gate of the place. They shall say to the elders of his city, "This son of ours is wayward and rebellious; he does not hearken to our voice; he is a glutton and a drunkard." All the men of his city shall pelt him with stones and he shall die; and you shall remove the evil from your midst.

Deuteronomy 21:18–21

Acknowledgments

To all those who so graciously and generously shared their knowledge: Janice Steinberg; Mary Hanlon Stone, Deputy District Attorney, for her legal acumen; Dr. Sara Teichman, for her psychological insights; my son, David, for his Talmudic lore; Dr. Barry Fisher, D.P. Lyle, and Mike Bowers, for their forensic expertise; LAPD Detective Al Delgado, Wilshire Division, and Detective Mark Fleishmann for some fine points of police procedure.

To Rabbi Yitzchok Adlerstein, Jessie's spiritual guide, and to Detective Paul Bishop, West L.A. Division, Jessie's mentor; they both help her "walk the walk" and keep her from stumbling too often.

To my agent, Sandra Dijkstra, for her wisdom and indefatigable enthusiasm.

To my editor, Jennifer Sawyer-Fisher, for her keen eye, warmth, and good humor, and for her patience while I was struggling with the title of this book.

To all the booksellers who have introduced me to new readers and have given me sound advice and support.

To the many readers who have brought me into their worlds and have entered mine.

To the special "buds" in my life, for providing cheer and laughs and virtual shoulders to lean on way into the night; and to the mah-jonggs, who make Mondays the highlight of my week and provide me with popcorn and laughs and friendships that I hold so dear.

Finally, to my family—truly, precious gifts.

Thank you.

Rochelle Krich
www.rochellekrich.com

SHADOWS
OF SIN

❖ 1 ❖

MINUTES BEFORE MARIANNA Velasquez's head slumped onto her desk, streaking blood into feathery fingers across the lined pages of the daily appointment book, she had been stamping envelopes while offering comfort through the phone to her eleven-year-old son, Alejandro, home from school with a stomach virus that had kept mother and son up all night.

The piercing whine of a saw coming from the adjoining offices had almost drowned out the chime announcing the opening of the door to the waiting room. Marianna looked up and pursed her lips, annoyed with this patient who had arrived late after insisting on the last appointment.

"No milk or cheese, just dry toast and tea," she reminded Alejandro. "I'll be home soon, *querido*." He sounded so miserable. She was loathe to hang up and wished she were home to comfort him.

Returning the receiver to the cradle, she forced her lips into a smile. She was not indifferent to the suffering of others but sometimes, like now, felt a twinge of impatience with patients—among them, she'd been surprised to learn when she'd first begun working here, a fair number of men—whose vanity made them risk cosmetic surgery and whose "emergencies" weren't always that. Envy, perhaps, she admitted, of those who could afford what was in many cases a luxury while she was just beginning to make ends meet.

And the boy had been so listless this morning, his dark brown eyes deep pools of sadness, his chalk white face a stark contrast to the thick, glossy black hair she had smoothed off his forehead while he was retching, poor thing.

All this flashed through her mind as she looked through the open reception window toward the door and the person who had entered. Her greeting froze in her throat, and she stared uncomprehending, mouth open, at the gun.

She had seen guns before in the gang-ridden East Los Angeles neighborhood of her childhood, and later, in Pico-Union, an area she had finally escaped as a single mother with Alejandro. She had shoved him countless times onto the threadbare carpet of the tiny bedroom they had shared, had covered his small body with her own when shots had rung out in the early evenings, a grim coda to her lullaby, or awakened them both in the middle of the night, leaving them huddled together waiting for a cease-fire. She had never thought to worry about her safety in the offices of a Century City plastic surgeon, and if she hadn't been so terrified she might have pondered the rich irony.

"Please," she whispered. Her heart was pounding against her ribs, her body stiff with fear. An inadequate, stupid word, she knew. She wanted to ask, "Why?" She wanted to say, "Let me help you, you don't want to do this," but the words wouldn't emerge, and she sensed that they, too, would be powerless against the dead expression of the eyes looking at her as though she didn't exist.

Inching her hand to the right, she pressed the intercom button to alert the doctor, who was in his office reviewing patient files with his nurse.

"Don't tell him I'm here." The voice was as dead as the eyes.

"I won't." Her fingers jerked back, as if singed by contact with the phone. She darted her tongue across her lips, terrified that at any second the doctor's response would testify to her lie.

The phone remained silent, and for the briefest moment she allowed herself hope—what did this have to do with her, after all? But the eyes told her she was deluding herself. She clutched the gold cross, embedded with tiny diamondlike glass chips, that Alejandro had proudly given her last Christmas, and she was praying for herself and for Alejandro, so young to be orphaned, when the bullets tattooed the hollow of her neck.

Her head fell forward, but she was aware that the door to the inner offices had been opened. Moments later, against the piercing aria of the nurse's hysterical shrieking, she heard the doctor's voice, steady and reasonable ("Let's stay calm, all right?" "If you put down the gun, I know we can talk this through, all right?"). Both voices were abruptly silenced by another round of gunshots (or was it the drilling next door?), followed by a duet of screams that subsided into a single moan.

Marianna's body was shaking with a leadlike cold that had begun to numb her fingers and toes but had not yet doused the needles of fire in her chest. She heard feet pounding past her toward the exit from the suite, the slamming of the heavy door. Finally, through the intercom, she heard the doctor's raspy voice—too late! too late!—increasingly desperate but more distant and faint with each "Marianna! Marianna!" like the dying, plaintive echoes of a bell tolling her name.

Or maybe it was her mother, calling her home.

❖ 2 ❖

THERE WAS SOMETHING obscenely incongruous, Jessie Drake thought, about finding bodies brutally shot to death in the beautiful twenty-fourth floor Century City offices of a plastic surgeon. She voiced this in an undertone to her partner, Phil Okum, who nodded but kept his attention fixed on the medical examiner's gloved hands, busy with their preliminary exploration.

Looking around, she tried to imagine the room's preshooting appearance and noted the decorative details that had barely registered when she'd arrived over an hour ago.

Lush yellow, maroon, and gray cabbage roses blooming in profusion on the chintz of the overstuffed love seat. A handsome mahogany desk and chair. Two wood-backed armchairs upholstered in yellow and burgundy stripes. A silver tray centered on the polished mahogany credenza held a floral porcelain tea set (the Limoges pattern was one that her mother, Frances, had long admired), and ornately framed reproductions of Cassat and Monet watercolors hung on two of the banana-colored papered walls.

A third wall was taken up by a picture window that on a clear day, Jessie supposed, offered a view of Santa Monica and a tantalizing hint of the Pacific. Not today, though. It had been a hazy November morning and afternoon, with the temperature in the low sixties and the timid sun held captive behind a semiopaque curtain of smog that had erased half the city.

The overall effect of the room's decor, inviting and gracious, had been fatally marred by gunfire that had riddled the love seat, armchairs, desk, and artwork with bullet holes, and by the presence of the two bodies being probed by the medical examiner while Scientific Investigation Division (SID) technicians finished dusting for fingerprints and collecting evidence. That, and the rank perfume of fresh blood and death that made Jessie's stomach churn even after fifteen years on the force and a generous protective dabbing of Vicks in and around her nostrils.

The tea set had survived intact, orphaned, its delicate beauty grotesquely out of place amid the shambles.

The diplomas—they, too, had come under assault—were on the wall behind the desk. From the pocked parchment behind the shattered glass, Jessie had learned that Ronald Bushnell, M.D., had been certified by UCLA and was a member in good standing of the American Board of Plastic and Reconstructive Surgery. He had also received an impressive number of awards and commendations, including one for his work with burn victims.

On the credenza, near the tea service, was a silver-framed photo of a grinning, tanned, strikingly handsome Bushnell in a gaudy Hawaiian print shirt, his thick, dark brown hair ruffled by a breeze coming off the wave-capped green ocean in the background. One arm was around the waist of a tall, broad-hipped blond woman, the other around a reed-thin adolescent blond girl. Wife and daughter, presumably.

The man on the bloodstained, pale yellow rug was Bushnell, but whatever tan he'd possessed had been leeched by death, leaving his face a sickly blue-gray. He'd apparently tried to get help—a phone lay next to him, the receiver off the hook, the transparent flat cord stretched taut across the desk, straining against the wall jack.

Blood had darkened the front of Bushnell's china blue shirt. It had forever stained the white blouse of the woman in the far corner of the room. More blood had been sprayed on the love seat, armchairs, and ceiling, and smeared in wavy rows along the wall down which the woman had slid to the hardwood floor. She had been found slumped forward, her head with its bright auburn curls bowed, a dejected Orphan Annie sent to the corner for some nameless infraction and for whom the sun would not come up tomorrow or any other day.

"I thought she was a patient," Edie Colton, one of the West L.A. patrol officers who had responded to an anonymous 911 call, had told Jessie and Phil when they'd arrived. "But the gal down the hall said she's a nurse. Nicole something. Doesn't know her last name, though."

Her name was Nicole Hobart, and she was thirty-five, Jessie had learned from the woman's driver's license, which she'd found in a purse in a lower cabinet in the small rectangular reception office. My age, Jessie had thought, with a flutter of discomfiture. The nose in the license photo looked fuller and longer, the cheekbones less pronounced. Bushnell's work, maybe. Perks of the job?

Jessie had found the other dead woman's purse, too. Marianna Velasquez, twenty-nine years old. The receptionist's head was obscuring the bloodied pages of the appointment book, but Jessie would have to wait until Henry Futaki, the M.E., had examined the body before she could check the book to see the entries of today's patients.

An SID crime scene tech had photographed the bodies, offices, and bloody shoe prints in Bushnell's office and on the patterned carpeting running along the hall. He'd placed lettered plastic tags next to the fingerprints on the doorknobs to the waiting room and Bushnell's office (probably a useless effort, given the number of patients and staff who had touched the knobs), the shoe prints, and the numerous bullet holes—evidence that couldn't be recovered and booked. Another tech had collected blood samples from the shoe prints with a cotton-tipped applicator dipped in distilled water. Numbered plastic tags, used to mark evidence to be picked up and booked, had been placed earlier next to the three dozen-plus bullet casings, which had already been secured in evidence bags.

Using graph paper and a tape measure, Jessie and Phil had drawn to scale both rooms and their furnishings and the positions of the bodies, which they had been careful not to disturb. Waiting for Futaki to finish, Jessie was studying the ceiling in Bushnell's office—you never knew what evidence you might find on ceilings, she'd learned—when the medical examiner rose from what must have been an uncomfortable squat.

After peeling off and disposing of his gloves, he approached Jessie and Phil, careful to avoid the lettered tags next to the footprints. He was thin and short—an inch shorter than her five feet six—and was dwarfed by Phil, six four and burly, an imposing figure even after losing fifteen pounds over the past two months through serious dieting and exercise prompted by an episode that turned out not to be a heart attack but could easily have been one.

Futaki had assumed his customary frown, merging his brows into one dark, unruly bush that overpowered his small, almost dainty face. He cleared his throat in a way that smacked of self-importance: pay attention because I'm not repeating this.

"The woman was shot in the chest and abdomen," Futaki began in his dour monotone, as though he were alone at his desk, dictating into a tape recorder. "It would appear that she died almost immediately. The man was shot at closer range, in the chest, head, and genitals."

"Ouch!" Phil grimaced and held his large hands over his crotch. "That's gotta hurt."

"Unless he was already dead?" Jessie glanced at the body and the black trousers camouflaging the bloodstains.

"The profuse bleeding in the genitals would suggest that his heart was still pumping."

Futaki directed this to Phil, clearly ignoring her, but she'd expected rudeness and refused to let it bother her.

"The head wound, however, appears to be postmortem. I

won't know for certain until the autopsy," Futaki continued. "The star-burst splitting indicates that there was direct contact between the barrel of the gun and the skin."

"Execution style," Jessie observed, addressing Phil.

The contact wound explained the bloody shoe prints leading from Bushnell's body out of the room and down the hall. The patterns of the soles suggested that the prints had been made by an average-size athletic shoe. One pair of shoes, as far as Jessie could tell. One shooter. An SID criminalist would make the determination.

"Definitely sending a message." There was no banter in Phil's voice now. "But what? And for who?" He played with his reddish brown mustache.

"That's your department, not mine," Futaki said. "Call Western Union—better yet, AOL. You might get a faster response." His short laugh sounded like a sea lion's bark.

Not even remotely funny, Jessie thought, suppressing a groan, but Phil chuckled and shook his head appreciatively, scoring a half smile from Futaki.

"Play the game," he'd urged her more than once. "Would it kill you to make nice?" Well, she'd tried "nice" over the years, and Futaki had never thawed. Maybe because she was taller than he was, maybe because she'd ended a relationship with a cop who was his close friend. Maybe because he thought women on the force should be sitting behind a desk or directing traffic. He wouldn't be alone in thinking that.

"What else can you give us?" Phil asked.

"I can't tell you which victim was shot first, and without an autopsy I can't determine cause of death. In all likelihood, the chest wound for the male, the abdominal wound for the female. But don't hold me to it."

"Time of death?"

"What do you have?" Futaki asked.

"Nine-one-one got an anonymous call at four forty-one. Aside from that, nothing. Most of the offices on this floor are closed for the day. The few that are open are way at the end of the hall. Plus there's construction going on in the office next to this one. Bottom line, no one heard anything." Phil shrugged. "Can you pin it down any closer?"

Futaki referred to his notebook. "No rigor yet in either of the victims. The body temperature of the male is ninety-six point seven. The female, ninety-six point nine. Based on that, the approximate time of death is an hour and a half ago, or a little after four. But there are variables."

Like the amount of clothing the dead person is wearing, or any illnesses he or she may have, or the room temperature. Following death, Jessie knew, the body cools approximately 1.5 degrees Fahrenheit per hour under normal circumstances, with the assumption that the body's temperature at death is 98.6 degrees.

"You mentioned that Bushnell was shot at closer range," she said. "How close?"

Futaki pursed his lips, as if annoyed at being reminded of her presence. "Without knowing the kind of weapon used, it's difficult to be exact." His tone implied that an experienced detective would have known that.

Screw you, she thought. "Was there stippling?"

"I *did* find stippling on his neck and chest, none on the woman," Futaki allowed grudgingly. "I'd say the woman was more than five feet away from the shooter. The male, between one and three feet."

"That fits." Phil nodded. "We found over three dozen casings just inside the room, about two feet from where Bushnell's blood trail starts."

"There's no blood on or around the doctor's chair," Jessie said, "or on the wall behind the desk. So he wasn't hit at all while sitting there. Maybe he approached the shooter to try to reason with him or her."

"Or disarm him," Phil added. "Any sign that they struggled?"

Futaki shook his head. "No defense or hesitation wounds. No tissue under Bushnell's nails. No scratches, bruises, et cetera. None on the woman, either. I found no powder smudging on the male to indicate he was close enough to struggle for the weapon when he was shot." He closed his notebook and slipped it into a pocket. "I'm going to examine the other victim. I'll try to do the autopsies by Friday."

"I was hoping for sooner," Phil said pleasantly.

Futaki glowered at him, his joined eyebrows forming a vee. "It's Monday, and I'm drowning in bodies. Do you have *any* idea how backlogged I am? We're understaffed, underfunded, and everybody wants answers yesterday."

"Me, I'm easy. I'll settle for tomorrow." Phil smiled.

"Everybody wants crimes solved fast," Futaki snapped, "no one wants to pay for it. You want quicker results, get voters to put the crime lab bond on the ballot next time."

He caught the attention of an assistant who was talking to one of the SID techs. "I'm done here," he announced crisply and, grabbing his satchel, strode out of the room. The assistant hurried behind him like a puppy.

"This doesn't feel like a random shooting by some punk out to have a good time," Phil commented to Jessie. "And there's no indication the shooter was searching for something. No desk drawers or file cabinets ransacked. Drug supply seems untouched."

She surveyed the room again. "*Somebody* was pissed off."

Phil followed her gaze, and nodded toward Bushnell. "Yeah, with the doc. He was a hunk. Suppose he was doing one of his patients, and the husband or boyfriend found out. Or maybe Bushnell's *wife* found out."

"Maybe." A basic rule in a homicide investigation: check out the victim's immediate family. "Could be Bushnell botched a face or owed a lot of money. Or what if he's involved with organized crime? That would explain the shot to the head."

"You're watching too much *Sopranos*. Shooting Bushnell in his privates says the killer's beef was personal, Jess."

"Or business. 'You screw with us, we screw you.' And

you're assuming that was intentional," she added, though she didn't disagree. "Could be the shooter had terrible aim or didn't know how to handle the weapon. That could account for the whole place being shot up like Swiss cheese. Even Bushnell's diplomas." Anger could account for it, too.

"Aim seemed just fine with the humans," Phil said.

She blinked away the mental picture of Bushnell and the two dead women—their gaping wounds, all that blood—and resigned herself to another night of restless sleep. She'd asked Phil how he dealt with the images, and he'd told her sometimes he didn't. Futaki, she guessed, slept fine. He probably never thought of bodies as ever having been alive.

"Bushnell must've thought he had a chance at talking his way out of this, or he wouldn't have approached the killer." Jessie studied the rug. "I think the nurse was on the sofa when the shooter arrived. The chairs are full of bullet holes, but little blood. Lots of blood on the sofa and the rug next to it, more blood leading to the wall where he shot her again."

Phil nodded. "Bushnell approaches the shooter. Shooter takes out Bushnell, then shoots the nurse. She runs to the back to open the bathroom door but doesn't make it. He finishes her off. *Or* he does her first, then Bushnell. Depends on who his main target was."

"Bushnell. The shot to his head says so. So why shoot the others?"

"Come on." Phil flashed her an impatient look. "Eliminate the witnesses. The shooter arrived around four, probably figured the place would be more or less empty."

"Only if he or she made an appointment for that time, or knew Bushnell's schedule." Jessie considered. "Or maybe he was acting on impulse and not thinking clearly."

"There you go." Phil smiled.

She stepped aside as two men entered the room carrying a gurney and an opaque plastic sheet to wrap the body. They approached the dead woman and unfolded the gurney.

Jessie returned her attention to Phil. "Suppose the shooter wasn't impulsive, Phil. Even if he came around four, and he was the last patient, he'd have to figure there would be staff here, right?"

Phil sighed. "Are we back to this?"

"If he was angry only at Bushnell, why shoot him *here*? Why not follow him home or take him out in the parking lot? It's a big place, poorly lit, lots of shadows. Not many people around when we parked. No witnesses to eliminate."

Phil shook his head. "The shooter couldn't count on that, Jessie. And what if a security guard happened to show? As far as why not at the doctor's house, it's easier to get into his office. No alarm or locks to worry about. Just waltz right in, do the deed. If he has to take out a few more people, he doesn't care. And if it's the wife, shooting the doc and the others at the office draws suspicion away from her."

"Makes sense. But we have to consider the possibility that the shooter had a problem with the doctor *and* his staff. An unhappy patient, or an angry employee."

Phil nodded. "Lots of office shootings these days. The lawyer in San Francisco, the day trader in the south, the other guy in Hawaii. That Boston Internet techie killed seven coworkers in seven minutes. What the hell's going on, anyway?"

"Ask the NRA."

❖ 3 ❖

THE LAST PATIENT Bushnell had seen, Georgia Vale, had arrived at three-thirty. Jessie surmised this from the penciled check next to the woman's name, neatly printed in the appointment book. There had been a patient scheduled at four, Clifford Bronte, but no penciled check. A no-show, or had Bronte killed the receptionist before she could check off his name? Jessie made out the letters N.P., written next to his name in red ink that seemed superfluous amid all the blood that had obliterated the area code and first five digits of his phone number.

She copied down Bronte's name and the names and phone numbers of the other patients Bushnell had seen that day. A total of nine, since he'd been in surgery most of the morning. She found the addresses in folders stored in a bank of wood-tone filing cabinets and copied those, too. Tedious, methodical work that might provide a clue or would prove worthless. She wondered with a flash of envy what Phil was learning. He'd left a few minutes ago with Officer Colton. A possible witness, the young woman had reported excitedly.

There was no folder for Clifford Bronte, which suggested that N.P. stood for "new patient." Could be Bronte was the killer—the timing was right. Or he hadn't kept the appointment. There was nothing necessarily sinister in that. He probably wasn't the first prospective plastic surgery patient to chicken out. At seventeen, Jessie had canceled two appointments to have her ears pierced before she'd finally mustered up the courage to have it done.

A payroll file revealed that aside from the dead receptionist and nurse, Bushnell's staff had included Leanne Fialkoff, a second nurse, and Suzanne Ord, the bookkeeper who also handled medical billings and insurance. Lucky for them that they hadn't been here during the shootings.

Too many techs were crowding the receptionist's small office. Jessie took the payroll file into the handsomely furnished reception room and was copying down Suzanne Ord's phone number and address when Phil returned. Accompanying him was a muscular, thirty-something man whose brown hair was dusted with whitish particles, as if someone had sprinkled his head with confectioners' sugar. He was wearing a too-short, smudged white T-shirt that strained over a beer belly and barely met the low-slung, paint-spattered jeans weighted down by the tools in his worn leather belt. A butt crack about to happen.

He stood with his feet apart, thumbs hooked in his jeans pockets, noisily chewing gum and gawking at the SID technicians. "So this is where it went down, huh? I heard there's three people shot dead." A loud smack of the gum.

The excitement in his voice disgusted her, and she wondered how excited he'd be if he saw the carnage.

"Mr. Hopper, this is my partner, Detective Drake," Phil said. "Jessie, Joe Hopper. He's remodeling the office next door. He just returned from getting supplies and told Officer Colton he may have seen the shooter."

"Hey, I'm not *sure* it was the shooter," Hopper said, facing Jessie. His jaw worked the gum hard. Smack, smack. "I was leaving to get more drywall and tape when I almost bumped into her. She comes running out this door"—he pointed to the exit—"and jumps when she sees me. I asked her was she okay. She says she's fine and hurries down the hall to the elevator. But like I told the lady cop, she didn't seem all that fine to me."

Jessie wondered whether Hopper was remembering, or inventing for the drama. "What do you mean?"

"She was all nervous. The two of us are waiting for the elevator, and she won't look me in the face. Keeps her head down like this." He imitated the movement, investing it with significance, then looked up. "She's jabbing the button, like that's gonna make the elevator come faster." Hopper snickered. "So I say, 'It never comes when you're in a rush, does it?' Just trying to be friendly, right? Next thing I know, she walks off and takes the stairs."

To escape Hopper, or recognition? Jessie doubted that the woman had walked down twenty-four floors. More likely, she'd exited on the next floor or the one after that and had taken the elevator from there.

"I thought, hey, you wanna be a snooty bitch, no skin off my nose." The man shrugged. "There's lots of women appreciate the Hopper charm." He sounded freshly aggrieved. "But now I'm thinking, maybe she was scared I'd finger her."

"Can you describe her?"

"Like I said, she kept her head down. But lucky for you, I have a good eye for the ladies." He winked at Jessie and smiled, displaying uneven nicotine-stained teeth. "She was pretty—but not as pretty as you, if you don't mind my saying." His eyes dwelled on her chest.

"You want to be careful with that Hopper charm," she said, her voice low and wistful. "You'll have me swooning right here, and Detective Okum won't be able to catch me."

"Bad back," Phil said with a straight face.

The man looked confused, then laughed uncertainly. Color crept up his thick neck and face. "Anyway . . ." He coughed. "My guess, she's in her forties. Blond hair, the kind that's got streaks in it, know what I mean?"

Jessie nodded. Her mother and sister had frosted blond hair. Lots of upkeep. "Did you notice anything about her clothes?"

"Like blood, you mean?" His eyes gleamed with ghoulish relish that would have done a vampire proud. "Nope. She was wearing a dark raincoat, holding it together like she was freezing or something. I thought maybe she had the flu."

Or postshooting shakes. Jessie hated getting her hopes up, but this sounded promising. "What time did you see her?"

He squinted and scratched his head. The motion scattered a sprinkling of particles and raised his T-shirt, exposing a roll of Hopper flab. "Four-thirty? It wasn't before, 'cause I was waiting to hear the sports update on the radio before I left."

"Would you recognize this woman if you saw her again?"

"Yeah, sure." A firm nod, accompanied by a satisfied clack of the gum. He narrowed his eyes. "So you think she's the killer, huh? Didn't look like one to me."

Looks didn't count, Jessie knew.

"Did you see anyone else suspicious entering or leaving Dr. Bushnell's office today?" Phil asked.

"No, but I've been working nonstop next door since a little before eight with my helper. The guy who leases the space, a lawyer"—Hopper wrinkled his nose—"he's paying me a bonus to finish fast. I could use the extra money, especially since the dot-com I invested in went south. My friends made out like bandits, but me?" He snorted.

"Maybe your helper saw someone," Jessie said. "We'll need to speak to him."

"No point. He left around three to the dentist's. Or so he said. He's kind of lazy, but his work's pretty good, and I figure the next guy's not gonna be better, you know?"

"What about before you left to get the drywall, Mr. Hopper? Did you hear anything that could have been gunfire?"

"I was using a saw and drill all day. There coulda been a war going on and I wouldn't of heard a damn thing."

She asked Hopper to wait, then walked the few feet to the receptionist's office, where she pulled the files on the five female patients Bushnell had seen that day.

Hopper took his time studying the color before-and-after snapshots of the first woman. "Look at that, would you?" He whistled. "You can't tell they're the same woman."

"Is she the one you saw?" Phil asked.

"Nope. Sorry." He worked the gum again.

More no's with the four other photos. There were hundreds of files, hundreds of photos to show Hopper. Jessie hoped the two surviving members of Bushnell's staff would be able to narrow down the field—assuming that the woman Hopper had seen was a patient, which wasn't necessarily so.

She asked Hopper to wait again while she retrieved the family photo from Bushnell's office. She watched his face carefully when he studied the blond woman Jessie assumed was the dead doctor's wife.

"That's not her." Hopper shook his head but continued looking at the photo. "Nice family, huh?" he added in a low voice. He sounded sad, as if he'd finally realized these were real people, not actors in a shoot-'em-up thriller.

Phil wrote down Hopper's phone number and address, gave him a card, and asked him to phone the West L.A. station if he remembered anything else. Hopper nodded, but his attention was on the SID technicians again, and Phil practically had to shoo him out of the room.

"He's going to be bragging about this at the bar tonight," Jessie said. "Drawing in all the women with his story about how he's helping in a police investigation."

"That plus the Hopper charm. You could go with him, Jess, be his *special lady*." Phil drew out the words and grinned. "Say the word, and I'll set it up."

"Don't tempt me." Two months ago she and her crime-reporter ex-husband, Gary, had ended a months-long relationship. The first few days had been hell, and she'd been tempted to phone him; the next weeks, difficult. Most days now she was certain they'd made the right decision, but she missed the companionship and wanted a man in her life.

She was returning the files when the receptionist's phone rang. Lifting the receiver, already dusted for fingerprints, Jessie said hello without identifying herself.

It was Bushnell's answering service, a male informed her. "I'm trying to locate Ms. Velasquez. Is she there?"

"No, I'm afraid not. Can you tell me who's trying to reach her?"

"Who am I talking to?" Caution had given his voice an officious edge.

"Detective Jessica Drake, LAPD."

The operator didn't respond at once. When he did, he sounded somber. "It's her son, Alex. He sounds around ten."

A little older than her nephew. Jessie sighed.

". . . says the mother was supposed to be home over an hour ago and he knows something's wrong. He's been calling every five minutes for the past half hour, and I felt sorry for him, so I figured I'd see if she was still there."

"Do you have him on the other line?"

"Yes. Do you want to talk to him?" The operator seemed eager to pass on this heavy responsibility.

"No. Tell him you want to speak to the adult in the house."

A minute later the operator was back on the line. "He's home alone, Detective. Apparently, there's no dad in the picture, and no relatives nearby. I'm afraid to ask more questions—he's shaky enough as it is."

No father, and now no mother. The shooter, of course, hadn't considered that he was orphaning Alex Velasquez when he killed his mother. Or maybe he had, and hadn't cared.

"Put me through, please."

She felt unbearably weary and wished someone else had answered the phone. But the responsibility would ultimately have been hers or Phil's. She had told other children that their mothers would never be coming home, and each time had found it painfully difficult to choose the right words. Not that there were any. At best she would manage to get this boy to a neighbor until she or someone else could tell him, gently, in person. And locate a family member.

And then what?

"Hello? Is my mom there?" The boy's voice wobbled with hope.

"Alex, my name is Jessie . . ."

❖ 4 ❖

"CHECK OUT THE Beemer." Phil pointed to the sleek black car as he walked with Jessie two hours later across a large flagstone driveway. "And this place. Bushnell was raking it in."

"Uh-huh." The house, a two-story light stucco with a Spanish tile roof and two wrought iron front balconies, was on Palm just south of Sunset in a prime area of Beverly Hills called The Flats. And Bushnell had owned another BMW—the security guard had identified the lonely black car in the parking lot.

She rang the bell at the side of the wide double doors, and her eyes automatically moved to the right doorpost. No mezuzah, which didn't necessarily mean Bushnell wasn't Jewish. Funny, how ever since she'd affixed the silver casement housing the scrolled, handwritten parchment to her own front door seven months ago, she'd become more aware of its presence or absence on other people's doors.

"The Expedition's not too shabby, either. And I wouldn't say no to the Range Rover." Phil was looking at the silver and black cars parked next to the BMW. "Maureen's Civic is falling apart," he said, turning back. "I just shelled out a couple of hundred for new shocks, and now the transmission's going."

"Hmmmn."

"I made chief of police."

She frowned. "What?"

"You weren't listening."

"Sorry." She smiled, embarrassed. "What'd you say?"

"That I just made chief of police."

"I heard that part. My condolences. Before that?"

"Maureen needs a new car." He studied Jessie. "Still thinking about the kid?"

She sighed. "Yeah." She couldn't get his face out of her mind. Pale, almost translucent skin; large, unblinking dark brown eyes that had stared at her as he listened with a solemn maturity that had made her heart ache.

"Yeah." Phil sighed, too.

"So where are you looking?" she asked after a moment.

"Maureen's checking out used cars on the Internet. Another Honda or a Toyota."

"My sister's addicted to surfing the Web. She's been buying maternity clothes on-line, although I think she returns more than she keeps." Jessie rang the bell again, rapped the lion-faced, shiny brass knocker on one of the doors, then hugged her arms against the wind. Three cars in the driveway—*someone* had to be home.

From a distance she heard a woman's voice calling, "Coming!" Then, closer, "Can I help you?"

"Mrs. Bushnell? I'm Detective Drake from the LAPD. My partner and I would like to talk to you."

"I'd like to see identification."

Always a good idea. Jessie removed her badge and held it up to the privacy window. A moment later one of the doors was opened by the blond woman in the photograph. Celeste Bushnell—that was the name beneath Ronald Bushnell's on the checkbook they'd found in his briefcase.

She was at least five seven and was wearing taupe slacks and a white sweater that emphasized the chunkiness around her waist and hips. Probably in her early forties, Jessie guessed from the fine lines at the corners of her hazel eyes and the deeper creases running from her nose to her mouth.

She had a pretty face, but her lips were too thin, her nose somewhat thick. Surprising that she hadn't asked her husband for a little surgical assistance. Or maybe after working at achieving perfection for his patients, Bushnell had gone for the natural look at home.

"I assume this is about that woman?" Celeste Bushnell said when Jessie and Phil were standing in the wide beige-marble-tiled entry. "She phoned here yesterday, and Ronnie told her he'd call the police if she did it again. I didn't know he'd actually done it."

"Which woman is that?" Phil asked.

"Carla Luchins. You don't know her *name*?" she demanded in a tone that suggested the police were incompetent.

"Mrs. Bushnell," Jessie said.

"Look, Detective," she began impatiently, but Jessie's expression must have alerted her, because she stiffened with a little gasp and her hands formed fists. She turned to Phil. "You're here about something else, aren't you?"

"I'm afraid we have some bad news, ma'am," he said gently. "Someone shot your husband in his office."

"Shot?" She repeated the word, as if trying to decipher a foreign language. Then her eyes widened with comprehension, and she pressed her knuckles against her mouth. "Is he badly hurt?" she whispered.

"I'm sorry to tell you he's dead, Mrs. Bushnell."

She made a low, keening sound and began to sway. Jessie steadied her and put her arm around her shaking shoulders.

She allowed herself to be led like a sleepwalker to a sofa in a spacious living room whose floral-patterned decor resembled that of Bushnell's office. She sat silently, hands gripping her knees, rocking slowly back and forth. Tears streamed down her face, but she made no move to use the tissue Jessie gave her.

"When was he . . . ?" Her voice trailed off.

"From what we know, about four hours ago," Phil said.

"I was beginning to wonder why he was so late. I knew he

was going to the gym from the office, but still . . ." She cleared her throat. "Did he suffer?"

"I don't think so," Jessie said, trying not to see the grisly images. "He probably died almost instantly."

The woman nodded and shut her eyes. Jessie was about to ask her something when she heard quick footsteps coming down the staircase and along the center hall.

"Mom, I'm driving to Rebecca's to study for a math exam," a girl called loudly, her voice echoing in the high-ceilinged entry. "I'll phone you when—oh, I thought you were in your office."

The tall, willowy, jeans-clad girl standing in the graceful archway looked almost the same as she had in the photo. Sixteen or seventeen, Jessie decided, maybe a little taller, and pale now that her tan was gone.

"Adrienne, I—"

"I'll phone you when I get there, okay? I should be back before eleven."

"Adrienne." Celeste attempted to push herself off the sofa but collapsed against the plump cushions. "Oh, God!" Her face was contorted in pain, and she stretched out her hand as if reaching for a lifeline.

"*Mom?*" Darting an accusatory glance at Jessie and Phil, the girl hurried to her mother's side. A curtain of straight blond hair hid her face. "Mom, what's *wrong*?"

"Daddy's been shot, sweetheart." Crying softly, the woman drew her daughter toward her and stroked her cheek. "He's gone, Adrienne, he's gone."

"He's dead?" The girl stared, uncomprehending. She jerked her head toward Jessie and Phil, then back to her mother, and with a sharp cry, collapsed in her waiting arms.

They were wailing, hugging each other tightly. Jessie sat, acutely uncomfortable in the face of grief, as she had an hour ago in the much smaller living room of the apartment Marianna Velasquez had made into a warm home for her son. Alex hadn't cried. He had sat like a statue, his slim hands folded in his lap, not responding to the rhythmic stroking of his elderly great-aunt, who was taking him to live with her because there was no other family in America. "At least for now," she had told Jessie. "Then we see."

Jessie looked at Phil. He was stoic as usual, his lips a grim line beneath the mustache. They waited until the crying had subsided into sporadic sniffles, and mother and daughter were facing forward, their red-rimmed eyes fixed on Jessie and Phil but not, Jessie guessed, really seeing them.

"We know this is a terrible time," Phil said, "but we need to ask you some questions. When did you last speak to your husband?"

"Sometime in the late afternoon. I phoned the office to find out if Ronnie was coming home straight after work. That's when he told me he was going to the gym."

"Did he sound upset or say he was having a problem?"

"No, nothing. He sounded normal."

"I talked to him this morning, for a second," the girl said. "He wanted to talk last night, to find out how I'm doing, but I didn't have time." Her face was screwed up in pain, and her eyes welled with tears.

Celeste stroked her daughter's cheek.

"Mrs. Bushnell, you mentioned that Carla Luchins was harassing your husband," Jessie said.

"She *threatened* my father!" The teenager's dark brown eyes were intense. "She killed him, I know she did!" Streaks of rose had flushed her pale skin, like a sky at sunset.

"Adrienne." Celeste sighed the word. "Ms. Luchins was unhappy with the results of surgery my husband performed, but I don't think she meant him any harm."

"Mom, she said Daddy was going to be *sorry* for what he did to her!" She turned to Jessie. "She came here and yelled at him. I was right there. It was *awful*."

"Did your husband report this incident to the police?"

Celeste shook her head. "He threatened to, to make her stop. But he wasn't really worried." She wiped her nose with the tissue. "Ronnie spoke with a doctor who'd given her breast implants. He'd done multiple surgeries to make the woman's breasts exactly even, but she was never happy. She threatened him, too, but nothing ever happened."

"What's this doctor's name?" They would have to warn him, in case Carla Luchins was on a deadly spree of revenge.

Celeste frowned. "He told me, but I don't remember. Marianna will know. Ronnie's receptionist."

"Ms. Velasquez is dead, Mrs. Bushnell," Jessie said gently. "I'm sorry. So is Nicole Hobart, one of the nurses."

"My God!" She covered her mouth and nose with her hands, then dropped them to her sides. "My God! Who could have done this? It's . . . it's unbelievable. Why would anyone kill Ronnie and the others? *Why?*"

"Can you describe Carla Luchins?" Phil asked.

"She was in the doorway, and I was farther back in the hall, so I didn't get a close look. She was in her forties, about average height. Her hair was blond, I think."

"She had highlights," the girl said.

Was this the woman Joe Hopper had seen? L.A. had no shortage of forty-something women with frosted blond hair. "Anything else you remember about her?" she asked Celeste.

"No, nothing. I only saw her that one time."

Jessie turned to the girl. "What about you, Adrienne?"

She shook her head. She was playing with the small gold necklace hanging around her neck and seemed lost in thought.

Phil said, "Mrs. Bushnell, were any other patients harassing your husband?"

"No. But some patients weren't totally satisfied," she said in a tone that implied the fault was theirs. "People have unrealistic expectations, so they're disappointed and angry." She shrugged. "Ronnie's a *terrific* surgeon. He's helped accident and burn victims and women with mastectomies. His patients *love* him." Her tear-streaked eyes were animated, her shoulders higher.

"My dad was written up in magazines," Adrienne offered

with shy pride. "A lot of his patients are movie stars, but he never talks about what they're having done."

It was sad, Jessie thought, hearing the mother and daughter still using the present tense about Bushnell. "Did your husband mention any patients who were dissatisfied?"

"Not by name. And I can't believe a patient would have killed him. I just . . ." Her shoulders slumped again.

Maybe Bushnell's other nurse and the bookkeeper would know. It would be a long night, Jessie though. So much for relaxing over dinner with her sister and brother-in-law and nephew. A good thing she'd told Helen not to wait.

Phil said, "Mrs. Bushnell, you mentioned you phoned your husband in the late afternoon. What time was that?"

"Around four."

"Can you be more specific?"

"Is this important?" Beneath the puzzlement was a hint of impatience.

"Just trying to fix the time of death." He smiled.

"I saw clients all morning and in the early afternoon—I'm an interior designer. But my last two canceled, so I came home. That was at two."

"That's when you phoned your husband?"

"No. I went shopping. I called him on my cell phone." She furrowed her brow, concentrating. "I'm not sure if it was before or after Neiman's, and I *think* I left Neiman's around four." She looked at him. "That's the best I can do."

"It was right *before* we left Neiman's," the daughter said. "I wanted to go to Bloomingdale's, but you wanted to see if Daddy was coming home straight from the office."

"Right, Bloomingdale's." Celeste nodded slowly, as if she were finally seeing the solution to a difficult puzzle. "Then we went out to dinner. Monday nights the housekeeper's off, so we eat out." She put her hand on her daughter's. "I'll have to tell my family and Ronnie's friends. They'll want to know about the funeral. When do you think . . . ?"

"We'll let you know when we can release the body,"

Jessie said. "It'll be several days, I'm afraid. Did your husband have any siblings?"

"He's an only child. His parents both died a few years ago. His mother had a heart attack, and his father died a year later. At least they were spared this." She sighed.

"What about your family, Mrs. Bushnell?"

"My parents live in Seattle. They *loved* Ronnie." She sniffed and dabbed at her eyes. "I have a brother, Andrew. He lives in Pasadena."

"Did he get along well with your husband?" Phil asked.

Celeste stared at him, clearly offended. "Yes."

"Unfortunately, in a homicide investigation, we have to suspect everyone. Aside from Ms. Luchins, did your husband have a falling-out with anyone recently?"

"No."

A firm, automatic no, but Jessie saw a flicker in the widow's eyes. In the daughter's, too. The girl bent her head and pushed at the cuticle of her thumb.

"It's vital that you tell us everything you know," Jessie said, "even if it seems unimportant."

Celeste shook her head. "No, there's nothing."

"What about business dealings, Mrs. Bushnell?" Jessie asked, thinking about the execution-style shot to the head. "An investment that went bad? A gambling debt?"

Celeste looked faintly amused. "Ronnie hates gambling. I made him take me to the Bellagio in Vegas. He played a little roulette and went back to the room to read. As far as investments, most of our money is in real estate and mutual funds. Ronnie took care of all that."

Jessie glanced at the girl. She was twisting a gold heart-shaped ring. Lots of fidgeting. "Adrienne, can you think of anyone who wanted to hurt your father?"

"Just Carla Luchins. If Daddy would've reported her to the police . . ." Her lips quivered. "Why did he have to be so *nice*? *Why*?" She started crying again and buried her head against her mother's chest. Celeste rubbed her back.

"Just a few more questions, Mrs. Bushnell," Phil said. "I know this is difficult." He waited while mother and daughter drew apart. "Adrienne, I'd like to talk to your mother alone for a minute."

The girl moved closer to her mother. "I want to stay."

"It's all right, Adrienne." Celeste squeezed her daughter's hand. "You don't need to hear all the details."

Adrienne glanced uncertainly at her mother. After an encouraging nod, she rose and walked toward the entrance, looking behind her several times as she left the room.

"She's trying so hard to be brave, but this is devastating her." The mother's anxious eyes were on the archway where her daughter had been standing. "She's always been Daddy's girl," she said, turning to Jessie. "Even more since she started her teens. And she's so much like Ronnie. Sometimes I think the only thing we share is blond hair and a shoe size." She sighed. "This is the age when it happens, isn't it—pulling away from the mother? And now it's just the two of us."

"She's an only child?" Jessie asked, thinking about the three cars in the driveway.

"We wanted to have more children, but it didn't happen. We considered adopting, but then . . . Anyway."

Phil said, "I have to ask you, ma'am, meaning no offense, did you and your husband get along?"

Celeste blinked rapidly, taken aback by the question, and eyed him with cool disdain. "So that's why you sent my daughter out of the room. The answer is yes. Ronnie and I loved each other and shared the same goals."

"Your husband was a handsome man. Is it possible a patient's spouse or boyfriend got it into his head that this patient was having an affair with your husband?"

"I *told* you." Her nostrils were pinched and whitened with anger. "We had a solid marriage."

"I understand." Phil nodded. "What I'm asking, is it possible someone would *think* he was having an affair? Did your husband mention anything like that?"

"No. Are you finished, Detective? I have to start making calls." She massaged her forehead. "God, I don't even know where to begin." She had the air of someone whipped, defeated. The angry edge in her voice was gone, and her shoulders were pulled down by despair.

"Can I come back now?" Adrienne stood in the archway, a forlorn figure slight enough to be blown away by a puff of wind. "I don't think my mom should be alone," she added with a hint of defiance.

"Actually, we're done." Phil pushed himself off the sofa. "We want to thank you for your help."

Jessie rose. "Again, we're terribly sorry for your loss, and we'll be in touch about the funeral arrangements. If you remember anything that may be important, anything at all, please call the station."

She handed her card to Celeste. The woman didn't even glance at it before dropping it onto the wood coffee table.

Adrienne had moved next to her mother. "Do you think. . . ." She bit her trembling lips. "Do you think I could see my dad?" she asked. "Just to say good-bye?"

❖ 5 ❖

CARLA LUCHINS REFUSED to open the door.

"I have nothing to say to you," she called in a bored, don't-bother-me voice, as if they were trying to sell her copper-bottomed pots she'd already rejected for a better product. "I was angry at Dr. Bushnell. He threatened to report me to the police if I bothered him again, so I let it go, okay? If he says I'm harassing him, he's lying."

"Ma'am, it would be better if we talked inside," Phil said.

"I don't *want* to talk to you, Detective, and you can't *force* me. I know my rights."

Everybody was an expert, thanks to all the cops-and-lawyers TV shows. Jessie enjoyed them (*Law and Order* was her favorite), but they made her job more difficult. She was thinking about *Hill Street Blues*, which she really missed, while Phil informed Carla Luchins that they had a warrant to search her apartment and asked her again to open the door.

"I don't think I should talk to you without my lawyer being present." The bored voice was gone.

"That's your right," Phil said, patient, "but you'll have to open the door so that we can conduct our search."

Judge Otterman had grumbled about shaky "probable cause"— Bushnell had never documented with the police the harassment his wife and daughter had described. But he'd issued a telephonic warrant based on Joe Hopper's identification of Carla Luchins as the woman he'd seen leaving Bushnell's office around the time of the murders.

("Bingo!" Hopper had exclaimed, jabbing a calloused finger at the face in the photo Jessie had removed from Carla's medical file. He'd smiled broadly, revealing again those tobacco-yellowed front teeth, and his eyes had sparkled with excitement. "So you're gonna need me to pick her out of a lineup, right?")

"You won't find anything," Carla Luchins said now.

"I'm counting to five, Ms. Luchins. Then I break down the door."

"This is police brutality!" she snarled, but her voice lacked conviction, and she jerked open the door.

She was wearing black open-toed mules, black latex leggings, and a tight pink sweater with a low V neckline that revealed the rounded tops of the breasts a doctor had embellished, though not to her satisfaction. The breasts looked even larger in contrast to her thin waist, slim hips, and thighs and threatened to topple her over. Probably liposuction, Jessie decided about the thighs, renewing her determination to lose the five pounds she'd put on in the past few months.

"I'd like to see the warrant," Carla Luchins demanded, thrusting out her hand. The skin wasn't as firm and baby smooth as that on her face, and the veins were pronounced. Jessie guessed she was in her midforties.

Phil gave her the face sheet of the warrant describing the place to be searched and the items to be searched for. "This is yours to keep."

"Gee, thanks. I'll keep it in my scrapbook, right next to my divorce papers." She studied the paper. Then she sighed. "Look, I'm sorry I gave you a hard time. I just freaked when you said you were police detectives."

"We can understand that," Jessie said.

"This whole thing is a misunderstanding." Carla ran a hand through shoulder-length, highlighted blond hair. "You can look around—well, you have that warrant, so you don't need my permission." She tried a tight, nervous smile that gave her a furtive look. "I want to clear everything up."

"We appreciate that, ma'am," Phil said.

They sat at an oak dining room table scarred with water rings and scratches and dulled with layers of furniture polish thick enough to play tic-tac-toe on.

"What do you want to know?" Carla squared her shoulders, thrusting her chest forward as if she were launching missiles.

"You've been harassing Dr. Bushnell," Phil said, his voice matter-of-fact, his eyes fixed above Carla's neck. Jessie gave him points. "You've been phoning his office constantly—five calls on one day, according to his notes. Then you showed up at his house and threatened him."

"The *reason* I phoned so *often* is because he wasn't taking my calls." She spoke with exaggerated patience, as if explaining a simple concept to a dull student. "I went to his house only *once*. I didn't know what else to do." She looked at Jessie. "I never threatened him."

"His wife and daughter say you did," Phil said.

"I was *frustrated* because he was ignoring me!" She glared at him, then took a calming breath. "I may have said 'You'll be sorry.' I meant I would *sue* him."

"When was the last time you spoke to Dr. Bushnell?"

"I went to his office this morning, but he was too busy to see me. I don't remember the last time I actually *spoke* to him." She narrowed her eyes in concentration.

She was very attractive, Jessie thought, but not beautiful—surprising, since her features were almost perfect: Large, dark gray eyes unmarred by crow's feet or even a hint of a sagging lid. Smooth, unblemished skin; a heart-shaped chin; high cheekbones. The nose—Bushnell's creation, according to the file—was thin and short, with a rounded tip. Jessie studied the nose to see what about it had so displeased the woman, and wondered how much of her face had been surgically improved.

Carla shifted her eyes and caught Jessie looking at her. She flushed. "It's grotesque, isn't it?" she demanded. "You were staring at my nose. *Everybody* does."

"I'm sorry," Jessie murmured, though she wasn't. "It looks—" She deliberately hesitated. "Very natural."

"*Natural?*" Carla's expression was grim. "The whole thing is crooked. It tilts to the right, can't you see that?" She leaned closer to Jessie.

"I see what you mean." The nose wasn't perfectly straight, but it was hardly grotesque. "I don't blame you for being upset."

Out of the corner of her eye she saw Phil's quick, almost imperceptible nod.

"It isn't just that," Carla said. "The tip has no shape because he didn't take out enough cartilage, and the nostrils are large enough to drive a truck through." She raised her head to display the offending apertures. "And they're not even the same size. He *butchered* my nose."

Jessie clucked. "Doctors." No talk of calling her lawyer now. The conversation would have been comical if the woman weren't so pathetically earnest.

"All I wanted was for him to fix my nose for free, but he denied there was anything wrong, can you believe it?" Her eyes filled with tears. "I can't afford any more surgery."

"You've had other procedures?" Jessie asked, pretending not to know.

"I've had a few things done. I paid for them by refinancing this dump, which was all I could afford with my measly divorce settlement, but that money's gone. My ex, of course, got to keep the Holmby Hills mansion."

"That's lousy. My ex robbed me blind, too," Jessie lied. "Left me without a stick of furniture and not a penny of support." She apologized mentally to Gary and wondered how he was doing. Curiosity, not longing.

"Men." Carla invested the word with disgust. She was oblivious now of Phil, one of the species, sitting a foot away.

"Three years ago he left me for a twenty-year-old law clerk." She sniffed. "That's my reward for putting him through law school and supporting us and our two kids for years on my salary. When he was living at home, he never spent time with the kids. Now he showers them with gifts, so no wonder they kiss up to him and his new honey. I don't exist. It's the typical story, isn't it?" She laughed bitterly. "I used to make fun of women like that."

"It's rotten," Jessie agreed with feeling, only some of it feigned. "So that's when you had plastic surgery?"

"You know how many women are out there, looking for good men?" Carla demanded angrily, as if Jessie were the competition. "You know how many women are looking for high-paying jobs? Looks *do* count, and not just in Hollywood."

"So you went to Dr. Bushnell, and he disappointed you."

"He promised he'd give me the nose I wanted, and then he did this!" She pushed her nose to the right, exaggerating the mild sway. "He said he could try to improve it, but according to the consent form I signed, I'd have to pay for the surgery and anesthesia and the surgical center again. Thousands of dollars!" Her voice shook.

"Consent form or not, he messed up." Jessie shook her head. "You spent all that money, you went through the discomfort of the surgery only to be disappointed with the outcome. And here he was just ignoring you." She clucked.

"The whole *office* ignored me! They treated me like I had some contagious disease. The receptionist kept saying she'd give Bushnell my messages, but I know she was lying."

"So that's why you went to Dr. Bushnell's home, huh? You were angry because he was ignoring you. And then he threatened to go to the police. Hardly fair, was it?"

Carla examined her ruby-lacquered fingernails.

"You called him after you went to his house, right? And

he still wouldn't talk to you. Is that why you went back to his office a second time today?"

She froze. "I didn't go back. I was there just once, in the morning. Ask the bookkeeper. She made me leave."

"Carla," Jessie chided gently. "A witness saw you leaving Dr. Bushnell's office at four-thirty."

She shook her head. "Your witness saw somebody else."

"He identified you from a photo." Jessie let the woman think about that for a moment. "You know Dr. Bushnell is dead, don't you?"

Carla's eyes opened so wide that the tips of her mascaraed lashes scraped her brows. "My God, what happened?"

"You *know* what happened, Carla." Jessie kept her voice reasonable. "You were in the office. You're frightened to admit it, but if you tell us the truth, we can help you."

"I wasn't there."

"You knew Bushnell wouldn't want to talk to you. He didn't, all those times before. So you took a gun to make sure he'd listen."

Carla stiffened. "I don't own a gun. Guns scare me."

"You probably didn't mean to shoot him," Jessie continued. "But when he refused to talk to you, you lost it. Is that what happened?"

"You're trying to get me to say I did something I didn't do!" She pushed her chair away and stood, shoulders imperiously straight. "I want you to leave."

Phil rose. "Not before we take a look around."

"Suit yourself, but you're wasting your time. And don't think I won't be watching you every second. This isn't Rampart, you know." The belligerence was back in her voice.

They would never hear the end of the scandal that had erupted over two years ago at Rampart Division and was still reverberating throughout the department. Corrupt officers framing suspects, planting evidence, shooting innocent people. Several convictions tainted by the scandal had already been overturned and there would be more. The city was facing major lawsuits. Morale in the department was low, and Jessie and every detective and patrol officer she knew had to contend with critical, suspicious citizens.

Which didn't exactly make her job easier.

❖ 6 ❖

THE PLACE WAS badly in need of refurbishing. The matted peach carpeting had several large stains, many of the ivory miniblind slats were bent, and there were networks of cracks on the walls and ceilings. More cracks threatened to break through the dated floral wallpaper in the two bedrooms and bathrooms. The paper was curling away from the seams, surrendering to the inevitable.

One less surgery could have paid for new carpeting and a paint job, Jessie thought, but she supposed everyone had his or her priorities. While Phil searched through the second bedroom, Jessie, under Carla's careful watch, rifled expertly with gloved hands through the dresser drawers and the clothes and shoes in her closet. She examined the hems of the skirts and slacks, but discerned nothing that remotely resembled bloodstains.

Under the queen-size bed she found a pair of white athletic shoes with a rust-colored substance on the soles. "Phil!" she called sharply with feigned excitement, even though the substance looked too brown and too aged to be hours-old blood. Too bad, because the shoe size—probably a nine—looked right.

"That's mud." Carla peered at the shoes. "I like to garden. Is there a law against that?" she asked, aiming for indignant but sounding anxious.

Phil appeared. Jessie showed him the shoes, gave him an

opening to nod somberly, then placed them into a paper evidence bag that she labeled and dated.

"When will I get those back?" Carla demanded.

"I'm going to give you a receipt," Jessie told her, ignoring the question as she signed her name on the bag.

Phil left. Jessie felt between the queen-size mattress and box spring, examined the contents of the medicine cabinet in the adjoining bath and all the other storage cabinets, lifted the lid of the toilet tank. She found sexy lacy lingerie that would showcase Carla's proud breasts, and countless face and throat creams with Retin-A and other ingredients that promised younger, firmer, plumper skin, but she saw no sign of a weapon or any incriminating evidence.

Phil had found nothing in the guest room or guest bath. He and Jessie searched Carla's car and garage and the trash cans in the small yard. Back in the house, they unfolded a sleeper sofa in the den, then rummaged through the closet and cabinets. A wicker magazine stand was filled with issues of *Cosmopolitan*, *In Style*, *Glamour*, and *Vanity Fair*. Jessie flipped through a folder with loose pages of ads of beautiful women whose features—sometimes the nose, another time the eyes or chin or cheekbones—had been circled with a red felt marker.

They searched the kitchen and paid particular attention to the full-length olive trench coat in the hall closet. There was nothing on the coat as far as Jessie could see, but Phil made a big show of placing it into another evidence bag.

"I don't understand why you're taking my things," Carla whined. "I told you, I stopped calling Dr. Bushnell after he threatened to go to the police."

"This'll keep the lab guys busy," Phil said to Jessie. "Looks like blood on the coat and on the shoes."

Carla paled. "I didn't kill Dr. Bushnell!"

"Lab tests don't lie," Phil told her. "If that's Dr. Bushnell's blood on your clothing, or his nurse's or receptionist's . . . We have an eyewitness, and now we have other evidence."

"But I didn't *do* anything!" She faced Jessie. "I want to tell you what happened, but I don't know if I should talk without a lawyer."

"Lawyers can complicate things, but if you're worried because you have something to hide. . . ." If the woman requested a lawyer, that would end the interrogation before it began.

"I don't have anything to hide!"

Jessie waited. Carla chewed on what was probably a collagen-enhanced lip.

"I *did* come back in the afternoon," she admitted in a low, shaky voice. "Dr. Bushnell was dead. So was his nurse, and the receptionist. There was a lot of blood, so much blood. I almost threw up." She swallowed hard.

"What time did you arrive?" Jessie asked.

"A quarter after four. I figured I'd get there after the last patient and make Dr. Bushnell talk to me."

"So you brought a gun, just to scare him." Jessie said this casually, as though it didn't matter.

"No!" Carla shook her head vehemently. "I *told* you! I hate guns! I wouldn't know what to do with one."

Jessie believed her. "Did you see anyone when you arrived? In the office, or in the hall?"

"No. I didn't even see the receptionist at first. Her head—" Carla stopped. "Her head was on her desk. I saw that later. I thought she'd gone for the day, so I went inside to Dr. Bushnell's office. Well, not inside. I stayed in the hall. The door was open and I saw them." She swallowed again.

"What did you do then?"

"I left. I didn't want to phone the police from there—I didn't want to be involved. And there was no point," she added defensively. "I knew they were all dead. I called nine-one-one from a pay phone a couple of blocks away from the building. My hand was shaking so hard I almost dropped the receiver."

The anonymous caller. "Why didn't you tell us the truth right away, Carla?" Jessie asked.

"I was afraid you'd think I killed him, because I showed up at his house and everything. You believe me, don't you?" She fixed an imploring gaze on Jessie.

Out of the corner of her eye, Jessie saw Phil's shrug. *Your call.*

"You'll have to come to the station and give a formal statement," she told Carla. "And don't leave town without letting us know." She would have units search the neighborhood trash bins for a weapon, just in case.

The woman nodded eagerly, her face flushed with relief.

"You were in Dr. Bushnell's office numerous times, Carla. Did you overhear him quarreling with anyone? With his patients? With anyone on his staff?"

Carla shook her head. "I never heard him yell at anyone. He was friendly with the staff, not all uppity like some doctors, and very easygoing. Well, except for this morning. He seemed really upset about something."

Jessie exchanged a quick look with Phil. "I thought you said you didn't see him this morning, Carla."

"I didn't, but I was standing outside his office, and the door was open. He was on the phone."

"What did he say?"

She concentrated. "Something like, 'My mind's made up. I should have done this a long time ago.' Then the bookkeeper saw me and practically threw me out."

Interesting—if Carla was telling the truth. Maybe she was making all this up to shift attention from herself. "What about his patients? Did anyone complain about him?"

"They were gaga over him. They'd talk about him all the time in the waiting room—you'd think he was a god." She hesitated. "I used to have a crush on him myself. The thing about Dr. Bushnell? He made you feel that he really cared about you." She sounded wistful.

Jessie raised a brow.

Carla blushed. "I didn't *hate* the man. I feel *terrible* that he was killed. I just wanted him to fix my nose." She frowned, then quickly smoothed her forehead before the lines could set. "I don't know who's going to pay for that now."

❖ 7 ❖

TWENTY AFTER ELEVEN, but the lights were still on in Helen's breakfast room, Jessie saw as she neared the house. She noted a champagne-colored Lexus in the driveway— Frances's new car, with a personalized license plate.

She wondered why her mother had come up from La Jolla and was tempted to drive home without stopping to say hello. After the long, tiring day she wasn't in the mood for fielding questions or criticism from Frances, who had been more snappish than usual during the last few phone calls.

Her brother-in-law answered the door barefoot, wearing a thick white terry robe, his wet black hair plastered against his skull.

"Sorry I kept you waiting," Neil said as she stepped inside. "I was just coming out of the shower."

A shower sounded good, Jessie thought. A bed, even better. "I hope it's not too late. I couldn't make dinner, but I promised Helen I'd come by tonight to help her choose wallpaper and furniture for the baby's room."

"Not too late at all, but we missed you." Smiling, he shut the door and briskly toweled his hair. "Helen's getting your mom settled in the guest house. She'll be thrilled you're here to save her. She looked wiped after she showed Frances the nursery. I take it a new case detained you?"

Jessie nodded. "Believe me, I'd much rather have been here." She followed him through the wide center hall and wondered what had possessed Helen to ask Frances for advice. Or maybe she hadn't asked. "Where's my dad? In the den?"

"He didn't come. Your mom showed up and told Helen she'll be here for a few days." Neil stopped at the foot of the staircase. "I'm not sure Helen's up to it. She's nervous around your mom, insecure. A year and a half of therapy down the tubes. Oh, well." He shrugged, making light of his comment, but he sounded concerned and annoyed.

She couldn't blame him. "Did my mom say why she was here?"

"I made the mistake of asking and she bit my head off, asked if she needed a reason to visit her daughter and son-in-law and grandson—who, by the way, rarely drove down to see her. So basically, I've been staying out of her way."

"Smart man."

"More like 'coward.' " His smile deepened the fine lines around his dark eyes that, along with the touch of gray in his hair, were a mild concession to his forty-four years. "See you later."

He generally managed to stay out of Frances's way and never rose to her bait. Solid, unflappable Neil. In many ways, Helen had married her father.

Jessie liked her brother-in-law but didn't know him well. He and Helen had lived in Winnetka, Illinois, from the time they'd married until a year and a half ago—to stay far away from Frances, Jessie assumed. Neil still traveled a great deal, sometimes around the world, consulting on engineering projects, though he'd cut down since they'd relocated.

He'd have to curtail his travel even more when the baby arrived in January, Jessie thought as she walked outside to the guest house above the two-car garage. Helen had a full-time housekeeper and had interviewed half a dozen nannies, but she would need Neil's moral support. Even then . . .

That was one major difference between Neil and her father. Neil tried to avoid unpleasantness, but he hadn't turned a blind eye to Helen's abuse of their son. Jessie felt a prickling of familiar resentment toward her father and tried to shake it off.

Frances, wearing a silk robe with a colorful exotic bird print on a burgundy background, was reclining Camille-like on one of the two twin beds, her neck propped up with several pillows, her slim bare legs crossed at the ankles. A headband kept her chin-length blond hair off her forehead and revealed hints of the almost invisible incisions of the facelift she'd had several years ago.

"Hey, Jess," Helen chirped, the unnatural brightness in her voice tinged with relief. She was standing in the bathroom doorway, resting a stack of thick beige towels on the ledge of her swollen belly. "I was beginning to think you weren't coming."

She looked worn, her rosy skin paler than usual, green eyes anxious, the glow of pregnancy somewhat dimmed—probably by Frances.

"Sorry I'm so late. Things got crazy." Jessie turned to her mother. "How are you, Mom?"

"Fine, thank you." Her tone grated like chalk on a board.

Not good. Bracing herself, Jessie approached her mother and leaned over to kiss her cheek, but Frances put up her hand, as if she were a school crossing guard.

"I just cleansed and moisturized." She crossed her arms. "Helen said you were coming for dinner. We waited."

"I didn't say for sure. I said *maybe*. And I said not to wait." Jessie shot her sister an irritated glance.

Helen flushed. "I told Mom it wasn't definite. How about some leftovers? London broil and mashed potatoes with sautéed onions."

"Sounds wonderful. I'm starved." In the last five hours she'd eaten only a granola bar and a twin-pack of Reese's Pieces.

"Well, Matthew was *very* disappointed," Frances said.

Her mother was a pro at laying on the guilt. Jessie adored her nine-year-old nephew and basked in his unabashed affection. "I'll phone him tomorrow."

"Unless something else comes up," Frances remarked. "Don't promise what you can't keep, Jessica."

Helen wisely disappeared into the bathroom.

"A phone call would have been nice," her mother continued. "Obviously, you couldn't tear yourself away. What was it? Paperwork, or another sordid murder?"

"Three, actually. But the victims are high-class, so you'll approve. A plastic surgeon and two of his staff."

Frances pursed her lips. "Your sarcasm is uncalled for, Jessica. I'm merely expressing my concern about the fact that you have no life."

"*Thanks* for pointing that out. That makes me feel *so* much better."

"I'm trying to help you, Jessica. You're my daughter."

Too bad, Jessie thought, biting back the retort. "Neil said you're here for a few days."

"I want to catch the trunk shows at Neiman's and Saks. What's the name of the doctor who was killed?"

She was surprised by her mother's interest. Then again, they were talking about plastic surgeons, people dear to Frances's heart. "Ronald Bushnell. Have you heard of him?"

"*Heard* of him!" Frances's eyes widened, and her hand was at her moisturized throat. "I almost *went* to him!"

"You're kidding!" Helen reappeared in the doorway.

"He did Charlotte's lift, you know," Frances told Helen. "A little tight, in my opinion. He did her eyes, too." She faced Jessie again. "Where was he killed?"

"In his office. It was gruesome, if you want to know."

Frances's shudder rippled through the silk robe and alarmed the birds, which seemed about to take flight.

"Do you have any idea who killed him?" Helen had remained in the doorway, leaning against the doorpost, as if undecided whether it was safe to stay.

"Not yet."

While waiting for the warrant to search Carla Luchins's

apartment, they'd talked to Steve Egerton, the surgeon who had enhanced Carla's chest. He had paled at the news of Bushnell's murder, had looked thoughtful when Phil asked him about Carla.

"I don't know," the doctor finally said. "She was annoying as hell, I'll tell you that. She'd phone five, six times a day and demand to talk to me. Didn't care that I was with a patient—she had to talk to me *now*. I redid her breasts three times, but there was no making her happy."

"Did she threaten you?" Phil asked.

"With a lawsuit. But physically?" Egerton shook his head. "Maybe she snapped. Is she in custody?" he asked, suddenly nervous.

"Not at this time," Phil told him.

Georgia Vale, the last patient Bushnell had seen, had been of no help. From the carefully combed silver hair, Jessie guessed she was in her sixties, though her face, still red from a chemical peel she said she'd had a few days ago, was relatively unlined. She'd been alone in Bushnell's waiting room until the doctor was ready to see her. No, she hadn't heard anything unusual.

"How did Dr. Bushnell seem to you?" Jessie asked.

"Charming, as always. He was such a dear." The woman sighed. "He did perfect work, absolutely perfect."

Not always, Jessie had thought. Carla Luchins had been a dissatisfied patient. Maybe there were others. "Do you know anything about Dr. Bushnell, Mom?" she asked now.

"Charlotte adores him. She says he's the sweetest, sweetest man. Gorgeous, too. Do you want me to ask her about him?" Her green eyes gleamed with excitement.

Frances Claypool, sidekick. She'd wear down suspects with a single raised brow. A sneer would have them begging for the hole. "Why don't you give me Charlotte's phone number, and I'll call her."

"I can't do that." Her mother drew back, horrified. "She doesn't want anyone to know she had anything done."

As if it weren't obvious. Jessie had seen Charlotte several months ago at a charity luncheon Frances had cochaired and had noticed the woman's suddenly youthful appearance. "Ask her if you can tell me, Mom. Explain that it might be important." Or not.

Frances deliberated. "All right. By the way, did Brian Lefton phone you for a date?"

With Frances, there were no freebies. She would have made a ruthless negotiator, Jessie thought, suppressing an admiring smile. "No."

"Roberta Kimmel gave him your number. You remember Roberta? She and I are chairing a dinner for the pediatric AIDS foundation, and I told her you're eligible again."

Desperate, Frances meant. "Mom—"

"This man is every woman's dream, Jessica. He's a highly successful stockbroker, cultured, and he looks like Harrison Ford. Divorced, but no children."

The Harrison Ford part was tempting. "I appreciate your efforts, Mom, but—"

"He's Jewish, if that's what you're worried about," Frances announced triumphantly. "That's no doubt important, now that you're so *involved* with your classes."

Her tone was snide, but Jessie decided to view the overall comment as promising—only last week, Frances had warned her against "becoming brainwashed by those rabbis you hang around with." She wondered how her mother would react if she knew Jessie had been attending Sabbath synagogue services for months and had begun keeping kosher, though not strictly, and only in her home.

"That's so thoughtful, Mom, but I'm not ready to date." A lie, but she'd barely exchanged more than a sentence with Roberta Kimmel, so how could the woman know what qualities in a man would interest Jessie? She sighed.

"Martyrdom is extremely unattractive," Frances said, misinterpreting the sigh. "And it's boring. You're thirty-five years old, Jessica. Your eggs are deteriorating as we speak.

When will you be ready?" She turned to Helen. "Maybe you can talk some sense into your sister."

"I'm going to warm up the leftovers, Jess," Helen said. "I'll buzz you on the intercom when they're ready."

Getting out of the line of fire, Jessie thought with envy and some amusement as she watched her sister make her escape. She turned back and found Frances studying her.

"You're interested in someone else, aren't you?"

Ezra. The name of her Judaic studies mentor stole into her consciousness and made her flustered. "No, no one."

"Then why are you blushing?"

"I don't like being grilled, Mom." Her mother had an uncanny knack for divining the truth, and punishing with it.

Frances didn't look convinced. She gazed at Jessie, appraising her. "I was really hoping that you and Gary would get back together. He's obviously crazy about you. I thought you loved him."

"We have issues we can't resolve, Mom." Conflicting careers, differing views about career versus family. About religion. How was *that* for irony? Gary was uninterested in Judaism. Ezra was defined by it. . . .

"*Issues.*" Frances wrinkled her finely shaped nose. "That's a ridiculous word." She cocked her head. "Sometimes it's helpful to talk to someone else," she said more kindly. "I'm a good listener, Jessica. All my friends tell me so."

She'd never considered her mother as a confidante, had never contemplated what she was like with her friends. "I appreciate it, Mom, but there's really nothing to say."

"I assume you told Helen what happened. You always do." There was pique in her mother's voice, and vulnerability.

"No, I didn't," Jessie lied. She moved to the other bed and sat down on the lilac-patterned comforter. "So how's Dad? Doesn't he mind that you'll be away for a few days?"

"I doubt it. Did Helen show you the baby furniture catalogue?"

Was her mother changing the subject? "Not yet. Is Dad all right, Mom?"

"Physically, he's fine. Why don't you call him? Maybe he'll tell *you* what's going on." She picked up an emery board and began filing a perfectly shaped nail.

"You and Dad had an *argument*?" She'd never heard her parents quarrel, primarily because Arthur Claypool always retreated from confrontation. *Whatever you want, Frances.* Jessie found the possibility that he'd stood up to her mother intriguing and not displeasing.

Frances glared at her. "We have *issues*. Isn't that the word you used?"

Jessie sighed. "Don't play games, Mom."

"I won't put up with his behavior, all *right*?" Her nostrils flared. "Your father's distant, Jessica. He barely talks to me. He spends more and more time at the office, or so he claims."

Whatever faint pleasure Jessie had felt disappeared, replaced by stirrings of unease. "What do you mean?"

"You're a detective," Frances snapped. "I'm surprised you haven't figured it out. I think he's having an affair. Are you happy now?" Her face was as red as Georgia Vale's.

Jessie scooted forward on the bed and took her mother's hand. "Dad loves you, Mom. He would never cheat on you."

"He's a man, Jessica. Men cheat." She removed her hand and crossed her arms again. "Last week he told me he'd be staying late at the office. I phoned him on his private line to ask him something, and he wasn't there."

"Maybe he was on the way home."

"He came home two hours later. He said he was probably in the rest room when I phoned, but I called four or five times. Am I supposed to believe he was in the bathroom every time? I'm the one with the weak bladder. The same thing happened two weeks ago."

Jessie frowned. "Did you confront him about it?"

"Yes. He made up some stupid story about the phone's ringer not working well, but I could tell he was lying."

Not my father, Jessie thought, her mind whirling.

"I've been a good wife." Her mother's tone was defensive, her chin high. "I worked hard to put your father through medical school. I agreed to stay in Los Angeles after his residency, even though the only family we had was back east, because it was good for his career."

Jessie nodded.

"You girls think I'm difficult about keeping the house just so, but I do it to create a beautiful home your father can be proud of, a home where we can entertain business guests and friends."

Jessie nodded again, wondering at what point Frances had convinced herself of this truth. Their two-story La Jolla house was a Lalique- and Baccarat-filled museum, and Frances its stern, unforgiving curator. Her father sometimes joked that there was nowhere to relax in the house, but never in front of Frances.

"And I've taken pains to keep up my appearance," her mother continued. "I know that's important to a man." She gave Jessie a sharp, reproving glance. "But I'm sixty-one years old. I have wrinkles the surgeon can't remove, my breasts aren't perky, I have to get up to pee several times a night, and that's just the way it is."

Too much candor, Jessie thought, shifting uncomfortably on the bed. "You look beautiful, Mom. Dad always *says* you're beautiful. You certainly don't look your age."

"Then why doesn't he want to have sex?"

Jessie's face was hot. "Mom—"

"I'm not a nymphomaniac, but we haven't been together in almost four months. He's always making some excuse. He's tired, his stomach is upset, he has paperwork. Now it all makes sense: he's having an affair."

"You don't know that. Maybe something's bothering him and he's afraid to tell you about it. That could affect him in . . . different ways." Thirty-five years old, and she was still blushing at the thought of her parents doing it.

"Afraid to tell me what?" Frances demanded.

"I don't know. Maybe he's having financial problems and doesn't want to worry you."

"Our finances are excellent." Frances paused. "I told him I needed a few days by myself, and he didn't ask me why." Her lips trembled, and her green eyes glistened with tears. "And he didn't try to stop me from leaving."

I should get up and put my arms around her, Jessie thought. But Frances's arms were still locked beneath her breasts. "He probably wanted to give you some time to cool off," she suggested.

"He was *thrilled*. I phoned the house to tell him I got here safely, but he wasn't there. He's out with his girlfriend."

"You don't know that."

The intercom buzzed. Jessie picked up the phone.

"Your dinner's ready," Helen informed her. "Ready to come out of the lion's den?"

"I'll be there in a few minutes."

"Promise me you won't tell Helen," Frances warned after Jessie hung up. "She can't handle something like this."

"I promise." Frances was probably right. "I know there's some misunderstanding here, Mom. Dad loves you. And you love him, right? I'm sure you'll work it out."

Her mother didn't answer, and Jessie was jolted. How strange to be anxious about her parents' marriage, when so often in the past, after suffering a beating at her mother's hands or a particularly cruel tongue-lashing, she had fantasized about life without Frances, had envied her friends, whose mothers and lives seemed normal.

"The second time I went out with your father, I knew I wanted to marry him," Frances said after what seemed like an endless silence. "He was tall and handsome, and so intelligent. He could have had any girl he wanted, and I couldn't believe he was interested in me." She spoke seriously, with no hint of coquetry.

"But that wasn't why I married him. I married your father

because he was confident and strong and kind. I married him because I knew that he would always take care of me, that I would always be safe. After everything I'd been through, I needed security more than love."

"Everything," Jessie had learned seven months ago in a stunning revelation, included being left for safekeeping by her parents, about to be taken by the Nazis, with a Polish family until the war would be over. "Everything" included being beaten daily by the wife for the crimes of being a Jew and a burden. There had been no reunion with her family, all of whom had perished in the concentration camps.

"So you didn't love Dad?" Jessie asked, trying to repress the sadness she felt. Always the romantic—that's what Helen told her, what her ex-husband Gary had told her.

"The love came later," Frances said. "That was a gift." She cleared her throat, and her face hardened. "I won't be made a fool of, Jessica. You can tell that to your father."

As a six-year-old, Frances had been abandoned twice: first by her father; then, after the war, by the Polish woman who had planted in her the treacherous seeds of uncontrolled rage. Maybe that was why she'd left her husband, Jessie thought—to preempt yet another abandonment.

"You want me to talk to Dad?"

"I don't really care. Only if you want to." Frances busied herself with the emery board.

As if Jessie had a choice.

❖ 8 ❖

LIEUTENANT KARL ESPES'S nose was swollen and clown red. His cheeks were flushed, his complexion pasty. The whites of his small brown eyes were glassy, and the pupils had almost disappeared behind his puffy lids.

"So you have zip, is that right?" the lieutenant said, addressing Jessie and Phil in a thick, nasal voice that distorted his words and made him sound like Elmer Fudd.

Jessie bit her lip to keep a straight face.

"I still like the Luchins woman," Phil said. "She was mad enough at Bushnell—at his whole staff, 'cause they ignored her, which would explain why she killed the others."

"We didn't find a weapon," Jessie countered. "There was no blood on any of her clothing."

They'd been over this again this morning, when she'd arrived at the station at seven-thirty, tired and irritable. Thinking about her parents had kept her awake much of the night, and she'd had difficulty concentrating on the morning prayers she had begun to recite (every day she challenged herself to add another few words in Hebrew), prayers that centered her and did for her spirit and soul what her daily exercise regimen did for her body. Today the prayers had failed her—or maybe she had failed them.

Espes sneezed.

"She dumped the gun and clothing where we wouldn't find them," Phil said. "She figured we'd search her neighborhood."

"She doesn't strike me as methodical, Lieutenant." Jessie turned to Phil. "Plus why would she shoot him in the head after he was already dead?"

"He messed up her face, she messes up his. Hopper puts her at the scene right when the doc was shot."

"She said they were dead when she got there. And don't forget the conversation she overheard. She said Bushnell sounded upset."

Phil snorted. "Sure, she said that—to protect her ass. What else is she gonna say—that she did it? They don't offer plastic surgery in prison. Yet."

"Enough," Espes growled, massaging his temples. "You sound like my in-laws. What about the wife and daughter?"

"They seemed really shook up." Phil looked at Jessie, as if waiting for her to challenge this, too.

"They did," she agreed. "But something's bothering the girl. I'd like to talk to her again, alone."

"Do it." Espes sneezed again. He yanked a tissue from the box on his desk and blew his nose like a trumpet, then lobbed the crumpled tissue into a trash can several feet away from his desk. "Find out who else had a grudge against Bushnell or his staff."

Phil said, "We're meeting with the bookkeeper at Bushnell's office at nine. I left a card last night, and she phoned the station this morning. Ditto with the other nurse. She was out sick yesterday, but she's been with Bushnell only about two weeks, so odds are she won't be much help."

"What about the Pervez case?" Espes reached for another tissue.

"We're still looking for the cousin," Jessie said.

Lily Pervez, a twenty-one-year-old Pakistani woman, had been knifed to death four days ago in a male cousin's one-bedroom apartment. There had been no evidence of sexual assault. The apartment manager had found the body when he went to collect the overdue rent. The cousin, Jamal Pervez, had apparently fled. His car was missing, and he'd emptied drawers and closets, leaving them open in his haste to get away. Two days ago he'd used his charge card to pay for gasoline at a station in Long Beach.

"The brother's calling me five times a day," Espes said, tenting the tissue over his nose. "He wants to know if this is what we call American justice."

"We're doing the best we can."

"Do better."

Marty Simms and Ed Boyd, West L.A.'s two other homicide detectives, were at their desks when Jessie and Phil returned from Espes's office. Simms was drinking coffee and studying the stock market listings in the *Times*.

"Catching up to Bill Gates yet?" Phil asked.

Simms looked up and smiled. "Getting there, getting there. I told you to invest with my guy."

Phil shrugged. "I have a mortgage and two kids and a wife who doesn't like stocks. Municipal bonds, yes."

"Ed listened, and he's making out like a bandit. Isn't that right?" He turned to his partner.

The twenty-eight-year-old Arkansas native smiled broadly and gave a thumbs-up. He had a talent for eliciting information from suspects who confused his winsome, boyish looks with gullibility, but in some ways he was naive and too trusting. Simms had taken Boyd under his wing. Jessie hoped he wouldn't lead him too deeply into the market or infect him with his sour view of women.

"I heard about your plastic surgeon," Simms said. "You get all the high-profile cases, we get crap."

"At least your crap is open and shut," Phil said. "We have zip on the surgeon, nothing on the Pervez woman, either. Espes wants both cases solved. 'Do better,' " Phil repeated, mimicking the lieutenant's nasal pronunciation.

Simms laughed. "Did he sneeze all over you? He was spraying me and Boyd like a showerhead."

Jessie grimaced at the image of invisible microbes invading her body. She would take extra vitamin C when she got home, she decided. Echinacea, too. Her neighbor Patti always touted the herb's curative powers.

"The man's got a cold," Boyd chided in his soft twang. "Not his fault."

"You're in a generous mood 'cause you had a hot date last night with Sheryl. You scored, huh?" Simms winked knowingly.

"None of your business." Boyd's freckled face had turned pink, and he looked even younger.

"You did, didn't you?"

"Ignore him," Jessie advised Boyd. "He's just jealous 'cause he hasn't had a date in months."

"Is it my fault you keep turning me down?" Simms grinned at her. "You won't be scoring much if you come down with Espes's cold," he told his partner. "See how forgiving you are then."

"Ten to one *I* come down with it," Phil grumbled. "My throat feels scratchy, my eyes itch. Why the hell doesn't he stay home?"

"He's probably afraid he won't have a desk when he gets back," Simms said. "I heard he was in Rampart before he went to Foothill."

The *R* word. Jessie sighed.

"No kidding." Boyd frowned. "Is the lieutenant in trouble?"

"The whole department's gonna be in trouble. It's just a matter of time. A few weeks, a few months. Don't you read the *Times*?" Simms tossed the paper onto his crowded desk. "You know what really pisses me off? O.J.'s using this to try to convince people that Mark Fuhrman framed him."

"Son of a bitch," Phil said.

"O.J. or Fuhrman?" Jessie asked.

"Take your pick."

Her phone rang. She walked the few steps to her desk and picked up the receiver. "West L.A., Detective Drake."

"Gary Drake, *L.A. Times* crime reporter extraordinaire. How are you, Jess?"

She hadn't spoken to him in two months and felt her stomach muscles tighten. "Fine. And you?"

"Great. Helen's in her seventh month, huh? She must be getting big. How's Matthew? Your parents?"

"She is, and he's terrific. My parents are fine, thanks." She made a mental note to phone her nephew when he came home from school. "What can I do for you, Gary?"

"Hey, I'm trying to be friendly. You're not interested, that's fine with me." He sounded hurt.

She sighed, regretting her terseness. "Sorry. This is awkward for me, Gary. Obviously you can handle it better."

"It's not easy for me, either, Jess. But I'm making the effort. We're going to have dealings. Your job, my job. We can't pretend we don't have a history."

"You're right." She took a deep breath and forced herself to relax. "Thanks for asking about Matthew and Helen. How are your parents?"

"They're good. I'm spending Thanksgiving in Phoenix with them. You?"

"I'll be with Helen and my folks. Give your parents my regards." She liked her ex-in-laws. That had been part of the pull to stay with their son.

"I will. So I heard you're investigating a triple-decker. Plastic surgeon and two of his staff. Anything you can tell me about it?"

She should have realized that was why he'd called. She was annoyed by the crassness of his term, though most cops she knew used similarly crude terms, and worse. "Not at this time, Gary. We've just begun the investigation."

"Cause of death?"

"Don't know. The M.E. said he hopes to do the autopsies by Friday." Something she wasn't looking forward to attending. Maybe Phil would go.

"Any suspects?"

"We're pursuing several leads."

He laughed. "Spoken like a true-blue official record. Off the record, any hunches, Jessie? For old times' sake?"

"I don't have anything at this time. I really *don't*, Gary." Even if she did, she'd never share it with him. With Gary, there was no "off the record."

"Call me if there's anything you can tell me? I'd appreciate getting the inside scoop."

"Okay," she agreed reluctantly. She didn't know how wise it was to maintain contact, but saying no was selfish.

"So how've you been? Seeing anyone?"

The tension was back. "No."

"Me, either. Lois is throwing Jim a birthday bash tonight at Benny's." A nightclub they'd frequented, on Sunset near Doheny. "Party starts at nine, goes on till they throw us out."

Jim was a financial reporter—a nice enough guy, from what she remembered. "Wish Jim a happy birthday from me."

"You could do it yourself. I was going alone, but I thought maybe you'd be my date."

"I don't think it's a good idea, Gary."

"No strings, no party hats. Just champagne and dancing, some gooey cake. This way I won't look like such a loser."

"Thanks, but I don't think so."

"If you change your mind, you know where I'll be."

SUZANNE ORD, BUSHNELL'S bookkeeper, and Leanne Fialkoff, the new nurse, arrived at Bushnell's office within minutes of each other.

"I don't like being here." Suzanne glanced around and grimaced. "It gives me the creeps." She looked for confirmation from Leanne, who was staring at the opening to the receptionist's room but said nothing.

They were both in their late twenties or early thirties, Jessie guessed, and were a contrast in colors and sizes. The bookkeeper was practically anorexic, with below-the-shoulder, stick-straight blond hair that made her long face look even longer and thinner. Leanne, curvaceous and zaftig in comparison, had long tousled black curls and crimson lipstick that gave her a sultry look.

Both women were very pretty. Nicole Hobart, the dead nurse, and Marianna Velasquez had been pretty, too. No accident, Jessie assumed, since beauty was probably a prerequisite for working in a plastic surgeon's office.

Phil remained with the nurse while Jessie accompanied Suzanne to her office. The bookkeeper shuddered as she stole a quick glance at the burgundy and gray diamond-patterned hall carpeting which camouflaged most, but not all, of the shooter's bloody shoe prints.

"I can't believe this happened," Suzanne said when she was seated at her desk. "I keep thinking if I hadn't left early yesterday to have my hair colored, I'd be dead." She hugged her arms, displaying a large, emerald-cut diamond wider than her waist.

"When did you leave?" Jessie asked.

"Three-thirty. The last scheduled appointment is at four, and we're usually out by four-thirty. Even if there's an emergency, only the nurses stay, and sometimes Marianna." Suzanne sighed. "Poor Alex! I met him once a year ago, when he was sick, and Marianna couldn't find a baby-sitter. He seemed more sensitive than other kids. I hope he's okay."

How could the boy be okay? Jessie wondered, irritated. To be fair, the bookkeeper probably didn't know what else to say, but something about her struck Jessie as false. "He's with his great-aunt."

"That's good." Suzanne nodded.

At least for now. It would be terribly sad if he had to go to foster care. "What happened to his father?"

"He and Marianna never married, and she didn't talk about him much. I don't think he kept in touch with the boy. I *know* he didn't pay for child care."

"Did she have a boyfriend?"

Suzanne frowned. "You think this is connected to *Marianna*?" The idea clearly startled her, and she pronounced the dead woman's name with greater gravity and more respect than she'd probably given her when she was alive.

"We have to check out every possibility."

"She was seeing someone a few months ago, but Alex didn't like him, so that was that."

"Do you know if the father was jealous?"

"She didn't tell me, but we weren't all that close."

"You seem to know about the boy's father and his relationship with Ms. Velasquez," Jessie pointed out.

Suzanne hesitated. "Actually, I know about the father and the boyfriend from Barbara Martin. She's the nurse Leanne replaced."

"Ms. Martin quit?"

Suzanne shook her head. "She was let go."

A great euphemism. For Jessie it had always conjured images of freedom, like a helium balloon released to float high up in the air; or the Israelites' leaving Egypt, a subject she'd studied with Ezra. *Let my people go.*

"Do you know why she was fired?"

"Dr. B. wouldn't talk about it. Barbara didn't want to, either, and I didn't want to pry." The bookkeeper shrugged. "She filed a workmen's comp suit, so maybe their lawyers told them not to say anything."

More likely the prying hadn't helped. Jessie sensed that Suzanne had no problem sticking her pretty nose into other people's business, soaking up gossip like gravy. "How long did Ms. Martin work here?"

"About a year and a half, maybe a little longer."

"Was she a good nurse?"

"Patients liked her, and from what I could tell she and Dr. B. got along real well until recently. The last few weeks, you could see something was bothering her."

"She must have been angry at Dr. Bushnell for firing her," Jessie said, in a tone that invited corroboration, not revelation. "Who wouldn't be?"

"She was *furious*," Suzanne whispered, as though someone could overhear. "I saw her right after Dr. Bushnell must have told her. I could see she was going to cry. She grabbed the key to the bathroom and ran out of the office, and I followed her. Not to pry, of course," the bookkeeper added quickly. "But what if something was terribly wrong?"

"Of course," Jessie murmured. "So that's when she told you she'd been fired?"

"She didn't say, but she took her things and left right after, and then Dr. B. said she quit, but we all knew she didn't. When she was in the bathroom, she was crying and calling him all kinds of names. Bastard. Son of a bitch. She said she hated him, and—" Suzanne lowered her eyes. "I'm really uncomfortable talking about Barbara. And I don't for a second believe she killed Dr. Bushnell, or anyone."

The woman was loving this. "Three people were brutally murdered, Suzanne. If you know something, anything, you have to tell us." Playing the game, giving her the out she needed.

"She wished him dead," the bookkeeper said a moment later with great solemnity. "I don't think she meant she would *kill* him. But she wished him dead."

Interesting that Celeste hadn't mentioned Barbara Martin. Maybe Bushnell hadn't wanted to worry his wife about his work problems. Jessie thought about the phone call Carla Luchins had overheard. *My mind is made up. I should have done this a long time ago.* Maybe Barbara Martin had been pleading to get her job back.

"Was she angry at Nicole Hobart, as far as you know?"

A puzzled look crossed the bookkeeper's face. "They got along. And she really liked Marianna." She sounded pensive.

"What do you know about Nicole?"

The dead nurse's family lived in Chicago, officers had learned from the apartment manager last night. Jessie had spoken with the stunned, grief-stricken parents this morning. Their daughter had been happy, the mother told Jessie. With her job, with her life, with Los Angeles, where she'd been living less than a year. Jessie had advised them to wait until the body would be released before coming out.

"She was here six months," Suzanne said. "I didn't know her well—she kept to herself. It's terrible that she's dead," she added perfunctorily, her mind clearly elsewhere.

"Was there a boyfriend?" According to the mother, she'd been amicably divorced from her ex, who lived in Chicago.

"I don't know." Suzanne checked her watch. Having revealed the Big Fact, she'd clearly lost interest in the conversation.

"What can you tell me about Dr. Bushnell?" Jessie asked.

"He was an *excellent* doctor. People came to him from all over the country, even from Europe and South America."

"Any arguments with dissatisfied patients?"

"You mean Carla Luchins." The corners of Suzanne's mouth curled up in disgust. "The woman's *intense*. She was driving Marianna crazy, phoning ten, twelve times a day, insisting Dr. B. fix her nose again, for free. There's nothing wrong with her nose." She leaned across the desk. "Now *she* is someone you should talk to! I had to throw her out of the office yesterday morning."

So that part of Carla's story was true, Jessie thought. "Were there other dissatisfied patients?"

"Not that I know of. I mean, people aren't always a hundred percent satisfied, but it's not a science, you know? And Dr. Bushnell was great at what he did."

"We spoke to Ms. Luchins," Jessie said. "She overheard Dr. Bushnell having an angry conversation on the phone when she was here yesterday."

"Oh, *please*." Suzanne sniffed dismissively. "The woman's scared and trying to get you off her back."

Exactly what Phil had said. "Did the doctor seem upset yesterday?"

She looked uncertain and took a moment before answering. "Now that you mention it, he *was* tense." She frowned. "Marianna and Nicole noticed it, too. We thought it was because Leanne was out sick. Dr. B. *hates* having his schedule disrupted."

"What about the doctor and his wife? Do you know if there were any problems?"

"No." The bookkeeper's frown had deepened and she seemed lost in thought.

Probably wondering whether something had slipped by her, Jessie guessed. "Was Dr. Bushnell friendly?"

It took her a few seconds to refocus. "Very friendly, but in a professional way. He was never inappropriate with me, if that's what you're getting at."

"No rumors that he was having an affair with a patient?"

Suzanne shook her head quickly. "Absolutely not."

So much for that theory, Jessie thought, disappointed. "According to Ms. Velasquez's appointment book, the last appointment yesterday was for a Clifford Bronte, but I couldn't find his file. She wrote NP next to his name."

"New patient. There wouldn't be a file yet."

There was no local phone number—listed or unlisted— for a Clifford Bronte, Jessie had learned. Maybe he was from out of town. Or maybe the shooter had used the name as an alias when booking the appointment. Or, she thought again, maybe the man simply hadn't shown.

At Jessie's request, Suzanne wrote down Barbara Martin's phone number and a Santa Monica address, and agreed to check the files for patients who had expressed dissatisfaction with their surgery results.

"Barbara may not be home," the bookkeeper said, handing Jessie a slip of paper with the information. "I phoned her last night after I heard about Dr. Bushnell on the news. I got her answering machine. Same thing this morning."

Interesting. "Do you have a phone number of a family member who may know where I can reach her?"

"Sorry, no."

"And you have no idea why she was fired?"

"No, I'm sorry." The woman sounded genuinely disappointed for having failed Jessie. Embarrassed, almost.

❖ 10 ❖

CELESTE BUSHNELL WAS resting, the petite, middle-aged Korean housekeeper reported in accented, broken English. She tried to shut the door.

Jessie braced it open with her palm. "I'd like to talk to the daughter, Adrienne."

The woman shook her head. "You come back later, h'okay? H'okay."

"I need to talk to her *now*." Jessie pushed the door open slowly, forcing the housekeeper to move back, and stepped inside.

"This here *sad* house, very-very sad," the tiny woman scolded. "Why you no come back later, show respect, hunh?"

"It's important," Jessie told her, impressed by the woman's fearlessness and loyalty, wondering whether she would have been as fearless confronting Phil, who was pursuing a lead on the Pervez murder. "Where is Adrienne?"

The housekeeper scowled. "You wait *here*. I be right back." She eyed Jessie suspiciously as she left the entry hall, as if putting a potential thief on notice.

A few minutes later she reappeared with Adrienne. The teenager had looked waiflike yesterday. Today she looked frail and frighteningly pale, as if the constant crying, evidenced by her red-rimmed, swollen eyes, had washed out all the color from her young face. She was wearing the same jeans and pale blue sweater she'd had on yesterday, and had slipped her long blond hair into a ponytail.

"My mom's trying to sleep," she said in a mechanical voice. "The doctor came last night and gave her some pills, but she didn't take any. But I think she took some now."

"I may her take *two* pill," said the housekeeper, who had remained to guard her charge. "I no like pills, but she need sleep. She is tired, very-very tired. You need sleep, too, Adri Anne." She pronounced the name as two words.

"I have a few questions to ask you," Jessie told the girl. "Where can we talk?" She ignored the housekeeper, who was glaring at her, her coal black eyes fierce as a bulldog's.

"The kitchen, I guess."

Her tone was listless, and so was her pace. With the housekeeper tagging along, Jessie followed the girl through the wide center hall to the back of the house into a country French kitchen with warm woods and yellow and blue ceramic tiles on the counters and backsplash. Wide French doors afforded a view of the pool and a tennis court near the rear of the large property, bordered by a hedge of tall trees Jessie couldn't name that provided privacy and serenity.

"Why don't we sit outside," Jessie suggested when the housekeeper made no move to leave.

"You go outside, you need sweater, Adri Anne," the woman warned. "You wait." She scurried out of the room.

Adrienne made no move to leave, either out of obedience or lethargy. Minutes later she stood, impassive as a mannequin, and allowed the housekeeper to lift one arm, then the other, and slip on the sleeves of a gray fleece zippered cardigan.

They sat at a round, glass-topped, wrought iron table on a brick patio filled with large clay pots of pansies, lobelia, and hot-pink azaleas. The weather was warmer today, less hazy, too. A mild breeze ruffled the bright flowers and brought an intoxicating whiff of jasmine. It was too beautiful a day to be talking about death, Jessie thought. She wondered whether the same thought had crossed Adrienne's mind, but a quick glance told her the girl was unaware of her surroundings.

"Were you able to sleep at all?" Jessie asked.

"Some."

"Is your family coming in?"

"My mom's parents are coming from Seattle today," she said in the same listless voice. "My uncle's coming later. He lives in Pasadena."

"That'll be good for your mom, seeing her parents."

"My mom couldn't sleep last night. The doctor gave her pills, but she didn't take any. This morning she did." She obviously didn't realize she'd told Jessie the same thing minutes ago.

"I know this is a difficult time, Adrienne, and I'm sorry to bother you. But I do have a few questions."

The girl didn't answer.

"Sometimes when people are in shock, they don't remember things right away. Big things, little things. I'm wondering, now that you've had time to think, whether you remember if your father quarreled with anyone recently."

"Just that woman. Did you talk to her?" Adrienne seemed suddenly animated, as if someone had switched on the light behind her brown eyes.

"Yes, last night."

She leaned forward, inhaling sharply. "Do you think she killed my father?"

"It's a possibility we're pursuing, but we'd like to investigate every lead. That's why I need you to think carefully. Did your father seem angry about something in the last few days or weeks? Was someone giving him a hard time?"

The girl shook her head, then lowered her eyes and fingered her necklace.

"His bookkeeper mentioned that he fired one of his nurses. Barbara Martin." The voice on the nurse's answering machine had invited Jessie to leave a message, but Jessie preferred to try again later. "Did he talk about that?"

"Not to me."

"Maybe he argued with a friend." No reaction. "Maybe with a family member. It doesn't mean this person killed your father. But it's information we need to know."

"Everybody has arguments," the girl said defiantly.

"Absolutely." Jessie nodded. "Especially among family. Did your dad argue recently with someone? With your uncle, maybe?"

"My dad and Uncle Andrew got along great. Everybody loved my dad." Her brown eyes glistened.

Something was bothering the girl. The mom? Mother and daughter had been together while Bushnell and two of his staff members had been killed, but what if Celeste had hired someone to do the job? Jessie had learned nothing to indicate that the marriage had been troubled, and everyone she and Phil had talked to—Carla, Suzanne, Leanne—confirmed that the doctor's relationships with his patients and staff had been completely professional. Still . . .

"Parents also argue," Jessie said casually. "I know mine do." She wondered again why her father hadn't returned either of the two calls she'd made to his office. Was he avoiding her? "People can't agree about everything. If they did, they'd be saints." She smiled.

Adrienne shrugged. She looked toward the French doors, where the housekeeper was keeping vigil.

"My dad's a doctor, just like yours," Jessie said. "My mom's upset with him sometimes because he comes home late." Because he's having an affair?

"My mom's pretty chill." Adrienne ran her finger across the glass tabletop. "My dad's more into rules. Curfew, homework, stuff like that, especially with—" She stopped. "They don't always see eye to eye."

Hardly a motive for murder. A monarch butterfly landed on a yellow pansy. Jessie watched it dance from flower to flower.

"It's not like he's *too* strict," Adrienne said quietly. "Even if he's mad about you for something, an hour later he's all over it." Tears flooded her eyes.

"You were close to your dad, weren't you?" Jessie said softly. "I'm sure you'd want to do anything to find out who killed him."

The girl nodded. The tears spilled onto her cheeks. "But I don't *know* anything."

"I have the feeling you do, Adrienne. I think you're afraid to tell me, afraid you'll get someone in trouble."

Color tinted her face. "No, I'm not."

The door opened and Celeste stepped onto the patio wearing a floral-patterned belted robe and white mules. Her eyes looked glazed, and she seemed to have trouble focusing. Side effects of the tranquilizer—or grief, Jessie thought. Lily Pervez's mother's dark eyes had held the same vacant stare.

"My housekeeper said you were out here, talking to Adrienne." Celeste sounded exhausted.

Jessie stood. "Just a few things I needed to clear up."

"Do you know who killed Ronnie?" She moved behind her daughter and placed her hands on the girl's shoulders.

"We're pursuing every lead, Mrs. Bushnell."

"I was hoping you'd have some news." Celeste smoothed the girl's hair. "Was there something you wanted to ask me, Detective?"

"Your husband's bookkeeper told me he fired Barbara Martin, one of his nurses. Do you know the circumstances?"

"Something about her not being professional, or not always careful? I can't remember. I know he was upset about having to find a replacement, and annoyed because she was suing him. Nowadays with workmen's comp laws, it's hard to fire anyone." Celeste's eyes narrowed. "Why? Do you think . . . ?"

"We're pursuing every possibility." Jessie debated, then said, "I had the feeling last night that you and your daughter were keeping information from me."

"No." Celeste shook her head and yawned. "No, we've told you everything we know."

"It may be something you think is insignificant, Mrs. Bushnell," Jessie continued, "or you may believe it has no bearing on your husband's murder. You may be right. Then again, you may be wrong. And if you are . . ."

Celeste was fidgeting with the edges of her robe and looked uneasy. Jessie wondered if she'd picked the wrong Bushnell to question.

"It's that *patient*," Adrienne said. "She threatened my dad, and she killed him. Why aren't you arresting her?"

"We're not ruling her out, Adrienne." Jessie returned her attention to the mother.

Celeste ran a hand through her hair and looked toward the pool.

"If you're keeping something from us, it'll come out," Jessie told her. "It always does. We're going to talk to your neighbors, to everybody who knows you and your family."

The woman sighed. "I can't do this anymore, Adrienne," she said in a low, almost inaudible voice. "I just can't."

"Mom—"

"It's Ethan," Celeste told Jessie. "Ethan Meissner."

The girl whirled around toward her mother. "Mom, *don't*!"

"Detective Drake is right. It's going to come out."

"You *know* Ethan didn't have anything to do with Daddy's murder!" Adrienne jumped up, her hands clenched at her side. "You *know* that!"

"Who is Ethan Meissner?" Jessie asked.

11

"ETHAN CAME TO live with us when he was eight," Celeste said. "He'd been through a terrible ordeal."

They were sitting in the kitchen. Celeste had urged Adrienne to lie down, but the girl had insisted on staying—probably to monitor what her mother revealed, Jessie assumed. The housekeeper had placed steaming oversize green mugs in front of Celeste and Adrienne—coffee for the mother, hot cocoa for the daughter. Nothing for Jessie, which came as no surprise, given the woman's hostility. Celeste, clearly distracted, hadn't offered. She had taken only a token sip of the coffee, while Adrienne poked with a spoon at the whipped cream that topped her drink.

"What happened to his parents?" Jessie asked.

"His mother killed herself," Celeste said somberly. "She'd suffered a nervous breakdown a year before, but no one realized how unstable she was. Lucy was always fragile, ever since her postpartum depression after Ethan was born. She couldn't take care of him until he was about two months old. I can imagine how guilty she felt. When Adrienne was born, we were separated because I had to be hospitalized for ten days with an infection. I cried all the time." She glanced at her daughter.

"You and your husband knew Lucy well?"

Celeste looked confused. "I thought I explained. Lucy was Ronnie's nurse. She was with him almost from the time he opened his practice. When Ronnie's receptionist quit, I took over until he could find someone else. Lucy and I became friends, and the kids spent a lot of time together." She had a distant, wistful look in her eyes, as if she were remembering happier days. "When she killed herself, we were devastated. Especially Ronnie. I think he blamed himself for not seeing the signs."

From her experience with suicides and their families, Jessie knew that seeing the signs and taking safeguards won't stop someone determined to take his or her life. "There was no father?"

"Oh, yes. Gideon." Celeste nodded. "But he was incapable of raising a child. He's a musician, and he was out of work most of the time. He could be extremely charming, but he was lazy and without direction, always waiting for his big break but not doing much to make it happen, always blaming everyone else for his failures. He had a drinking problem, too, and a temper. I think Ethan was afraid of him." She picked up the mug with both hands and held it without drinking, as if the warmth emanating through the ceramic were comfort enough. "Gideon was relieved when Ronnie and I offered to take Ethan. Everybody was."

"What about Lucy's family?"

Celeste put down the mug. "They died in a car accident just before she killed herself. I think that's what broke her. And Gideon's family lived in Israel. So we decided to have Ethan live with us. We'd been so close with Lucy and Ethan, and it was wonderful for Adrienne to have a brother." She looked tenderly at her daughter, who had rested her head on her arms.

Ethan had been fortunate to have options. Jessie wondered again how Alex Velasquez was doing, whether the great-aunt would decide that taking care of a young boy was, in spite of family obligations, too difficult.

The housekeeper had been at the sink, wiping dishes. Now she approached the table. "You need eat something," she told Celeste. "I give you bowl of soup, h'okay? Ve-ge-ta-ble." She pronounced the word as having four syllables. "Very good soup. I just made."

"Thanks, but I'm not hungry, Kim. Maybe later."

The woman's frown wrinkled her already lined flat face. "You no eat, you get very-very *sick*, and what I tell your mother when she come? And what happen to Adri Anne, hunh? I bring you soup, you be *strong*."

"All right."

The housekeeper sniffled and shuffled away.

"She's very protective," Jessie remarked.

"She's like family." Celeste smiled wanly. "Kim worked for my parents since my brother and I were kids, first in my dad's dress factory, then, when she had back problems from sitting at the machine all day, in our home."

"It's unusual for Koreans to work away from their family, isn't it?"

Celeste nodded. "Before my dad hired her, she worked in her family's sweatshop, but she hated it." She glanced at the housekeeper, whose back was toward them. "My mother told me she thinks Kim's husband beat her," she whispered. "Anyway, she's fiercely loyal to my family. When my parents moved to Seattle, I inherited her. She's bossy, but she'd do anything for me. When Ronnie and I were dating, he worried more about winning Kim's approval than my parents'." She smiled again and brushed away tears. "She's very worried about Ethan."

"You didn't adopt Ethan?"

"Gideon wouldn't agree. Until a few years ago, he kept talking about straightening out his life and having Ethan come live with him. We all knew it would never happen. Gideon knew it, too, but I guess talking about it made him feel like less of a failure as a father. It didn't really matter. Adoption or not, Ethan was our son."

"Which is why he'd *never* hurt Dad!" Adrienne's head jerked up like a marionette's. "He *loved* Dad."

"I know, sweetheart." Celeste patted her daughter's hand.

"Did Ethan and your husband quarrel recently?" Jessie asked.

Celeste nodded. "Ronnie was extremely concerned about him. Ethan was—" She broke off and looked thoughtful, as if searching for the right words. "Ethan's been going through a difficult time. He told Ronnie he wanted to drop out of high school and get an equivalency degree, and—"

"A lot of kids do it," Adrienne interrupted. "It's not the end of the world."

"Ronnie felt it was a terrible mistake. Ethan's so bright. He could get into any of the Ivy Leagues."

"It's *his* life, Mom. He should be able to make his own decisions."

Celeste silenced her daughter with a weary look. "The point is," she said to Jessie, "my husband felt Ethan was getting bad advice from his friends. Last year he earned straight A's, even in his AP courses. This year began fine, too, and then something happened. I don't know what. I think he was hanging around with the wrong crowd."

"Was he on drugs?" Jessie asked.

"The school thought so, and Ronnie found paraphernalia in his room." Celeste sounded more sad than angry. "Ethan was drinking, too. He hit a pole and smashed up the front of my car. Adrienne was with him, and when I think that they could both have been killed . . ." She shuddered.

"Nothing *happened*, Mom. I wasn't hurt. *No one* was."

"That was luck," her mother told her sternly. "God was watching over both of you." She faced Jessie. "There were other things. I'd be missing cash—twenty dollars, fifty. And jewelry."

"You're always misplacing cash." Adrienne seemed on the verge of tears. "You said so yourself, so you can't blame Ethan! You leave your earrings all over the house. Kim found your emerald ring in the trash with papers you threw out!"

"I tend to be careless," Celeste admitted. "It drove Ronnie

crazy. But lately he thought Ethan was taking the cash and pawning the jewelry to buy drugs. He accused Ethan of stealing and warned him he wouldn't tolerate the drugs or the drinking. Ethan denied stealing anything. He told Ronnie that he was going to live his life the way he wanted, that Ronnie couldn't tell him what to do."

"He was scared," Adrienne insisted quietly. "He didn't mean it."

"Maybe." The mother nodded. "Ronnie lost his temper. He told Ethan that as long as he was living under his roof and eating his food and taking his money, Ethan would have to abide by his rules. Ethan called his bluff. He packed a few things in his backpack and walked out, just like that. I begged Ronnie to stop him, but Ronnie can be stubborn."

"When did this happen?"

"Three weeks ago. It was horrible, just . . . horrible. The next day Ronnie tried to find Ethan to talk him into coming back home, but none of his friends knew where he was. His *old* friends, I mean. Ethan phoned a day later to tell us he was okay, but he wouldn't say where he was. He's called a few times since then."

"Could he be with his father?" Jessie asked.

"He isn't. We phoned Gideon the night Ethan left. He promised he'd let us know if he heard from him. I'm not surprised he hasn't. Gideon hasn't been in touch with Ethan for months, and Ethan's never been able to depend on him."

"So you have no idea where he is?"

"He's probably staying with one of the bums he's been hanging out with, but we don't even know their *names*." Celeste stared into her mug. "Sometimes I wonder if he's living on the street, like one of the homeless. He didn't take his car, and Ronnie took away his credit card, he was so angry. Ethan didn't have much cash on him. I wanted to give him a few hundred dollars, but he wouldn't take it."

Too proud, Jessie thought with a twinge of empathy, too angry. She'd repeatedly refused financial aid from her father when she'd moved to Los Angeles to escape Frances—in part, she'd realized even before therapy, to hurt him for his passive complicity.

"Have you filed a police report?" she asked Celeste.

"No. Ronnie wanted to at first, but Gideon said no, and legally, he's Ethan's guardian. He said it would be better not to have anything on Ethan's record. Then Ethan called. He hasn't shown up at school, but he's eighteen, so I guess he can do what he wants." Celeste played with the collar of her robe. "Before he called, we checked the area hospitals, just to make sure he hadn't been injured or . . ." She didn't complete the thought. "Last night, when you said you had bad news . . ." Again she stopped. "I don't know if he's heard about Ronnie. He'll feel awful, just awful." Her eyes filled with fresh tears.

"The whole thing's crazy!" Adrienne exclaimed. "So *what* if Ethan had a fight with my dad and moved out? That's not a reason for him to kill my dad."

Unless, Jessie thought, Ethan, high on drugs or booze, had been persuaded by his friends that he'd been given a raw deal by Bushnell. Jessie had never understood what had prompted Lyle and Erik Menendez to kill their parents one summer day. Greed, claims of abuse. Who knew what resentments Ethan had harbored against his foster parent? Or had one of Ethan's friends done the deed for him?

"Do you have a gun in the house, Mrs. Bushnell?"

"Ethan didn't kill my dad," Adrienne repeated.

Celeste was staring at Jessie. "No, no guns. Ronnie hated guns. And Ethan . . ."

"Do you know who Ethan's new friends are?" Jessie asked the daughter.

"No."

She studied the girl. "Adrienne, if Ethan hasn't done anything wrong, he won't be in any trouble. And what if he needs help?"

"Adrienne, if you know *anything*, tell Detective Drake." Celeste sounded frustrated, impatient.

The girl chewed on her lip. "He mentioned someone who goes by the name Torro, another is Big M.," she finally said, clearly reluctant. "I only know their nicknames. They're older and not from around here. I don't know where Ethan met them, or how to find them. There's a girl, too, but he didn't tell me her name."

"Do you know where Ethan hung out with them?"

The girl shook her head.

"I'm sure he doesn't know about Ronnie, or he'd be here," Celeste said. "Can you find him, Detective? I don't want him out somewhere, alone. There's no telling what he'll do to himself."

"You'll have to file a missing person's report," Jessie told her. "Then we can enter him into a national computerized system."

Celeste nodded. "But in the meantime? Is there anything you can do?"

To search for incriminating evidence, Jessie needed a warrant. To try to find information just to *locate* a missing person, she didn't. And if, in the course of seeking information that would lead to his whereabouts, she came across incriminating evidence, that evidence would still be admissible.

"I could take a look in Ethan's room, with your written permission," Jessie offered. "And I'll need a photo."

12

THE ITEMS IN the airy second-floor bedroom seemed to belong to two different boys. There was the Ethan who owned a guitar and an electronic keyboard, who had won too-shiny, gold-look plastic trophies in tennis and swimming and debate, and had brightened his gray walls with sports pennants and a pegged rack displaying caps from various teams and sports. A basketball lay on the Berber-carpeted floor beneath a knotty pine computer desk that held a laptop and above which were two shelves containing a twelfth-grade literature text, a thesaurus, a large dictionary, and a collection of fiction.

Jessie glanced at the spines: *The Canterbury Tales, The Three Musketeers, Madame Bovary, Wuthering Heights, Hedda Gabler, Vanity Fair, Crime and Punishment, House of Mirth, The Sufferings of Young Werther, The Bell Jar.* There was a slim copy of *Hamlet,* in addition to a text of Shakespeare's complete works, and a biography of Virginia Woolf. Not a Cliff's Notes in sight—she was impressed.

There was a darker Ethan, an eighteen-year-old who played Dungeons and Dragons, read *Hannibal* and *American Psycho*, and had hidden beneath the extra pillows in his closet a videotape collection of chillingly violent films: *Eight MM, Natural Born Killers, Pulp Fiction, Reservoir Dogs, The Basketball Diaries, Seven.*

"Why would he watch those?" Celeste asked plaintively

when Jessie stacked the videotapes on the desk, and Jessie had no answer.

Ethan's taste in music was equally eclectic: Mozart, Beethoven, Debussy, Chopin, and a host of other classical greats ("You should hear him play the piano," Celeste said. "He's gifted."); a large collection of jazz; heavy metal groups like Ozzy Osbourne, Marilyn Manson, Limp Bizkit, and some Jessie had never heard of; heavy rap like Eminem and DMX; softer rap. Another stack of CDs—Backstreet Boys and others—the kind of music Jessie would have adored fifteen years ago and still liked but didn't prefer ("I grow old . . . I grow old . . . I shall wear the bottoms of my trousers rolled.").

Was this what her nephew would be listening to three, four years from now? And what then? Did the music change along with the adolescent, or did it induce the change?

Something had definitely changed for Ethan. Paging through his spiral school notebooks, she noted that sometime in late September his neat, tight handwriting had taken on a more erratic, jagged style, and where he'd usually written copious notes, he now barely jotted down more than a few sentences, sometimes only a word or two. She found no references to any of the friends Adrienne had named or to Bushnell, but from the paper curlicues remaining in the spiral binding she knew several pages had been ripped out. She wondered what Ethan had written, why he'd felt the need to dispose of words he'd committed to paper.

Above a pine armoire hung a framed collage of photos. She studied the tall, lanky, dark-haired teenager who had clearly been a central part of the Bushnell family: Ethan in green basketball shorts and jersey and a knee brace, his face shiny with perspiration and pride. Ethan in swim trunks, his curly hair flattened, standing next to a grinning Ronald Bushnell. Ethan and Adrienne sticking their tongues out at the camera. The two on a roller coaster. The family at a park, in Disneyland. The four of them, layered in parkas and disguised with sun goggles, propped up on ski poles against a background of blinding white snow.

"He looks like a happy young man," Jessie remarked.

"He was, until recently." A sad expression clouded Celeste's face. "It's almost like he was reverting to the little boy who came to live with us. Ethan was anxious then, moody. He didn't communicate much, and didn't like to be hugged or touched. It wasn't just the suicide. Between Lucy's depression and Gideon's temperament, he didn't have an easy time."

Jessie thought about her nephew. When she'd met Matthew, he'd also been an anxious eight-year-old—silent, afraid to be touched. He was better now, but sometimes she worried about the long-term effect of Helen's abuse.

In one of the desk drawers she found a family photo. The background of sun and sea was identical to that in the photo in Bushnell's office, one of the few objects that had escaped the gunfire. Bushnell was wearing the same print shirt, the same smile. Ethan, standing between Bushnell and Adrienne, was smiling, too, his brown eyes warm.

"I was looking for that." Celeste sounded puzzled. "It's supposed to be in the family room." She took the photo from Jessie and set it, face up, on the desk.

In a middle drawer, under a stack of notebooks, Jessie found a manila envelope inside of which were several sheets filled with musical notations and lyrics. Like his CD collection, the aspiring musician's poetry ran the gamut from sentimental to sinister: there were odes to nature; a series of tentative declarations to an unnamed love that became exultant and rhapsodic when "boy got girl"; reflections on death (no mention of his mother), despair. One, titled "Endings," was particularly ominous:

> There's no real point to go on any longer,
> The pain's so huge, and it's only getting stronger.
> Put a bullet to my head
> But before that, kill 'em dead
> In the house and in the school
> 'Cause they played me for a fool.

My existence is a lie,
How many times can I die?
Kill 'em all
Watch them fall

Celeste paled when she read the words. "I had no idea he was so depressed." She sounded mournful, frightened. "Did he show you this?" She handed the sheet to her daughter.

Adrienne shook her head. "He fools around with gangsta rap, but it's not what he's really into. I don't think he meant any of this," she added but didn't sound convinced.

"We wanted him to start therapy again," Celeste said. "He went a few times but refused to continue."

The therapist might have interesting information but would probably claim patient confidentiality. Still, it was worth a try. Jessie asked Celeste for the therapist's name and phone number and wrote them down.

"Does Ethan have a girlfriend?" she asked, thinking about the love poems.

"He was dating someone, but they broke up a while ago," Celeste said. "I don't think there was anyone new, and then he started with these other people." She glanced at her daughter, but the girl shrugged.

The songs weren't dated. Jessie wondered if he'd written them to his old flame or to the new girl whose name Adrienne didn't know. "I'd like to check the files on Ethan's computer, Mrs. Bushnell. He may have written something that will help us find him." She'd received permission before looking through the boy's notebooks, too.

"It's an invasion of his privacy, Mom." Adrienne turned to Jessie. "You're treating him like a criminal, and he didn't *do* anything!"

"What if he needs help and is too proud to come home?" Jessie said gently. "Those lyrics say he's very troubled." What if he'd *tried* to come home, and Bushnell had refused? *I've made up my mind. I should have done this long ago.*

Celeste ran a hand through her hair. "You really think he might kill himself?"

"You have good reason to be concerned, Mrs. Bushnell. And you should take precautions here, too."

She stared at Jessie. "Ethan wouldn't hurt us!" Her voice shook. "We've done everything for him—given him love, security, a home."

"He talks about killing people, at home and at school. Your husband's been murdered. I don't think we should treat this lightly." Jessie would have to alert the school.

Celeste nodded. "Go ahead," she said wearily.

Adrienne stood with her arms folded tight against her chest, her young face sullen.

Sitting at the desk, Jessie switched on the computer and waited until the humming and soft clicking subsided. She accessed the main directory first. Ethan had loaded Doom, Tomb Raider, Metal Gear, and Kingpin. In videogame parlance, Phil had told her, they were known as multiplayer "first-person shooter" games, or FSPs—they featured on-screen weapons that severed targets' limbs and sprayed blood on walls, providing violent thrills and high body counts and doing God knew what to the player's psyche.

The diskettes in Ethan's desk drawer were disappointingly tame—they contained only school-related files. The Recycle Bin was empty.

There was an Internet icon at the top of the computer screen. "Did Ethan go on-line often?" Jessie asked.

"More and more, especially lately," Celeste said. "Ronnie thought he was spending way too much time on-line. He warned Ethan that he was going to cancel his account if he didn't concentrate on his studies."

"He used it mostly for his *school* stuff, Mom." Adrienne's tone was patronizing, impatient. "It's easier than going to a library."

It would be interesting to see what sites Ethan frequented, and whom he E-mailed. Jessie clicked on the icon and waited again until the screen prompted her to enter the password for the member using the screen name EMCATZ2.

"It's his initials, and it's M-CATS," Celeste said. She was looking over Jessie's shoulder. "The qualifying test for med school? Ethan was planning to follow in Ronnie's footsteps."

If necessary, Jessie would obtain a court order that would compel the server to reveal Ethan Meissner's password. Right now she didn't know if she was dealing with an unhappy, rebellious teen who could be suicidal, or a murderer. Or both.

"I'll need a photo of Ethan," she reminded Celeste after she had shut off the computer.

"Right." The woman looked uncertain and left the room. A moment later she returned and handed Jessie a small headshot of the teenager. "This is an extra of the photos he took in July. He had to redo his passport when he turned eighteen, and we were planning to go to Cancun again this winter during school break. We have a condo there."

"When was that taken?" Jessie pointed to the family shot whose near duplicate she'd seen in Bushnell's office.

"In Maui, this past summer. We had the best time." Celeste picked up the photo and gazed at it, touched her dead husband's face. "Ethan's the photographer in the family. He asked this cute little old man to take it, so he could be in it. We didn't think it would come out focused or centered."

"Your husband has one just like it in his office, but Ethan's not in it."

"I know." She sighed the words. "The day after Ethan left, Ronnie was hurt, and he tore up the photo in his office. He said if Ethan didn't want to be a part of our lives, that was fine with him. He was sorry right after he did it, but we only had the two prints, and I couldn't find this one. So he took the one without Ethan." She put the photo back on the desk. "It was just temporary."

Now it was final. Three years ago, when her separation

had been permanent, Jessie had removed every photo of Gary from their house. She recalled the wrenching heartache, the numbing sense of loss, almost like bereavement, that she'd felt analyzing Gary's smiling face in each picture, trying to discern whether film had captured the moment their marriage had begun to unravel. Pictures can lie, she'd realized. Smiles can deceive, something she should have known from the happy faces of her mother and father and Helen in their family photos. Her own face, too.

She'd stored the photos of Gary in a box, along with their wedding album, not quite sure what to do with them. She knew a detective in Sex Crimes who had made a bonfire of all the photos of her ex. Jessie couldn't bring herself to do that. She wasn't angry at Gary anymore, had never been that angry to begin with, just terribly sad. But maybe it was time to remove the photos and the nostalgia that teased her and made her second-guess what she knew in her heart was right.

"Three weeks ago we were so happy," Celeste said.

❖ 13 ❖

SIMMS AND BOYD were out on a new carjacking turned homicide, Phil reported when Jessie returned to the station. Espes had gone home for the day.

"After he infected everyone." Phil took a long swig from the plastic water bottle that was now a constant companion. "FYI, Carla Luchins came in and gave her statement. I was real popular while she was here." He grinned.

"I'll bet." Jessie kicked off the flats she'd bought last week and hadn't quite broken in and checked her desk. No messages. "Did anyone call for me?" Meaning her father.

"Not since I got back from Oxnard, which was a total waste of time. I drive all the way to this supermarket where Jamal Pervez supposedly tried to buy groceries this morning and get some cash. The clerk who handled the transaction can't tell me much, just that the guy looked nervous when the clerk asked him for his ID, and lit out of there."

"Was it Pervez?"

"The clerk says maybe, maybe not. The guy was standing two feet away from him, and he can't say for sure." Phil grunted. "He should've signaled the guard before he asked for ID."

"We still don't have a motive." Jessie flexed her aching toes. "According to Jamal's friend, Jamal was grateful to Lily's parents for sponsoring him when he emigrated from

Pakistan. And he was fond of Lily. She visited his apartment all the time."

Phil smirked. "Maybe he was *too* fond."

She shook her head. "There was no sexual assault."

"He didn't *assault* her. He *loved* her. He withdrew ten thousand from his bank the day before the murder, right?" They had learned about the cash withdrawal this morning. "Suppose her parents disapproved. Jamal wants to elope and move away. Lily says no—she can't go against her folks. Jamal flips and kills her. Then he panics and runs."

Jessie thought for a moment. "Let's say you're right. Pervez is a bright guy, a computer whiz with more in his bank account than most twenty-year-olds."

"More than me," Phil groused.

"So why use the credit card knowing it can lead us to him? And if he's a fugitive, why hasn't he left the state?"

"He feels guilty. Maybe he wants to be caught." Phil swiveled in his chair. "Shit, *I* don't know. Maybe he *didn't* kill the cousin, but knows it looks bad for him. He's hiding out till we find the person who did. That's what the family thinks."

"Okay, but we're back to the credit card. And why did he withdraw the ten G the day before the murder? Don't tell me it's coincidence, Phil. You can't have it both ways."

He pulled at his mustache. "What if he's using the credit card to let the family know he's alive? He can't risk phoning them—what if their lines are tapped?"

"Maybe." Jessie nodded. "Or someone else is using his card to make us *think* Pervez is alive."

Phil shook his head. "A, his car is gone," he said, ticking off points with his fingers. "B, he packed a suitcase and emptied his drawers. C, the only blood we found in Pervez's apartment belongs to Lily."

"D, he could've been kidnapped and killed elsewhere. Everything else could be part of the setup."

"Including the money? Why'd he withdraw ten thousand

the day *before* he was killed, Jess? You can't have it both ways—that's what you told me."

"Why not?" She drew dollar signs and question marks on a sheet of paper. "Maybe the ten G is *why* he was killed, Phil. Suppose Jamal had to pay someone off. Drugs, gambling, whatever. The person shows up. Lily arrives unexpectedly—she's at the wrong place at the wrong time." Like Bushnell's nurse and receptionist? Or was one of them the main victim? "So this person has to kill Lily, too, but he does Jamal somewhere else to pin Lily's murder on him."

Phil considered and nodded. "*Or*, Lily shows up at Jamal's while he's out. This person arrives, kills her. Jamal shows, finds her dead, panics and skips."

They would have to talk again to Lily's parents and brother—Jamal's only American family—and to his sole good friend. Jamal was pretty much a loner, they'd learned.

"What about you?" Phil asked Jessie. "Learn anything from the girl?"

"From the mother, actually." She told him about Ethan Meissner, about a childhood traumatized by the tensions of an habitually out-of-work father and a mother's suicide, about the quarrel with Bushnell that had precipitated his leaving home, about his interest in dark music and cinema. She showed him the lyrics—Celeste had photocopied the page in her husband's office.

"The father had a temper and a booze problem," Jessie said. "The mom killed herself. Maybe it's in the genes."

" 'Kill 'em all, watch them fall.' " Phil expelled a deep breath. "You hear about these screwed-up kids knocking off their parents, their teachers, their classmates, girlfriends, but it never makes sense, does it? Kinkel, Johnson, Golden, Carneal, Woodham, Williams. A teenage hall of horrors. And nobody ever sees it coming, not even the parents. How is that, huh?"

Jessie didn't answer.

"They say the Harris boy who did the Columbine killings

was making explosives in the family garage. *In the garage!*
I said to Maureen, no way his parents didn't know. How
could they not *know*? Were they too busy with their own
lives? Too lenient? Too trusting? But it's easy to blame the
parents. I don't want to be some smug son of a bitch when
the bottom line is, it could happen to anyone."

"Come on, Phil. You have terrific boys. You and Maureen
are so involved with them. You spend so much time together.
And there are warning signs." Moodiness, isolation, fits of
anger or depression, a sudden drop in grades.

"You don't always want to see them, not in your kid. You
make excuses. And it's tough out there in the school yard."
Phil hesitated. "A couple of weeks ago Brian got suspended
for punching a kid who called him a dummy," he said, not
looking at Jessie. "He has a special tutor now, so I hope he'll
feel better about himself, but he's still sensitive 'cause he
has a hard time with school."

"Kids have fights, Phil." He'd mentioned a while back
that his younger son might have a learning disability. He
hadn't brought up the subject since, and Jessie was pleased
to hear that the boy was getting help.

"Look, I don't think my kids are headed for trouble, but
do I really *know* them? And what about their peers? Maureen and I are seriously considering private high school.
Brian's only ten, Chris is twelve, and we're already worrying about who they'll hang out with. Will they be pressured
into trying pot or booze or having sex just 'cause it's cool?"

"That's a far cry from killing people."

"You think Harris was screwed up when he was ten?" Phil
demanded. "Something changed him."

"I think he was probably screwed up when he was
younger. There are kids who do bad things for no reason.
Bad seeds."

"Usually there are reasons." He paused. "You see a park
playground filled with little kids—black, white, Hispanic,
Asian. You look at them playing together, all of them with

faces so innocent, and it breaks your heart 'cause you know at least one of them is going to end up pulling a trigger."

"So what's the answer?"

"You want to watch over them, but you don't want to smother them," Phil said, as if counseling himself. He sighed. "You end up praying a lot."

14

THE PRIVATE SCHOOL Adrienne and Ethan attended was on a winding, tree-shaded side street in Westwood off Sunset, not far from the West L.A. station on Butler, and within walking distance of UCLA. Let your grasp exceed your reach, Jessie thought with apologies to Browning, although if this were anything like other private schools, most of its students and parents probably aspired to the Ivy Leagues.

Frances had. She'd practically sat in mourning when Jessie hadn't earned the necessary grades. "Your teachers all say you're not working up to your potential. You're doing this to spite me!" she'd cried. Maybe so. Jessie had known how important this was to her mother, so it was a small, though stupid, victory. And why allow herself to contemplate the haven that would be hers if she attended college back east when she would never abandon Helen to Frances's mercies?

The campus and three-story building were hidden behind a fortress of Italian cypress trees. Phil drove halfway up a driveway to a wide iron gate and showed his badge to the guard stationed at a booth. A few years ago Jessie would have been surprised at the high security, but the shootings at Padukah and Columbine had forever shattered the illusion that schools were invulnerable to terror. Buford O. Furrow had brought the terror closer to home recently when he opened fire at a Jewish community center in L.A. county's West Valley, injuring three small children, a teenager, and a middle-aged receptionist and later killing a postal worker. Now many schools had armed guards, security cameras, metal detectors, all the latest technology.

The parking area was crammed. So many cars, so few spaces, especially in Southern California high schools, where most teenagers assumed that getting a license entitled them to their own set of wheels and to whom taking a bus was as anachronistic as riding a horse and walking was unthinkable. With school lots unable to accommodate all the automobiles, students hogged spots on neighborhood streets, prompting ir-ritated residents to retaliate with restricted parking.

To live and park in L.A.

Phil found a lone spot for his Buick Cutlass between a Jeep Cherokee and a Mercedes. With the exception of a Sat-urn, an old Chevy Lumina, an Altima, and several older model Hondas and Toyotas, the place was an advertisement for Infinitis, Lexuses, Land Rovers, Expeditions, BMWs, and other luxury cars.

"La crème de la chrome," Jessie commented as they headed toward the main entrance. Phil was glaring at the ve-hicles as if they'd personally offended him. "Stop drooling."

"Ten bucks says the teachers own the crappy ones."

"Yeah, but they have the gratification of knowing they're shaping the minds of tomorrow."

It was 11:20, and the grounds were empty. Inside the building Jessie and Phil passed a boy in navy slacks and white shirt in conversation with two blond girls wearing identical green-and-yellow-plaid pleated skirts and white blouses. A harried-looking receptionist, wedging a phone re-ceiver between her ear and shoulder, motioned to Jessie and Phil to wait.

"Can I help you?" she asked after hanging up the phone.

Jessie introduced herself and Phil. "It's about Ethan Meissner."

"Poor Adrienne!" The woman assumed a grave expres-sion. "I heard the terrible news about Dr. Bushnell on the radio this morning. Parents have been phoning all day, wanting to know whether that was Adrienne's family." She frowned. "Ethan hasn't been here in several weeks. We filed a truant report and notified his parents. Apparently he's left home."

"We'd like to speak with the principal," Jessie said.

"Headmaster," the receptionist corrected with a hint of condescension. "I'll see if Mr. Alpert is available." She spoke to someone on the phone, then directed Jessie and Phil to an office at the other end of the large lobby.

Alpert was standing behind his paper-filled desk when they entered, and leaned over to shake their hands. He was probably in his late thirties or early forties, Jessie guessed, though his receding hairline made him look older. He was wearing a dark suit, a pale blue shirt with monogrammed French cuffs, and what looked like a Zegna tie. Very Brooks Brothers.

"A terrible business," Alpert said, motioning to them to sit. "Such a shock. I met Dr. Bushnell several times. A fine man, a concerned parent. I take it Ethan hasn't returned home?"

Jessie wondered if he always spoke in fragments. "Mrs. Bushnell has no idea where he is. We're hoping one of his classmates may know."

"Doubtful." Alpert drummed his fingers on his desk. "Ethan's estranged himself from his classmates this semester. From his teachers, too."

"He was doing well until recently, I understand."

"He showed great promise. Did Mrs. Bushnell tell you he scored a fifteen sixty on the S.A.T's? He was being courted by the Ivy Leagues and was planning on early admission to Harvard. We had high hopes for him." Alpert shook his head.

For the school, too, no doubt. "What happened?"

"He began the semester well, but he started cutting classes. He failed one exam, then another. He also had a physical altercation with another student."

"Did you talk to him?"

"*Several* times." The headmaster's tone implied that the question was stupid. "We're highly involved with our students." He opened a manila folder and glanced at a filled-out form. "During our first talk he said he'd skipped classes because he hadn't been feeling well. That was in mid-September." Alpert thumbed to the next page. "Two weeks later we spoke about his grades. He explained he'd been groggy during the exams because he was taking antihistamines for a chronic allergy."

Or maybe he was trying to explain the sluggishness and runny nose that indicated drug use, Jessie thought.

Alpert looked at another page. "The last time we talked was after he fought with another student. Ethan insisted the other student had instigated the argument." The headmaster shut the folder. "I warned him that he was jeopardizing his chances of getting into Harvard. He told me he didn't care, that nothing mattered." Alpert hesitated. "You know about Ethan's background?"

Jessie and Phil nodded.

"Tragic, really. The mother's suicide affected him greatly. Ethan's never been gregarious or easygoing, but the day I spoke to him he was markedly different—closed, edgy, angry. I asked him point-blank if he was taking drugs. He denied it, but I didn't believe him."

"Do you have a drug problem here?" Phil asked.

Alpert smiled grimly. "Detective, every high school in America has a drug problem, and any principal who tells you otherwise is lying or out of touch with reality. It's insidious. Ours isn't large, thank goodness. We're vigilant. We've trained our staff to detect overt signs, and we act immediately. A student caught using is expelled. But some students are more careful, and parents don't pay seventeen thousand a year to send their darlings here to have their urine tested. That's not to be quoted," he added quickly.

She did the math. Sixty-eight thousand for a high school

education. She glanced at Phil—he looked depressed. "You don't notify parents if you have only suspicions?"

The headmaster eyed her sadly, as if she were clueless. "We do, if they're strong suspicions backed up by data, but we have to phrase our concern carefully and avoid accusation, or we could be sued. And we don't always get thanked. Some parents are in denial and react with anger. Whether they follow up?" Alpert shrugged. "Even when there are overt signs, some parents blame the school or friends. It's never their child's fault, or theirs."

"What about the Bushnells?" Jessie asked.

"I have to say, their attitude was refreshing. We'd talked before on the phone about Ethan's falling grades, but this isn't something you do on the phone. I asked them to come in. I told them about the boy's mood changes, about his belligerence. When I asked if they thought the problems could be drug related, they didn't argue, and Dr. Bushnell assured me he would speak to Ethan. The next day Ethan was absent. I assumed the Bushnells had taken him to a doctor. Dr. Bushnell phoned a day later and told me Ethan had left home." Alpert sighed. "A sad business, and such a waste. And now this. Do you have any idea who killed Dr. Bushnell?"

"We're pursuing several leads," Jessie told him. The stock answer. "Who were Ethan's friends, before he changed?"

"Ethan was always a loner, more interested in his studies than in friendships. Again, I'd say that was a result of his childhood trauma." Alpert thought for a moment. "There *is* one student with whom I've seen him, Jason Knowles. A fine young man. And, of course, he's close to the Bushnell's daughter, Adrienne. Actually, I'm afraid Ethan's behavior was affecting her. Her grades were also slipping this semester, and she seemed unmotivated, tired. Since he's been gone, her teachers tell me she's been quieter than usual, but she's keeping up with her assignments."

Another reason for Bushnell to take a tough stand with the boy and not allow him back home, Jessie thought. It was hard enough to protect your child against peer pressure, harder yet when the peer was living in your house.

"What about Ethan's teachers?" Phil asked. "Is he close to anyone in particular?"

"Tim Croton," Alpert said without hesitation. "He teaches AP English. He's fond of Ethan and extremely worried about him."

Maybe Croton would know more about Ethan's friends, Jessie thought. "What's the name of the boy he fought with?"

The headmaster frowned, and she wondered if he was annoyed because she'd ended her sentence with a preposition.

"Kevin Hayes. In retrospect, we shouldn't have accepted him. He's had a negative influence on some of our students, including Ethan. His grades weren't stellar, but he seemed eager to succeed, and his brother had done so well here."

And seventeen thousand a year was tempting. Although judging by the filled parking area and what she'd heard from Helen, who was already researching private high schools for Matthew, Jessie assumed hundreds of parents would be vying for the school's slots. "Did Ethan express any anger toward the Bushnells?"

Alpert's face registered consternation. "I assumed you were trying to find him to tell him about what happened to Dr. Bushnell," he said, his tone wary. "You think he might be involved in the murders?"

She wondered if he was worrying about Ethan Meissner, or the impact of notoriety on the school. Probably both, and who could blame him? "We have no idea. We're pursuing every possibility. He wrote some lyrics that hinted at violence at home and at school."

"Here?" Alpert's eyes widened with shock.

"It may be just talk, but you'll want to alert your security and staff."

"Of course." The headmaster nodded nervously.

"Did Ethan say anything that hinted at violence toward

any of the other students, or toward the Bushnells?" she asked again.

"I wouldn't want to take anything out of context." Alpert formed a steeple with his hands. "The last time we talked, I tried to persuade Ethan not to waste everything he'd worked so hard to achieve. I told him that he'd regret it, that it would be an act of ingratitude to the Bushnells, who had been so loving and generous." He paused. "Ethan became irate. He was yelling, saying that he didn't owe a thing to Dr. Bushnell, that Bushnell didn't give a damn about him and was ruining his life."

"Did he threaten to harm Dr. Bushnell?" Phil asked.

The headmaster frowned. He tapped the steeple against his lips. "The problem is, I can't be certain. Ethan mumbled something when he stopped yelling. I thought he said, 'I wish I was dead'—that's what I told Dr. Bushnell. But he *could* have said, 'I wish *he* was dead.' "

Either way, not the correct grammar, Jessie thought, and not an emotionally well young man.

15

JASON KNOWLES HAD long legs and arms and a thin, elongated face that hadn't yet filled out to accommodate his aquiline nose and expressive brown eyes. He looked gawky and uncomfortable, a teenager who knew he wasn't a jock.

"I haven't hung out with Ethan in weeks," he told Jessie and Phil in Alpert's office, where the headmaster had left them. "I don't know where he could be."

"You guys have a falling-out?" Phil asked.

"No. One day we were cool, the next day we weren't." Jason shrugged. "Ethan's a flake like that. I figured he was going through some stuff he didn't want to talk about." His pronounced Adam's apple was threatening to push through his slender neck.

"Did he seem different to you in class lately?"

The boy considered. "He had attitude when he talked to the teachers—he never did before. He wasn't into classes much, and half a dozen times he just didn't show."

"But you weren't worried about him?" She'd expected more sophisticated vocabulary, and decided the boy probably wanted to be cool with the cops, something that would earn him points with his peers. "You didn't ask him about it?"

The boy flushed. "I was worried, but I'm not his parents. Anyway, Ethan likes to keep his private stuff to himself."

"Hey, I can relate." Phil nodded. "I have two boys, I can

tell when it's time to back off. So do you think he was taking drugs, Jason?"

He didn't seem surprised by the question. "I thought about it. If he was, he didn't tell me."

"If he was taking drugs, where do you think he might have gotten the stuff? We're not looking to arrest anyone for using, just trying to find Ethan."

Jason had tensed but met Phil's eyes with his own earnest ones. "No idea."

"Big M? Torro?"

The boy frowned. "I don't know those names. Should I?"

"Adrienne says Ethan's been hanging out with them."

He shook his head. "No clue. Sorry." He sounded sincere.

"Kevin Hayes?"

Jason snorted. "Hayes talks big. He probably uses, but I don't think he deals. He talks up a *lot* of stuff."

"I heard they had a big fight. What about?"

"Adrienne. Hayes has been wanting her, but she won't give him the time of day, so he told everyone they got it on. Ethan heard and told Hayes to shut his fu—" Jason stopped himself. "To shut his mouth. So Hayes says Ethan's pissed 'cause he wants to do her himself. That's when Ethan punched him."

"Does he?" Phil asked, his tone casual, as if he were asking whether Ethan liked the Lakers. "Want to do her?"

"No way." Jason glanced at Jessie, then back at Phil. "They're practically brother and sister. Gross." He grimaced. "Anyway, Ethan and Hayes were okay after that. Thick, actually. Ethan was helping him with his term paper, stuff like that. I can't figure it."

Jessie thought she heard a note of jealousy in the boy's voice. She'd had a few relationships in high school that had left her feeling wounded, inadequate: a best friend one day, a nonperson the next.

"Kevin Hayes is absent," she commented. A fact she and Phil had found even more interesting when the receptionist had phoned the boy's home and talked to the housekeeper, who had assumed the boy was in school. Of course, he could be munching on popcorn in a movie theater or shooting targets at an arcade. "Do you think they might be together?"

The boy thought about that. "Maybe." He looked unhappy.

"Did Ethan have a girlfriend?" Celeste had said no, but teens don't always confide in their parents, especially about girls. And there had been all those love lyrics.

"No one special, as far I know."

"He was dating someone last semester, right?"

Jason nodded. "Gillian Logan. She's a senior, too. But that was over a few months ago. She dumped him."

Lesser events could plummet a teen into despair, Jessie thought as she wrote down the name. "Did he take it hard?"

"I couldn't tell. Like I said, with Ethan, you don't really know what he's thinking."

"Did Ethan get along with the Bushnells?"

"Pretty much. I mean, the dad has all these rules, but it was no big deal." Jason hesitated. "The mom's more chill, and half the time she's not home, and the doc's usually out late. So the rules don't matter, you know?" He smiled for the first time since he'd entered Alpert's office.

Phil gave the boy a card and pressed upon him the importance of calling the station if Ethan contacted him. "We're worried about him," he said.

Which was true.

"It's been a while since I've been called into the principal's office," Tim Croton said. "I can't say I like it any better now."

He was younger than Alpert, probably in his late twenties, and less formally dressed—beige slacks instead of a suit, a blue Oxford shirt with button-down collar, a solid blue tie. His manner was less formal, too, his smile easy and engaging. Jessie found herself liking him and realized why: he made her think of Ezra. But then, everything lately was having that effect.

"We're trying to get a handle on Ethan Meissner," she said. Speaking for herself and for Phil, who was taking advantage of the lunch hour to talk to other students who might know Ethan's hangouts, or Kevin Hayes's.

"I figured you weren't here to check out my AP course. Though if I do say so myself, it's damn good." Another smile. "You're trying to find him?"

Jessie nodded.

"I hope you do. I wish I could help." The instructor was all seriousness now. "Ethan's a terrific young man, but something's been eating at him. And yes, it *could* be drugs—I figure that's what you're going to ask. That would explain the mood swings, the hostility, the I-don't-give-a-crap attitude. But if he's using, something drove him to it, and it's not peer pressure."

"He wrote some love songs to an unnamed girl, but I understand he broke up with his girlfriend, Gillian Logan, a while ago. Do you think that could have made him despondent?" Jessie would have liked to question the girl, but she and her parents were back east, checking out college campuses. Alpert had said she would return tomorrow.

Croton looked pensive. "I don't think so."

"Any guesses?"

"His mother's suicide. I'm not a shrink, but if you analyze enough literature, you get a sense of what motivates people, what maims them, what makes them run. Ethan's never gotten over the violent nature of her death."

"I saw a biography of Virginia Woolf and Sylvia Plath's *The Bell Jar* in his room. Both writers committed suicide. So did the heroines of four of the books on his shelves. Emma Bovary, Hedda Gabler, Ophelia, and Lily from *House of Mirth*, whose last name I can't remember."

"Bart. An extraordinarily dreary heroine, Wharton's Lily, an extraordinarily dreary death." He looked at her with interest. "I'm impressed. Were you an English major?"

She was glad Phil wasn't here—he would have teased her, told her she was showing off to score points with the teacher, which she supposed she was. Talking books with Tim Croton was far more interesting than fielding passes from Joe Hopper.

"Political science. But I've always been an avid reader, thanks to my dad." Whom she still hadn't reached. "Were those books on your syllabus?"

Croton shook his head. "For his term paper. He chose the topic, probably expecting me to talk him out of it, but I didn't. I figured he was looking for answers." The teacher hesitated. "The work he circled around like a hawk, not quite sure whether it was safe to nibble at yet, was *Hedda Gabler*. It frightened and repelled him, and fascinated him."

"Why?"

Again the teacher paused before answering. "Ethan's mother had a copy of the book on her nightstand when she killed herself. Like Ophelia, Virginia Woolf drowned herself. Lily Bart and Emma Bovary used poison. Sylvia Plath used cooking gas. But Lucy Meissner used one of her husband's guns, just like Hedda. 'Having the strength and the beauty to get up and leave life's feast.' But of course, suicide isn't beautiful at all, especially not from a gunshot wound. It's bloody and ugly. Did they tell you he found her?"

Jessie shook her head. In her mind she saw the eight-year-old boy discovering his mother's still form, heard his scream. "Ethan told you this?"

"About a month ago, in a rare moment of openness that I stupidly mistook for a sign of healing but was really a cry for help. I was *so* pleased." He averted his gaze, but not before Jessie saw the sorrow in his eyes.

She felt like a brazen trespasser but had to continue. "What prompted him to confide in you?"

"We'd developed a relationship. And he had to talk to *someone*. He'd locked his mother's death into a little compartment in his mind, but of course, it wouldn't stay put."

Croton nipped at the pleat of his slacks. "I don't feel comfortable revealing what Ethan told me in confidence. It would be violating his trust."

She nodded. "I respect that. But his family's extremely concerned about him, and any light you could shed on his state of mind might be important."

"I don't see why. It won't help you find him, and it may give you the wrong impression. Obviously, you're wondering if he killed Dr. Bushnell, and you're trying to figure out why he'd do it."

"You're right." No point in denial. "But he's not our only suspect, and we believe he may be suicidal."

Croton was startled. "What makes you think that?"

She debated, then showed him Ethan's lyrics.

He read the page and blew out a deep breath.

"It would help us to know how to talk to him when we *do* find him. Not to say the wrong things." She was encouraged when Croton didn't immediately refuse. A soft sell was better, she decided. She waited.

"He's consumed by guilt," the teacher finally said, still sounding uncomfortable. "The day it happened, he'd nagged his mother into letting him play at a friend's house after school, and he blames himself for leaving her alone."

"She would have found another time."

Croton nodded. "You and I know that. Ethan doesn't. It didn't help that his father told him he was at fault. Ethan didn't say that outright, but he implied that's why his father didn't fight to keep him—he wasn't worthy."

God, the pain! Children of divorce, Jessie knew, often blamed themselves for their parents' breakup, and interpreted a parent's leaving as a rejection. But this was worse. "Mrs. Bushnell said Ethan was happy until recently. And they seem devoted to him. They treated him like a son."

"But he *isn't* their son. That's part of the problem," Croton said earnestly. "He felt guilty about everything they did for him—the expensive clothing, the car, the fabulous vacations, the tuition. They were planning on paying for college and med school, too. Harvard isn't cheap."

Jessie frowned. "Are you saying the Bushnells held all that up to him?"

"No, but Gideon did. He's Jewish, the Bushnells aren't. He accused Ethan of selling out his religion for a Range Rover and a Tommy Hilfiger wardrobe, of being ashamed of Gideon because he didn't make a six-figure salary."

My existence is a lie. "Mrs. Bushnell said Gideon didn't want to parent Ethan, that he talked about having Ethan live with him only to save face."

Croton shrugged.

Jessie contemplated what she'd learned. It still didn't explain the sudden change in the boy's behavior. She asked Croton what he thought.

"Applying for college put the pressure on," he said. "Dr. Bushnell wants Ethan to follow in his footsteps—Harvard, med school, although I don't think he's insisting on a specialty in plastic surgery." He smiled wryly. "If Ethan goes that route, he's betraying his birth father."

"And Ethan wants to be a doctor," Jessie added.

"Actually, he doesn't. He wants to be a musician like good ole dad. But then he's betraying Bushnell."

She thought for a moment. "So Ethan cuts classes, messes up his grades to make sure he doesn't get into Harvard—then the choice isn't his."

"Go to the head of the class, Detective. That's my thought, too, for what it's worth."

"And he uses drugs?"

"Because he's trapped, and it's a way out," Croton said quietly. "Because he's angry but he doesn't know at whom. His father, the Bushnells, maybe even his mother for killing herself and creating this whole mess."

"How angry?"

He stared at her a moment. "You're asking me did he kill

Dr. Bushnell?" Croton sighed. "Two months ago, I would've said, no way in hell. And now? I pray he didn't."

"If he didn't kill Dr. Bushnell, why hasn't he shown up? The murders have been all over the media. He must have heard about them by now."

"Not if he's stoned out of his mind. I hope you find him, Detective, before he kills himself."

Or someone else.

❖ 16 ❖

EZRA WAS LEANING against his desk, his long legs crossed at the ankles, his right hand raised to emphasize a point. She usually attended in the evenings, and he must have been wondering why she'd shown up halfway into his two o'clock class. He responded with a quick smile to her mouthed "Sorry," and was looking her way when she sat down behind a bearded young man who was nodding at Ezra's every word.

". . . no Jewish holidays in Cheshvan, but a number of sad events took place in that month. Which is why it's called *Mar*cheshvan. *Bitter* Cheshvan. The death of Methuselah; the death of Rachel, Jacob's beloved wife. And, of course, the Big One. Not an earthquake—the Flood."

The comment elicited a ripple of laughter. Ezra caught Jessie's eye, and she smiled. She felt a shy pride in the way he connected with his students, as though she held a claim to him the others didn't. *Teacher's pet,* the school secretary often teased. Maybe something more. Her mother's prodding last night ("Is there someone else?") had started her wondering again. Sitting in the headmaster's office, she'd felt a need to steal a few minutes to see him.

("Errands," she'd told Phil, turning down his offer to grab a quick lunch after interviewing scores of Ethan Meissner's classmates and putting out an APB on the boy, now that Celeste had filed a missing person's.)

"The Flood began on the seventeenth of Cheshvan," Ezra said, "and lasted forty days. Basically, God decided to wipe out humanity and start again, sparing only Noah and his family. Mankind was hopelessly debased, flagrantly committing idolatry and immorality. But their fate was sealed, the Torah tells us, because of *chamas*."

He sounded saddened, as though he were describing current events. Jessie found herself drawn to the discussion, though this was not why she'd come.

"What's that?" asked a young woman Jessie had never seen before. She was wearing jeans and a T-shirt and had a stripe of purple in her black hair. "Can you spell it?"

"*Chamas*." Moving to the blackboard, Ezra wrote the word in Hebrew in white chalk. "According to some, it means antisocial acts. Others say it means rampant thievery."

Chamas. Jessie repeated the word silently, making the guttural *ch* sound as though she were clearing her throat.

"God thinks thievery's worse than idolatry and immorality?" a gray-haired man challenged, his skeptical tone just shy of rudeness.

Adults of varying ages, Jessie had come to learn, attended classes in this school on Pico Boulevard near Robertson, in the heart of the Orthodox Jewish community that was becoming more and more familiar to her. And they attended for varying reasons. Some, Jewish like Jessie, were exploring a religion about which they knew little and were unsure where it would take them. Some were *frum* (observant) from birth—FFBs, they called themselves—returning after having strayed and seeking a spiritual jump start. Others, like Melinda, the twenty-six-year-old woman two rows ahead with whom Jessie often talked in their evening Hebrew class, had grown up in an unaffiliated Jewish home. She had committed to a faith-based observance but was lagging in knowledge behind her husband, an FFB. She was modestly dressed—ankle-

length olive skirt, high necked, long-sleeved, beige che-
nille sweater—and had tucked her blond hair into a crocheted navy snood.

Then there was the gray-haired retired math professor, Sid
Epstein—Jessie had seen him several times in her evening
Jewish history class. He had come to discover how his
twenty-one-year-old son had been brainwashed into practic-
ing Orthodox Judaism, and kept returning. Jessie tried to
imagine her mother sitting in on Ezra's class, trying to understand what had captivated her older daughter's head and
heart.

"An excellent question, Sid." Ezra resumed his place in
front of the desk. "The commentaries ask the same thing.
After all, according to Torah law theft doesn't incur the
death penalty, whereas immorality and idolatry do. Yet God
executed an entire population because they stole."

"Okay, I'll bite." Epstein nodded. "What's the answer?"

"Rabbi Meir Simcha of Dvinsk, a turn of the century
commentator, explains that immorality and idolatry are pun-
ishable by death only in the case of the individual, when he
has examples of moral behavior from the majority. When the
majority has succumbed, there's no example, hence God is
merciful. And in essence, immorality and idolatry are
against God, not man. But with *chamas,* even if *everyone* is
stealing, it's still clear that the act is wrong. And when theft
becomes rampant—a sin of man against man—society and
civilization can't exist, so God steps in."

"Like Sodom and Gomorrah," the girl with the purple
streak offered.

"Exactly." Ezra nodded. "Thievery became so common
that people walked around naked because they were afraid
others would steal their clothes. We're talking thievery and
other antisocial behavior on a communal scale, without
shame or remorse because it became the norm."

There were neighborhoods in Los Angeles, Jessie knew,
that frightened residents had been forced to cede to brazen

gang members who sold crack on street corners in full day-
light and sprayed bullets at members of other gangs, all too
often wounding or killing innocent bystanders. No shame,
no remorse. The norm. But how does it *become* the norm?

"I don't know," Epstein said, as if voicing Jessie's
thought. "If everyone's stealing, how does anyone know it's
wrong?"

"They *knew* it was wrong, Sid, because they were careful
to steal in a way that exempted them from punishment."

Like Ethan Meissner? Jessie wondered whether he'd re-
lied on Celeste's carelessness with money and jewelry to
cover his pilfering. If, in fact, he'd stolen anything . . .

Epstein snorted. "How could they be *exempt?* Stealing is
stealing—right, Rabbi?"

He insisted on calling Ezra "rabbi," even though Ezra had
explained that he wasn't ordained. Epstein had argued—
rabbi meant *teacher,* didn't it?—so Ezra had dropped the
issue. Sometimes Jessie sensed that the professor was mocking Ezra, but Ezra didn't seem to mind.

He smiled patiently. "The classic example is of a man carrying a basket full of peas. People would surround him, each
taking a few peas worth less than a *pruta,* a small coin, until
the basket was empty. But the victim had no legal recourse,
because each thief would argue that he'd stolen an amount
so minute he wasn't liable to punishment."

"Very clever." The math professor sounded pensive.

"And insidious. *Chamas* is a nullification of the other.
Chamas says, 'You don't exist, so what you have doesn't belong to you.' *Chamas* says, 'You don't exist, so I can do
what I want to satisfy my goals.' Men nullified one another,
so God nullified the world."

Murder was the ultimate nullification. Jessie wondered
what goal had driven Bushnell's killer. Revenge? Rage?
Envy? Fear? Or maybe there had been no real goal. Maybe
it was all about drugs. Too soon to tell. Bushnell, at least,
had existed for the killer, if only as someone to be elimi-

nated. Nicole Hobart and Marianna Velasquez had probably been an inconvenience, flies casually swatted to their deaths. And Lily Pervez—had she been the target or an inconvenience? And what about her cousin?

"God brought the Flood, and a new beginning," Ezra said. "He promised Noah He wouldn't destroy the world again and sealed His promise with the rainbow. In fact, when we see a rainbow, we recite a blessing and regard it as a cautionary sign: God doesn't like what's going on, but He's honoring His promise. Which doesn't give us carte blanche to mess up."

"Heavy stuff, Rabbi," Epstein commented. "Robbery, murder, the Flood. No wonder it's called a bitter month."

"Things improve, Sid." Ezra smiled. "Next week we read about Abraham, the lonely man of faith who left his father's home to found monotheism."

What if you didn't have faith? Jessie thought. What if you were a lonely young man, depressed, angry, torn between two fathers pulling you in different directions?

Ezra had given her insights about the Torah that had helped her deal with the depressing complexities of her profession. She wanted to talk to him about the case, and about personal things that had nothing to do with the class or the Torah.

Her pager beeped. She took it out of her purse and checked the message on the dial, wondering wryly if God knew she had come under false pretenses and was warning her to back off. But it was only Phil.

"I CAN'T IMAGINE where Kevin is," Sally Hayes said. "He slept at his father's last night, and I left early this morning to take a deposition, so I didn't speak to him. Kevin didn't say anything about not feeling well, and I know he had a math test today."

She looked every inch the lawyer, Jessie thought: tailored navy suit, cream camisole, navy pumps. She wore a necklace of large pearls spaced about an inch and a half apart by twisted string and smaller pearls in her ears, behind which she'd pushed chin-length, straight auburn hair cut at a blunt angle.

She was all angles and emitted a bristly quality—sharp chin, nose, cheekbones. Even the pearls rested hesitantly against the vee of her protruding neck bones. Approach at your own risk. The furniture in the room they were in was angular, too—straight-backed, straight-armed gray leather sofas; a rectangular glass-and-chrome table with a triangular piece of rusty copper that was supposed to be art. Not an inviting room, and not an inviting woman.

"We talked to his friends," Phil told her. "No one's seen him in school today."

The woman's thin lips formed a stern line. "This is his father's doing. Donald coddles Kevin. I'm the bad one, but that's all right," she said grimly. "I still don't understand the emergency. Kevin's probably vegging out in front of Donald's TV, watching videos."

"Your ex-husband says Kevin decided to sleep *here* last night." They had talked to Donald Hayes before coming here.

"Well, it's nice of my ex-husband to let me know! I was out for the evening." She frowned, Phil's words apparently having registered. "You're saying Kevin's *missing?* Why wasn't I called earlier? He could be dead somewhere, or unconscious." Her voice had risen to a shrill pitch that echoed in the spartanly furnished room.

"We checked with the police and all the hospitals," Phil told her. "There haven't been any reports about anyone resembling your son."

Sally sighed her relief. "Well, he's going to be a sorry young man when he returns!" she promised, her eyes flashing. "Scaring me to death like this!"

"Has he been truant before?"

"Once or twice. He went to the beach with some friends from school. He's not the student his brother is," she added, as if that explained Kevin's problem. "His brother is a sophomore at Columbia."

"Do you know the names of these boys?" Jessie asked, wondering how many times Kevin Hayes had heard himself negatively compared to his brother.

She named two boys that Jessie and Phil had questioned. Neither one had spoken to Kevin since yesterday. Neither had any idea where Kevin, or Ethan, might be. Or they weren't telling. The honor code, Jessie thought—the precursor of the Blue Code of silence in the police department.

"The headmaster warned Kevin he'd be expelled if he ditched again," Sally said, "but I don't think Kevin believes him. Thanks to my ex, he doesn't seem to understand consequences." She was brooding now, not really focused on Jessie and Phil.

"Has he ever mentioned Ethan Meissner?"

"Ethan's been here several times to help Kevin with his schoolwork. He seems like a studious young man, and I was pleased to see that he and Kevin were friends." She cocked her head. "Why? Is *that* who he's with? But that doesn't make sense."

"We're not sure," Jessie said. "Would you mind taking a look around Kevin's room to see if he left some indication of where he was going." Maybe with Ethan.

Sally Hayes's eyes narrowed, and the tip of her tongue touched her upper lip. "This isn't about Kevin being absent, is it?" she asked in the careful voice of an attorney.

"We're trying to find your son," Phil said. "He may be a material witness to a crime. He may be playing hooky."

"May I see your identification again?" She examined the card he handed her. "Homicide detective," she read. "What the hell is going on here? You come here pretending to be truant officers, and—"

"You assumed that, ma'am," Phil interrupted.

She was glaring at him. "And you did nothing to correct my assumption!"

"I can see you're upset, Mrs. Hayes," Jessie said. "But I'm sure your main concern is your son's safety. If he's in trouble, you want to find him. We can help."

She didn't answer immediately. "What is it that you think he's done?" she finally asked, her tone guarded.

"We don't think he's done anything, Mrs. Hayes. But we think he may know where Ethan Meissner is."

"Exactly why do you need to find the Meissner boy?"

"He may be implicated in a homicide that took place yesterday. You may have heard about it on the news—Dr. Bushnell and his nurse and receptionist. Ethan was living with the Bushnells until three weeks ago."

"I heard about it. I had no idea Ethan was connected with the Bushnells." The woman thought for a moment, then shook her head. "You can fool me once, Detectives. You think Kevin's involved in this murder, and you want me to help you find him. Kevin is lazy and spoiled and he's learned to play the son of divorced parents to the hilt, but he's not a murderer. So no, I'm not going to search my son's room, and you certainly can't do it."

"Mrs. Hayes," Phil began.

"Kevin is playing hooky somewhere, having the time of his life. He'll come slinking home sometime tonight, and *believe* me, I'll make him understand that there are consequences. He will *never* do this again." She tightened her lips.

"Your ex gave him six hundred dollars last night."

"What!" She stared at Phil.

"Kevin said he had a one-time chance to buy an entertainment system—a thousand-dollar value for six hundred, cash only. He promised your ex-husband he'd pay him back over the next five months."

"Donald is such an idiot!" she hissed. She sat back against the unforgiving sofa cushion.

"Mr. Hayes told us he'd given Kevin an ATM card to use for emergencies. At our suggestion, Mr. Hayes checked with his bank. Kevin used the card last night and withdrew three hundred dollars. He withdrew another three hundred this morning. So he is *not* playing hooky, Mrs. Hayes."

She smoothed a strand of her hair behind her ear. "I need to think."

Phil nodded. "Take your time."

"I can't believe he's involved in this."

"He has a jacket, but you know that. Petty theft, vandalism, DUI with a suspended license. He's not just spoiled, Mrs. Hayes."

She flushed but met his eyes. "The divorce was hard on him, and he was lashing out. But therapy has helped a great deal. He's a changed boy."

When she was working Juvenile, Jessie had heard this so many times. "Would you agree it's too much of a coincidence that both Kevin and the Meissner boy disappeared the day after the murders?"

The attorney stiffened her posture. "I'll agree that it seems like a strong coincidence, but until I know otherwise, I'm going to assume that Kevin has a good reason for what he's done."

"Do you own a gun, Mrs. Hayes?" Phil asked.

The question took her by surprise. "Yes, I do. It's registered, and I've taken lessons. I'm alone in the house quite a bit, and although Beverlywood is a safe area, I don't care to take any chances."

"What kind is it?"

"A Glock nine millimeter." There was a touch of pride in her voice.

Not a typical woman's gun, Jessie thought. Phil had called Futaki in the morning and nagged him into doing the autopsies Thursday, but if the recovered bullets were shattered, Ballistics would have to determine the caliber. More time lost. "May we see it?"

"No, you may not."

Either she was worried that the gun was missing, or that her son had used it. Jessie could threaten to return with a search warrant, but the woman was an attorney and would know she was bluffing. No probable cause.

"If you hear from your son, please urge him to talk to us," Jessie said. "We're not trying to railroad him."

The woman stood and smoothed her skirt. "If I hear from my son, I'll listen to what he has to say. And at that time I'll make a decision as to what course of action to follow. I'm not going to jeopardize his future with a baseless arrest for something he didn't do."

"We don't intend to arrest him. We just want to talk to him. I would think that you'd want him found, too. If I were in your shoes, I'd file a missing person's report."

"So that you can put out an APB on him?" She sneered at Jessie and shook her head. "I don't think so."

"With or without the missing person's, we're going to send out a Teletype to all our divisions, advising them to be on the lookout for your son." A BOLO, in cop talk. One of

Jessie's favorite terms. "You don't want us to have to hunt him down," she said kindly. "Believe me."

Sally Hayes frowned, and when she spoke, her voice had lost some of its cool assurance. "If I hear from him, I'll let you know." She paused. "He's a teenager, Detective. Please remember that. He'll be frightened if the police surprise him, he may do something stupid. He—" She stopped. "He's a good boy."

So are they all, Jessie thought sadly. All good boys.

❖ 18 ❖

FROM BEVERLYWOOD IT was a short distance to the Pervez house in Palms, near Venice and Overland. Phil was uncharacteristically silent during the drive, and Jessie left him alone. She assumed he was thinking about Kevin Hayes and Ethan Meissner, about teenage boys in general, about his own kids.

Several lights were on in the Pervez house, but there was no car in the driveway and no one answered the door. Phil left a note in their mailbox, asking them to phone the station.

"Just as well," he said as they walked back to his car. "It's past four. I've put in more than my hours, and Espes said to hold off on the overtime. I'd love to get a warrant for the Hayes's place. Ten to one the mom's Glock is missing along with the kid."

"That doesn't mean it's the murder weapon. We don't have anything to connect the Hayes kid to the murders except that he's missing. So far, he's a truant."

Phil grunted. "So we send a BOLO to all the divisions. Good thing we have his mug shot from his jacket."

"The dad's not as tough as the attorney-mom. Maybe we can talk him into filing a missing person's, then we can put out an APB."

"Good idea. I'll call him when I get home." Phil opened the Cutlass's door and got in.

Jessie did the same. "I'd like to know where the hell Barbara Martin is. I've been leaving messages all day."

"Probably out looking for a new job."

"She wished Bushnell dead."

"And then she filed a workmen's comp suit. Probably figured she'd hit him where it hurts most—in the wallet."

"Maybe. What do you say we talk to Meissner's dad before we call it quits for the day?" Jessie had been thinking about the father on and off all day. "Maybe he's heard from his son. And what if he's on Ethan's hit list?" *Kill 'em all, watch them fall.*

"Tell you the truth, I feel like shit. I know I'm coming down with Espes's bug."

"It won't take long. Mrs. Bushnell gave me the address. He lives in Woodland Hills, so it's on your way home." Phil lived in Thousand Oaks, a graceful, sprawling community in Ventura County. "We stop by the station. I get my Honda and follow you."

"What if Meissner isn't in? Going back you'll be hitting all the rush hour traffic for nothing. It's a bitch."

"My problem, not yours. And I don't want to call ahead and alert him." It wasn't as though she had a family waiting for her to come home, she thought, and told herself to cut the self-pity.

Twenty minutes later she was in her car behind Phil's Cutlass, merging onto the 405 Freeway. Traffic slowed as they neared the Sepulveda Pass, the route most people took from West Los Angeles to the San Fernando Valley and parts north. Rummaging through the center armrest compartment, she chose an ABBA CD and sang most of the words to "Chiquitita" as the cars inched obediently forward.

A Cadillac just like her father's pulled in front of her. Using her cell phone, she dialed his office and spoke to Diane, his receptionist of fifteen years.

"Hasn't he returned your calls, honey? I gave him the messages. He's with a patient now, but I'll make sure he calls you the minute he's done. That man!" She sighed.

"He can reach me for the next fifteen minutes or so in the car on my cell phone. After that, I won't be available."

"I'll tell him, honey. Drive carefully, now. I don't like it that you're driving and talking at the same time."

"I'll be careful. Thanks, Diane."

Diane had no cause for concern. Jessie loved to drive fast, especially on open stretches of road, but the traffic remained bumper to bumper on the 405. Even if it hadn't, Phil would have grumbled if she'd passed him.

The address Celeste Bushnell had given Jessie belonged to a faded gray stucco, two-story building overpowered by oleander and century and by mushrooming agave plants whose sharp points promised menace. An enormous palm tree obscured part of the FOR RENT sign on the front lawn. Two bedrooms, one bath, central air, pool. If interested, see manager in 2G. For anyone living in the Valley, where summer temperatures averaged ten degrees higher than in the city, the central air was a necessity, not a luxury.

2G was Gideon Meissner's apartment, on the second floor toward the rear. While Phil rang the bell several times in succession, Jessie eyed the large varnished wood mezuzah on the doorpost.

"*Ma'shehu bo'er,* Yoram?" a male called in an irritated voice. "*Mashiach higiah?*"

From the modicum of Hebrew Jessie had learned, she understood the few words: Was something burning? Had the Messiah arrived? Ezra would be proud, she thought.

The man yanked the door open. He was around five eight and wearing jeans and a Polo shirt that was snug over his paunch. His handsome features must have wowed the ladies once: jet black curly hair, a strong chin, sensual lips, eyes the color of bittersweet chocolate. But his skin was puffy and his face looked shopworn and jowly—probably the booze, if Celeste Bushnell was right.

He looked startled but quickly flashed a lukewarm smile. "Sorry. I was expecting somebody else. You're here about the apartment, yes? I can show it to you fast, because I have an appointment, and you can take an application, okay?" He spoke with an Israeli accent and didn't sound overly enthused or eager to fill the vacancy.

"I'm Detective Okum, LAPD," Phil said. "This is my partner, Detective Drake. We'd like to speak to you about your son, Ethan."

"Celeste Bushnell told you he's missing, yes?" Meissner sounded irritated. "I told her if I hear from him, I'll call her." His face darkened. "Something happened? He's in trouble?"

"It's possible. May we come in, please?"

They entered a small room filled with the acrid scent of cigarette smoke and a hodgepodge of furniture that, like their owner, had seen better days: a tan Naugahyde sofa; a square black leather ottoman; a torchère whose brass coating was peeling. Ashtrays had been placed throughout the room like votive candleholders. In spite of them, the sofa and a teak coffee table and the brown spinet piano near the front window were scarred with cigarette burns, hostages tortured to yield their secrets. Against one wall stood two tall bookcases crammed with books—many of them Hebrew texts, the rest English-language classics. Ethan had obviously inherited his father's love of literature.

Meissner frowned. "Celeste said my son called and told her he's okay. You're saying he's not?" He settled himself on the ottoman, leaving the sofa for Jessie and Phil.

She wondered if he knew about Ronald Bushnell. "As far as we know, he's all right. We don't know where he is. That's why we're here." She sat down, careful to avoid the foam peeking through a torn cushion. "When was the last time you spoke to Ethan, Mr. Meissner?"

"Eitán," he corrected, accenting the second syllable. "It means *strong* in Hebrew. My wife wanted him to be like all the other kids, so she called him *Ethan*." He pronounced the name with disdain. "I talked to him a month ago. If you spoke to Celeste, you know the whole story, that I'm not the best father. I'm not proud of it. If I could do things over, I would do them differently." He reached for the cigarette pack on the coffee table. "Do you mind?"

"Actually, I do," Jessie said. At least he'd asked.

"Americans." He snorted. "You don't smoke, you worry about what you drink, about your cholesterol. In the end, what good does it do except to make your life miserable?"

"You're not an American?" Phil asked.

"I'm living here twenty-one years, but I'm an Israeli citizen. I should have returned twenty years ago. Everything would be different then." He sounded sad, and the corners of his mouth were pulled down.

"Why didn't you?"

"What can I tell you? I thought I would make a big success with my music and go back with enough money to live well and show my parents they were wrong about their son." His smile was ironic. "There was a point when I was ready to give up and go home, but Lucy was already in a depression and needed her family. After she died. . . ." He looked upward and shook his head slowly. "I thought to take Eitán to Israel, but who would be his mother? A boy needs a mother, I told myself, and my parents were elderly. The truth? I was selfish, I was lazy. But also, I was terrified of the responsibility. And I wasn't thinking straight. Lucy's death, the terrible way she died . . ." Meissner sighed. "I made many mistakes, many."

The man sitting across from her sounded sensitive, sincerely remorseful, not like the Gideon Meissner Celeste had described. "I understand that you blamed your son for your wife's death."

Meissner flinched and bowed his head. "I was half drunk," he said quietly after a moment, not meeting her eyes. "I didn't know what I was saying. I was angry with Lucy for killing herself, angry at myself because I should never have left her that morning. Eitán knows I didn't mean it."

Jessie considered telling him he was wrong, but kept silent. He was directing most of his comments to her, not Phil, and she didn't want to interrupt his narrative. There were times when Phil asked the questions and she listened.

"Who told you this?" Meissner demanded with a flash of anger. "Celeste? Ronnie? They like to remind themselves what a bad father I am. It makes them feel better about what they did." He grunted. "So now Eitán ran away from their perfect home. Did Celeste report him missing? This is why you're here?" He seemed oddly pleased.

Jessie avoided the question. "How did Ethan sound when you spoke to him?"

"How should he sound? Like a teenager. Bored, in a hurry to end the conversation." Meissner picked up the cigarette and held it between his fingers.

"Did he mention he was having trouble at school?"

"Eitán does not confide in his father." His tone was bitter, self-deprecating. "Celeste told me, when she called that night to see if he was here. She was hysterical. Eitán ran away, he was taking drugs, he was ruining his life."

"You don't seem terribly concerned," Jessie said, puzzled by the father's indifference. Maybe it was a facade.

"I should sit shiva because he won't go to Harvard?" Meissner shrugged. "When I was Eitán's age, I ran away, too. My parents are *dati*—religious. This wasn't a life for me. I did drugs, I drank, I had sex with a lot of women." A smile flitted across his face. "I straightened out. Most kids do." He eyed the cigarette longingly and dropped it onto the table.

According to Celeste, Meissner hadn't given up the liquor. Who knew about the drugs and the sex? Maybe Lucy Meissner's depression had been caused by her husband's behavior. "You aren't worried that the Bushnells have no idea where he is? That he's probably hanging out with the wrong kind of people?"

"He called and told them he was fine, didn't he? He called

a few times." The father hunched forward. "Look, he was under a lot of pressure in that house. They were always pushing, pushing. Eitán had to get all A's, he had to be a star in tennis, in debate. He had to practice piano two hours a day. He had enough."

"Your son told you he resented being pressured?"

"He would never criticize the Bushnells, *chas ve'shalom*. God forbid." Meissner smiled grimly. "But I could hear what he did *not* say. They paid for his braces and private school. They bought him expensive clothes, a television, a stereo system, a car. They took him to Mexico and Hawaii and all over. He *knew* there was a price tag. He *knew*." The father was brooding now, his voice filled with sorrow.

"Celeste said you were relieved that they took Ethan to live with them after your wife died."

"They *stole* my son! For this I should thank them?" Meissner's face was flushed. "I'm not *dati*, but Rosh Hashana and Yom Kippur, I go to the *bet knesset*, the synagogue. Maybe for my parents, maybe for myself. I don't know." He shrugged. "But I go. Lucy went, too. For her, too, this was important."

"Your wife was Jewish?"

"Yes, from both parents." He nodded. "We met on the kibbutz where I was working. Her parents were not thrilled she fell in love with an Israeli who wanted to be a musician. They told her I was marrying her to get a green card. Not true. I loved her." The sad, distant look was back in his eyes. "The first Rosh Hashanah after Lucy died, I wanted to take Eitán to the *bet knesset,* but he wouldn't go. 'He's too upset,' Ronnie said. 'The psychiatrist said not to force him. Next year he'll go.' I should argue with a psychiatrist? Already everybody's saying I'm a terrible father, that I give up my son. The next year Ronnie tells me Eitán is confused about religion. Ronnie's Jewish—he wants to raise his daughter in Celeste's religion, that's *his* business, and Celeste's." Meissner shrugged. "Eitán is *my* son, *my* business. The year after that, he told me some other bullshit, I don't remember what exactly. Finally I gave up."

The man was a picture of dejection—elbows on his knees, shoulders slumped, eyes focused on the threadbare carpet.

"Dr. Bushnell is Jewish?" Not what Croton had told her.

"From his mother's side. But he wasn't raised Jewish, so he doesn't consider himself Jewish. When Eitán was twelve I wanted him to study for his bar mitzvah. He doesn't have to be religious, but he should know about his heritage, yes? A boy should know where he comes from. In Israel, the children learn in school about the Torah and the *chagim*— the holidays—so you don't have to be religious to know. But not here. Eitán wasn't interested, and Ronnie and Celeste said, '*Gidón,* he's been through so *much.* Even without a bar mitzvah, he knows he's Jewish. We tell him all the *time.* Don't *pressure* him.' " He had mimicked a whine. "*I* shouldn't pressure him!" Meissner's voice had escalated gradually, and now he was yelling, his face mottled with anger.

This was the temper Celeste had mentioned. He smacked of self-pity, and Jessie was annoyed. What connection with Judaism had he expected when he'd allowed his young, traumatized son to be raised in a non-Jewish home? She remembered what Celeste had said, that Meissner always blamed others for his failures.

"You could have taken Ethan to live with you."

"I tried. He didn't want to live with me. It was supposed to be temporary, his staying with Ronnie and Celeste. But they made life too good for him, gave him too many things. Why would he want to leave? But in the end, he wasn't good enough for them anyway, was he?" Meissner laughed bitterly. "A cruel joke, yes?"

"Because he wasn't doing well in his studies, you mean?" Deliberately, according to the English teacher.

The father looked puzzled, then nodded. "Yes, of course. They made him feel he was a disappointment."

She sensed that her question had surprised him and wondered what he'd really meant by Ethan's not being "good enough." She wished she'd played it differently, but it was too late now. She took the page with the lyrics from her purse and showed it to Meissner. "Your son wrote this."

He read the words silently and tossed the sheet onto the table. "I should be impressed with this? It's *charah*—shit. He listens to the angry garbage they call music today, what do you expect? He listens to Eminem. You heard Eminem? He hates women, he hates gays, he hates everything. For this, they give him three Grammys." Meissner glowered. "He's poison, him and others like him."

Jessie didn't disagree. "Ronald Bushnell was murdered yesterday," she told him.

His eyes widened and he stared, open-mouthed. "What happened?" he finally asked in a subdued voice.

He seemed genuinely shocked, but for all she knew, he was a great actor. "He was shot to death in his office, along with his receptionist and one of his nurses. Mrs. Bushnell didn't tell you?"

"Could be she phoned. I was out most of the day, and I didn't listen to my messages." Meissner ran his hand across the faint dark stubble on his chin. "So that's why you're here. You think Eitán did it." He shook his head. "My son is not a killer."

Sally Hayes had said the same thing about her son. "We need to talk to him, Mr. Meissner."

"I don't know where he is. I told you."

The phone rang. Meissner glanced toward the kitchen, which was visible through the doorway at the end of the dining area. "Excuse me a minute. I'm expecting an important business call." He jumped off the ottoman, but instead of going toward the kitchen, he hurried down a hall to his left.

"Maybe he thinks it's the kid, and he wants to talk freely," Phil said.

She would love to eavesdrop, but Meissner would certainly hear the click if she picked up the receiver.

She tiptoed into the kitchen, thinking Meissner's voice might carry, but heard nothing. She hoped he was a better musician than a housekeeper. Unwashed dishes with the gooey remains of what looked like macaroni and cheese were stacked in the sink, and the tile counter, covered by beer cans, was caked and grimy. Stacks of Hebrew-language newspapers, magazines, and sheet music lay on the small round white melamine dinette table. Meissner had written something above the masthead on the top newspaper and circled it.

An 800 phone number, and two short Hebrew words. She sounded them out and realized she was looking at the number for El Al, Israel's official airline. Underneath that, today's date and 12:55 P.M., with a question mark next to it. Below that, 2:10 P.M. There was another, longer word, also in Hebrew, and what looked like a ten-digit phone number. Not a foreign prefix, from what she could tell.

She had her notebook open and was about to copy the Hebrew letters and numbers when Meissner appeared in the doorway.

She slipped the book into her purse and walked toward him. "Could I trouble you for a glass of water? I have a pounding headache and need to take something." She winced and gave what she hoped was a convincing pained smile.

His eyes went to the newspaper. "It's no trouble." He took a glass from a cupboard, filled it with tap water, and handed it to her.

"Thanks."

"Excuse my mess." He walked around her to the table, placed the sheet music onto the newspaper, and straightened the stack.

In the living room, she took two Advil tablets from the pill box she always carried in her purse and downed them with the water, trying not to notice the film on the glass.

"That was Celeste." Meissner resumed his perch on the ottoman. "She sounds terrible, poor woman. She wanted to know if I heard from Eitán. She's worried how he'll react when he hears about Ronnie, so you see, she also does not believe that Eitán killed him."

Or doesn't want to. "I think Ethan knows. I'm surprised he didn't phone to tell you."

Meissner shook his head. "Like I said, he doesn't confide in me."

Jessie didn't believe him. The El Al information, Meissner's attempt to keep Jessie from seeing it. Having been thrown out of the house by Bushnell, where else would the boy have turned? She said as much, in more diplomatic words, to Meissner.

The man shrugged in response.

"If you know where he is, and you think you're being a good father by protecting him, you're making a huge mistake, Mr. Meissner. If your son killed Dr. Bushnell, and you helped him flee, you're an accessory."

"What is all this talk about 'fleeing'? It's ridiculous!" Meissner shook his head. "Eitán had no reason to kill Ronnie. He didn't *hate* him. He wasn't happy, so he left. End of problem."

"Then where *is* he, Mr. Meissner? Why hasn't he come forward? Maybe he was using drugs at the time and not thinking clearly. The district attorney will take that into consideration. Or maybe he didn't do it. A classmate of his is missing, too. Maybe they went to Dr. Bushnell's office together, and the other boy did the shooting. We're looking for him, too. In any case, we need to talk to Ethan. But if your son remains a fugitive, they'll hold it against him. Running away makes him look guilty."

"That doesn't mean he is. Maybe he's afraid you won't believe him."

"If he didn't kill Dr. Bushnell, he has nothing to fear."

Meissner snorted. "In books, maybe. The Los Angeles Police Department doesn't have the best reputation. Anyway, Eitán didn't kill anyone, and I don't know where he is."

Jessie handed him a card. "If you hear from him, urge him to turn himself in for questioning. And if you decide you have information for us, please contact us immediately."

He studied the card and slipped it into the pocket of his jeans.

"If he meant what he wrote, Mr. Meissner, other people may be in danger, including you. You might want to think about that."

❖ 19 ❖

"WHY WOULD HE put his kid on a flight to Israel?" Phil asked when they were standing next to his car. "Sure, it drags things out, but we'll get him back eventually."

"Just a sec. I want to do this before I forget." She took out her notepad and wrote down what she could recall of the Hebrew word on Meissner's newspaper and the area code of the phone number. 909. Where the hell was that? "Not necessarily, Phil. Gideon Meissner's an Israeli citizen."

"So?"

"There was a case a while ago in Maryland, near D.C. Two boys killed this other kid. One of the boys fled to Israel. He wasn't born there, but the Israeli court ruled that because the dad was born there, the kid had all the rights of a citizen. The law of return, I think they called it."

"We can still extradite him."

She shook her head. "Depends on what the D.A. goes for. Israel doesn't have the death penalty. In this Maryland case, they wouldn't extradite the kid because the prosecutor was going for a capital charge."

"So what happened?"

"The Israeli court tried and convicted him. I don't remember what the sentence was. The other kid was arrested in Maryland. He hanged himself in his jail cell." A grim crime, a grim ending.

Phil grunted. "You think the Meissner kid's headed for his

grandparents? Meissner said they're elderly. Why would he bring heavy shit like that on them?"

"Meissner said a lot of things. Anyway, the boy doesn't have to stay there. He could disappear. I'm sure there's a whole network of family."

Using her cell phone, she learned from the Pacific Bell operator that 909 was the area code for Riverside and San Bernardino counties. She obtained the toll-free number for El Al. After punching in the numbers and being connected, she identified herself as a police detective to a female agent who spoke with a heavy Israeli accent.

"I need to know whether you have an Ethan Meissner on your twelve-fifty-five P.M. flight to Tel Aviv," Jessie told her.

"Sorry, I cannot give out that information over the phone. I would have to see proper identification." Polite, but firm.

"Is that flight a nonstop to Tel Aviv?"

"No. Our nonstops fly Wednesday and Saturday. This flight stops in JFK at nine-fifteen P.M., and departs for Tel Aviv at ten-forty P.M., arriving Tel Aviv at four-oh-five P.M."

It was five-fifteen, L.A. time. If Ethan was on that flight, he'd be landing in New York in an hour. Jessie would have two hours to contact airport security to prevent him from boarding the flight to Tel Aviv.

Jessie thanked the agent and ended the call. "I have to go down to the terminal," she told Phil, and repeated what she'd learned. "If he's on the flight, the New York police will take him into custody."

"Could be a wild goose chase." He sounded tired, and his eyes were red.

"I can handle it on my own. Go home, get some rest."

"You're sure?" He sounded relieved. "I'll call Hayes about filing the missing person's for his kid. I can make calls to area hospitals and stations, see if anyone has word on the kid. Let me know what happens."

"Sounds to me like I'm getting the better deal."

*   *   *

Traffic was a bitch, as Phil had predicted, but the drive was mindless, a straight run south on the 405 to Century. She played the ABBA CD again and tried her father. The recorded message told her the offices were closed for the day and gave her instructions if she had an emergency.

She didn't, but she was alternating between being annoyed with him for not returning her calls and concerned. She tried the house and heard her mother's overly articulated voice directing her to leave a message.

Century was a wide, multilaned street lined with large convention-size hotels and a marquis that advertised live nude dancers. As opposed to the dead kind? Driving west, she was awed as always by the aircraft that seemed to skim the tops of the buildings. Minutes later she entered the horseshoe-shaped airport, congested with cars, taxis, and way too many buses and minivans. She parked in a white zone at the top of the horseshoe, in front of the Tom Bradley International Terminal with the green glass overhang.

An airport parking official swaggered over to her Honda as she was exiting the car.

"No stopping, no parking," he told her in a surly, bored tone. "No excuses."

No shit, she thought. She showed her badge, feeling a flicker of satisfaction as he mumbled an "Okay, then," and walked away. She pitied his next victim.

The El Al counter was quiet, and she was able to speak with an agent immediately.

"Detective Jessica Drake, LAPD." She showed the man her badge and her department photo ID. "I need to find out if Ethan Meissner is on today's twelve-fifty-five P.M. flight to Tel Aviv."

The agent studied the badge and Jessie's photo and looked at her curiously. "A moment, please." He conferred with a fellow agent and returned to his station. "Let me check. Spell the last name?" His fingers flew over the computer keyboard as she gave him the information. "An Ethan Meissner was a standby for that flight," he told her.

She caught her breath.

He continued typing. "That flight arrived in New York's JFK early at nine-oh-eight P.M. It's scheduled to depart at ten-forty P.M., arriving in Tel Aviv at four-oh-five P.M. tomorrow."

She checked her watch: 6:14. Still more than enough time to alert security at JFK and stop Meissner from boarding the plane for Tel Aviv. Her heart beat faster.

"But I see from the passenger manifest that he didn't board the aircraft," the agent said.

Jessie frowned. "He didn't make it?"

"Apparently not. It was a full flight."

"You have a two-ten flight to Tel Aviv, right?"

"Tomorrow afternoon. Nonstop service from Los Angeles to Tel Aviv. We offer that on Wednesdays and Saturdays."

"Can you see if he's booked on the Wednesday flight?"

"I'll check." Less than a minute later, the agent glanced up at her. "Yes, he is."

She felt a thrill of excitement, immediately tempered by Gideon Meissner's reaction when he'd found her in his kitchen. Had he worried that she'd seen his notations on the newspaper? If so, it was unlikely that he'd put his son on the 2:10 flight.

"What other airlines fly to Tel Aviv from Los Angeles?"

"Continental does." More typing. "They have a daily flight departing Los Angeles at seven A.M., arriving in Newark at three-sixteen P.M. Departing Newark at five-twenty-five P.M., arriving Tel Aviv the next morning at eleven. They have a later flight departing Los Angeles at twelve-forty P.M., arriving Newark at nine P.M. Departing Newark at eleven-thirty-five P.M., arriving Tel Aviv at five-ten P.M. And American connects with British Airways. Do you want me to check that as well?"

"Please." If Ethan had taken the earlier Continental flight, he'd left Newark and was in the air, headed for Tel Aviv. The later flight gave her enough time to intercept him, but why would he delay—unless, of course, the earlier flight, like the El Al one, had been fully booked.

There were several possibilities on American via British Airways, the agent informed her a minute later. The 9 A.M. sounded promising for Ethan, frustrating for her: it arrived at JFK at 5:24 P.M. and departed again at 6:20 P.M. for London, where it connected the following morning with British Airways. Britain, as well as most of the European countries, had no death penalty. She didn't know but assumed there would be complications extraditing the teenager. England was preferable to Tel Aviv, though. Meissner wasn't a British citizen.

"There is also an American six-fifty P.M. flight from Los Angeles, direct to London," the agent said. "That connects with British Airways, too."

It was 6:19. Ethan may have taken the earlier flight, or he may have intended to take El Al's nonstop tomorrow. But what if he was taking the 6:50 American?

She thanked the agent and raced out of the terminal. Traffic was heavier than when she'd arrived, and she could see a double lane of cars queued up in front of the American terminal, four or five hundred yards to her right.

She ran toward the terminal, her new shoes pinching her feet, and arrived breathless at the ticket counter after elbowing her way around passengers who glared at her.

The ticket agent was frowning, too. "Ma'am, you'll have to wait your—"

"Detective Drake, LAPD." She showed her badge, explained what she wanted, and spelled Ethan's name. 6:27.

"He's ticketed for this flight," the agent told her a moment later. "Gate forty-three."

Her heart thumped. "Have they started boarding?"

"The flight's on time, so they should be boarding now."

Calling a quick thank-you behind her, Jessie ran down the crowded lobby and up the escalator steps, alarming a white-uniformed, white-capped woman who was collecting donations for a Christian mission. At the security check, the alarm rang as Jessie passed under the gate. She showed a husky male officer her badge and ID and the new Beretta in her purse and explained what she was doing. He compared her photo and face carefully and called over a supervisor, who did the same before letting her go.

Seven more minutes lost! She reached the gate at 6:38 and found a sea of people and luggage and crying babies. The terminal was being renovated and was encumbered with metal scaffolding that made her feel claustrophobic. Some passengers were still sitting on the rows of attached seats. Most had joined a line leading to the open doorway to the aircraft. Three people were standing in front of the gate counter.

Jessie moved to the far left of the area, near the huge plate glass window, and studied the crowd. She saw no one who resembled Ethan Meissner. There were quite a few Orthodox Jews—not surprising, since this flight's destination was Israel. The men wore yarmulkes or black hats. The women looked more vibrant, their heads covered in wigs of all hair shades, or colorful hats or snoods. A short, stout, black-hatted man with a dark beard put his arm around a younger man also wearing a black hat and pulled him tightly to his chest. She heard the words "heart attack" and "serious," and the bearded man was patting the back of the pale, shaking younger man, who had covered his eyes with his hands. They hurried away from the terminal.

She walked to the front of the desk and showed her badge to the agent, whose eyes widened with concern.

"I need to know whether Ethan Meissner has boarded this flight," she said in a low voice.

The woman studiously avoided looking at Jessie as she typed on her keyboard. "I don't know if he's boarded, but he's seated in twenty-seven B."

Jessie showed her badge again to the gate attendant collecting the boarding passes, and yet again to the flight attendants standing just inside the aircraft's entrance.

Twenty-seven B was the aisle seat on the right side of the aircraft, in the rear third. Jessie squeezed past passengers stowing luggage in the overhead compartments, ordering those who wouldn't move aside to get out of her way.

A young woman was sitting in twenty-seven A, the window seat. The adjoining seat was empty.

"Does this seat belong to anyone?" Jessie asked. Maybe he was in the lavatory. Or maybe he hadn't arrived yet. She would have to wait until all the passengers were seated.

"I'm not sure. There was a young guy sitting here when I came, but then he left."

Jessie frowned. "He left the aircraft?"

The woman nodded. "I think his father had a heart attack. That's what the flight attendant told him. He looked scared and hurried off the plane."

The black-hatted man. A perfect disguise.

Muttering "Shit!" under her breath, Jessie turned around and forced her way to the front of the aircraft. By now they were most certainly gone, but she ran down the ramp and out the door to the seating area, ran along the concourse and down the escalator steps, almost colliding with another white-uniformed woman collecting donations.

Less than a minute later she stood at the curb, searching right and left for the two black-hatted men.

Nothing.

She was about to give up and return to her car when she saw the bearded man several hundred feet to her right. She hadn't recognized him because he and his companion had removed their hats. Now they were sprinting for the open front and back passenger doors of a maroon minivan.

She started running and held up her badge. "Police! Stop that maroon van!" she yelled to an airport security person near the van, gesturing toward the vehicle, but her words were drowned out by the honking of cars. For a second she considered drawing her weapon, but there were too many people between her and the targets.

"Ethan Meissner!" she screamed, her feet pounding on the sidewalk.

The young man turned to look at her. The bearded man shoved him into the backseat, yanked the door, and slammed it shut. A second later he had disappeared into the front seat and pulled the door shut as the van drove off, tires screeching on the asphalt.

EZRA WAS TALKING to a young woman with curly blond hair who was gazing at him adoringly. Hovering nearby were three other women Jessie recognized—all single—waiting their turns. She sat impatiently while each one lingered an impossibly long time.

Finally, she was alone with him. He walked over to her.

"You left before class was over," he said, taking the seat next to her. "Everything okay?"

"My partner paged me. I had to go."

To Sally Hayes, to the Pervez family, to Gideon Meissner, to the airport. She felt as though a week had passed, and her feet were still sore from running in shoes she doubted would ever be comfortable. Her pride hurt, too, about losing Ethan Meissner—she'd been *that close!* Phil had said all the right things when she'd phoned him, but she was annoyed with herself. Espes would be annoyed, too. Marty Simms would rib her. She didn't even have the van's license plate number.

"Did I miss much?" she asked.

"Just a wrap-up. So what brings you back—aside from the Nathanson charm?" He smiled. "Obviously, not tonight's class, which was over by the time you got here."

"It's the charm, definitely." Which was the truth.

She was glad she'd come here instead of driving home to lick her wounds and polish off a pint of Ben & Jerry's ice cream. She wondered again when she'd first starting noticing how sexy his smile was, how his dark brown hair curled against the nape of his neck.

"It's deadly," he said. "All the males in the family have it. So, really. Something on your mind, Jessie?"

In her head this had played so easily, but her palms were suddenly clammy. "I thought we could grab a cup of coffee and talk."

"Sure." He looked at her, curious. "I haven't had dinner, and I have an hour before my next class. Why don't we go to the deli?"

The deli was a few blocks away, on Pico near Doheny. It was crowded, as usual, with families with small children and a few solitary diners. She smelled fried onions and French fries and hamburgers and steak and everything else she shouldn't be eating. Her stomach rumbled.

The thirty-two-year-old owner waved at her. "How's it going, Jessie?"

"Great, Danny. How's Ayelet?"

"Two new teeth," he said proudly. He showed her a photo of the nine-month-old, her bright red hair identical to her father's. "Try the shnitzel. It's good."

She smiled. "All your food is good, Danny. I have you to blame for the weight I've put on."

She came here to buy takeout for the Sabbath, and sometimes for dinner—alone, but not as lonely as she'd felt at first. She was beginning to know people, to belong.

"Let's sit there." Ezra pointed to one of the few unoccupied tables at the back of the long, L-shaped room.

Danny looked at Ezra, then at Jessie. "You're with him?" He had an odd expression on his face.

"She's my student," Ezra said.

"Oh, okay." He nodded. "Treat her nice—she's a special lady." He handed Ezra two laminated menus.

"He looked relieved," Jessie remarked when they were seated. "He disapproves of me because I'm not observant, doesn't he?" She was surprised at how hurt she felt.

"No way." Ezra smiled. "Danny's been trying to set me up with his sister. She's nice, but not for me."

"Oh." She felt foolish over her insecurity, relieved that the friendliness had been sincere. "Well, his sister has lots of competition. I noticed you have groupies."

He laughed. "Hardly. I'm not exactly Tom Cruise."

"Oh, I don't know." She rested her chin in her cupped hands and pretended to assess him. "Your smile is just as good—better, 'cause you don't have those big, scary teeth."

"Gee, thanks."

"A nice mouth," she continued, "a nice nose, even with that little bump. All in all, not bad looking for a teacher." His hazel eyes looked almost blue against the navy of his blazer. "I'll bet they're hot for you, Ezra."

"You're making my head swell. My yarmulke won't fit." His tone was light, but the color in his face had deepened.

The waitress came over. Ezra ordered a pastrami burger— "The best in the kosher world," he told Jessie, who resisted temptation and ordered roast chicken and salad.

"For your information, those women wanted details about next weekend's San Diego Shabbaton," Ezra said after the waitress had filled their water glasses and left. "We're having lecturers from all over the country, Jessie. I think you'd find it inspirational."

"No thanks. I like getting my inspiration at Shabbat lunch with Dafna."

During the past few months she'd enjoyed several postsynagogue meals at Ezra's sister's West L.A. home. She'd accepted invitations from other synagogue members, too, and enjoyed feeling connected to people and community in a way she never had before. She still felt most comfortable with Dafna and her husband and their two young sons, and the occasional guests who joined them. And Ezra. She'd been keenly disappointed last weekend when he hadn't shown up.

"Think about it," he urged. "You'll meet a lot of people."

"Group events aren't my thing." She ran her finger around the rim of the glass. "They take me back to high school dances and feeling gawky and ugly and sorry for myself 'cause the popular guys didn't know I existed and even the nerds didn't make me their first choice."

He smiled. "Funny, I would've figured you for prom queen."

She exaggerated a sigh. "Where were you when I was a senior? Oh, that's right. Probably in yeshiva—and you wouldn't have been allowed to dance with me anyway. No touching women, right?"

"Actually, I was a freshman at NYU, and I wasn't all that strict when it came to touching women."

"No kidding?" She knew so little about him.

"I told you before, Jessie, I'm a teacher, not a rabbi. I certainly didn't behave like a rabbi back then. Ask Dafna. On second thought, don't." He grinned.

"A wasted opportunity for both of us, then. Too bad, huh? It would have been nice."

"Too bad." He rested an arm on the top of his chair. "So am I reading something into this, or are we flirting?"

Something fluttered in her stomach. "I think we're flirting."

He was silent a moment. "What about your ex-husband? I take it he's no longer in the picture?"

"We broke up on Rosh Hashanah." A painful start to the new year, but with it, she'd realized, came the possibility of new beginnings.

"I'm sorry it didn't work out, Jessie."

"Me, too," she said simply.

He was looking at her with an odd expression. "I don't know what to say." He moved his arm off the chair back. "Four months ago I would've jumped at the chance to go out with you."

"You're seeing someone else?" Her face was warm with embarrassment.

"No. There's no one else, despite Dafna's valiant efforts, and my grandmother's." Ezra's smile was strained. "The thing is, Jessie, I don't want to be the guy you're turning to on the rebound."

"Gary and I ended things two months ago, Ezra." She flashed to this morning's phone call. If Gary wasn't ready to let go, that wasn't her problem, or her fault.

"You were married to him for three years. Are you sure you're over him?" Ezra asked quietly.

"*Yes,* I'm sure." What the hell was she doing, pleading her case as if she were desperate? "Obviously, this is making you uncomfortable, and I don't blame you. Let's keep it simple. Me student, you teacher."

"I've hurt your feelings." He sounded distressed. "I'm sorry, Jessie, but it's—"

"Look, it was just a thought." The last thing she needed was pity. "You're right—two months isn't all that long. The truth is, I'm probably using you to avoid going out with Brian Lefton. And our friend Danny will be happy. I wouldn't want to push his sister out of the picture." She was trying to rescue both of them from awkwardness, but felt stupid and humiliated.

Ezra looked puzzled. "Who's Brian Lefton?"

"A guy my mom wants to set me up with." He'd left a message on her machine last night—at first she'd forgotten who he was. "Tall, dark, handsome, wealthy, and he looks like Harrison Ford. He's Jewish, too."

"Sounds like every woman's dream." Ezra smiled.

"My mom's words exactly."

The waitress brought their orders. Jessie busied herself with the roast chicken, which was tender and juicy, but she could have been eating leather for all she cared.

She would give Brian Lefton a chance, she decided. And if he didn't work out, there was always Joe Hopper, the man of a thousand charms and a spare middle tube. And Frank Pruitt, the detective she'd dated before reconnecting with

Gary. The last time she'd seen Pruitt, he'd told her to give him a call. So what if he was interested in her (okay, and she in him) just for the great sex? So what if he was a teensy bit anti-Semitic?

"How'd you like class today?" Ezra asked.

Jessie was only too happy to change the subject. "Epstein gave you a run for your money, as usual."

"I like him." Ezra smiled, his eyes earnest. "He's tough, but fair. And he's trying to understand his son."

Unlike my mom or sister, Jessie thought again.

"At bottom, I suppose he's relieved," Ezra said. "If his son's going to flip out, at least he's flipping out with religion, not drugs. Things could be much worse."

Jessie nodded. "The new homicide I'm investigating? One of the suspects is an eighteen-year-old boy who may be on drugs." She told him about Ethan Meissner without mentioning his name. "One day he has the world at his fingertips, the next day he throws it away."

"It's never that simple, Jessie."

"You're right, of course. It seems this boy's been consumed with guilt over his mother's suicide. And he grew up with a father who has a drinking problem and a temper. Now apparently the boy is into drugs and alcohol. He left home when his foster parent laid down the law."

Ezra sighed. "And you think this teenager is a killer?"

"Killers are getting younger and younger, Ezra. A first grader killed his classmate because he didn't like her."

"I read the papers, Jessie. I'm not cloistered." He sounded mildly annoyed.

"Sorry. I didn't mean to sound patronizing." Or did she? She was still smarting from his rejection, although she could hardly blame him for being cautious. Maybe she *was* on the rebound.

"I have to believe that little boy didn't know what he was doing, Jessie, that he didn't realize death was permanent."

"You don't believe there are children who are intrinsically

amoral?" She'd been thinking about this all day, since her conversation with Phil.

Ezra considered. "I don't know. I believe parenting and environment have a lot to do with it."

"So the kid's not responsible?"

"I didn't say that." He took a bite of his burger. "You know, the Torah talks about teen violence—'a wayward and rebellious son who does not hearken to the voice of his father and the voice of his mother, and they discipline him.' The Hebrew term is *ben sorer u'moreh*."

"What happens to him? Forty lashes?" That was a typical biblical punishment, she had learned.

"He gets lashes, but he continues in his wanton ways." Ezra hesitated. "Eventually, the parents take him to the city elders and declare him a wayward and rebellious son, a glutton and a drunkard. And all the men of the city stone him to death."

"Whoa!" She grimaced. "This country has a bad rep for executing young killers, but a *thirteen*-year-old?" She frowned. "Define 'wayward and rebellious.' "

"Not exactly dinner conversation, is it?" He put down the burger. "The commentaries list specific criteria. The boy has to be within the three months after he turns thirteen. He has to steal money from his parents and use it to buy a certain type and quantity of meat and wine."

"You're kidding me, right?" Jessie stared at Ezra. "That's *it*? He didn't *kill* anyone?"

"The boy is executed *now*, when he's relatively innocent, rather than later, when his wantonness and unbridled lust will escalate to violent crimes, even murder."

"That's just *wrong!*" Her outcry caught the attention of the couple at the next table. She lowered her voice. "No offense to the Torah, Ezra, but you can't kill someone because you *think* he's going to be a killer."

"You're looking at the body, Jessie. The Torah is looking at the soul."

She shook her head. "I don't buy it. How do they know he's not going to do a one-eighty and become a law-abiding adult? God says a person can always repent, even on his deathbed."

"That's absolutely true." Ezra nodded. "And if the parents forgive him, the boy isn't executed. This is an exceptional case. The criteria are strict: the age, the exact nature of the theft, the amount of liquor and food he consumes and where he consumes it, how many times the boy repeats his actions, the relationship between the parents, the physical character- istics of the boy and the parents."

"Meaning?" She found this fascinating and troubling.

He picked up a fry. "For one thing, the parents' voices have to be identical."

She stifled a laugh. "That's impossible, even if the dad's castrated."

"Exactly. Some commentaries explain that it's a metaphor—the parents have to be consistent in how they raise their child, in the values they teach."

She had no argument with that.

"The point is, Jessie, the criteria are so difficult to meet, that there's no established case in the annals of Jewish law of the execution of a *ben sorer u'moreh*."

She prodded a piece of chicken with her fork. "So why include the section in the Torah?"

"You're asking all the expert questions." He ate the fry. "Most commentaries say the section is an exhortation. 'This is what can happen if. . . .' "

She thought about that. "Okay. But if the boy meets all these criteria, why not lock him up and rehabilitate him?"

"The Torah doesn't have a penal system. And the *ben sorer u'moreh* is beyond rehabilitation—unless, as I said, his parents forgive him and establish a relationship. I suppose the modern equivalent would be the sociopath. Most psy- chologists agree that sociopathy isn't curable."

Two months ago she had fatally shot a man whom the police psychologist had called a sociopath. She had looked into his eyes and been terrified by the emptiness.

"So this boy is born amoral?" she asked. "A bad seed destined to be killed?"

"No. If that were the case, there would be no free will, and Judaism is based on free will. The boy *chooses* to act a certain way. But the parents have to be talking with the same voice. What if one is indulgent, the other rigid? One respects authority, one doesn't? One has faith, one is a cynic? What kind of role models have they been? What values have they set? How involved were they before they realized the boy was drinking and stealing? We don't know what took place in that home, Jessie."

She thought about the teenage killers who were making the headlines too often, about the parents who had raised them. About Ethan as a toddler and little boy, growing up in a home with a depressed mother who killed herself and an alcoholic father with a bad temper. And the second home? From everything she'd heard, Ronald Bushnell had been tough, Celeste a pushover. But what did it all mean?

"Your teenage suspect," Ezra said. "What's he like?"

"According to his English teacher, he's a terrific kid tormented by his mother's suicide. His foster mom feels sorry for him but thinks he's into drugs and alcohol and theft. His real dad hardly knows him. He blames the foster parents for that—the opposite of what they say—and for cutting the kid off from his Jewish roots."

Ezra raised a brow. "The boy's parents are Jewish?"

"The mom was. So is the dad. He's not observant, but tradition's important to him."

"A tough situation." He looked distressed. "So what's your take on the boy?"

"I haven't talked to him yet. He's on the run, maybe suicidal. I almost caught him trying to take a flight to Israel. That's where his grandparents live." She told Ezra what had happened at the airport. "He was ten feet away! I never suspected he'd be disguised as a Chasidic yeshiva boy. Smart move." She had to give them credit.

"Not all Orthodox Jews who wear black hats are Chasidic. What about the bearded man? Was he the father in disguise?"

"No. The dad obviously knew I suspected what was going on. He must've phoned someone to get the boy off the aircraft before I could arrest him." Or before the London police did. "There's a third guy involved—the driver of the van. Twenty people around, and not one of them got the license plate."

"Now what?"

"We put an APB on the boy and a classmate who's also been missing since the murders. He may be an accomplice." Phil had taken care of that. They would have to notify all the airports and train stations to be on the lookout.

"And if you don't find them?"

"We have some ideas." She'd phoned the station from the airport and asked the Watch Commander to put a tail on Gideon Meissner. In the morning she hoped to get a warrant to tap his phone and search his apartment. "Sorry, I can't tell you any more."

"Frankly, I don't want to know. Your work sounds so depressing—three murders, two teenage suspects. And that's just one case." Ezra shook his head. "Doesn't it get to you?"

Gary would have wanted to know all the details. He would have pressed, and she would have told him to back off, and they would have argued again about her not trusting him. "It gets to me all the time. What about your *ben sorer u'moreh?*" she countered. "Talk about depressing."

"That's a case of a possibility that was never actualized. This is your daily reality."

"I guess that's why I come to your classes. A spiritual salve for my battered soul."

She was finishing the chicken when she remembered the Hebrew letters beneath the flight information on Meissner's newspaper. She mentioned this to Ezra and took out her notepad.

"I couldn't write them down immediately, but I'm sure the first letter was a *reish*." The equivalent of an *R*. "There was an accent mark to the left, and the letter was separate from the others. Probably a first name."

"From the accent mark, I'd say it was short for Rav or Rabbi. What are the other letters?"

She handed him the notepad. "I had difficulty making it out because there were no *nekudot*," she explained, referring to the marks below the letters that represented vowels. "And I'm not sure I have the letters in the right order."

"I like doing jumbles." He took his pen and copied the letters in different combinations. "Linkregman? Linkgerman? Nikleregman?" He looked up. "Let me work on this. And I'll show it to some people, okay?"

"That would be great. Thanks, Ezra."

"Glad to help."

He tore off the page, and she held out her hand for the notepad. Their hands touched.

"Your *ben sorer u'moreh*," she said a few minutes later when they were walking to her car. "If I were the parent, I couldn't do it. Have him executed, I mean."

Ezra looked at her. "I don't think I could, either."

❖ 21 ❖

HER FATHER HAD phoned. She listened to his formal voice telling her he was sorry he'd missed her call and would try again later.

Frances had phoned, too. "Just wanted to know how your day went, dear. I saw a little red Michael Kors dress that would look *fabulous* on you. Neiman's is holding it until tomorrow night."

Not a hint of anxiety in her voice—it was as though last night's conversation had never taken place. But that was typical of her mother. She had swooped into their rooms in a fury, shredding a too tight or too short skirt or dress, raising welts on her daughters' thighs and backs, twisting arms almost to the breaking point and gouging them with sharp fingernails that had often drawn blood. The storm spent, Frances would be pleasant and composed, magnanimous in her forgiveness. As a child that had been more frightening and confusing to Jessie than the assault itself. As a teenager and young adult, it had filled her with anger and hate, which in turn had compounded her guilt.

She checked the mail, watered the Chinese evergreen in the den that looked as wilted as she felt, then phoned her father.

"How are you, sweetheart?" he said when he answered. "Diane told me you phoned several times. Sorry I didn't get back to you sooner—it's been a hectic day."

"I tried you at the house around six, Dad. I figured you'd be home from work. Where were you?"

"My daughter, the detective." He chuckled. "I went to the market for milk and cereal. So how was your day?"

Talk about The Pretenders. She felt a surge of irritation that had nothing to do with Frances's worries. "Mom's upset, Dad," she said, in no mood to begin with subtleties. "She said the two of you are having problems."

"We're not having problems. She's in one of her moods."

"She's hurt, Dad. She says you're distant."

"So she's been telling me." He sighed. "She has too much time on her hands while I've been busier than ever with the practice. And I have things on my mind."

"Like what?"

"I'm considering cutting down on my hours, maybe retiring in a year. I'm not getting younger, you know."

She felt a twinge of alarm. "Are you feeling okay?"

"I'm fine. There's nothing for you or your mother to worry about. I didn't want to discuss this with her until I decide what I plan to do. Maybe that was a mistake, but you know how she is—if I even hint about retiring, she'll have us booked on cruises all year long." He laughed.

She thought he sounded nervous. "Mom says she phoned you a few times at the office after hours and you weren't there."

"I was in the men's room."

"She phoned you last night, after she arrived at Helen's. You weren't home."

"Am I supposed to check in with her every ten minutes?" He was annoyed now. "I went out to dinner."

"By yourself?"

"Are you interrogating me, Jessie? If your mother wants to talk to me, let her call me up."

"She thinks you're having an affair." Jessie wished she could see her father's face.

"That's ridiculous!"

"She's convinced of it."

He was silent a moment. "I'll call her."

"You don't have office hours Wednesdays. I think you should drive up and talk to her, Dad."

"I wish she hadn't involved you, Jessie. What else did she say?"

That you don't want to have sex with her. "She didn't go into details. So are you coming?"

"I'll think about it."

"Dad—"

"I said I'll think about it!"

She was unaccustomed to hearing him yell, and her face burned as though he'd slapped her.

"I'm sorry—I didn't mean to raise my voice. This isn't what you think, Jessie."

"Don't tell me—tell Mom."

"I heard you, Jessie. Good night."

He hung up abruptly, and she was left listening to a dial tone.

The house was chilly. She turned up the heat and changed into a white T-shirt and a pair of red-and-white plaid pajama bottoms. The seams had opened, and the threads had started to unravel at the hem, but she couldn't bring herself to toss out the pajamas—they were too comfortable, they were her uniform. She thought again about the box filled with photos of her and Gary, about their wedding album. She would have to do something about that.

She threw a load of laundry into the washing machine, went into the kitchen, and poured a glass of milk. She was about to take a sip when she remembered she'd had chicken for dinner. According to the laws of kashrut, she had to wait six hours after eating meat or poultry before she could eat dairy.

"It's not about health reasons," Ezra had explained. "Although nutritionists have found benefits to the wait. It's a commandment that isn't explained—a *chok*."

The cold milk was tempting, and she wondered whether

her deepening attraction to Orthodoxy was mixed up with her feelings for Ezra. She held the glass for a moment, then poured the milk back into the container and drank cranberry juice instead.

Feeling like Madeleine Albright, she phoned Helen's house, and listened to her sister complain about being exhausted after accompanying Frances on her shopping spree. Then she spoke with her mother.

"I talked with Dad," she said after a few seconds of chitchat. "He's not having an affair, Mom. He's preoccupied because he's thinking of retiring." She didn't care that she hadn't asked her father's permission to repeat this.

"That's nice, dear. Did you get my message about the dress? I think you'll like it."

This was theater of the absurd. "Talk to him—hear what he has to say."

"He knows where to find me if he's interested, Jessica. By the way, you didn't call Matthew, did you?"

So much for her first attempt at shuttle diplomacy. "I forgot. Can you ask Helen to put him on?"

"He's sleeping. Luckily, Helen didn't tell him you were going to call. Are you going to look at that dress?"

"I'll try." She wanted to scream.

"What happened with that plastic surgeon?"

"He's still dead."

There was a beat of silence. "You complain when I don't take an interest in your job, Jessica, and when I do, that's not good, either."

She sighed. "You're right. I'm sorry." In her morning prayers she'd acknowledged her obligation to honor her parents, but she wondered whether God knew what a challenge he'd given her with Frances. "Phil and I have been working on the case all day, and I'm exhausted."

"I spoke to Charlotte. She said she has something to tell you—honestly, I think she wants to sound important. Anyway, it's too late to phone her now. You can reach her early in the morning or after eleven, because she has an eight o'clock Tae-Bo class. Do you want her number?"

"Thanks, Mom." Jessie doubted that Charlotte would have much to add about Ronald Bushnell, but she took down the phone number. "Brian Lefton phoned," she offered, wanting to make amends. "I think I'll go out with him."

"That's *very* nice, Jessica," her mother purred.

Life was so easy when you did things Frances's way. After wishing her good night, Jessie did twenty minutes of stretches and sit-ups in her bedroom while watching TV. She transferred the laundry to the dryer, then sat at her desk and wrote a preliminary report of what she'd learned that day.

Putting things on paper helped clarify her thoughts and reminded her to phone Barbara Martin again. The fired nurse still wasn't in. Jessie left a message and the station phone number. "It's important," she said, though she didn't know whether that was true.

She wondered what Gideon Meissner had meant when he'd said the Bushnells hadn't considered Ethan "good enough." Not because of his grades—that hadn't been it, judging from Meissner's surprised expression. Ethan's low-life friends?

She phoned Sally Hayes. The woman answered on the first ring, her "Yes?" high-pitched and fraught with anxiety.

"You've found Kevin?" she demanded.

"No, we haven't. I take it you haven't heard from him?"

"No. Neither has my ex. Something terrible must have happened, or he would have called! What are you doing about finding him?"

Not the same woman they'd talked to earlier. "We're doing everything we can. We're continuing to check hospitals in the area and all the police divisions for reports of any accidents." And the morgue, she added silently. "Is your gun in the house?"

The woman didn't answer.

"Your ex-husband filed a missing person's, so there's an APB out on Kevin," Jessie told her. There would probably be war between the two ex-spouses over that, but it wasn't her problem. "If your son has a weapon, that information should be available to any officer who might apprehend him. We don't want any tragic accidents."

"It's not in the house," the woman admitted reluctantly. "But that doesn't mean he took it."

Dream on. "Does Kevin know where you keep your gun?"

"Yes. But he knows it's not a toy."

"Do you keep it loaded?"

"I don't see much point in having a gun for protection and having to load it in an emergency," she snapped. "What am I supposed to say to an intruder—'Please wait while I get some bullets'?"

"When was the last time you saw your gun?"

"About a week ago. *None* of this makes sense. Why would Kevin—oh my God, maybe the *Meissner* boy took it! I'm sure Kevin told him about it. He probably showed it to him. You know how teenage boys are. They want to be cool."

An interesting possibility, Jessie had to admit. She wondered whether Ethan had stopped there after he'd left the Bushnell home and dropped out of sight. And if so, why. "When was the last time Ethan was at your house?"

"I don't remember exactly."

"Was it *after* you saw your gun?"

"I said I can't remember! I'm sure that's what happened. Ethan took my gun! Who knows what he did with it!"

Looking through the photos had been a mistake. She was by nature sentimental and a hoarder and couldn't bring herself to toss into the trash the captured memories of what had been, after all, an important part of her life. But they made her melancholy, and the house felt intensely lonely.

It was past eleven, but she chucked the pajamas and

slipped into a short black skirt with a flared hem and a black spandex top with a deep V neckline. Strappy black sandals with thin high heels. No bra, no stockings. She put on makeup and perfume, tousled her naturally wavy hair, and left the house.

She wasn't sure where she would go—an upscale bar, maybe, though she wasn't much of a drinker and would be driving home. She decided to go dancing in one of the clubs on Sunset, but knew she was fooling herself long before she drove toward Doheny and parked in the lot behind Benny's.

Music, laughter, a haze of cigarette smoke that stung her eyes. She looked around but didn't see Gary or Jim or Lois or anyone else she knew. So the party was over. Just as well, she thought. She sat at a small table, nursing a glass of white wine, watching the couples on the crowded dance floor. Hip-hop, swing, reggae—they knew all the moves. Her foot tapped along with the rhythm.

A man at the bar smiled at her. She smiled back. He slid off the stool and walked over. He was younger than she'd thought, probably in his late twenties, and taller. Well dressed, dark brown hair, brown eyes, chiseled features. So good-looking he could have been a model.

"Hi, I'm Brad." He smiled. "Want to dance?"

"Jessie."

She gave him her hand. He drew her to her feet and led her onto the dance floor. She felt a little clumsy at first, and nervous, but the wine had given her a buzz, and he was a practiced dancer. She found herself unwinding with the music—a disco beat first, then a rock 'n' roll oldie that had her laughing as he spun her away from him and drew her back like a coil.

The song ended. Michael Bolton began to croon "When a Man Loves a Woman."

"Okay if I cut in?"

She turned her head and her heart skipped a beat when she saw him. So damn handsome and sexy, it wasn't fair. Brad looked at her questioningly. She nodded and thanked him, and watched him walk back to the bar.

Gary's hand was on her waist, as if it belonged there. "I didn't see you come in. I'm glad you're here."

"Me, too." His blue eyes were staring into hers, and she felt light-headed, maybe from the wine. "I didn't see you, either. I thought you'd left."

"I was waiting till midnight, for Cinderella. You look unbelievably hot, Jessie."

He pulled her close, one hand holding hers, the other, warm through the thin spandex, on the small of her back, which was slick with perspiration. His cheek was against hers. She smelled his cologne and the scotch on his breath and realized how much she had missed being held by a man.

She shut her eyes. They were dancing so slowly, barely moving, and at some point his lips grazed hers.

"I missed you, Jessie. I missed you so goddamn much," he whispered.

He kissed her, his lean body pressed so close that she could feel the muscles in his thighs and the thumping of his heart. She kissed him back, arms around his neck, feeling pleasantly achy and flushed and aroused as she knew she would be when his tongue explored her mouth and his hands moved slowly up and down her hips, then underneath the spandex top.

"I want you," he said. "Let's go."

She wanted him, too, because he knew her body, knew all the right places. She wanted him because it had been almost three months since she'd kissed a man, seven months since she'd had sex with anyone, and she was lonely and needy and horny, and terribly sad, because she couldn't do this, she didn't want to hurt him, because going to bed with him was stupid and dishonest and would leave her feeling cheap and pathetic.

Because it was Ezra she wanted to be with, Ezra's mouth she wanted on hers, Ezra's hands touching her, pressing her close.

ESPES HAD CALLED in sick, Ed Boyd reported when Jessie arrived at the station in the morning. "The first time I remember him doing that."

She'd forgotten to take vitamin C and echinacea. Too late now. "Poor baby." She no longer disliked Espes but doubted she'd ever feel the closeness and mutual regard she'd shared with Jack Kalish, who had taken a leave of absence to take care of his wife.

She'd awakened with a mild headache, and the Advil hadn't kicked in yet. Filling her mug with boiling water from the urn at the end of the long detectives' room, she returned to her desk and prepared her morning drink: strawberry-kiwi and two packets of artificial sweetener.

She sat down. "Where's Simms?"

Boyd looked up from the Blue Book he was scanning, filled with reports and photos of the investigation he was working. "He said he'd be in soon. I think he's with his broker." He looked pensive.

"You're not getting in too deep, are you?"

"Not me." He smiled. "You sound like my mom. She'd kill me if I lost more than a couple of hundred on the market. If she had her way, I'd be back in Arkansas, working in the family dry goods business."

She tasted the tea. Too hot. "You didn't like Arkansas?"

"I liked it okay, but I always hankered to see California. I don't know why. I do get homesick, though." He sounded wistful. "Can I ask you something personal?"

"Okay. But I may not answer." She blew gently over the tea, curious.

"This girl I'm seeing, Sheryl? She's terrific. Pretty, sweet, real smart. I think I could be serious about her," he said, a hint of shyness beneath the drawl. "But they say it's tough, being a cop and being married. There's a high divorce rate," he added awkwardly.

"True." He was a sweet young man. She knew he was referring to her and was touched by his sensitivity. She smiled to relieve his discomfort. "So what's the alternative? You never get married?"

"I know." He sighed. "I want a wife, a family. My folks are asking when they're going to have grandchildren."

It was nice to know that Arkansas parents laid the same guilt as those in Southern California. "It can work. Look at Phil—he and Maureen are happy. Espes is married, although who could be happy with him?" She was rewarded with a smile. "Lots of cops stay married, Ed. I'm not saying it's easy—the hours can be erratic, the work's dangerous. Not every wife is willing to put up with that."

Or husband. Gary had worried about the danger, though as a crime reporter, his hours had often been more unpredictable than hers. But now it was over. Finally, definitely over.

"Was that what happened with you? If it's none of my business, just tell me to shut up." He was blushing.

Mamma Boyd had raised her son right. "That was part of it." The miscarriage, which Gary had blamed on a fall resulting from her chasing a suspect, had been a final crack, but she wasn't prepared to talk about that. "The bottom line, we weren't clear about our expectations before we married, and we didn't communicate well. And our careers often put us in conflict."

Boyd nodded. "Marty told me your ex is a crime reporter. That had to be tough."

What else had Simms said about her? She found a granola bar in her purse and tore at the wrapping.

"Sheryl's a pediatric nurse," Boyd said. "I know she worries about me, but she respects what I do. But Marty says getting serious is a big mistake. He says I should be having a good time, playing the field."

"You aren't Marty." According to Phil, Simms's mother had skipped, leaving him and his brother with the father. Not something that would make you overly fond of women, but she didn't feel right talking to Boyd about his partner. "You have to do what's right for you."

"You're right. Thanks for being so open, Jessie."

She could have been talking about herself. She felt transparent in her embarrassment, as though Boyd and the entire world knew about last night. She felt so sorry for the hurt she'd caused. *"Why'd you come here, dressed like this, if you weren't interested?"* Gary had demanded angrily when she'd pulled away and apologized. *"Why don't you figure out what the hell you want and stop playing with my mind?"*

It could have been worse, she thought. They could have been in bed.

". . . ask you something else?" Boyd said.

She forced herself to concentrate. "Okay, but that's your quota for the day." She smiled.

"Sheryl's birthday is coming up. Is it all right to get her jewelry?"

She had a difficult enough time choosing gifts for her own family, and she was hardly an expert on successful relationships. "Earrings are okay, but not too expensive. Perfume's always safe. And flowers." Jessie loved flowers.

She spoke to Nicole Hobart's parents and left a message for Myra Borden, Ethan's therapist. Phil arrived late and blamed a four-car pileup.

"Another accident thanks to a cell phone." He looked accusingly at Jessie.

"I see *you're* feeling better," she said. "You should have stayed home."

He set a thermos on his desk. "I'm okay. I'm doped up on cold medication." Sitting down, he checked his messages and scowled at them. "No one from the Pervez family phoned?" he asked, uncapping the thermos and releasing a plume of coffee-scented steam.

"Nope." She inhaled the rich aroma. She loved the smell of coffee, but not the taste.

"Maybe they heard from the nephew and went to meet him," Phil said.

"Assuming he's alive. Or maybe they went into hiding."

Phil's scowl deepened. "Why the hell would they do that?"

"Makes sense if they're afraid of whoever killed Lily— and possibly Jamal."

"Or if they're afraid *of* Jamal."

"The family *sponsored* the guy, Phil. Why would he want to kill them?"

"Who knows what goes in families? Bushnell took the Meissner kid in, treated him like a son. And the boy is our *numero uno* suspect." Phil took a swig from the thermos. "If we don't hear from them by this afternoon, we'll have to go by there again. Any news?"

"Futaki's doing the Bushnell autopsies tomorrow. And I spoke to Sally Hayes last night." Jessie repeated what the woman had told her. "She phoned this morning to tell me her housekeeper said Ethan came to the house Sunday afternoon. He claimed he'd forgotten something in Kevin's room and needed to get it. Sally and Kevin weren't home, but the housekeeper knew him, so she let him look around."

"So maybe Ethan stopped by to pick up the Glock."

"*If* Sally Hayes is telling the truth. How come the housekeeper didn't mention this to her before? Maybe mom's making it all up to get us off her son's back. We'll have to talk to the housekeeper."

Phil grunted. "More fun."

"I spoke with the cop who's watching Gideon Meissner's place. No sign of the boy. But Ezra Nathanson is going to try to make sense of that Hebrew name I saw at Meissner's. It was right below the El Al info."

"Could be the name of an Israeli relative or friend."

They flipped a coin to see who would get the warrant to search Gideon Meissner's house.

Phil lost the toss and grumbled. "I'll give Judge Otterman your regards. What about you?"

"I'm going back to high school."

She finished the granola bar and her tea, and walked down the stairs with him and outside and looked at the Pizza Hut orange-tiled entrance to the adjacent parking lot. The sky was still overcast, and dark gray clouds threatened rain.

"Don't get detention," Phil said.

Like many of the girls Jessie had seen yesterday, Gillian Logan was extremely thin, even in plaid, which Jessie had given up pounds ago. She had gray eyes, shiny straight long black hair parted in the middle, and white teeth that had probably benefited from braces and bleach.

"I don't know if Mr. Alpert explained why you're here," Jessie said. "Here" was one of the cubicles where teachers and students conferred. The headmaster hadn't offered the use of his spacious office. He'd been unhappy to see her again, reluctant to pull Gillian out of class. It was highly disruptive and upsetting to the students and the parents, he'd complained.

Gillian nodded. "He said it's about Ethan. Is he in trouble?" She sounded more curious than concerned.

"He's missing, and we have to find him."

"Because Dr. Bushnell was murdered, right?" Her voice had dropped. "Do you think he did it?"

"Do you?" Jessie countered.

The girl was startled, and chewed the gloss on her upper lip. "I don't know Ethan all that well. He was never rough with me, and he never yelled at me."

"How long did you two date?"

"About six months, on and off."

Jessie raised a brow. "In six months you didn't get to know him?"

Gillian shrugged. "He didn't like to talk about himself much. You never really know what's going on in his head."

"Did he get along with the Bushnells?"

"I guess. They expected a lot, but Ethan's brainy, and he wanted to do well. So it wasn't a big deal." She frowned. "He changed this semester, though. He's moody a lot of the time, pissed off. I heard he's been getting into fights."

"With Kevin Hayes. Do you know what they fought about?"

Gillian shook her head. "Kevin's a jerk. He likes to mess with people's heads, push their buttons. Probably makes him feel like less of a loser." She made a face. "He was this close to flunking out last semester." She held up her thumb and index finger with barely a gap between them.

Jessie nodded. "I understand he and Ethan were friendly lately."

Gillian looked surprised. "No *way*. Why would Ethan hang with Kevin?"

A good question. Jessie had hoped the girl would have the answer. "So why did you break up with Ethan, Gillian? Because he was angry and moody?"

"He wasn't like that back in September. That's not why we split up." She sounded uncomfortable. "It kind of fizzled out over the summer, but then in September we were dating again. Then it was *really* over." She flipped her hair behind her ear.

"Do you think that's why he was angry, Gillian? Because you ended it?" Which came first, the chicken or the egg?

The girl hesitated. "It wasn't exactly like that."

"It was mutual, you mean?"

"Not really." Gillian bent her head and traced a box of the plaid print on her skirt.

I'm an idiot, Jessie thought, feeling sorry for the girl. "He was interested in someone else?"

The girl nodded, her head still down. "I found out he was *using* me." Her voice quivered with hurt. "He was telling the Bushnells he was out with me so he could be with *her*. He knew they wouldn't approve."

A friend of Torro's and Big M's? "Do you know her name?"

Gillian looked up at Jessie, her face flushed with anger. "Sure, I know her name. Adrienne. Adrienne Bushnell."

Not good enough.

"You lied to me," Jessie told Tim Croton.

She'd appropriated the headmaster's office to give herself an edge of authority. She wasn't feeling so kindly toward the English instructor today and had felt like dragging his AP butt out of class.

"I didn't lie," Croton said calmly. "You asked me if he was upset about breaking up with Gillian Logan. I said no."

"Don't play games." She leaned forward. "This is a murder investigation, Mr. Croton, not a literary exercise. Withholding information can get you in serious trouble."

"I'm sorry. I honestly didn't think it was important, and I didn't feel I could violate Ethan's confidence."

"Am I missing something here, Mr. Croton?" Jessie cocked her head and squinted at him. "You're not his lawyer, are you? You're not his shrink? You're not his rabbi?"

"I'm a teacher concerned about his student. I did what I thought was in his best interests." Croton's voice was cool but his face was flushed.

"Sounds very noble, but you withheld information that

could give Ethan a motive for murdering Ronald Bushnell."
She glared at him, annoyed that her anger didn't seem to affect him. "What did Ethan tell you?"

"Basically, you know what I know. He and Adrienne fell
in love over the summer, but her father disapproved."

"Before or after Ethan's grades started slipping?"

"Before. When Dr. Bushnell found out, he went ballistic.
He made Ethan promise to stop seeing Adrienne. Ethan
tried, but he couldn't keep his promise. So he pretended to
be interested in Gillian again. He felt terrible about using
her."

"But that didn't stop him from doing it." Jessie swiveled
in Alpert's chair. "So all this stuff about Ethan being depressed about his mom's suicide, and being angry because
he was pressured about college applications and pleasing
Bushnell and his dad—all of that was crap, huh?"

"No, it's all true," Croton said slowly. "Dr. Bushnell's disapproval just added stress. Ethan felt that no matter what he
did, in Bushnell's eyes he'd never be good enough for his
daughter. So he figured, why bother? Then he'd decide to
prove to Bushnell he *was* good enough. It was heartbreaking, listening to him. He was devastated. I think that's why
he turned to drugs."

"And then Bushnell found out and threw him out. Did
Mrs. Bushnell know about Ethan and her daughter?"

"I don't know. Ethan didn't say."

Thwarted love, drugs, a father's rejection—they added up
to a strong motive. Jessie flashed to Jamal Pervez and wondered if Phil was right. Maybe the young man had loved his
cousin, maybe her parents had disapproved. Had he killed
her when she'd refused to defy them?

"Where does Kevin Hayes fit into this?" Jessie asked.

Croton frowned. "What do you mean?"

"He's missing." So is his gun, she added silently. "He and
Ethan may be together."

"As far as I knew, they didn't get along." The teacher

sounded puzzled. "In fact, Ethan told me he was angry at Hayes for spreading rumors about Adrienne."

That corroborated what Knowles had said. "According to Jason Knowles they patched things up. Ethan was helping Hayes with his schoolwork."

Croton shook his head. "I don't know anything about that. Hayes isn't in my class."

"Ethan tried to leave the country last night."

The teacher sighed. "You're sure?"

"I saw him. He left the airport with a man dressed like a Chasidic Jew—black hat, beard. Any idea who that is?"

"No. I advised him to talk to a minister or a rabbi, because he was conflicted about his religious identity. He told me he wasn't interested. Maybe he changed his mind."

"What about Adrienne? How did she react to her father's disapproval?" Jessie would have to consider the girl as a suspect, too. She'd been agitated about Ethan's leaving the home, passionate in his defense.

Croton sighed. "Ethan said she was terribly upset. But she's very much daddy's girl, so she obeyed."

"Not Juliet to her Romeo?"

"More like Catherine and Heathcliff. *Wuthering Heights?*" he prompted when Jessie didn't respond.

She nodded absentmindedly. In her mind she was in Ethan's room, touching the spine of the book on his shelf. She tried to remember what it was that—

"Clifford Bronte," she said, unaware that she'd spoken.

"You mean Emily," Croton said. "There were two other sisters, Charlotte and Anne. Charlotte wrote *Jane Eyre*. There was also a brother, Patrick, but no Clifford."

"No," she agreed. Not a new patient, but a hybrid of the truncated name of a pathetic fictional orphan turned tortured adult and that of his creator. Ethan, or whoever had made the appointment, had probably felt quite clever.

"I talked to Ethan's math and history teachers," she said. "They both think he was trouble waiting to happen."

Croton shrugged. "That's not the way I see him. Troubled, yes. Trouble, no. There's a difference."

"Could he have been fooling you? Putting on an act?"

The instructor thought for a moment. "I don't know. I thought I knew him." He sounded unhappy.

❖ 23 ❖

"YOU FOUND EITÁN?" Gideon Meissner asked anxiously when he opened the door for Jessie and Phil. "He's all right?"

"You know he is. Cut the *charah*, Mr. Meissner," Phil said, pushing the door open. "That's the correct word, isn't it?"

"I don't know what you are talking about, or why you are so angry. But Eitán is all right—that's all that matters." Meissner raked his hair with his fingers. "If you know where Eitán is, why are you here?"

"Your neighbor saw Ethan coming out of your apartment Monday morning, the day of the murders," Jessie said.

"Who told you—that snoop, Mrs. Montenido?" He snorted. "She can barely see. For your information, I am working on a new album with a talented young man. *That's* who she saw."

"At two-thirty in the morning?" Luckily for them, Mrs. Montenido was an insomniac. "This witness identified Ethan from a photo." Not an absolute identification, but the woman had been reasonably certain.

Meissner frowned. "Two-thirty *Monday* morning? I wasn't home then, it happens to be. So maybe Eitán came and left— he has a key to my apartment."

"Where were you so late?"

He arched a brow. "What, I'm a child, I need a curfew? I went out for some drinks. Alone," he added pointedly. "Then to Coffee Bean. Sometimes I get my best ideas when I'm by myself in a noisy place full of smoke and people. Funny, no?" He flashed a smile that under other circumstances would have charmed.

The man was a quick thinker, Jessie had to admit. "Maybe Ethan stopped by and borrowed your gun."

Meissner shook his head. "I don't have a gun."

"What happened to the one your wife used to kill herself?" Phil asked.

Meissner winced and gave Phil a wounded look. "I threw it into the ocean," he said softly. "I didn't want it in the house, after what happened. You can understand." He cleared his throat and faced Jessie. "Is that it?"

"Not quite. We have a warrant to search your apartment." She extended the paper to him, but he waved it away.

"You don't believe me?" He sounded offended. "Please, come in. Search." He invited them in with a deep flourish, like a maître d' ushering VIP guests to the finest table. "See for yourself that I have nothing to hide."

A half hour later they had to concede he was right. They had found more proof that Meissner was a slob—the place was grimy, filled with cobwebs, and littered with empty beer and whiskey bottles and piles of soiled laundry that gave off the musty odor of damp socks. There was no sign that Ethan had been there, and no weapon.

"So, you believe me now?" Meissner said when they were back in the living room. "I told you that you would find nothing." He smiled.

The smile—it was more like a smirk—irritated her. So did his complacency. "Where's your son, Mr. Meissner?"

He sighed. "How many times do I have to tell you—I don't know."

"You wait-listed him on an El Al flight yesterday, but he didn't get on."

He laughed. "You're joking, yes?"

"You had him booked for today's flight, and you bought a

ticket for him on yesterday's six-fifty American Airlines flight." All the airlines with flights to Israel had been alerted, just in case the boy tried to leave.

Meissner had been shaking his head while she talked. "If Eitán decided to go to Israel, Detective, that's his own idea, and his own business."

"And he used what money to buy the ticket? I was in your kitchen, Mr. Meissner. I saw the El Al flight times that you wrote on the newspaper."

He narrowed his eyes, puzzled. "The newspa—oh, *now* I understand." He nodded. "This is because I am thinking of visiting my parents. It's a long time since I have seen them, and they are not getting younger."

"You saw me in the kitchen and worried I'd figured out Ethan was planning to leave the country. So you had someone get him off the American flight before I could arrest him."

Meissner looked bemused. "Detective, I don't know what you're talking about, but it sounds like a good movie. You are finished looking around, yes? Then excuse me, but I have things to do." He walked to the front door and opened it.

"Do you have a storage locker?" Jessie asked.

"Yes, in the garage. You would like to see this too, of course." He sounded bored.

They followed him to an old red Porsche at the far end of the underground parking structure. Above the parking slot were padlocked dark brown cabinets. Meissner opened the combination lock. Jessie and Phil searched through black canvas suitcases, boxes of sheet music, more boxes filled with flatware and car parts. They checked the car, too, including the glove compartment and trunk.

"What'd you think you'd find?" Phil asked her when they were walking back to the street. "Jimmy Hoffa?"

"The gun. I'm not convinced he tossed it. Or if he did, maybe he bought another one. Did you see how smug he was?"

Phil pulled a tissue from his pants pocket and sneezed violently into it. "I *should*'ve stayed home." He folded the tissue and put it away. "So Meissner was smug. He knew we were wasting our time 'cause he was telling the truth."

"He was playing with us, Phil."

When they passed the front of the building, she stopped abruptly. "There's a vacancy." She pointed to the FOR RENT sign.

"You're looking to move?"

"He's the manager. He figured we'd search his place, so he hid something in the empty apartment."

Phil frowned. "You think the kid is staying there?"

She shook her head. "Too risky. But maybe he was here yesterday."

They walked back up the stairs to 2G, and she rang the bell. Meissner opened the door.

"Now what?" he asked impatiently. "I have a life, you know."

"We'd like to see the vacant apartment," Jessie said.

He blinked rapidly. "You're interested in moving in? It's not such a great place." He tried a smile.

"Please get the keys, Mr. Meissner."

He put his hands in his jean pockets. "You have a warrant to search my apartment, fine. You searched. You want to search anyplace else, I cannot make that decision. It is not my building."

"Let's get permission from the owner. What's his name?"

"It is not a *he*, it is a company. Kenworth Realty. What do you think you will find, a dead body?"

The more Meissner resisted, the more certain Jessie was that she was right. "Why are you nervous, Mr. Meissner? Are you hiding something or someone?"

Meissner scowled. "I'm hiding nothing. You're wasting my time, that's all."

She waited with Phil while Meissner disappeared into the kitchen. A moment later he returned, shaking his head.

"They are not answering. I get the machine. Maybe later."

"Let me try." She took her cell phone from her purse and flipped it open. "What's the number?"

He massaged his chin. "Look, I don't want to bother them. If they know the police are asking me questions about a murder, you think they will keep me as a manager?"

"What's the number, Mr. Meissner?"

"Fine." He grunted. "You want to see the apartment, you can see it. You have a job, you don't care if I lose mine, but what the hell, this is America."

"Do you have control over the apartments, Mr. Meissner?" Jessie asked. "You're authorized to allow entry?"

"Yes, yes," he said, impatient now.

She took out her officer's notebook with the buff cover on which the Miranda warning was printed and had him sign that he'd authorized the search.

The vacant apartment was on the ground floor at the rear of the building. Holding a large ring with enough keys to be a deadly weapon, Meissner tried two keys until he found the one that opened the door.

The place smelled of new paint. Brown paper runners, dampened in spots by footprints, lay on the shampooed beige carpeting, and the cream-colored open-weave drape panels were still tied together with string to preserve the pleats. There was no furniture in any of the rooms, no food in the refrigerator. Jessie was disappointed to find no evidence that Ethan had stayed there.

They searched the bedroom closets, bathroom cabinets, and the linen closet in the hall. Phil was checking the kitchen cabinets while Jessie, kneeling, examined the cabinet under the sink.

That's when she found the gun, taped behind the garbage disposal motor. A nine-millimeter Walther.

She lifted it out carefully and held it up. "It's amazing what tenants leave behind nowadays."

◆ **24** ◆

"I KNEW YOU would think the worst," Meissner said.

He was sitting across from Jessie and Phil in the drab yellow interrogation cubicle, his hands curled into balls, eyes intense.

"You've been doing so well making up stories," Jessie said. "I'm fascinated to hear what you come up with now."

"Give the guy a chance, Jessie," Phil said. "He obviously wants to cooperate. He's here, right?"

Meissner had accompanied them voluntarily to the station. Phil had explained that they weren't taking him into custody, that he wasn't under arrest. They hadn't Mirandized him, and Meissner hadn't asked for an attorney.

Jessie faced Meissner. "I'm listening."

"It's my gun." The man nodded, clearly uncomfortable. "It was stupid to lie, to hide it, but I was afraid. Already you are thinking Eitán killed Ronnie and the others."

"You bought this after you disposed of the other gun?"

Meissner hesitated. "It's the same gun."

"So that was another lie?"

"Yes, another lie. When you have a child, Detective, you will do anything to protect him."

Especially when you'd failed him so many times in the past, Jessie thought. "Ethan was at your apartment the morning before the murders. Did you see him?"

"No. Believe me, I have been thinking about this. Eitán

came to see me—he *needed* me. And I was not there for him." He sighed.

"Maybe he came for your gun," Phil said.

"No." He shook his head. "No."

"Did you see the gun on Monday?"

"No. But I didn't look for it, so how can I say if it was there or not?"

"When *did* you look for it?" Jessie asked.

"After you left yesterday."

"Because you thought Ethan might have taken it."

"Yes. But he did not, obviously. The gun was there where I keep it."

"He could have taken it and put it back. You said he has a key. Did you see him Monday night? Tuesday morning?"

"No."

"Where is he now?" Phil asked.

Meissner exhaled deeply. "I told you again and again. I don't know. How many times do I have to say it?"

"We're having a credibility problem here, Mr. Meissner," Jessie said. "I think you can understand why."

"Now I am telling the truth."

"Are you? Where were *you* on Monday at around four P.M.?"

He stared at her. "Home."

"Was anybody with you to corroborate that?"

"Four o'clock?" He frowned in concentration. "Four o'clock, I was showing a couple the apartment."

"Then you'll have their name and phone number from the application."

"They did not fill out an application. The apartment did not suit them."

"That's unfortunate, Mr. Meissner. Because I'm thinking that maybe you *are* telling the truth about your son. *You* were angry at Ronald Bushnell, right?"

Meissner glanced at Phil, then back at Jessie. He laughed nervously. "You think *I* killed Ronnie?"

"Your son came here early Monday morning. If he didn't come to get the gun, he came to talk to you. I think he was upset with the Bushnells. I think he told you why, and you were furious."

"I did not see him. I was out."

Jessie leaned toward him. "They stole your son from you, and in the end he wasn't good enough for them. Your words. He wasn't good enough for their daughter, either." She'd surprised him and took pleasure in the fact. "He loved Adrienne, she loved him, but Ronnie said, no way is that boy good enough for our baby. That infuriated you, didn't it?"

Meissner snorted. "I heard all this when Eitán left their house, Detective. If I was so angry, why would I wait three weeks to do something?"

"I thought you haven't talked to your son in over four weeks."

His rubbed his chin. "Celeste told me this."

"Celeste told you she didn't think Ethan was good enough for her daughter? A little cruel, don't you think?"

"She wanted me to know why Eitán left."

Jessie shook her head. "I don't think so. I think Ethan told you all this on Monday. You have a temper—everybody knows that. You decided to have it out with Bushnell."

"Yes, of course." He smiled grimly. "I killed three people because my son's heart was broken."

"You were just going to yell at Bushnell. But you started drinking, and you became angrier and angrier. And you drank some more. So you took your gun along. You thought Bushnell would be alone in his office, but his receptionist and nurse were there, so you killed them, too."

Meissner shook his head sadly. "A very good story, Detective. Too bad it is not true."

"You had a motive," Jessie said. "You had opportunity. You had a weapon. Ten to one the gun we found is the one that killed Dr. Bushnell and two of his staff. And your prints are probably all over it."

He sighed. "Of *course* my prints are on the gun. It's mine."

"Why did you hide it?"

"I *told* you why," he said with exaggerated patience. "I knew it would look bad for Eitán."

"Or for you. You've been lying from the start. You hid the gun. Those aren't the actions of an innocent man."

Meissner folded his arms across his chest. "I want to see a lawyer. That's my right, yes?"

"Where's Ethan, Mr. Meissner?"

He glared at her, his face turning purple. "So that's what this is?" Half rising from his chair, he leaned toward her, his weight on his hands. "You think I'm stupid? Go ahead—lock me up. I still won't know where Eitán is."

She wished she could. "If the gun we found turns out to be the murder weapon, Mr. Meissner, that's exactly what we'll do. Don't leave town without letting us know."

He stood. "Where would I go?"

"Israel? You have an unused ticket, don't you?"

"Maybe Meissner *doesn't* know where the kid is," Phil said, returning to his desk. He handed Jessie a roast beef sandwich and a small carton of coleslaw from the brown bag he was carrying, and put a plastic container with salad and a yogurt on his desk.

"Thanks." She paid him for the sandwich and slaw. "He knows. If we could arrest him on a felony charge, we could hold him for forty-eight hours. Odds are Ethan would hear about it. With all the guilt he feels about his dad, maybe he'd surface and turn himself in."

Phil opened the container and stabbed at the salad. "Suppose he doesn't? Suppose he's thinking, 'Screw you'?"

"Then we're no worse off. By the way, I spoke with Ethan's shrink. She cited doctor-patient privilege, wouldn't even confirm she knew him. I reminded her that if Ethan told her he planned to harm himself or someone else, she was legally bound to tell us. She wouldn't comment."

"Why don't you arrest her *and* Meissner? Pacific Station has a couple of empty holding cells."

"Better yet, I'll put her in *with* Meissner—she can give him Prozac."

Jessie unwrapped the sandwich, hesitated (was it better to recite or not recite a blessing over food that wasn't kosher?), then silently recited the blessing and took a bite. She tasted the coleslaw. Phil was watching her, and she wondered whether he'd noticed. "What?"

"Do you have any idea how much mayo they put in that?" Phil pointed his fork at the carton. "Regular, not low-fat."

"Can I enjoy this, please? You're like a reformed smoker."

"Hey, it's your arteries." He speared a cherry tomato. "Any other news?"

"Ezra Nathanson phoned. I called him back, but he's teaching. Maybe he figured out the Hebrew name Meissner wrote down."

Phil's phone rang. He picked up the receiver, and she ate her sandwich, doodling on a paper and half listening as he spoke to Lily Pervez's brother.

"They're home," he told Jessie after he hung up. "They spent most of yesterday planning the funeral. They haven't heard from the nephew. I told them to stay put, that we'd be there within the hour."

"I've been thinking, Phil."

"What they pay you for." He tossed the empty salad carton into his trash can.

"Seriously. What if Meissner *did* do it?"

Phil uncapped the yogurt and took a spoonful. "So why send the kid out of the country?"

"To make it look like he's shielding the kid, when in reality he's shifting attention from himself."

"They're chintzing on the fruit lately, have you noticed?" He stirred the yogurt. "Assuming you're right, why would Meissner go to Bushnell's office instead of his home? This is personal, not business."

"You could ask the same thing about Ethan." She thought for a moment. "Maybe he didn't want to involve Celeste or Adrienne. Maybe he wanted to have it out, man to man."

"Man to man and gun. I don't buy the motive, Jessie. So Bushnell doesn't want the boy for his daughter. Big effing deal. You don't kill over that."

"You're the one who thinks maybe Jamal killed Lily for pretty much the same reason."

"That's different. With Jamal, the hurt is bigger."

"You're talking ten years of resentment, Phil. Ten years of being make to look like a loser who can't take care of his own kid, ten years of having to swallow that the Bushnells are giving the kid everything he can't, that they *stole* him—his words. And then they toss the boy out. And won't take him back—if that was the call Carla overheard."

Phil swiveled back and forth in his chair. "I could buy it if he did it on an impulse. But the killer made an appointment to see him. Clifford Bronte, right?"

"Meissner would have *loved* that touch. He's a literature lover—you saw his books. He made an appointment under a false name because he wanted to make sure Bushnell would be there. But the more he thought about it, the angrier he got. So he took a gun with him. Maybe he just wanted to scare Bushnell."

"Maybe." Phil considered, then shook his head. "But why would he wait three weeks to make a move against Bushnell?"

"He brooded about it, Phil. The more he thought about it, the more pissed off he became. That, plus a few drinks." Jessie shrugged. "And maybe he didn't know all the details weeks ago. Why did Ethan show up at his dad's place at two-thirty in the morning the day of the murders?"

"Guess we'll have to ask him when we find him. Suppose you're right. Where does Kevin Hayes fit into all this?"

She frowned. "Good question. The mom called again, frantic. She thinks Ethan killed her son, with her gun."

"Could be. 'Kill 'em all, watch them fall.' But why kill the Hayes kid? They were getting along. And why would Ethan steal the Glock when he had access to his dad's gun?"

"We have to talk to the housekeeper, see if Sally's telling the truth about Ethan stopping by on the morning of the murders."

Phil went to the rest room. Jessie wiped her mouth with a tissue and crumpled the sandwich wrapper, then remembered she hadn't phoned Charlotte. Frances would be annoyed if she didn't follow up.

Charlotte sounded the way she always did, her piercing voice too loud—probably because she was hard of hearing, Frances said, but Charlotte wouldn't admit it.

"Your mother told me what happened, dear. It's so awful, isn't it?"

"Terrible," Jessie agreed, moving the phone a few inches away from her ear. "My mom said you wanted to tell me something about Dr. Bushnell."

"I don't know if it's important. Your mother was asking me questions—like whether the doctor had seemed nervous lately, or anything like that."

Jessie sighed. Bless Frances. The temptation to play detective had been too strong. "Did he?"

"Well, actually, he did. I went to him a week ago for a collagen injection. He's usually so friendly and charming, but he was so terse! And preoccupied."

No wonder. Jessie picked up her pen and drew a box.

"I told him so. I said, 'Dr. Bushnell, if you're not careful, I'll have collagen in my ear instead of my lip.' That shook him up! He apologized. Of course, he didn't say what was bothering him, and I didn't ask."

"Of course not." So much for Charlotte's big news. "Well—"

"But I think it had something to do with his nurse."

Jessie's interest quickened. "Barbara Martin?"

"Yes. How did you know?" Charlotte's voice was sharp with disappointment. "They said she quit." Dramatic pause. "But *I* think she was fired."

Jessie took pity on the woman. "*Really?*"

"When I was there the time before, she was assisting Dr. Bushnell. This time there was a new nurse. Very pretty girl. I'm not surprised."

Jessie was confused. "That's she's very pretty?"

"Well, that, too. Everyone in that office is beautiful, and young." Charlotte sighed. "No, I mean that the other nurse was fired. The last time, she was *very* unprofessional. The doctor was in the middle of the procedure and he had to tell her *three times* to hand him something because she wasn't even looking at him! So Dr. Bushnell said her name *very* sharply, and she just glared at him and turned so quickly that she knocked down the tray with the instruments. And she left the room. Just like that! Can you imagine?"

"Did Dr. Bushnell say anything?"

"He apologized for her. He said she had a lot on her mind."

Nothing new here—Celeste had thought the nurse had been fired because she'd been unprofessional. And the book-keeper had offered no clue. "Charlotte, thanks so much for talking to me. This has been very helpful." She held her hand over the disconnect button, ready to end the call.

"I'm sure Dr. Bushnell felt terrible letting her go. They worked so well together. But it was really for the best. I think she was in love with him."

Jessie drew back her hand. "What gave you that idea?"

"The way she looked at him when she didn't realize anybody saw. The way she'd hand him instruments."

"Do you think something was going on between them?"

"Goodness, no!" Charlotte sounded appalled. "Dr. Bushnell was *totally* devoted to his wife. He talked about her all the time. But I think Barbara was making him uncomfortable. When I had liposuction two months ago, she was in the recovery room with me. I was just waking up when I heard Dr. Bushnell come in and ask how I was doing. She said fine. She must have thought I was asleep because I wasn't talking, and my eyes were closed. She *kissed* him."

"If your eyes were closed, how do you know?"

"Because he told her to stop what she was doing. He whispered something like, 'Are you crazy?' and 'This can't happen again.' He was *very* upset."

Upset, or nervous that Charlotte had witnessed the embrace?

❖ 25 ❖

THE PERVEZ FAMILY had heard nothing from their nephew.

"We are very worried," the son told Phil and Jessie. "We don't believe he killed my sister. And now maybe something bad has happened to him."

He was the spokesman for the family. Mr. Pervez had listened with fierce concentration while his son talked and had nodded from time to time. Mrs. Pervez hadn't uttered a word since they'd arrived. She kept her head bowed to avoid eye contact with Phil and Jessie, and her clasped hands had disappeared in the folds of her ankle-length skirt.

They expressed surprise about the ten thousand dollars Jamal had withdrawn from his account the day before Lily had been murdered. They had no idea why he'd needed the money, the son said, no knowledge about his cousin's business dealings, but they knew he was always involved with different projects.

"Computers," Lily's father volunteered. "Very much money in this."

"Was Jamal in love with Lily?" Jessie asked.

"In love?" The brother shook his head. "Jamal loved Lily like a cousin, nothing more. Something bad has happened to him."

"Lily is a good girl," the mother said. "Jamal, he is good, too."

The father frowned.

Phil asked again if they knew whether Lily had gone to visit Jamal for a particular reason that day. The son shook his head, then the father, then the mother.

"See no evil, hear no evil, speak no evil," Jessie said when they were back in Phil's Cutlass. "I couldn't tell if they were covering up about Jamal and Lily. You?"

"Me, either. Something's off, though. They were all wide-eyed when we told them about the ten grand, but I got the feeling that they knew. And did you see how nervous the mother was the entire time we were there? She wouldn't even look me in the eye."

"That's a modesty thing," Jessie said. "It's their culture. Women don't talk to nonfamily males. So if they know something, why aren't they telling us? The son's been calling the station nonstop, Espes said."

"Could be they're afraid of retribution, like you said." Reaching over, he pulled a tissue from the box in the glove compartment and covered his nose when he sneezed. "They want us to find their daughter's killer, but don't want to lead us to him."

"Maybe. I'd like to have a chance to talk to the mother alone."

The potbellied manager of the Santa Monica apartment building where Barbara Martin lived had no idea where she was or when she'd be back.

"So what's this about?" he asked, eyes narrowed. "She in trouble or something?"

"No trouble," Jessie said pleasantly. "We need her help with an investigation we're conducting."

He nodded, but looked doubtful. "Try 2F. She's taking in the Martin woman's magazines and newspapers."

And watering her plants, Melinda Kramer, the chatty ponytailed tenant in 2F told Jessie and Phil, apparently not all that curious as to why police detectives were looking for her neighbor.

"She left in a big rush around six on Monday evening, said she needed to get away for a few days. She wasn't even going to tell me, but I saw her taking a suitcase to her car and asked her if she wanted me to water the plants. She must've forgotten all about them, so it's lucky I did."

Jessie exchanged a quick look with Phil. "Did she seem upset?"

"Kind of. Well, she's *been* upset, for weeks, about losing her job. Maybe she needed to figure out what to do next. Plus she wasn't feeling well. She had a bad stomach flu, couldn't keep anything down. Probably the same thing I have, which is why I'm here talking to you instead of working." Melinda smiled. "Actually, I'm feeling much better, but don't tell my boss."

"Did Ms. Martin say where she was going?" Phil asked.

"No. She loves Santa Barbara and this little place up the coast. I can't remember the name. She's not really a sun person—I guess because she worked for a plastic surgeon. She's always on me about using the highest number sunscreen, warning me about melanoma and wrinkles. Well, melanoma's scary, that's the truth," Melinda said, her tone serious. "But you can't worry about wrinkles. I told her when I have too many on my forehead, she can treat me to a few Botox injections, and I'll do her ultrasound for free. I'm a technician," she explained.

"I read that this Botox stuff works by paralyzing your muscles," Phil said.

"Barbara said it's only a temporary side effect," Melinda assured him. "You can't frown for a while."

"Sounds like good bartering," Jessie said, wondering whether the woman talked this much on the job.

Melinda smiled. "Barbara thought so. She said she'd take

me up on it soon. Well, that was before she was fired. She used to bring me skin cream samples." She shrugged.

"Do you have any idea when she's coming back?"

"Nope. Her mailbox is overstuffed, so I've been putting everything in her apartment. And today something came registered from a lawyer. I signed for it."

The "something" was probably connected with the workmen's comp suit, Jessie guessed.

"I would've called to tell her," Melinda continued, "but she wasn't sure where she'd be staying. She said she'd call me when she got there, but she never did."

Maybe because she'd intended to disappear, Jessie thought. More likely, she'd just wanted to escape from Melinda's exhausting garrulousness. "It's important that we get in touch with Ms. Martin. Could you look around to see if she left anything indicating where she might be staying?"

Melinda frowned. "That's *snooping*."

"She left you a key, right? What if that registered mail needs her immediate attention? I'm sure she'd want you to find out where to reach her."

The woman looked uncertain. "I don't know."

"She said she'd call you to let you know where she was staying. She hasn't. What if she's in trouble, Melinda? What if she's hurt?" Which was a definite possibility.

"She got something from a doctor, too," the young woman said, thinking aloud. She sighed. "Okay. I'll take a look."

She went back into her apartment and returned with a key. Jessie and Phil followed her down the concrete hall and waited while she unlocked and opened the door.

She stood on the threshold and glanced at them dubiously. "I guess you can come in. But you can't take anything, okay?"

"Okay." Jessie wouldn't want to take anything that might be evidence—without a warrant, it would be inadmissible.

The place looked like a page from a Pottery Barn catalog:

straight-backed sofa with a beige cotton slipcover; mul-
tidrawered chest that served as a coffee table; monochro-
matic woven wool rug. Bunches of dried and silk flowers in
pewter vases added color to the room, and tab-topped drap-
ery panels in a gauzy fabric hung on the windows.

"That's Barbara, with her folks. I think they live in St.
Louis." Melinda pointed to a brushed silver-framed photo
sitting on a wood lamp table.

Jessie picked up the frame and studied the young woman
in the photo. Like the rest of Bushnell's staff, she was slender and strikingly pretty, with thick, shoulder-length auburn
hair. She was smiling at the camera, one arm around her
mother, the other, around her father.

Jessie and Phil remained in the living room while Melinda
went into the kitchen. A pile of envelopes and magazines lay
on the coffee table. Jessie picked up the envelopes and
scanned them. Bills; the registered letter from the attorney;
a letter from a medical group at the Cedars-Sinai towers.
Jessie copied down names and addresses.

"I can't find anything," Melinda said a few minutes later,
coming back to the living room. "If she wrote down where
she was going on something, she took it with her."

"Thanks, anyway." Jessie gave the woman a card. "In case
you hear from her, or remember something."

Walking to the street minutes later with Phil, she pulled
out her cell phone and punched in the numbers for the medical group.

"Doctors Kemper, Edelstein, Le Grange, and Wallace," a
woman announced.

More like a summit conference than a doctor's office.
What happened to Marcus Welby, M.D.? "Can you please
tell me what kind of practice this is?" Jessie asked.

"OB-GYN. Did you want to make an appointment with
one of the doctors?"

"I'll call back, thanks." She ended the call and turned to
Phil.

"So?"

"So I think Barbara Martin's stomach flu was morning sickness." Jessie smiled. "Maybe the workman's comp suit wasn't hitting him where she *really* wanted to hurt Bushnell—in the groin."

❖ 26 ❖

MATTHEW'S FACE LIT up when he saw her.

"Aunt Jessie!" He slipped off the desk chair and ran toward her, then wrapped his thin arms around her.

"Hey." She hugged him tight, feeling a rush of uncomplicated joy, and kissed the top of his head. She pulled back and examined him. He was a younger version of Neil— black hair, dark brown eyes. "You've grown."

He stood taller and beamed, revealing the gap where his two front baby teeth used to be. "You think so?"

"Definitely. Your mom said you were doing homework, but I begged her, and she let me come up here." Not far from the truth. "So how's it going?"

"Almost done. I have a spelling test tomorrow. Can you test me, Aunt Jessie?"

She smiled. "Sure. I'm sorry about the other night, Matthew. I really wanted to have dinner with you and your parents, but I had to work late."

"I know. Grandma said you work too hard, and your work is dangerous. Can you stay tonight?"

"Uh-huh." She wondered what else Frances had said in front of him.

She tested him on the chapter, taking pride in the fact that he got every word right. It never ceased to amaze her that this person was Helen's child, her flesh and blood, a product of a union between a sperm and an egg. In a few months he would have a brother or a sister. She wondered how he would react; wondered, too, whether she would ever be re-viewing spelling words with her own child.

On the way downstairs he took her to the future nursery, an airy, generous-size room with a bay window. Wallpaper samples were taped to the walls.

"Are you excited about the baby, Matthew?"

Matthew nodded. "I like this one." Jumping, he stretched his right arm high and touched a border with a pastel print of farm animals. "Mommy said I can help pick out all the toys for the baby."

The movement revealed a purple bruise below his elbow. "What happened to your arm?" she asked, trying to sound casual.

"I fell when I was Rollerblading. It doesn't hurt. Mommy says it's a good thing I was wearing my helmet."

"She's right." She had to stop watching him, assuming the worst, but though Helen was a different person now, Jessie couldn't erase the image of her wielding a hairbrush, out of control. Hardly fair. She wondered how Neil handled a new bruise or welt or sprain, and felt sorry for her sister.

"What's up with Mom and Dad?" Helen asked Jessie after sending Matthew to the guest house to tell Frances dinner was ready. "She's been in a mood since she got here, and when he phoned about an hour ago, she wouldn't talk to him."

"I have no idea." Jessie straightened a place setting.

"Liar." She flashed Jessie a hurt look. "Mom said to ask you. She didn't want to 'go over the ugly details,' as she put it. Thanks a lot for telling me."

That was just like Frances, Jessie thought, her face flushed. "I'm sorry, Helen. She made me promise not to say anything. She didn't want to worry you."

"I'm not a child. Why does she always treat me like one? Just because I'm a few years younger than you are?"

Jessie sighed. "Helen—"

"I'm not blind, you know." She rested her hands on her belly. "The other night, when you came down after talking to her, you looked like the world was coming to an end. Is Dad ill? If he is, I have a right to know."

"Mom thinks he's having an affair."

Helen looked stunned. "Come on! *Dad*? He *adores* Mom."

"That's what I told her. Anyway, I spoke to him. He swears he's not having an affair. He's just preoccupied with work and trying to decide whether he should retire."

Helen scowled. "Well, what made Mom *think* he's having an affair? There has to be something."

Jessie repeated what Frances had told her. "That's all I know. I advised him to drive up and talk to her in person, and he basically told me to mind my own business."

"*Dad* said that?" Helen was about to say something else when Frances appeared with Matthew.

"Jessica." She offered her cheek, and Jessie kissed her. "Matthew tells me you're staying for dinner."

"How are you, Mom?"

"Absolutely perfect, and enjoying time with my grandson." Frances ruffled Matthew's hair. "You didn't get the dress, did you?"

Jessie smiled sweetly. "As a matter of fact, it's in the trunk of my car. Thanks, Mom. I love it." The off-the-shoulder, long-sleeved, below-the-knee red silk jersey clung to her curves and made her feel sexy and sophisticated. She hadn't loved the price tag but had decided to splurge.

Frances nodded approval. "You won't be sorry. A good dress is an investment."

Helen brought a steaming pan of spinach lasagna to the table. Jessie felt a little guilty with every delicious mouthful of the tangy cheese and meat dish, and wondered how her family would react if she ever decided to be strictly kosher. Helen and Frances would be upset and tell her she was crazy. Her father probably wouldn't care. It didn't really matter. So far she'd made a commitment only to *trying* it, and only in her home. She hadn't invested in new dishes. She could stop at any time. . . .

"You look like you're a million miles away," Frances said, annoyed. "I wish you'd stop thinking about your work, just for a few hours."

"How's the case going, by the way?" Helen asked.

"Slow." No leads on Kevin Hayes or Ethan Meissner. Confusing, too, now that she'd spoken to Barbara Martin's neighbor. She didn't know what to make of the nurse's sudden departure.

"Did you speak to Charlotte?" her mother asked.

"Uh-huh."

"Well, did she have anything *important* to tell you?"

"Not really." If she said yes, Frances would press. "But thanks for trying."

Brian Lefton had phoned again and left his number. She wrote it down, listened to her other messages, and looked through her mail. Just bills.

She had a qualm about having spent so much on the dress. She tried it on and looked at herself in the full-length mirror at the back of her closet door. Expensive, but so nice. She put on a pair of black silk dress shoes and her pearl necklace, shook out her hair, and touched up her blusher and lipstick. Nicer.

All dressed up and nowhere to go, but there was definitely something therapeutic about buying a great dress. She sat at the edge of her bed, swinging her leg, and phoned Brian Lefton.

"Hi, Brian. It's Jessie Drake," she said when he answered. God, she hated this.

"Hey, I'm glad you called. Roberta Kimmel gave me your number, but I guess you know that. She's a friend of my mother's."

He had a nice voice. "Of mine, too. Where do you live?"

"I have a condo in Westwood, very close to work. I'm with Merrill Lynch, in Century City. But that's pretty boring compared to what you do. I've never gone out with a police detective before."

"Well, the good news is that I don't usually arrest a guy on the first date unless there's probable cause."

He laughed. "Well, listen, would you—"

The doorbell rang.

"There's someone's at my door," she told him. "Can I call you right back?"

"No problem."

She hung up, walked to the entry, and after glancing through the privacy window, opened the door.

"You're going out," Ezra said, looking at her dress and frowning. "Sorry. I should have called first."

She wondered if the off-the-shoulder neckline was making him uncomfortable. Well, this is who she was. School was out. "Actually, I was just trying on a new dress."

"Great dress. You look beautiful."

She smiled. "Thanks. I returned your call, but you were teaching. I hope you're here to tell me you figured out the name I copied down. I could use a break in this case."

"Klingerman, Rabbi Bezalel Klingerman. He runs a boys' yeshiva in Big Bear. He's not Chasidic, by the way."

Jessie nodded. Big Bear was in San Bernardino County. "That makes sense. The phone number I saw had a nine-oh-nine area code. Thanks, Ezra."

"I can drive up with you tomorrow, if you want, smooth the way. Zach Abrams said he'd take my classes. But—"

"That's sweet of you, Ezra. I don't know if I can let you do that."

"Jessie—"

"It's not that I don't appreciate the offer. I'm sure it would help if you were there. It's just that—"

"Can we discuss this later? I'm not here about Klingerman. I could have *phoned* you about Klingerman. Look, can I come in?" He was gazing at her intently.

"Sure." She moved aside to let him enter, then shut the door behind him, wondering why he sounded so nervous. "Is everything okay, Ezra?"

"This is for you." He held up a boxed corsage and removed the plastic top. "For the most gorgeous girl in high school."

Her heart skipped a beat. "This is so sweet of you, Ezra." She lifted the white orchid and pinned it with fumbling fingers to her dress. "It's beautiful."

"I'm an idiot," he said. "I haven't stopped thinking about what you said—about you. I can't believe I turned you down."

Her face tingled. "I don't blame you for being cautious. I thought about what you said, Ezra, and—"

"Forget what I said. I've learned there are no guarantees, Jessie. You can't protect yourself from life. When Carol was killed, I didn't think I'd survive. But even if I'd known when I first met her what pain her death would bring, I would have wanted to know her, to have her be a part of my life."

She felt a pang of sadness and something that wasn't quite jealousy. "You still love her."

"I'll always love Carol," he said simply. "Does that bother you?"

She considered. "I don't know."

"I've dated a number of women in the past few years—attractive, witty, intelligent—but I was just going through the motions. Then I met you. When you walk into a room, Jessie, I have to catch my breath, every time. When you don't show up for class, I wonder where you are, what you're doing, who you're with."

Her heart fluttered. "I saw my ex-husband last night. He invited me to a party, and I wasn't going to go, and then I went. But I wanted to be with you, Ezra." She said all this quickly, the words rushing out of her mouth, because she wanted him to know, didn't want him to misunderstand. "I danced with Gary, but I wanted it to be you."

"I'd love to dance with you, Jessie," he said softly.

The way he was gazing at her made her knees feel weak. She wanted to touch him, to be touched, but of course he wouldn't do that. Yesterday she had been the pursuer. Now she was reminded again of how different they were and felt suddenly nervous.

"About religion," she said. "I can't promise you where I'm going."

"It'll be interesting to find out." He smiled. "God brought you into my life, Jessie. I'm sure He has a plan."

She hoped so. The phone rang, and she remembered suddenly about Brian Lefton. "I was on the phone when you rang the bell," she told Ezra. "The guy my mom's friend is trying to set me up with? That's probably him."

He reached out his hand, and she thought he was going to touch her after all, but he ran his finger across the flower's petals.

"Tell him your dance card is filled, Prom Queen."

AS A YOUNG girl, Jessie had enjoyed vacationing in Big Bear. While her mother relaxed at the lodge's large aquamarine pool or played mah-jongg with some of the other women, Jessie would go into town with her father and Helen. Boating, horseback riding, playing games at the arcades—every day was filled with fun. More special than the activities, though, was the fact that Frances was usually in a better mood away from home, less demanding of her daughters, less apt to explode in a rage over a minor infraction of the perfect world she needed.

Ezra's apartment was on Cardiff south of Pico, a short distance from the school. He was waiting at the curb when she pulled up, and she thought about the last time she'd been here, seven months ago, when she'd come to question him as a suspect. Things had certainly changed.

He put a small Styrofoam ice chest into the back of the car and a Macy's shopping bag at his feet. "I brought sandwiches for lunch and some snacks."

"This isn't a picnic date," she warned. "It's police business."

"That's why I didn't bring wine." Ezra smiled. "It's a five-hour round-trip, Jessie. I figured we have to eat." He looked at her. "You sound tense."

"Sorry. My lieutenant gave me a hard time."

"About my coming along?"

"That, and a few other things."

Espes had been in a surly mood this morning. "You're all over the map, Drake," he'd snapped. "You're threatening to arrest Meissner. You have an APB out on his kid, even though you have no physical evidence to connect him to the murders. You have another APB on the Hayes kid. You're not sure if the nurse, who Bushnell may have knocked up, is on the lam. So now what? You plan to arrest a rabbi?"

"Is it a problem?" Ezra asked.

Jessie shook her head. "I convinced him Klingerman's more likely to open up if you're with me. And you might pick up on some stuff I wouldn't notice. Plus my partner, Phil, has to attend the autopsies. The main thing is, follow my lead, okay, Ezra? The department could be in serious trouble if you got hurt."

"Can't you deputize me or something?"

She laughed. "I don't think so." Her laugh turned into a yawn. They'd sat in her den, talking, until two in the morning. About his childhood and hers (she left out significant details), about his love of teaching following the realization that he didn't feel passionate about pursuing the law career he'd always talked about; about the need for justice and order that had driven her to become a homicide detective in spite of her family's objections.

"I kept you up too late," Ezra said. "Want me to drive?"

"Only if you want me to vomit."

"There's a charming picture." He made a face. "You've never even been in a car with me."

She smiled. "It isn't you. I'll be sick if I'm not behind the wheel."

What Jessie hadn't liked as a girl about vacationing in Big Bear, and didn't like any better now, was the trip itself. It wasn't long, about two and a half hours each way, and the first hour from L.A. to San Bernardino was fine—straight freeway. But Big Bear was almost at the top of the San Bernardino National Forest. During the ascent Jessie would clutch the edge of the car's backseat, her head frozen straight ahead, hands clammy, fighting the waves of nausea that rose higher with each sharp curve of the one-lane road, terrified of looking to the side, where, except for occasional lookout stations, nothing protected them from falling over the sheer cliff into the rocky abyss below. The descent was no better.

She took Robertson and headed to the 10 Freeway, then switched on the radio. Elton John was singing "A Candle in the Wind."

"I heard him years ago at the Hollywood Bowl," Ezra said. "Just him and a percussionist. Fabulous."

"I love Elton. You like the Beatles?"

"I have every record they cut. Crosby Stills?"

She nodded. "What about the oldies?"

"Love 'em. So I guess I passed the first test." He smiled. "That calls for a treat." He reached into the Macy's bag, pulled out a package of Pepperidge Farm Sausalito cookies, and ripped it open. He extended the package to her.

Pepperidge Farm Sausalito cookies were her undoing. Along with Ben & Jerry's ice cream, cheesecake, and a host of other things. "These are kosher?"

"Kosher dairy. So are Nabisco Oreos and tons of other products. I'd show you the certification, but I think you should keep your eyes on the road, especially at the speed you're going."

"I like driving fast," she admitted with a sheepish grin.

Elton John had finished saying good-bye to Norma Jean. Celine Dione was singing the hit song from *Titanic*.

"The music kids listen to is so different today," Ezra said. "Hip-hop, gangsta rap. A lot of it is so angry, so violent, misogynistic. You can't help wonder what effect it has on them."

"Ethan Meissner listens to gangsta rap, but he's also into jazz and classical music. I can't figure him out." She described what she'd found in his room—the videos, the books, the sports pennants. "It's as if he's two different people."

Ezra nodded. "Either he's confused, or complex. There's just much more out there for kids. My parents weren't happy with some of my choices when I was a teenager, either. The music I liked, the films I saw. But the R-rated stuff then would be rated G today."

His father, he'd told her last night, had been an accountant; his mother, a retired elementary school teacher. They'd lived in the same house for thirty-five years, attended the same Modern Orthodox synagogue where Ezra and his twin brother, Joel, had been bar-mitzvahed. Adele and Herman Nathanson had burned to death in that house, Jessie knew, along with their pregnant daughter-in-law—victims of neo-Nazi arsonists.

"Were your parents strict?" he asked.

"My mom more than my dad." The simple, sanitized version. Someday she'd tell him the truth, she thought, and wondered whether her father had talked to Frances.

Ezra handed her another cookie.

"I've stopped eating pork and shellfish," she told him. "And I haven't been eating dairy and meat together for two weeks. At least at home."

"So how's it going?"

"I keep forgetting." She smiled ruefully. "And there are things I *know* I'd miss. Oysters, cheeseburgers, bacon. A glass of milk with a hamburger. I feel like a condemned woman having her last meal."

He smiled. "Some delis use a pareve—nondairy—cheese for the burgers. I'm sure it's not as good as the real thing. I've had stuff that's supposed to taste like shrimp, but I don't know how authentic it is. As for milk, there's nondairy creamer, but I doubt you'd want to guzzle it."

She made a face. "Hardly."

"This is a wonderful step, Jessie."

"A *small* step." She hesitated. "To be honest, Ezra, for me keeping kosher isn't about the rules. I like the feeling it gives me, the spirituality. The idea that I'm investing something as mundane as eating with a kind of nobility."

Ezra nodded. "That's certainly part of it."

"Maybe in a few months or so I'll be ready for the rules."

He smiled. "Whenever you're ready."

She stole a look at his face. "You're disappointed."

"No, not at all." He shook his head.

"But it would make things easier for us if I kept strict kosher, right? What if I *never* want to keep kosher, Ezra? Have you considered that?"

"Yes. And I have no answers. Like I said, Jessie, there are no guarantees. Why don't we focus on getting to know each other instead of worrying about the future?"

"You're right." She sighed. "My sister says I'm always looking for problems."

"Is that why you're frowning?"

"Am I?" She made an effort to relax her forehead. "I guess I'm nervous about how to tell my family."

"They're opposed to your interest in Orthodoxy?"

"They're opposed to my interest in *Judaism*."

He tilted his head. "Opposed, or perplexed?"

"You know that my mom was a hidden child during the Holocaust. She doesn't want any reminders, and my sister, Helen, who insists she's one hundred percent Episcopalian, keeps warning me not to tell her son he's Jewish."

"I guess that qualifies for 'opposed.' " Ezra smiled. "Do they know you're taking classes?"

"Uh-huh. My mom brings it up in a snide way from time to time. Helen won't discuss it." We are all great at denial, Jessie thought. "I think they're hoping this is a virus I'll get out of my system."

He munched on a cookie. "Once they see you're committed, they may be more supportive, Jessie."

She laughed. "You don't know my mom. She'll freak. So will Helen."

"Where's your dad in all this?"

"He hasn't commented." Par for the course. "I can control what I serve in my home. But what do I do at my parents' house, or my sister's? Or when we're all eating out together? Thanksgiving is two weeks away. I'm thinking I should wait to keep kosher until the holiday's over, so I don't have to figure out what to do. Dumb, huh? But then there's Christmas."

"Not dumb at all. Would it make you feel better to know there are hundreds of people in your situation? Kids, adults, even seniors?"

"Not really. What's the answer?"

"There's no one answer. You have to figure out a way not to be insulting or excluding. You have to explain in a loving way that you're not rejecting them or their beliefs, that you're not saying your way is better. Because that's exactly how they'll feel, Jessie. It's a human, defensive reaction, especially between a parent and a child."

She nodded. "So what do you say?"

"You say that it's no different than if you decided to be a vegetarian, or if you were diabetic or lactose intolerant. That this way rings true for you, that it makes you happy and fulfilled, that you hope they'll support you in this path and share in your happiness." Ezra paused. "Look, it's not easy. It takes months, sometimes years to work things out. But if at bottom there's a loving relationship in the family, most people look to find solutions."

A huge "if," Jessie thought with a twinge of sadness. She wasn't prepared to reveal her family dynamics to Ezra. He'd probably run the other way. "And if that doesn't work?"

"You assume another identity and move to a different state."

She laughed. "I'd better start packing, then. But seriously, what do I do about Thanksgiving?"

"I can't answer that, Jessie. My answer would be based on the rules. I can't talk in half measures."

"Guess I'm on my own, huh?" She finished a cookie and reached for another.

"So can I assume that your family won't be wild that we're seeing each other?" he asked a moment later.

"The only thing worse would be if I were seeing Howard Stern or Saddam Hussein. Sure you're up for the challenge?"

"Wouldn't give it up for the world."

The way he was looking at her made her tingle. "Tell me more about Klingerman."

"Police business, right," he said with mock sternness. "Basically, it's what I told you last night. According to my friend, Klingerman's a *bal teshuvah*—he wasn't observant until fifteen years ago. He studied in an Israeli yeshiva, then started his own place here. Etz Chayim. Tree of life. He takes in troubled teens, tries to turn them around."

"An Orthodox twelve-step program?"

"Six hundred thirteen steps—that's the number of Torah commandments, or *mitzvot*." Ezra smiled. "It's a mix between rehab and a halfway house. The kids he takes are postrehab—his goal is to keep them from going back on drugs or alcohol, or running around with a wild crowd. Some of his boys are on probation. The deal is they stay and straighten themselves out. If they leave, they do jail time."

"Pretty good deal."

"He has a psychologist on staff and a nurse. He's very sincere, very committed. From what I hear, he's having a pretty good success rate."

"He has a police file." Jessie had checked him out this morning under the legal name Ezra had given her: Bernard Klingerman. "Possession, DUI. Before that, resisting arrest at an antiwar demonstration in Berkeley."

"I'm not surprised. But that's why he's so effective, Jessie. His past helps him understand the kids, and helps the kids relate to him."

"You said he isn't mainstream."

"He's definitely off the beaten track. Most of his kids don't come from observant homes. He's more concerned about their connecting spiritually than following rules. I'd say he has a Chasidic bent—more heart than head."

"Not necessarily a bad thing."

"Not bad at all, as long as there's balance. My point is, he doesn't care what the mainstream Orthodox rabbis think of him or his program. He's not politically correct."

"How do the kids end up at his place?"

"Word of mouth. Klingerman also recruits aggressively. He and his staff visit rehab centers, jails, hospitals, twelve-step programs. If a kid is Jewish and interested, Klingerman takes him in. No questions asked. I heard he checks out bars and homeless shelters, but I don't know if that's true."

Had the rabbi or one of his staff come across a stoned or drunk Ethan? Or had Gideon Meissner sent his son to Klingerman as a last resort? "Who pays for all of this?"

"If the parents can pay, that's great. But if they can't, or if they're not willing to, Klingerman doesn't throw the kid out. Apparently, he has generous benefactors who think he's just short of being the Messiah."

Jessie frowned. "Is he a cult figure?" Cult figures made her nervous.

"I don't think so. But he's a godsend to a number of wealthy parents whose kids almost OD'd. Klingerman saved them. The parents can't do enough to show their gratitude."

"Orthodox parents?"

"Some. Some of them know nothing about Judaism, and don't care to. They may not be thrilled that their kids are observant—it's definitely an adjustment. But they probably figure better a black hat than a body bag."

❖ 28 ❖

THE AIR WAS cool and clear and crisp. Jessie stood at the side of the car with her eyes shut, inhaling greedy gulps and waiting for her stomach to stop churning. Despite being at the wheel, she'd tensed once she headed north on the strip of highway that stretched from the city of San Bernardino to the foot of the mountains. For the hour and a half of the serpentine drive up, she'd barely spoken a word and had been grateful for Ezra's sympathetic silence.

"Feeling better?" he asked.

"Much." Taking one last deep breath, she glanced up at the towering pine trees that seemed to scrape the robin's-egg blue sky. "It's gorgeous up here, isn't it?"

"Breathtaking."

"I suppose there's a blessing to recite."

"Actually, there is." He smiled. "Why take God's gifts for granted?"

There were no sidewalks, and no sign of a yeshiva. She had parked the Honda at the side of the narrow road behind a row of other cars. Following Ezra's friend's directions, they walked along the road, their shoes crunching on dried leaves and pine needles. A hundred feet ahead was a clearing, at the end of which she saw a three-story building. The maroon van was parked at the side, next to a dark blue Suburban and several midsize cars.

A serious-looking young man wearing a white shirt,

black slacks, and a black velvet yarmulke opened the door.

"I'd like to speak to Rabbi Klingerman," Jessie told him and introduced herself.

He let them in. "Just a minute, please. I'll tell the Rav." He walked to a room at the left end of the hall and entered, pulling the door shut behind him.

"He didn't even seem curious," Jessie remarked to Ezra. "I could have said I was here collecting for a charity for all the reaction I got."

"I'll bet Klingerman deals with police and social workers all the time. Like I said, some of these boys are on probation and have to stay on the premises."

A skylight bathed the large entry with sunshine. She looked around, taking in the polished wood floor and cream-colored, texture-papered walls. To her right was a reception area with sofas and chairs upholstered in a navy fabric. "Not a bad place to stay."

The young man returned. "The Rav will see you now."

Rabbi Bezalel Klingerman's office was dominated by built-in walnut bookcases filled with neatly arranged, handsomely bound volumes of what Jessie assumed were Judaic primary texts and commentaries. The books were of varying heights and rich colors (burgundy, hunter green, black, brown). Most had gilding on the spines. The taller tomes, she guessed, were Talmud tractates.

More texts were stacked on the massive walnut desk behind which Klingerman sat in a high-backed burgundy leather armchair. He had greeted Jessie and shaken hands with Ezra.

"How can I help you, Detective Drake?"

He was definitely not the man Jessie had seen at the airport. His thick, curly hair was graying, not black, his long beard more salt than pepper. And he was taller, with a physique that exuded vitality even while he was sitting, and penetrating electric blue eyes that made Jessie feel he could read her thoughts.

"I'm here about Ethan Meissner, Rabbi. I'd like to speak to him."

The rabbi turned to Ezra. "You're with the police, too, Mr. Nathanson? Or is it *Rabbi* Nathanson?"

"I'm not a rabbi, and I'm not with the police. I'm a teacher."

"We need good teachers. So what's your role here? Facilitator?"

"Something like that," Ezra said easily.

Klingerman stroked his beard. "Eitán is part of our program," he admitted. "But he won't talk to you, Detective."

"I'd like to hear that from him."

"You think I've got him locked up somewhere?" The rabbi smiled wryly. "Eitán is a free agent. He comes and goes as he pleases. But I can't let you talk to him."

Espes had warned her to be diplomatic. "With all due respect, Rabbi, that's not your choice to make. His foster father, Dr. Bushnell, has been murdered, along with the doctor's nurse and receptionist. We have to question Ethan about the murders."

"I heard about what happened. It's a terrible tragedy—*Hashem ye'rachem.*" May God have mercy. "But Eitán doesn't know anything about the murders, and to pull him away from his studies would be highly damaging. He's making terrific progress, terrific, and I don't want to mess with that. He's not the same kid who came here three weeks ago."

Klingerman's body language and diction were less formal than she'd anticipated. Maybe he'd never outgrown his more unorthodox past—or maybe he hadn't wanted to. That was part of his charisma. "How *did* Ethan find you?"

The rabbi shrugged his broad shoulders. "It's not important. What's important is that he's here, that he's healing. When he arrived he'd hit rock bottom. His life had no meaning, he was fooling around with drugs, alcohol. Now, through his study of the Torah, through a return to his roots, his life has started to take on meaning and value. He has hope. And he's been clean."

"A major transformation in three weeks?" Jessie asked, not bothering to hide her skepticism.

"It's a start. His addiction wasn't heavy to begin with. A lot of the boys who come here have been through rehab before and relapsed. The problem is, when you're weaning someone off the drugs or alcohol, or the sex, you're treating the symptom, not the problem. The *problem* is the void that makes these kids seek chemical or sexual highs because their lives are profoundly lonely and empty, because there's no spiritual foundation."

"And Torah is the answer?"

"*Etz chayim he la'machazikim bah.* 'The Torah is a tree of life for those who grasp onto it.' That's what this place is all about, and the kids seem to be responding."

"Maybe they're grasping because it beats the alternative—jail, parents who nag, conventional rehab."

"*Mi'toch lo lishma, ba lishma.*" Klingerman smiled. "If a person initially learns Torah or observes the *mizvot*, the commandments, for the wrong reasons, he may eventually come to do them for the right reasons, from the heart. My job isn't to analyze why these boys are here, Detective. My job is to help them find their hearts, to bring to life the spark of their Jewish souls."

"I appreciate your concern for Ethan's emotional well-being, Rabbi Klingerman. And it's great that he's finding himself here. But that doesn't absolve him of responsibility from his previous life. Despite what he may have told you, we have reason to believe he may be involved with the murders, or know something about them."

The rabbi shook his head. "Eitán isn't a killer. He told me so, and I believe him."

Jessie took out the photocopy of the lyrics Ethan had written and handed it to the rabbi. "This is Ethan's."

Klingerman read the words and handed back the paper. "He wouldn't be the first kid to imitate gangsta rap."

"Not every kid's foster father is murdered, Rabbi. 'Kill 'em all, watch them fall.' The person who wrote this sounds angry, desperate."

"Like I said, Eitán isn't the same person who came here three weeks ago."

"He tried to flee the country. But you know that." She smiled pleasantly, though the memory still rankled. "Your people got him off the aircraft before I could apprehend him."

"My 'people,' as you call them, went to the airport because Eitán changed his mind about leaving. I was against his leaving to begin with, and relieved when he came back."

"Your man heard me call Ethan's name, Rabbi. He shoved Ethan into the maroon van sitting in your driveway. I'd call that obstruction of justice."

"Obstruction?" Klingerman raised a brow. "I'd call it prudence. My assistant saw a screaming woman running toward him. How could he know you were a cop?"

"I identified myself."

"You hear so many frightening stories about people who pretend to be with law enforcement. How did he know you were legitimate?"

She felt her frustration growing and realized she wasn't going to win this one. "If Eitán doesn't know anything about the murders, why was he fleeing, Rabbi?"

"That's your *evidence*?" Klingerman snorted. "Do you have eyewitnesses who saw Ethan committing these murders?"

"No."

"Not even one?"

"Not even one," she said, annoyed with the baiting.

"According to Torah law, you need *two* eyewitnesses to find a person guilty of a capital crime." He raised two fingers. "*And* they had to have warned him of the consequences." He turned to Ezra. "Am I right?"

"This is the United States," Jessie said, making an effort not to snap. "We follow a criminal justice system, not the Torah, and in that system, we don't require two eyewitnesses to convict a person of murder. And as far as I know, neither does the Israeli judicial system."

"Yes, but Israel doesn't have the death penalty. Why do you think Torah law requires two eyewitnesses in a capital case, Detective? Because *one* witness can lie or be mistaken. Because circumstantial evidence can be misleading."

"And if the suspect is guilty? He just walks?"

"If there are no eyewitnesses, no warning, God will exact punishment. With rare exceptions, it's not our job to be executioners. And with good reason. You saw a boy trying to leave the country after his foster father was killed, and you automatically thought, 'He did it!'" The rabbi clapped his hands. "There are other reasons why a boy runs away."

"You said he loves it here, he's doing so well."

"He was making remarkable progress until the murders. When he heard what happened, he fell apart. He was sobbing inconsolably. He's grief stricken, Detective."

"Maybe he was crying out of remorse, Rabbi," Jessie said not unkindly.

"Yes, he felt remorse. Yes, he blamed himself."

Jessie felt a prickling of excitement. "Then what—"

"Suppose as a child you nagged your mother to let you go to a friend's house to play," Klingerman said quietly. "Suppose when you returned home, you found her dead of a self-inflicted gunshot wound. Suppose your father blamed you." He gazed at her with those eyes. "Suppose, Detective, that years later you storm out of your foster father's home and a few weeks later this foster father is killed. Would you blame yourself? Whether it's logical or not? Would you?"

Jessie didn't answer immediately. "Did Ethan tell you this? Or is this your assessment?"

"He told me Monday night, when he found out. I heard the news on the radio. Of course I had to tell him. He was shocked, distraught."

"Or maybe he was pretending, and gave you a bill of goods. Maybe you're being blinded by compassion for the kids you're trying to help."

Now it was Klingerman who didn't answer.

"The father admitted he made the flight arrangements," Jessie lied. "But you helped out."

"He spooked Eitán." Klingerman sounded unhappy. "He was afraid the police would suspect him because he quarreled with Dr. Bushnell, because he left under such bad terms. I begged Eitán not to go. I begged the father, too. Eitán was determined to go, so I sent some people with him to make sure he was all right."

"Did you pay for the ticket?"

"No. I assumed Mr. Meissner paid."

"Was Ethan here all day Monday?"

"I'd have to check with his mentor. I saw him at *ma'ariv*, evening prayers."

"When exactly was that?" The times for reciting prayers, Jessie knew, were dependent on sunrise and sunset. Last Friday night she'd lit Sabbath candles at 4:33, so *ma'ariv* on Monday could have been recited as early as 5:30. But it could have been recited much later.

"The boys *daven ma'ariv* after their evening sessions. Usually, around nine-thirty. It's a long day," he added.

So Ethan could easily have made it in time from Bushnell's office to the yeshiva. "What time is *mincha* here?" she asked, referring to the afternoon service.

Klingerman's eyes showed surprise. "Usually at two, unless we have a special program, like today. Then it's earlier."

"Did you see Ethan then, or at *shacharit*?"

He regarded her with interest. "I seem to recall he wasn't feeling well on Monday. I assume he was in his room."

"But you don't know that. What are the transportation

arrangements here, Rabbi? I mean, if someone wants to go to L.A., how does that work?"

"Our driver goes to the city once a day Sunday through Thursday, and sometimes one of the staff drives down, too. Not today, though. There was a problem with the large van. Anyway, we discourage the boys from leaving the grounds—we feel it's better if they stay within the complex. But we don't disallow it. They need to feel that they're here by choice, that they're free to make their own decisions. The only thing we require is conservative dress. Button-down shirts and slacks, a yarmulke, *tzitzit*—an undergarment with fringes at the four corners worn under the shirt. You'd be surprised what a difference clothing makes."

Not really. Jessie had read that some public schools were instituting uniforms to create an atmosphere of serious learning and to get away from gang colors. "Do the boys sign out if they leave the premises?"

"Technically, they're supposed to, but we're not strict about it. It's never been a problem. And we don't want our yeshiva to feel like a prison."

"So Ethan could have gone to L.A. on Monday, right? The van's driver will know."

Klingerman hesitated. "Yes, probably."

"Ethan's father told us Ethan was in L.A. on Sunday. What time did he leave here?"

"Right after *shacharit*."

Mrs. Montinedo had seen a young man resembling Ethan going into Meissner's apartment late Sunday night. What had he done all day? "He went to see Adrienne," Jessie said, stating her sudden guess as if it were fact. "Did you think that was a good idea, considering that her father was opposed to their dating?"

"He needed to explain why he couldn't see her anymore. He wanted to tell her he'd found himself here, with his own people. I advised him against it, of course. I didn't think he was ready. And he wasn't. The pull was too strong." Klingerman sighed. "But when I spoke to him Monday night after *ma'ariv*, he told me it was over between them."

"*After* Dr. Bushnell was dead," Jessie pointed out. "Did he say why?"

The rabbi shook his head. "What Eitán told me, he told me in confidence."

Guilt, Jessie guessed. "Bushnell found Ethan and Adrienne together, didn't he? They quarreled again."

"Again, I can't discuss what Eitán told me."

But it made sense. Meissner had correctly articulated the problem: if Bushnell had thrown Ethan out three weeks ago, why had Ethan waited to act out his anger? But if he'd quarreled that Sunday . . . She still couldn't imagine why he'd suddenly shown up at his father's apartment. She asked Klingerman, but he wouldn't say.

"Let Ethan tell me, then," Jessie said. "If he didn't kill Dr. Bushnell and the two women, he has nothing to fear. But he may have information about who *did* commit the murders."

"You'll only upset Eitán more than he already is. He's trying to return to his spiritual roots, Detective. He's begun to purge himself of the taint of the outside world and its temptations. Sex, drugs, alcohol."

Patience, she told herself. "I don't see how my talking with him will plunge him back into that world, Rabbi Klingerman. Where is he?"

"He swears he's innocent, and I believe him. Arresting him won't serve justice, but it will jeopardize his soul."

"I'm not talking about arresting him, Rabbi."

"Oh, but you will." The rabbi nodded. "Because he quarreled with Dr. Bushnell, because he's in love with the daughter. More 'evidence.' "

"We have other suspects." Meissner, for one. Barbara Martin for another. Jessie wondered where Kevin Hayes fit into the picture. Still no sign of him. "This is a homicide, Rabbi," she said sternly. "You're interfering in a police investigation."

"I'm not interfering. I'm just not willing to do your work for you. I'm trying to protect Eitán's soul, Detective. It's in a very fragile state, and sitting in a jail cell for a crime he didn't commit won't help."

"I can have you arrested, Rabbi Klingerman. That's not my preference." It wouldn't be Espes's either. She could imagine his face when she told him. And the news would probably make headlines.

"It isn't mine, either. But if that's what you have to do, that's what you have to do." He shrugged.

"You've been there before, right, Rabbi? Berkeley, in the sixties. You still enjoy resisting authority."

"Enjoy? No." He shook his head sadly. "But I still do what I believe is right."

"What if you're wrong? Let's say Ethan *was* making progress. Suppose something happened Sunday that undid all that progress, something that sent Eitàn's over the edge. Maybe he needs help. Or maybe he's totally innocent. Won't he feel better talking to me and clearing all this up?"

The rabbi tapped his fingers together.

"And if he's not innocent. Suppose he's a threat to others, Rabbi Klingerman. Do you want to be responsible if he kills someone else?"

His eyes were brooding. "Let me talk to Eitán, Detective," he said quietly. "Privately."

"YOU WERE A big help," Jessie said when Klingerman left the room.

Ezra shrugged. "You instructed me not to say anything. Just listen, you told me. Remember?"

"I know. But couldn't you have come up with something Talmudic to twist Klingerman's arm?" she asked glumly.

"Nothing that he couldn't have refuted. Anyway, you heard him—he's prepared to go to jail to protect Ethan. But you did fine without me. Obviously you had an impact—he's talking to the boy right now."

"Telling him what?"

She felt restless. Standing up, she walked to one of the large bookcases, took down a heavy tome, and opened it. In the past months she'd felt pride at the progress she was making learning Hebrew, but it all looked foreign to her now, unfathomable.

"It's ridiculous." She slammed the volume shut and put it back on the shelf. "So is this two eyewitnesses and a warning stuff. Let's wait outside."

"Why?"

"In case Ethan decides to skip while we're sitting here in this nice office."

They left the building. Jessie considered, then walked to the maroon van. Leaning against it, she had a clear view of both front and side entrances.

Ezra was gazing at her. "You're angry at Klingerman."

"Yes."

"Disillusioned with the Torah."

She hesitated. "Yes."

"What about Mexico? Are you disillusioned with that country? Or with England? Or Switzerland?"

She frowned. "What are you talking about?"

"None of those countries have capital punishment, and they won't extradite murder suspects to California, or other states that *do*, if the district attorney's going for the death penalty."

"I deal with homicides every day, Ezra," she said, feeling the anger and frustration rising. "In how many cases do you think I have two eyewitnesses who gave the suspect a previous warning?"

"Probably none," he agreed. "That's why there's God and life prison sentences. How many death row cases have been overturned in the past ten years because of exonerating DNA evidence, Jessie? The governor of Illinois just put a moratorium on executions. Want to place bets that other governors are going to follow suit?"

She eyed him thoughtfully. "I take it you're against the death penalty."

"Actually, I'm on the fence. Emotionally, I'm for it. Intellectually, too. But I worry about the possibility that a jury could make a mistake, about misleading circumstantial evidence, about inadequate representation. I read about a recent Texas death row case where the defense attorney was *asleep* during much of the trial. Can you believe it? And then there's the *halacha*, Torah law."

"There's still room for doubt even with two witnesses, Ezra. Two witnesses can lie."

He nodded. "But the judges grilled them exhaustively. And executions were rare. A *bet din*, or court of law, that convicted in a capital crime more than once in seventy years was called a bloody *bet din*."

"You think Klingerman's resisting because of that?"

"If you were in Singapore, Jessie, and you saw a kid throwing a sunflower seed on the ground, and the police asked you to finger the perpetrator, would you do it, knowing he'd be severely caned?"

She'd read about the American teenager whose back had been lacerated for just that offense. "Come on, Ezra. It's not the same thing."

"If you were in a country where the punishment for theft is having one's hands chopped off, would you turn in someone if you saw him stealing?"

"So what are you saying? That laws are arbitrary?" She frowned. "I don't like this."

"I didn't think you would."

"If Klingerman doesn't produce the kid, I have half a mind to have him arrested."

"Go ahead."

She scowled at him. "Don't humor me, Ezra."

"I'm not. You do your job, Jessie, and understand that Klingerman has to do his."

Fifteen minutes later Klingerman exited the building and approached her.

"I'm not sure where Eitán is right now," he told Jessie, his face filled with consternation. "I've looked everywhere. He may have gone into town earlier."

Jessie gave him a withering glance. "He ran away."

"I don't know," the rabbi admitted.

Klingerman could be lying. She hadn't seen anyone leave, although Ethan could have left while she was in the rabbi's office. The young man who had opened the door for her and Ezra could have spread the word that police had come to talk to the rabbi.

"I want him found," she snapped. "I've already advised the San Bernardino sheriff's department that I may need their help. I'm calling them in now."

Klingerman nodded, unhappy but resigned.

Using her cell phone, Jessie spoke with the sheriff's deputy she'd contacted earlier, who promised he was immediately dispatching several deputies to the seminary and would obtain a search warrant as quickly as possible for Ethan's room and the premises.

"Where is everyone now?" she asked Klingerman after she finished the call.

"The boys should be finishing *mincha* in the *bet midrash*—the study hall. Believe me, Detective, I hope as much as you that Eitán hasn't run away."

She didn't bother to respond. "Wait by my car," she told Ezra.

Entering the building, she followed Klingerman to the study hall and stood in the doorway. Tables and chairs and a few lecterns occupied the bottom half of the large wood-paneled room. The top half was probably unfurnished to accommodate the boys, who were standing in the area, rocking back and forth and occasionally bending their knees and bowing. Leading them in prayer was a young man in a white shirt and black slacks. He was standing in front of a lectern, facing a navy curtain, decorated with gold Hebrew lettering, behind which Jessie assumed was a cabinet housing one or more Torah scrolls.

Like the leader, most of the boys were in what Ezra had told her was typical yeshiva garb—white shirts, black slacks, velvet yarmulkes. A few wore light blue shirts and black suede yarmulkes, like Ezra's, instead of the velvet. Three yarmulkes crocheted in bright yarn stood out like bobbing spots of color in a black-and-white movie.

The service was over, and the boys were walking to the tables. Holding the photo Celeste had given her, she entered the room. "Ethan Meissner," she called loudly.

A few heads turned toward her, but Ethan's wasn't among them. She called his name again.

"He isn't here," a white-shirted boy told her.

"Where is he?"

The boy looked behind Jessie, at Klingerman, then back at her. "I don't know. He didn't come to *mincha*."

She checked every boy in the room, then walked back to Klingerman, who had waited near the doorway. "Where else could he be?" she demanded.

"In his room, in the cafeteria, in the gym. But I looked in all those places."

She ordered the boys to remain in the study hall and followed Klingerman to Ethan's second-floor room. It was vacant. His bed was made, the books neatly stacked. According to Klingerman, Ethan had been in the seminary Monday night. She was itching to check his closet and drawers for bloodstained clothing, but without a warrant anything she found would be inadmissible.

He wasn't in the gym or in the cafeteria. The Brunehilde-like blond cook, her face reddened from the steam rising from the pot she was vigorously stirring, told Jessie she'd chased Ethan out of the kitchen an hour ago when she'd caught him taking sandwiches out of the refrigerator.

"They're always hungry, these boys," she said with more pride than displeasure. "I let him take two sandwiches, even though he knows the kitchen's off-limits." The cook frowned. "He's a nice boy. He's not in trouble, I hope?"

Jessie was barely able to control her anger. "I could have you shut down," she warned Klingerman when they left the kitchen. "Aiding and abetting a fugitive won't sit well with parents and probation officers and social workers."

"Excuse me, Detective, but since when was Eitán a fugitive? You told me yourself you weren't necessarily going to arrest him. I told you I would talk to him, and I tried. Was I supposed to know he would run away?"

Four sheriff's deputies arrived and began to search the seminary building, the storage structure at the back, and the woods behind the property. Returning to the study hall,

Jessie questioned the boys, all of whom were vague about when they'd last seen Ethan. Another code of silence. Either the teenager hadn't been here when she'd arrived, or he'd learned of her presence and left while she was in the rabbi's office.

Klingerman seemed sincerely concerned, but she was furious and regretted not having asked the sheriff's deputy to bring a warrant for his arrest. In truth she had shaky grounds at best and would have accomplished nothing, aside from angering Espes, and she realized that part of her anger was really her own nervousness. She didn't know how she would explain having lost the boy a second time.

The short, watery-eyed Russian driver/handyman was repairing a screen when she found him. He hadn't seen Ethan today, he told Jessie in a heavy accent, but had driven him to L.A. Sunday morning and dropped him off at the Beverly Hilton Hotel on Wilshire and Santa Monica.

Walking distance from the Bushnell home. "When did you drive him back here?" Jessie asked.

The man wiped his perspiring face with his shirtsleeve, leaving a streak of dirt. "He is supposed to be by hotel five o'clock. I waited twenty-five minutes, maybe more, then I leave." He shrugged. "Maybe he has other person take him."

More likely he'd gone to his father's apartment. "Did you see him the next day?"

"I am not seeing boys all the time. This does not mean he is not here."

She was running out of patience. "When *did* you see him?"

The man squinted into the bright sunlight. "Tuesday afternoon? I see him going with others to the van. Then he comes back."

A round-trip to the airport. Maybe Meissner had driven his son back to the yeshiva on Monday, in time for evening prayers. So that the boy would have an alibi? And in that case, maybe Ethan had disposed of any bloodstained clothing before he'd returned to the seminary.

And now he'd disappeared again.

The black-bearded teacher who'd whisked Ethan away from the American Airlines gate was uncomfortable talking to her and revealed with great reluctance that Ethan had asked to stop by the Bushnells before heading for the airport. The boy had been inside the house for a few minutes at most, and had been upset when he'd returned to the car.

"I'd like to see Ethan's file," Jessie told Klingerman when she was back in his office.

He shook his head. "That's confidential."

"His application, then. He may have listed information that would help us find him."

The rabbi hesitated.

"You owe me," she told him. "And if Ethan's in a seriously upset condition, he shouldn't be on his own."

Klingerman frowned, then walked to the gray filing cabinet, tabbed through the files, and returned to his desk, holding a single sheet of paper.

She scanned the application. Ethan had written NONE in all capital letters for home address but had listed Gideon Meissner as next of kin. In the space next to REFERRED BY he'd written GOD. The form had also asked him to state his reason for coming to the seminary ("It beats sleeping on the street") and his goals: "to get my head straight."

"Who referred him to you?" she asked Klingerman again. "And please don't give me your 'It doesn't matter' line."

The rabbi hesitated. "The father."

There was a knock on the door.

"Come in," Klingerman called.

The door opened, and the black-bearded teacher entered. "Can I speak to you, Bezalel? It's important."

"Excuse me a minute," the rabbi told Jessie.

She turned to the teacher. "Does this concern Ethan Meissner?"

The man hesitated. "I don't know." He looked at Klingerman.

"What's the problem?" Klingerman asked impatiently.

"Mrs. Angelman's car is missing."

"The cook," Klingerman explained to Jessie. "She's sure?" he asked the teacher.

The man nodded. "She wanted to get something from her car and noticed that her keys were missing. So is the car."

"Where does she keep her keys?" Jessie asked, though she had a reasonable guess.

"In the kitchen, in her purse."

"Looks like Ethan helped himself to more than a few sandwiches," she told the rabbi.

❖ 30 ❖

THE GOOD NEWS was they had grounds to arrest him on a felony charge. The sheriff's deputies issued an APB on the cook's white Corolla and informed the San Bernardino authorities to be on the lookout. If Ethan had driven off when she was in Klingerman's office over an hour ago, by now he was probably past San Bernardino.

Headed where?

Jessie phoned West L.A. and relayed the information, which would be disseminated to all the departments. She also alerted the two officers watching Meissner's apartment. This time they would get him, she told herself. She pictured the Corolla leading a string of black-and-whites on one of the car chases that was becoming an almost nightly staple of local television news.

"I'm sorry," Ezra said when she returned to her car and told him what had happened.

"Not your fault." She turned the Honda around. They would get him, but she wouldn't be part of it, because she was stuck here on top of a damn mountain.

"You're not going to speed, are you?"

She shook her head. "I don't have a death wish. Although the thought of facing my lieutenant doesn't thrill me." In that first instant she'd had an urge to give chase, had wondered whether she had the mettle to brave the winding road. Now she wouldn't know.

"You definitely think the boy did it, don't you?"

"If it looks like a duck, and walks like a duck, it's a duck, Ezra."

"Maybe he's just a scared teen."

"Maybe. By the way, Klingerman told me the father's the one who sent the boy here. Interesting, since Meissner's not religious."

"Like I said, Klingerman gets a lot of kids whose parents aren't observant. They just want him to work his magic."

She drove for a while without speaking. "Actually, it makes sense. I mean, here's the dad, who's been out of the loop all these years—his fault, according to the Bushnells, but he doesn't want to see that. So when the son comes crying to him that the foster parents tossed him out, he feels he can finally do something for his kid, and stick it to the Bushnells at the same time."

Ezra frowned. "What do you mean?"

"They're sick to death with worry—at least Mrs. Bushnell is—and Meissner lied and told them he hadn't heard from Ethan. He probably loved being in control, turning the tables on them. Plus who does he send Ethan to? An Orthodox rabbi! He claims that for years the Bushnells have prevented him from teaching Ethan about his Jewish heritage."

"Maybe it's more simple than that, Jessie. Maybe he was grasping at straws, trying to figure out what was best for his son."

"Nothing about this family is simple, Ezra."

They were on the main road. She turned on the radio and braced herself for the descent. "Here we go."

"My cue to stop talking?"

She smiled. "You're a quick learner."

She drove slowly, her foot on the brake, hugging the side of the road that abutted the mountain. She tried not to look to her left, even though she couldn't see the sheer drop, and every time she turned a curve, she had a lurching sensation until she knew the road was clear and she wasn't going to crash with an oncoming car.

They were nearing the fork in the road that would take them to Lake Arrowhead or San Bernardino when traffic slowed. Soon they were part of a caravan of creeping cars.

"Probably an accident ahead, or a stalled car," Ezra said.

She nodded. Part of her didn't mind the slow pace. The other part wanted off of the mountain, safe on the flat stretch of freeway. She didn't want to think about having to pass a disabled vehicle on the left, about the possibility of veering off the mountain's side or crashing head-on into an oncoming car. She told herself she would be following the other drivers, all of whom would be proceeding carefully.

Now the cars weren't moving at all. She tried using her cell phone to contact the Big Bear sheriff's department and make sure they were aware of the traffic situation, but she couldn't get a line. Probably out of cell range. Finally, she got through and spoke to one of the sheriff's deputies who had shown up at the seminary.

"We've been trying to contact you on your cell phone, Detective Drake," he told her. "We got news about twenty minutes ago that the disabled car causing the traffic pileup is the white Corolla."

She felt her stomach muscles tighten. "What happened?"

"The car seems to have broken down. No sign of the boy."

Damn. "Nobody saw anything?"

"Don't know that for sure, Detective. You'll want to ask the officers at the scene."

She thanked the deputy and ended the call, then turned to Ezra. "Take the wheel, okay? I want to check out the accident up ahead. If traffic moves, drive to the next lookout spot and wait for me there."

He nodded. "It's Ethan?"

"It's the cook's car. They don't know where Ethan is."

She put the Honda in park, set the brake, grabbed her

purse, and got out as Ezra walked around the car to the driver's side.

"Be careful," he said with a quiet intensity that touched her.

She sprinted alongside the cars, the cool air sharp against her face, and was aware of curious looks from the drivers and passengers she passed. The queue of cars seemed endless, and she was getting a little tired when she rounded a curve and spotted the Corolla fifty feet ahead.

The car was stalled in the middle of the road. The driver's door was open wide, the hood up.

Two patrol officers were directing traffic around the vehicle, which was blocking the single ascending lane and impeding the flow of cars in the descending lane. With her badge in her hand, Jessie approached one of the officers, identified herself, and explained her interest in the car.

"Jerry Light," he told her. He had thick, dark brown hair, black eyes, and a reddish tint to his tanned face. "How'd you get here?"

She pointed backward. "My friend's driving my car. He's about half a mile up. When did this happen?"

"We had a couple of reports about a disabled car around forty minutes ago. We're still waiting on the tow truck, and we've been instructed not to move the vehicle until someone from the sheriff's department checks everything out, in case it turns out to be a suicide."

Goose bumps dotted her forearms. "What makes you think that?"

"One guy who called in about the car said he saw a kid standing at the edge of the cliff. He stopped and asked the kid if he needed help. The kid said no, the car was just overheated. But he looked like he'd been crying. The guy left, but the more he thought about it, the more uneasy it made him, so he turned around and drove back. The kid was gone, but the car was still here."

"Maybe he hitched a ride." She pulled her wind-tousled hair away from her face.

"Maybe." Jerry Light nodded. "The kid left a note in the car, under the keys. 'I'm sorry.' "

Sorry for having stolen the car? For having killed three people? For what he was about to do? "Did you see anything that would suggest he killed himself?"

"Nope. But it's not always easy to make something out. I don't think he's there, but you'll want to take a look yourself, right?"

"Sure," she lied.

Her stomach was in knots, her palms clammy. Taking a deep breath, she followed him across the asphalt to the front of the Corolla.

The officer moved impossibly close to the edge of the cliff, squatted, and peered down. "There's something down there that got caught on a branch. Black cap, maybe. Could be from today, could be from three months ago."

She wished he would move back.

"Tell you one thing. If your boy fell, no way is he alive. There's not much brush, and those stones are unforgiving." He stood up. "You won't see anything from there."

"Okay." She took a tentative step forward.

"Afraid of heights?" He nodded. "My wife, too. I'm part Indian, so this doesn't bother me." His smile was friendly, encouraging. "Here, I'll hold on to you." He extended his hand, his short shirtsleeve billowing in the cool breeze.

Pride falleth before a cliff, she thought. Clutching his hand, she walked toward him gingerly until she was at his side and welcomed the tight fit of his arm around her waist.

"I've got you," he promised.

She felt dizzy and a little nauseated, and her upper lip was dotted with beads of sweat. She took deep breaths, exhaling white circles of air from her mouth, and pretended that a crystal clear glass existed between her and the empty space just inches form where she was standing.

She looked down. The grandeur of the stark scenery awed her, and she felt tiny, inconsequential, humbled. Terrified.

"You'll need these." He handed her a pair of minibinoculars from his pants pocket.

She raised the binoculars hesitantly to her eyes and swept the area, going from left to right. She moved them too quickly at first, compounding her dizziness, then scanned the area with a methodical slowness that gave her a sense of control. She spotted something partially covered by brush and drew in a sharp breath.

"Find something?" he asked.

She handed him the binoculars and showed him where she'd been looking. "Could be the back of a head."

"That's nothing," he said a moment later. "Just a rock. The mind plays tricks."

She viewed the area again. "I don't see anything."

"Look over there." He pointed down, to her right.

Following his finger, she used the binoculars again. She still didn't see anything. The third time she did, about fifty feet down the mountainside, hanging from a branch. Something black and round and small that glinted under the sun's rays. Something that could be a velvet yarmulke.

"See it?" Jerry asked.

She nodded. She wondered whether the stiff breeze that was whipping her hair into a frenzy had blown the yarmulke, if in fact that's what it was, off Ethan's head, or whether he'd flung it off in futility or anger or despair or renunciation. She felt the frightening pull of the abyss and wondered how close he'd come to taking a step into nothingness; wondered, too, why she felt an uncomfortable pity for a young man who may have killed three people and was on the run.

She scrutinized the black object again and returned the binoculars. "Thanks."

"Had enough for today, huh?" He smiled again and released her. "You get used to it when you live around here. You may even come to like it."

She didn't think so.

She inched backward from the cliff's edge and followed the footprints that made a twenty-foot diagonal line from where she'd been standing and disappeared into the asphalt.

❖ 31 ❖

"I'M SORRY." CELESTE Bushnell ran a hand through her hair that, like everything else about her, was limp and lackluster. She was wearing the same robe she'd had on when Jessie had seen her two days ago, a floral print that almost disappeared against the chintz of the living room sofa. The purplish circles under her eyes were more pronounced and made her look like a bruised fighter.

"It's difficult enough conducting an investigation when people are cooperating fully," Jessie told her. "When you withhold information, you make it that much harder for us to identify your husband's killer. Unless, of course, you don't *want* us to find your husband's killer."

Celeste's head jerked back, as if Jessie had slapped her, and her face was flushed. "Of *course* I do!"

"You knew Ethan and your daughter were in love. You knew your husband disapproved. That's why Ethan left—it wasn't just about drugs or alcohol. That was something we should have been told."

She could say almost the same thing about the Pervez case, Jessie thought. She was frustrated with Lily's parents and brother, who were almost certainly withholding information. She was exasperated with Celeste Bushnell, with the daughter, with Meissner and his son, with the whole damn extended family for lying and evading and for the fact that Espes had glared at her with his watery, beady, cold-reddened eyes and asked her whether she was up to the task of finding an eighteen-year-old boy or would prefer paperwork.

"I was afraid you'd suspect Ethan even more than you did, and then you wouldn't search for the *real* killer," Celeste said. "I know it looks bad. Ethan's confused and a little rebellious, but so are a lot of kids."

"Most kids don't write about killing themselves and other people. Most kids whose foster fathers have been murdered don't run away and don't steal cars to do it."

Celeste's eyes welled with tears. "He's *scared*! Can't you understand that? His mother killed herself, and now the man who's been like a father to him for the past ten years has been murdered!"

Basically what Klingerman had said. Maybe it was true. The San Bernardino deputies had found no incriminating evidence in Ethan's room. She and Phil had found nothing in Gideon Meissner's apartment, and no bloodstained clothing in the vacant apartment. They had found the Walther, though. Ethan or his father could have tossed any bloodstained garments over a cliff on the way up to the seminary.

"He's a good boy, Detective," Celeste said, wiping her eyes with her fingers. "He would *never* kill anyone, especially Ronnie. Ronnie *loved* him and was so proud of him. Ethan knew that. He knew Ronnie would come around."

"Even about Ethan's relationship with your daughter?"

Celeste hesitated. "I don't know," she admitted. "Ronnie was extremely upset. The kids have always been so close, so I guess we should have seen it coming. I thought it was sweet, but Ronnie worried that one of them would be hurt, and that would damage the family."

A valid argument. "And Ethan was having a negative influence on Adrienne, right? The drugs, the drinking, the late nights. Her grades were falling, too."

"I was worried." Celeste nodded. "But Adrienne's a

strong girl. I thought she could be good for Ethan." She fingered the collar of her robe. "The more I think about it, the more convinced I am that Carla Luchins is the killer."

The woman was desperate, Jessie thought. "When did you last see Ethan?"

"The night he left the house, over three weeks ago."

"We have a witness who saw him enter your house Tuesday afternoon, the day after the murders."

"Tuesday afternoon," Celeste repeated, her face screwed in concentration. Her expression cleared. "I wasn't home. Adrienne and I went to the airport to pick up my parents."

"Your housekeeper must have let him in. She didn't tell you he'd been here?" Jessie asked, skeptical.

Celeste shook her head. "She may have been marketing. But Ethan has a key. He probably came to say good-bye, and I wasn't there," she said mournfully.

"Because he was going to Israel."

"Yes."

"How did you know Ethan was going to Israel, Mrs. Bushnell?" Jessie asked softly.

The expression on her face froze. She blinked rapidly. "I don't—" She stopped. "Gideon told me."

"Mr. Meissner claims he doesn't know anything about Ethan going to Israel."

"Well, he must have told me about it," she said with a flash of irritation. "How else would I know?"

"Is that when he asked you to pay for the ticket?"

Celeste frowned. "I don't know what you're talking about."

"Mr. Meissner couldn't afford to buy a last-minute ticket to Israel. And you told me your husband took away Ethan's credit card. I checked with the airlines, Mrs. Bushnell. Both the El Al and American Airlines tickets were charged to your card."

"I don't understand how that's possible. Unless . . ." She tapped a finger against her lip. "Ethan must have had a receipt with the card number. He must have felt desperate to do something like that." She sighed.

"I spoke with the credit card company, Mrs. Bushnell. With large transactions, they generally check with the card holder to verify authorization." In San Bernardino Jessie had allowed Ezra to take the wheel so that she could save time and make phone calls in the car: to American Airlines, to El Al, to the credit card company. "Which you did on Tuesday morning at eleven-oh-six. You authorized the tickets. Or Adrienne did. She probably knows your mother's maiden name, too, which is something they always ask."

Celeste's eyes darted like those of a trapped animal. "I couldn't bear the thought that they'd lock him up!" she whispered, her lips trembling. "I just couldn't. Adoption or not, I'm his *mother*. He's my *son*. I *had* to protect him." She was crying, hugging her arms.

"From what? You said you don't believe he's capable of murder."

"He was so depressed, Detective. He felt so hopeless, so alone. I was afraid if he was jailed, he might kill himself," she said in a low voice, as if stating the fear might make it fact. "Gideon was afraid of that, too."

"Like mother, like son?" Jessie asked.

Celeste flinched. "Yes, like mother, like son."

"What about Barbara Martin? You lied about her, too." Hit 'em when their defenses are down, Jessie thought, watching the widow carefully.

The woman looked perplexed. "What do you mean?"

"We have a witness who says the nurse and your husband were having an affair."

She drew herself up stiffly. "I don't know what you're talking about."

"Celeste, are you all right? I heard crying."

Jessie turned to the living room arch and the tall man standing there.

"I'm fine. This is Detective Drake. She's investigating Ronnie's murder."

He approached the sofa and put his hand on Celeste's shoulder. "I'm Andrew Hepley, Celeste's brother. Will this take much longer, Detective?"

"We're almost done," Jessie said pleasantly. "I'd like to talk to your sister privately."

"I'm not leaving."

"Andrew, please. It's okay."

He shook his head.

Celeste faced Jessie. "All I know is that Ronnie fired the nurse, and she was suing him. I don't know why people are so cruel. Isn't it tragic enough that he's been murdered? Do they have to spread vile rumors?"

"Ethan was here on Sunday, too," Jessie said. "The day before the murder. We suspect that he fought with your husband about Adrienne. We know he went to his father's house late that night, very agitated." Speculation, but it could be true.

Celeste shook her head. "Ronnie played golf Sunday morning and spent the rest of the day at the health club. I was out shopping, and then I went to a movie with friends. A chick flick. Ronnie wasn't interested." She smiled lightly.

"So you don't know that your husband didn't come home and argue with Ethan."

"No, I don't *know*," she said, annoyed. "But he would have told me if Ethan had come by."

"Where was Adrienne?"

"She had plans to visit a friend."

At the Beverly Hilton hotel? It was easy to fool parents, Jessie knew from her own high school years. And nowadays, when parents were even busier with their own lives, their own careers . . . "I'll have to talk to her."

"Adrienne isn't home. My parents took her out to dinner. Why do you have to bother her?" she cried with a surge of anger. "You know everything there is to know. She's lost her father, and Ethan. I don't want her harassed!"

"Detective, what's the point of this?" the brother demanded. "From what I can see, all you're accomplishing is upsetting my sister."

"Mr. Hepley, please don't interfere." Jessie fixed him with a reproving glance. "I don't intend to harass Adrienne, Mrs. Bushnell," she said quietly. "But if she saw Ethan the day before the murders, I need to talk to her."

"I know." Celeste sighed. "I know you're just trying to do your job. But this is so painful, for all of us. I'll have her phone you when she comes back."

"Do you know anything about Kevin Hayes?"

She looked puzzled. "He and Ethan got into a fight at school, and the headmaster called us. Ethan wouldn't say what it was about. Why?"

"He's been missing since Monday night, along with his mother's gun. It's too much of a coincidence that Kevin disappeared right after the murders."

Celeste's eyes widened. "Are you saying . . . What *are* you saying? That the *Hayes* boy killed Ronnie? But why?"

"It's possible Kevin and Ethan were both involved in the murders. It's also possible that Ethan killed Kevin." With everything that had been going on, Jessie hadn't had a chance to stop by the Hayes's house and question the housekeeper.

"This is a nightmare!" Celeste moaned. "I don't believe this is happening."

"Where is Ethan now?" Jessie asked.

"I don't know." Celeste ran a hand through her hair. "Gideon phoned late Tuesday to tell me Ethan didn't leave the country after all. He said he was in a safe place. He said it was better for Ethan if I didn't know the name."

"An Orthodox Jewish seminary for boys in Big Bear," Jessie told her. "He's not there anymore. He's on the run."

Celeste looked stupefied, as though Jessie had informed her that Ethan had traveled to the moon.

"Where would he go, Mrs. Bushnell?"

She shook her head. "I have no idea."

A quaver in her voice told Jessie otherwise. "I'm running out of patience, Mrs. Bushnell. Ethan is a fugitive now. There's a felony warrant out for his arrest. If you know where he is, you're an accessory after the fact. You can be arrested." Too bad she couldn't have the entire family locked up. Group rates.

Celeste paled. She looked quickly at her brother.

"Don't say anything, Celeste," he cautioned. "You may need an attorney."

"If you tell me where he is, I can try to persuade the D.A. not to press charges against you," Jessie told her.

She glanced at her brother, then at Jessie. "I need to think."

"You have five minutes. Then I'm taking you to the station. Maybe you'll be able to think more clearly there."

She looked stricken. "I don't want Adrienne coming home to an empty house."

"Your call." Jessie made a point of checking her watch.

"If my sister tells you where the boy is, the D.A. won't press charges?" Andrew Hepley asked.

A quick about-face, Jessie thought. "I'll do my best. I'll tell him she's cooperating."

"If you know where Ethan is, tell her, Celeste," the brother urged. He increased the pressure on her shoulder. "He's been trouble from the day you and Ronnie took him in. You've protected him enough. Now you have to protect yourself, and Adrienne. She needs you."

Celeste licked her lips. She looked around her, as if seeking an escape. "There's an aunt in San Diego, Gideon's sister. Gideon was thinking of sending him there."

"Why San Diego?" Jessie wondered aloud. Not very far away, if you were trying to escape. Something was tickling her memory, something—"Cancun," she said. "You have a condo there, if I remember."

Cancun was in Mexico, a country that might not extradite on a capital crime. Tijuana was just a walk across the border from San Ysidro, which wasn't far from downtown San Diego. And boarding a foreign carrier on foreign soil was easier and safer than trying to board an American carrier in Los Angeles or San Diego. Meissner had probably assumed—correctly—that Jessie had alerted all American carriers to be on the watch for the boy. If Ethan crossed into Mexico, he would be untouchable, at least temporarily.

"Is that where he's headed?" she asked.

Celeste nodded. She bowed her head.

"What flight? *What flight*, Mrs. Bushnell?" Jessie repeated sternly when the woman didn't answer.

She looked up. "I don't know for certain. Gideon said he'd take care of the arrangements."

"And you would pay for it. What airline?"

"Mexicana," she said, her voice almost inaudible.

"Was Mr. Meissner driving him to San Diego?"

Celeste shook her head. "He thought you might be having him watched."

"So how is Ethan getting to San Diego?"

"The train. I don't know which one."

"Is he there yet?"

"I haven't heard from Gideon."

"Call him," Jessie instructed. "Find out if Ethan arrived, and if he hasn't, what time he's supposed to arrive. Don't say anything else."

Celeste nodded. She rose shakily from the sofa, and her brother gripped her arm to steady her. Jessie followed them into the study and waited while Celeste, her hand trembling, picked up the phone on the desk and punched the numbers.

"Gideon?" she said a moment later. "It's Celeste. Has he arrived? Not yet? No, no news. No, nothing. I'm fine. What train is he taking? Why not? Oh. Okay, call me when you hear something."

She hung up the phone, her hand still shaking, and faced Jessie.

"He's not taking the train. Gideon thought it would be better if he took a nonstop bus instead. There's a four o'clock that arrives in San Diego at six-fifty-five P.M. He should be on it now."

Jessie checked her watch. 5:06. Ample time to contact the San Diego police and arrange for them to apprehend Ethan. "If you're lying to me, Mrs. Bushnell, I'll have you arrested."

"I'm not lying! I'm tired of all the lying."

"Don't call Gideon. Don't call his sister-in-law. If you do anything to interfere with this investigation, you'll do time in prison. I promise you."

"I won't." She started crying and pressed her hands against her lips. "Please don't hurt him. *Please*."

❖ 32 ❖

ETHAN HAD DONE himself a great disservice, and Jessie a great favor, by stealing the cook's car. Without a felony charge, and with no probable cause to arrest him for the murders, all she could have done was drive to San Diego and try to persuade him to talk to her—if she could have reached him before he disappeared across the border.

Using the Bushnells' phone, Jessie contacted the San Diego Police Department and spoke with Detective Larry Masters.

"I'll enter the arrest warrant on NCIC as soon as I get to the West L.A. station, probably within the half hour," she told Masters after she'd explained the situation, using the acronym for the National Crime Information Center. "I'll fax you a copy of the warrant and a photo of the suspect. If you have any questions, call me at the station."

"Don't worry. We'll pick him up at the bus station."

"You might want to stake out the aunt's place just in case. Her name is Orit Yardeni." Jessie dictated the address Celeste had given her. "I've lost this suspect twice, Detective. I don't want to lose him again." She was embarrassed and wondered what Masters must be thinking.

"Understood. We'll check out the address, keep it under surveillance until we have him in custody. What about the murder charges?"

"We don't have the physical evidence. We're waiting for

a ballistics report on a weapon we recovered." She'd checked with Phil after returning from Big Bear—Ballistics promised to have an answer in the morning.

After thanking Masters, she phoned West L.A. and informed Espes about the developments. She also arranged to have a uniformed officer come baby-sit Celeste to insure that the woman didn't contact Meissner or the sister-in-law. Or Ethan—he probably had a cell phone.

"I gave my sister a sedative and she's resting now," Andrew Hepley told Jessie when he returned to the study.

"For her sake, I hope you make sure she doesn't phone Gideon Meissner or the aunt in San Diego, or Ethan. I meant what I said about arresting her." Jessie intended to keep her eye on the three-line phone. If Celeste tried to call anyone, Jessie would know.

"That boy." Hepley shook his head.

She looked at him with interest. "I take it you don't like Ethan."

"He's very bright and he can be charming, but he's caused my sister and brother-in-law grief. Drinking, drugs. He's pulled Adrienne down, too. And now this." He sighed.

"Your sister is obviously totally devoted to him."

The brother nodded. "To a fault. Spare the rod, and all that. This is killing her. Celeste's the one who insisted Ethan come live with them. Ronnie resisted, but she convinced him. She wanted another child for so long, and even as a little girl Adrienne was always so attached to Ronnie. Celeste *adores* Ethan, can't see anything but good in him. Ronnie's the same way with Adrienne. Spoiled her rotten." He shrugged.

"Your sister's loyal to her late husband, too, in spite of the fact that he had one or more affairs."

Hepley stiffened. "I wouldn't know about that. Would you excuse me? I want to check on Celeste."

Nothing ventured . . .

The uniformed officer arrived. Jessie talked with him privately, then went into the kitchen, which was redolent with the scent of sautéing onions. She found the housekeeper standing at the counter.

"I have to ask you a few questions," Jessie told her.

"More questions?" She glared at her with narrowed eyes. "Why you cannot leave this house alone, hunh?"

"Were you here on Tuesday?"

"Yes. H'okay?"

"Did you go out at all?"

"No. Why you ask?" she demanded, her small hands expertly peeling a potato with a short knife. "I have citizen papers. I am legal, one hundred *per* cent."

"Ethan came to the house Tuesday afternoon," Jessie said. "What did he want?"

A crafty look passed over the woman's face. "Who say?"

"The person who drove him here and waited while he went inside. What did he want?" Jessie repeated.

She pared a long russet strip. "He want to talk to Adri Anne. I tell him Adri Anne no home. Missy Celeste no home, too."

"But he didn't leave." According to the teacher, Ethan had stayed a few minutes, she remembered.

The woman hesitated. "He not believe me. He go upstairs to Adri Anne's room." She frowned her displeasure. "I follow."

"You were upset because he didn't believe you?" Jessie clucked sympathetically.

"Upset, yes. I say, 'Where you are all this *time*, hunh'?" Her eyes were flashing, and she had warmed to the subject. " 'This family do e-very thing for you. Dr. Bushnell dead, Missy Celeste and Adri Anne crying much tears all the day. Very-very sad time, and where you are?' " She pointed the knife accusingly at Jessie.

This was not a woman to cross, Jessie decided. "What did he say?"

"He not talk. He go downstairs and leave." She took a vicious swipe at the hapless tuber.

"Why didn't you tell Mrs. Bushnell Ethan was here?"

She snorted. "For what? Make her sad? She plenty sad already. She try hard with him, and now she cry all the time."

"Do you like Ethan, Kim?"

"Missy Celeste say he is son. Missy Celeste good woman, like her mother. I work many-many years for her mother. She is very good to me."

Talk about evasive. "But what do *you* think about Ethan? Do you think he could have killed Dr. Bushnell?"

The housekeeper darted a glance toward the doorway to the dining room. "He different boy, *some* times. Some times very-very nice. Some times make Missy Celeste cry, make doctor very angry." She pursed her thin lips.

"Dr. Bushnell was angry because Ethan wanted to be Adrienne's boyfriend, right?"

The woman shrugged. "Is not my business." She gouged an eye out of the potato and scrutinized the tuber before plunking it into a glass bowl filled with water.

"Was Adrienne upset with her father?"

"Adri Anne is very close to *her* father. He is very much loving Adri Anne. What she want, he give her. *I* think, if she wait, he say is h'okay." The housekeeper nodded sagely.

"We know Ethan came here the Sunday before the murder," Jessie said. "We know he and Dr. Bushnell argued. Was it about Adrienne?"

"Could be. How I should know?" Her tone was guarded.

"Did Ethan threaten Dr. Bushnell? Did he say he was going to hurt him?"

Kim picked up another potato.

"I'm sure you want to protect Mrs. Celeste, Kim. She loves Ethan like a son, so you're not sure what to do. But if Ethan killed Dr. Bushnell, he might hurt himself. Or someone else. Like Mrs. Celeste, or Adrienne."

The woman's dark eyes were clouded with uncertainty.

"Who came here first on Sunday, Ethan or Dr. Bushnell?"

"E-tan, with Adri Anne," she said after a moment. "They

come here *five* o'clock. The doctor, he come maybe *one* hour later."

"Then what happened?"

"He see Adri Anne's car in driveway. I tell him Adri Anne in her room."

"With Ethan?"

The woman nodded.

"Then what?"

She shrugged. "He come down, with E-tan. They go in doctor's office and close door. I don't hear what they say. Later, E-tan come out. He walk right by me, out door, like he don't see me."

"Did he seem angry?"

"He look sick." She held the potato in her hand and contemplated. "He look like my father when he find out he has cancer. Like he sure to die."

33

MEXICANA AIR HAD a 1:20 A.M. Friday flight from Tijuana to Cancun, and another at 9:45 A.M. She could always become a travel agent if she lost her job, Jessie thought, back at her desk.

She had faxed the warrant and a photo of Ethan to the San Diego police and phoned Detective Masters to confirm that he'd received both.

"I'd like to drive down to San Diego tonight," she told Espes. "Pick up the Meissner boy."

"Do it in the morning. You've had enough driving today. San Diego PD will baby-sit him for us."

"I'd feel better if we had him up here in custody, sir. And I'd like to hear what he has to say."

The lieutenant looked at her thoughtfully. "No overtime."

"No overtime," she agreed.

"You can't go alone. I'll have Kolakowski drive you down in a black-and-white. Easier to transport the suspect back up here, anyway."

"Thank you, sir."

"What time did you say the bus arrives?"

"Six-fifty-five, sir."

She contacted San Diego and gave Masters her cell phone number, then met Stan Kolakowski downstairs in the lobby and walked with him to the Butler parking lot. She'd worked with him several times and didn't mind the prospect of being in a car for two hours each way with the veteran patrol officer.

She and Ezra had finished the tuna sandwiches on the way home from Big Bear, but there were a few Sausalito cookies left and a bag of potato chips. She retrieved them from her Honda and joined Kolakowski in the black-and-white. Using her cell phone, she left Ezra a message telling him she had to cancel their dinner date because of police business.

"I'll call you when I get home, if it's not too late," she told the machine.

She checked her home phone messages. Her sister had called, and her mother. Nothing from her father. Well, she couldn't do anything about that now. Maybe tomorrow. She phoned her sister, told her she'd be out late, and was relieved to hear that Frances was out having a facial.

At a quarter to six rush hour traffic on the 405 South was predictably heavy. She tapped her foot impatiently.

"A parking lot," Kolakowski said. "Are we in a hurry?"

"Yeah." They couldn't reach San Diego before the bus did, and Jessie felt confident that the police had everything under control, but she wanted to be there as quickly as possible, to see this teenager she'd been hunting for three days and had lost twice.

Kolakowski flipped on the siren and lights. He found open pockets in the traffic, weaving in and out of lanes with a smoothness that impressed her. Ten minutes later he was doing over ninety. Night had fallen, and the only scenery was the glare of the headlights of the oncoming cars and the well-lit billboards on either side of the freeway.

At 6:10 they were nearing Long Beach, and she phoned Masters.

"We have plainclothes detectives at the aunt's house," he told her. "We have four units at the bus station, waiting. Don't worry, Detective Drake. We'll have your guy gift-wrapped for you."

She thanked the detective and hung up. She was tired, emotionally and physically, but she chatted with Kolakowski for a while until the yawns overpowered her.

"Why don't you take five," he told her. "I'll wake you when we get there."

It was nice to be able to relax. She shut her eyes and thanked Espes silently for giving her Kolakowski, who was a pleasant cop and good driver, not like some who hit the brakes often and made her stomach churn.

She hadn't planned to fall asleep, but she must have, because Kolakowski was calling her name.

"Your cell phone's ringing," he told her.

She flipped open the phone and checked her watch. 7:04. "Detective Drake."

"Detective, this is Larry Masters. I hate to tell you this, but your guy's not here."

Damn Celeste Bushnell for lying! "He's not on the bus?" Jessie sat up straight, rigid with tension. Her heart was pounding.

"Nope. I talked with the driver. He made no stops, so no one got off. We have the aunt's place under surveillance. There's a man inside, and two kids. A car in the driveway."

What the hell was going on? "Can you leave two units at the bus station, in case he took the next bus? And send two units to the train station?"

"Already done. We'll alert the border officials and give them copies of the suspect's photo."

"Thanks. But no roadblock, okay? If he hasn't crossed yet, I don't want to alert him that we're on to him. This may be our best chance to catch him." It was probably too late, she thought. Too damn late. "Where's the international airport in Tijuana?"

"Right across the street from the border. Where are you now?"

She turned to Kolakowski. "Where are we now?"

"We just passed Oceanside. Should be in San Diego in less than twenty minutes."

She repeated that to Masters. "We're heading straight for the border crossing in San Ysidro. I'll be in touch when we get closer. Sorry about this. The foster mother swore he was on that bus."

She would personally handcuff Celeste Bushnell and cart her off to jail, Jessie told herself. Unless Gideon Meissner had given Celeste the wrong information—intentionally. Maybe something in her voice had alarmed him. Or maybe he just didn't trust her.

"One more thing," she told Masters. "Can you find out whether the aunt has another car, and if so, the license plate number."

"Will do."

She phoned Greyhound. The next bus from Los Angeles had left at five and was to arrive at eight. From AMTRAK she learned that Ethan could have taken a 4:15 train, which would have arrived in San Diego at 6:50, or the 5:05, which would arrive in half an hour at 7:35. There was a 3:00 bus, but the teenager couldn't have made it from Big Bear to downtown L.A. in time. Ditto for the 2:00 train.

She contacted Masters and relayed the information just as she spotted the first of several warning signs picturing a family, holding hands, running. The signs were intended to alert motorists to pedestrians, usually illegal aliens, who might be running across the freeway, trying to elude a border patrol that would capture them and return them to Mexico.

Not many people tried to escape the other way, she thought as she settled back against the seat.

They were nearing San Ysidro when her phone rang again.

"He's not on the seven-thirty-five train," Masters reported. "My guess is he took the earlier one, which arrived at six fifty."

"So he could have crossed by now."

"Could have. But they had to drive from downtown San

Diego to San Ysidro. That's twenty miles. Plus there's usually traffic when you near the border."

She hoped so.

There were six long rows of cars heading toward the border crossing booths under the white concrete overpass that announced MEXICO in large letters. There was also a long queue of pedestrians. As a young girl Jessie had visited Tijuana once with her parents and Helen. Frances had complained about the dirt and the noise and the children hawking souvenirs, but she'd been delighted with a marble chess set and a leather bag that she'd picked up cheap.

Kolakowski drove the black-and-white between the two outer right lanes and parked ten feet from the border. Exiting the car, Jessie shivered in the cold night air and wished she'd worn something warmer than her light navy jacket. With Kolakowski behind her, she approached the Mexican border official sitting inside the booth and presented her badge.

"One moment, please," the dark-haired woman said in a clear, accented English.

Jessie scanned the lanes of vehicles but didn't really expect to see Ethan Meissner in one of them. Most visitors to Tijuana parked in one of the day lots near the border and walked across. It was easier, and cheaper than having to obtain Mexican auto insurance, which was mandatory. It was less complicated, too, in case you did have car problems or an accident. From everything Jessie had heard, you didn't want to have to deal with the Mexican authorities.

And getting out was faster. The cars were moving toward the Mexican border at a quick pace, but from the road trip her family had taken deeper into Baja California, she knew that entering the United States could take over an hour. Sitting in her father's air-conditioned Cadillac that crept forward at a snail's pace along with all the other cars, the windows firmly closed at Frances's insistence, she'd been fascinated by Mexican vendors of all ages weaving around the cars, tapping on windows ("Ignore them, they'll go away"), trying to make a last-minute sale. A turquoise bracelet, a wallet, a handwoven rug, a poncho.

A husky man wearing a denim jacket walked over to Jessie and extended his hand. The breeze had tousled his light brown hair. "Detective Drake? Larry Masters. You made good time."

He had a pleasant smile and seemed unreasonably relaxed, she thought as she shook his hand and introduced Kolakowski. Then again, Ethan Meissner wasn't his to lose a third time.

"We've alerted all the border crossing officials," he told her. "They all have a copy of Meissner's photo and his name. He can't cross by foot or by car without showing a birth certificate or passport."

Unless he'd done so before they'd arrived. "Where are your units stationed?"

"One at every booth. No roadblock, per your request. Good call, by the way." He smiled again. "There *is* another car—a tan Dodge Caravan. Hasn't been spotted yet."

She nodded, eyeing the crowd of pedestrians walking toward her. Couples, a few families with young children, though most families probably visited earlier in the day. Tourists eager for a taste of Mexico and some bargains.

"I'm going to search the crowd," she told Masters.

"I'll come with you. You take the right, I'll take the left."

After asking Kolakowski to remain at the booth, she began walking against the human traffic, the photo of Ethan Meissner in her hand.

Twenty feet ahead was a tall boy wearing a black jacket and black baseball cap. With his head kept low, he was studying the ground as he shuffled forward with the line.

Her heart skipped a beat. She opened her purse and slipped her hand around the handle of her gun.

When she was two feet away, she signaled to Masters, who immediately crossed to her side.

She touched the boy's arm. "Can I see your passport, please?"

He looked up, startled, and jerked his arm away. "Don't they do that up there?" he asked, pointing toward the booth.

Brown eyes, black hair, a thin mustache she hadn't expected. He didn't look exactly like the boy in the photo, but with the mustache she couldn't be sure.

"Passport, please," she repeated.

He fished inside the pocket of jeans too tight to conceal a gun and produced a passport.

Seth Winters. The photo ID matched.

Feeling a sharp jab of disappointment, she thanked him and moved on. Masters returned to the other side of the line.

Fifty feet ahead she spotted another boy wearing a visored cap, this one navy. White sweatshirt with a sports logo, the straps of a black backpack visible around his shoulders. Their eyes locked. He couldn't have known who she was, but he froze, like an animal instinctively sensing that the hunter is near. He turned around suddenly and pushed his way into the crowd.

She shoved her way through to Masters. "He's here," she whispered excitedly. "He's wearing a navy sports cap and a white sweatshirt."

She moved back outside the line. Her heart pounding, she sprinted between the gawking pedestrians and the cars and searched for the blue visor, aware that by now he could have tossed it.

She reached the end of the line at the same time Masters did. Nothing. Her heart was racing.

"He couldn't have disappeared." Masters said.

He had probably waited until just before she'd passed him, she decided, then reversed direction and continued toward the booth. She said this breathlessly to the detective and asked him to wait at the end of the line while she checked up ahead.

This time she worked inside the crowd. She elbowed around people, ignoring their protests, until she spotted the white sweatshirted tall figure with a black knapsack strapped to his back.

He was about fifteen rows ahead of her.

She narrowed it to ten. "Police!" she yelled. "Step aside!"

The crowed parted like the Red Sea.

He darted to his left, weaving in between the cars as he moved away from the booths.

She raced after him, her weapon drawn.

"Stop or I'll shoot!" she yelled.

Masters was running toward the boy. From the booths at the border crossing, Kolakowski and uniformed San Diego police converged, forming a circle around him.

The boy stopped suddenly in front of a car and raised his hands.

"Don't shoot!" he screamed. "Don't shoot!"

Holding her gun with both hands, Jessie approached cautiously. Masters, Kolakowski, and two uniformed police followed, tightening the circle.

A tall woman wearing a short quilted jacket over her jeans came running from the parking lot area. "Don't hurt him!" she shrieked. "Please, don't hurt him!"

One of the uniformed officers stopped her. "Stand back, ma'am."

"That's my nephew! Why are you holding him?"

"You'll have to wait here, ma'am."

"There are five weapons aimed at you," Jessie warned the boy. "Don't move a muscle. Search him," she instructed Kolakowski.

"Eitán, I'm here!" the woman yelled.

The officer walked up to Meissner and patted him down. Unzipping the backpack compartments, he checked the contents and shook his head. "He's clean."

"Lower your hands slowly, Ethan, and place them behind your back," Jessie ordered.

The teenager obeyed.

She removed the backpack, slipped on the handcuffs, and locked them. "Turn around slowly."

Finally she was face-to-face with Ethan Meissner. She had been prepared for sullenness, defiance, possibly even a smirk. But his pale face was expressionless, his brown eyes glazed, as if he didn't know what had happened.

"You're under arrest," she told him.

He didn't answer, didn't make a gesture. He looked like a scared kid about to cry, but she refused to feel an ounce of sympathy. Holding the gun to his back, she walked him to the black-and-white, opened the back door, and ordered him inside.

"Where are you taking him?" the woman cried. "Eitán, don't be scared, Eitán!"

"Doesn't look like you'll be going to Cancun after all," Jessie told him. "*Que lastima*." What a pity.

Wasn't *that* the truth.

34

ORIT YARDENI, ETHAN'S thirty-six-year-old aunt, was slender, with olive skin, dark brown eyes, and black hair like her brother's. Her Israeli accent resembled his, too, though her syntax was more American. She was concerned about her nephew but apparently unintimidated by the fact that she was being questioned. She insisted she'd known nothing about Ethan's being a fugitive.

"Gidón phoned me in the afternoon," the woman told Jessie in an interrogation room at the San Diego police station. "He asked me to meet Eitán at the train station and drive him to the border crossing. He said Eitán was flying to Cancun for a week or so."

"You didn't think it was odd that Ethan was going to Mexico in the middle of November?"

"Gidón said Eitán was traumatized by Ronnie's murder, and the family thought he needed to get away from all the publicity."

Jessie looked dubious. "Why not fly from L.A.? Why from Tijuana?"

"I asked him. Gidón said there were no last-minute flights available from L.A, and the San Diego flights connect to Cancun through L.A., so that left Tijuana."

A great story. Jessie wondered whether Gideon had sold this bill of goods to his sister, or whether they'd concocted it together in case Ethan was caught. She'd learned nothing from the teenager himself. He'd refused to say a word to Jessie or to anyone else and was in a holding cell, where he would stay until Jessie and Kolakowski delivered him to a Culver City jail cell.

"You and your brother are close?" Jessie asked.

"Yes, sure." Orit nodded. "We're the only two here in the States. I wish I lived closer to Los Angeles, so that we could see each other more. Especially now, when he is going through this terrible time."

"How long have you been living in San Diego?"

"Eight years. My husband is teaching economics at the university here. It's not Israel, but it's nice." She smiled quickly, then frowned. "I still don't understand what has happened. You arrested Eitán. Why?"

If she was pretending, Jessie thought, she was doing a credible job. "He stole a car, Mrs. Yardeni. And he may be involved in Dr. Bushnell's murder and the murders of his receptionist and nurse."

The woman clucked.

"You don't seem shocked," Jessie said.

"To be honest, I haven't spent much time with my nephew. What I know, I hear from Gidón. Even when Eitán was little, he was a problem. Angry much of the time, unhappy, getting in fights in school. He stole candy from a store once. Lately I hear the boy is troubled. He's drinking, doing drugs. I'm sad, but not surprised. The whole thing is sad. And for my brother, another tragedy." She sighed.

"You're referring to his wife's suicide."

"Yes. I moved here two years after. But I came to stay with Gidón for a few weeks when it happened. He was broken. He couldn't function, couldn't take care of Eitán. So I took care of the boy. But eventually I had to go back to Israel, to my family. And then Ronnie and Celeste took him in." She shrugged.

"Your brother says they stole his son."

Orit nodded. "Gidón likes to be dramatic—he's an artist,

yes? But in this he is right. Oh, he helped them do it. I *begged* him to take Eitán and move back to Israel. But he wouldn't. He didn't want to let the boy live with Ronnie and Celeste, but Celeste pushed and pushed, and Gidón knew he could not take care of him by himself. So what choice did he have? And he wasn't thinking clearly for months after Lucy killed herself. A thing like that, it leaves scars. It's no wonder Eitán is troubled."

"I understand that Ethan found his mother's body."

"Can you imagine the shock?" The woman's eyes flashed. "Even now, when I think of it, I am angry. That she should be so selfish, that she would allow her child to find her! I cannot understand how a mother can do this. But Lucy was always selfish."

Interesting. This was the first time Jessie had heard any criticism of the dead woman. "She was depressed."

"Yes, sure. *Depressed*." The sarcasm was unmistakable. "Look, I didn't know Lucy so well, okay? I met her once before the wedding, then a few times when I came to visit them in Los Angeles. But I heard from my brother all the time that he is having problems. Do you know after Eitán was born, for *two months* she did not take care of him?"

There was a great deal of resentment here, Jessie thought. Why? "She had postpartum depression. You can't really blame her for that."

"And after? Gidón wanted very badly to come back to Israel. A wife should support her husband, no? But Lucy refused. A wife should help her husband in his career, but for Lucy, it was always about what *she* needs, what *she* wants. Even if it ruins her marriage." Her mouth curled in derision. "I'm sorry. Gidón would not like that I am telling you this."

"Celeste Bushnell says your brother has a drinking problem, that he hasn't really held down a real job, that he has a temper. Maybe that contributed to your sister-in-law's depression." She was deliberately goading the woman, although she wasn't sure what she would learn.

"Gidón is not perfect." The sister leaned forward. "But *why* was he drinking?" she asked, her voice low, urgent. "Why was he unhappy? Ask Celeste *that*!" She moved back angrily against the chair. "But of course, she won't tell you. And maybe, to be fair, she doesn't know."

"Doesn't know what?" Jessie asked.

"If a wife is not behaving like a wife, what should a man do?" Orit Yardeni demanded. "If a wife cheats on a husband, maybe he doesn't have the mind to be creative, the drive to succeed. So he starts to drink, to forget his problems. But it's easier to blame Gidón. Safer."

"Lucy was unfaithful to your brother?"

"He wasn't sure, but he suspected. In his heart he knew." She tapped her chest. "A thousand times he cried to me. A thousand times I told my brother to divorce her, but he refused. He was terribly in love with her, even though she made him crazy with jealousy. I feel sorry for Eitán, growing up in that home. You asked me why I wasn't surprised when you said he might have killed someone? This is why."

"Did your brother know who she was having an affair with?"

The woman laughed and shook her head. "My God, you still don't get it? It was Ronnie. Always, it was Ronnie."

❖ 35 ❖

"I'D LIKE TO help you," Jessie told the teenager. He was sitting at the other side of the small, scarred table, in the same chair his father had occupied yesterday.

The tape recorder was running, though she wasn't sure why she'd bothered. The boy still had not said one word. He hadn't asked for an attorney, though Jessie had read him his rights. He hadn't asked to make a phone call, either, not in San Diego, not here in West L.A., where he'd been booked. Phil had offered to come in, but Jessie had told him to stay home. If the boy talked at all, he'd be more likely to do it if Jessie was alone.

"I'm sure you'd like to clear all this up," Jessie said. "I can tell that it's weighing on you. You left a note in the car you stole. You said you were sorry. I believe you, Ethan. I believe you *are* sorry."

Silence.

"You're scared, Ethan, and I don't blame you. You're scared of what will happen to you if you tell the truth, but you'll feel much better getting things off your chest. I know I would." She paused a moment, but there was no reaction. "You've been through a great deal, Ethan. We know that. We talked to your father. We talked to Mrs. Bushnell. She told us about your mother's tragic death. She loves you, Ethan. She's concerned about you." Still no response. "Adrienne's worried, too. I know how much the two of you love each other. I can imagine how devastated you were when Dr. Bushnell forbade you to see her."

Something flickered in his brown eyes.

"You must have been depressed. You must have been angry. I would have been," Jessie said softly. "All these years he said you were like a son to him, and now he's telling you you're not good enough for his daughter! That's a terrible feeling, isn't it? To feel rejected by the people who said they loved you. Maybe you thought they were always lying.

"Sometimes people have terrible feelings that make them do things they normally wouldn't do," she continued when he didn't answer. "They feel trapped, desperate. We understand that. We take it into consideration. Do you want to tell me where Kevin Hayes is, Ethan? His family is anxious about him. They would appreciate anything you could tell them."

It was as though she were talking to a mannequin. She wondered whether he was listening, or whether he'd tuned her out. From the glassy expression in his eyes, she couldn't tell. "We know you're sorry for what happened, Ethan. You said so in the note. You were standing at the edge of the cliff, crying. You were thinking of jumping, weren't you? Of ending it all. I can understand that feeling, Ethan. I know how scary it is, standing next to a cliff, feeling the pull. Those roads make me very nervous. But you didn't jump, Ethan. Your family's glad. I'm glad, too. We all want to help you."

He clasped his arms and stared at a spot above Jessie's head.

"Rabbi Klingerman thinks very highly of you, Ethan. He believes in you."

A spasm pulled at the boy's cheek. His lips trembled. She felt gratified at having elicited a reaction, though small.

"The rabbi told me you've made remarkable progress in the three weeks you were with him. He's concerned about you. We all are."

"Can you talk to him for me?" His voice was low and

husky and without urgency or intonation, as though he were under hypnosis or talking in his sleep.

"You're entitled to make a phone call, Ethan. Is that who you want to call?"

"I want you to tell him that I'm sorry about the car. That I'm sorry I disappointed him."

"You must have been frightened, or you wouldn't have stolen the car. Why were you frightened? Because of what happened to Dr. Bushnell? To Kevin Hayes? If you tell me, I can try to help."

He didn't answer. Not that question, nor any of the others she posed in the next few minutes. When she saw there was no point in continuing, she called for the guard.

Her father showed up at eleven-thirty, not long after she arrived home, bone weary and ravenous, irked again with the budget cuts that had eliminated the West L.A. jail a while back and made it necessary to transport Ethan to the jail at Pacific Station on Culver and Centinela.

She opened the door wearing her raggedy pajama bottoms and a fleece top. Her hair was pulled into a messy knot, and a pimple was threatening to erupt on a cheek scrubbed free of makeup. Frances would have criticized, but her father never did. His unconditional acceptance usually pleased her, but sometimes, like now, she felt as though he didn't care enough about anything to be bothered.

He hugged her and kissed her as always, but there was something tentative about the embrace. "I've been calling and calling from Helen's," he told her with the forced casualness of a man who had to share something unpleasant. "Then the line was busy, so I knew you were still up."

She'd been on the phone with Ezra when she heard the doorbell. Talking, laughing. Now the tension was back, along with the stinging hurt she'd felt at her father's uncharacteristic sharpness the day before. "I got home a short while ago—from San Diego, as a matter of fact. When did you get to L.A.?"

"Around eight. What were you doing in San Diego?"

"Chasing a fugitive."

"I hope you got him." He smiled.

"I did." She hoped a night in a jail cell would encourage Ethan Meissner to talk.

She stood at the counter and spread tuna on the English muffin she'd toasted to an almost charcoal state. "Want one?" she offered. "I haven't had supper." Not real food, though she'd polished off the cookies and the chips. So much for attaining Carla Luchins's slim thighs in this lifetime.

"No, thanks. I ate at Helen's." Her father glanced at her critically. "You look exhausted. Are you getting enough sleep, sweetheart?"

Her mother could say almost the same thing and make her bristle. "I'm okay. It's been a long day." She placed a slice of tomato on each muffin half and took the plate and a glass of nonfat milk to the table. "Did you talk to Mom?"

"I haven't seen her yet." He sat down across from Jessie. "She went to the theater with friends and isn't back. It's just as well. I wanted to talk to you first, Jessie. I felt bad about the other night."

She felt bad, too, but refused to make it easy for him. "Mom's the one who's upset. She deserves an explanation, Dad. She's very hurt."

"I know. I'm just not sure what to tell her."

She gazed at him. "So you *are* having an affair?"

"Don't be ridiculous!" He looked annoyed, then sighed. "I didn't want to bother anyone with this, but I guess I have no choice."

She felt a twinge of fear, and her appetite was suddenly gone. She'd been harboring resentments for years toward her father, and especially during the past few days. Now God was going to punish her.

"With what?" she asked quietly, bracing herself as she ran through a catalog of dire possibilities.

"I have Parkinson's, Jessie. I've had it for a while."

Parkinson's, she repeated silently. Parkinson's, she consoled herself, could be ultimately debilitating, but it wasn't as bad as Lou Gehrig's or a host of other catastrophic illnesses. Still, she felt as though she'd slammed into a wall. Tears stung her eyes, but she forced them back. Her father needed optimism, not pity.

She moved to the chair next to him and squeezed his hand with both of hers. "How long have you known?"

"About six months. I noticed a twitch in my finger. I ignored it—that's a doctor for you. We always make the worst patients." He smiled lightly. "But the twitch spread to my entire hand. So I had Mark run some tests."

Mark Ohlmeyer was his best friend and a fellow internist. In her mind she reviewed her father's appearance on the dozen or more times she'd seen him in the past six months. Aside from a few more lines around his eyes and a little more gray in his thick hair, she'd noticed nothing.

"What does Mark say, Daddy?"

"He said my condition's not bad at all. He put me on something called Mirapex, which is controlling the shaking, thank God." He held up his hand to demonstrate its steadiness. "The drug has possible side effects—hallucinations, extreme drowsiness." He grimaced. "Not fun, I'm sure, but I've been lucky so far, and maybe I'll continue to be lucky."

Jessie nodded. And if he wasn't?

"If the symptoms worsen, there are other drugs and new surgeries, including fetal-cell implantation. Mark says there have been amazing results. But that's premature."

"Absolutely." She tried to absorb what her father was telling her, tried not to imagine this handsome, distinguished-looking man shaking uncontrollably, falling. "The times Mom phoned you at the office and didn't find you there—you were at Mark's?"

Her father nodded. "That, and a therapist. Depression is one of the symptoms of Parkinson's. I suppose that's why your mother says I've been distracted. I told you I'm considering retiring. That's true. Right now I'm functioning fine, but I can't predict how long that will last. Mark says not to do anything rash, but I need to have a plan."

"I think he's right. You should stay busy, active."

"If I can, I will."

"Why haven't you told us, Dad?"

He sighed. "I wanted to wait until it was necessary. I didn't want any of you to worry."

"I'm a big girl, Dad. If you're not well, I want to know. I want to help."

"I know. That's why I'm here." He put his arm on her shoulder and kissed her cheek. "Helen's pregnant—I don't want to ruin what should be a happy time for her. As for your mother, she won't be able to handle this. That's why I don't want to tell her now, or your sister."

"They'll find out eventually, Dad. They'll be hurt that you didn't share this with them, and angry with me for hiding the truth."

"I'll tell them the truth—that I made you promise. I don't want to upset your mother if I don't have to, Jessie."

She felt a flicker of impatience. "No, of course not. We don't want to upset Mom."

He frowned. "What?"

"Nothing. I'm sorry." Now wasn't the time. "She's your wife, Daddy, not your child. She has a right to know."

Her father shook his head. "She'll be terrified. She's always counted on me to be there for her. She calls me her rock. If I tell her, she'll imagine the worst."

"You can explain it to her, the way you just did to me. There are drugs, there are surgeries. They're doing more and more research to find a cure."

"You're being rational, Jessie. Your mother won't be able to do that."

"She isn't made of glass, Dad. She's strong. She's a survivor."

"She's a woman who to this day needs to know where I am almost every minute of the day. She was like that with you girls, too."

"She's controlling, Dad." The words flew out of Jessie's mouth. It was the first time she'd ever criticized her mother to her father.

He gave her a hard look of disapproval. "Yes, she is. The war did that to her. Losing her parents, her siblings, her extended family. Her father promised he'd come back, but he never did. Can you imagine what your mother must have felt?"

"No, I can't," Jessie said quietly. It was another piece of the puzzle that was her mother.

"Well, try to remember that the next time you think your mother's controlling." He paused. "When I was in medical school, your mother would wait up till three or four in the morning, sometimes all night, just to see me. She was *sure* that I wouldn't be coming home, that something terrible had happened to me. Even now when I'm ten minutes late, she's phoning the hospitals. She's been living her life expecting disaster to strike, Jessie, but she's not really prepared for it. And that's how she'll see my illness."

It was confusing, hearing things that made her want to cry for her mother when she still couldn't let go of the anger. "Did you ever suggest therapy, Dad?"

He nodded. "She was insulted. She told me she wasn't crazy. People from her generation and background are suspicious of psychologists, Jessie. They don't think anyone can help banish their demons and don't see the point in trying."

"Too bad. It might have helped all of us." There, she'd said it. She felt a thrill of fear and heady excitement, like an acrobat taking a step onto a tightrope without a safety net to catch him.

"What are you talking about?"

"Come on, Dad. You know what I mean. It's the way we've lived our lives, pretending that we're this perfectly happy family, that there are no skeletons in the closet."

"We *are* happy, Jessie. Look, every family has differences. And yes, we've had our share. I wish that Helen had had an easier time of things, but she seems to be doing fine. She and Neil are happy about the baby, and Matthew is doing great. I wish you and your mother were closer, but things between you seem much better lately."

He was either clueless or in denial. She wanted to say no, wanted to *demand* that he acknowledge the truth: that Frances had abused her daughters; that he had known and done nothing about it. But she couldn't. Not now, not tonight when he was so vulnerable. Maybe never.

"Promise me you won't tell your mother or sister, Jessie."

"I don't want to be part of another lie, Dad."

"Do it for your mother's sake, Jessie."

"Mom's better off hearing the truth. She's convinced you're having an affair."

"I'll convince her otherwise. She'll believe me."

Jessie hesitated. "She thinks you're not physically attracted to her. That you're not . . . interested." God, this was awful. Her cheeks were hot.

"She told you that?" Her father was blushing, too. "It isn't that I'm not interested. I'm just . . . well, there are other symptoms."

"Tell her, Dad."

He kissed her again and pushed his chair back. "I'll think about it."

The muffins were cold and tasteless but she downed them with a cup of Red Zinger tea. After brushing her teeth, she shut off all the lights and went to bed. The new down comforter she'd bought at Strouds was heavenly, and she luxuriated in the instant warmth, but she had difficulty falling asleep. She couldn't stop thinking about her father.

She padded into the den, chilly with the heat turned down, and switched on the TV. Wrapped in a brown-and-cream afghan her friend Hilda, an elderly Holocaust survivor, had crocheted for her, she flipped through the cable channels looking for a movie, but nothing appealed to her.

A book, she thought. Rising with the afghan, she stood in front of the built-in, overcrowded wood bookshelf and scanned the outer row of paperbacks. Behind them she spotted her college texts. Joyce's *Ulysses*, *Eleven Plays of Henrik Ibsen*, the works of Kurt Vonnegut, Tennessee Williams . . .

She pulled down the Ibsen and turned to the contents. *Hedda Gabler*. The play Lucy Meissner had been reading before her suicide.

Curled up on the den sofa, Jessie read about the unhappy wife and her strange relationship with her father; about the way she played with people to ease her boredom; about the lover she urged to kill himself "beautifully"; about the blackmailer who learned her secret and made her desperate enough to take one of her husband's pistols and put a bullet to her temple.

Lucy Meissner had killed herself with her husband's gun. Nobody had said, but Jessie suspected that the woman had shot herself in the temple, too.

And someone had put a bullet to Ronald Bushnell's temple, Jessie recalled with a shiver only partially caused by the room's frigid temperature. Probably after he was dead, according to Futaki.

Which made it all the more interesting and disturbing.

❖ 36 ❖

FUTAKI'S FAXED AUTOPSY results reported no surprises.

Marianna Velasquez had died from carotid arterial hemorrhaging. Nicole Hobart had bled to death from her abdominal wounds. Bushnell's aorta and liver had been perforated. His head wound, the medical examiner confirmed, had been postmortem, and bullets recovered from all three victims had come from a nine millimeter weapon.

But not, according to a Ballistics tech that Jessie talked to early in the morning, from Gideon Meissner's Walther.

She scowled at the receiver as though it were responsible for the bad news and slammed it down.

"What?" Phil asked. He'd come to work achy and congested and had littered his desk with tissue boxes and a pharmacy of lozenges and pills.

"Meissner's gun isn't the murder weapon."

He grunted. "Shit."

Jessie brooded for a while, doodling on a pad. "Remember how smug the dad came across when we grilled him? He wasn't worried, because he *knew* the Walther wasn't the murder weapon. That's why he didn't make that big a deal out of letting us search the vacant apartment."

"How could he *know*, Jessie?"

She smiled grimly. "Exactly."

Phil snorted. "*That* again? You spent the whole day chasing the kid, you finally catch him, and now you're saying the *dad* did it?"

"According to Meissner's sister, Lucy Meissner and Ronnie Bushnell were having an affair for years. Meissner suspected all along."

"So why off Bushnell now, ten years after the fact?"

"Because he's enraged that Bushnell, who did his wife and stole his son, is now rejecting the son. It's the last straw." She was encouraged by Phil's nod. "So he killed Bushnell in an alcoholic rage and tried to ship the kid out of the country 'cause the kid knows something that would implicate him." Jessie paused. "Or, he wants to make the kid look guilty to deflect suspicion from himself."

"Nice dad." Phil crunched the lozenge he'd been sucking.

"He knows there's no physical evidence connecting the kid to the murders."

"So why'd he try to hide the Walther?"

"He didn't want questions. But ultimately he wasn't worried."

"Even if my head didn't feel like a wet towel, I'd have a hard time keeping up." Phil kneaded his forehead. "Okay, say it's the dad. Why would he kill Kevin Hayes? Or are you saying it's just one big fat coincidence that Kevin and the mom's Glock disappear right after the murders? Did you talk to the housekeeper?"

"I stopped at the Hayes's house on the way to the station this morning. Sally says the woman didn't show up. She thinks she's nervous about being questioned by the police—apparently, she's an illegal. Hayes gave me a phone number for the housekeeper, but no one's answering."

"So we don't know who took the Glock. You asked Ethan about the Hayes kid, right?"

"He didn't respond. But I've been giving it some thought." She'd had plenty of time last night when sleep had eluded her. "We've been checking hospitals and police reports and the morgue, and there's no sign of the kid. I think he's alive."

"So why is he on the lam?"

"Suppose the Hayes kid heard about the murders Monday night when he was at his dad's. It was all over the news, or maybe a classmate phoned and told him."

Phil held his coffee mug to his mouth, inhaling the steam. "Go on."

"Suppose he thinks Ethan's the shooter. Suppose he thinks Ethan snapped and is planning to take out everyone who ever pissed him off, and he thinks he may be next. He panics. He cons his dad out of six hundred bucks and takes another six from the ATM. He goes home, takes the gun for protection, and goes into hiding."

"Very nice theory, Jess, but didn't that Knowles kid tell us Hayes and Ethan had squared things? Ethan was helping him with his homework, stuff like that."

"Right. But no one can figure out why. Not Knowles, not Croton, not Ethan's ex-girlfriend, not Celeste Bushnell. Why *would* Ethan suddenly make nice with this kid who was spreading nasty rumors about Adrienne?"

"Okay, Sherlock." Phil smiled. "Why?"

"Hayes knew that Ethan and Adrienne were getting it on. That's what they fought about, right? I think he threatened to tell Bushnell unless Ethan helped him. The ex-girlfriend said Hayes was practically flunking out, and Ethan's a brain."

"So why did Hayes panic?" He tasted the coffee, then took a few sips.

"Because he *told* Bushnell, and Ethan found out." Jessie couldn't read her partner's expression. Only his eyes were visible over the rim of the mug. "Maybe he didn't keep his part of the bargain, or maybe Ethan didn't want to play anymore. Bushnell kicks Ethan out of the house. The rest we know. Another possibility: The mom's telling the truth about Ethan stopping by the house. Kevin hears about the murders. He goes home, finds the gun missing. He knows Ethan took it, 'cause he'd showed it to him, bragged about it. So now he's thinking he's in big trouble with the cops, *plus* Ethan could be gunning for him."

Phil drained the mug and set it down. "Assuming you're right, he should be coming home to mama as soon as he hears that Ethan's in custody."

"When he feels safe." Jessie nodded. "Trouble is, we have no physical evidence tying the dad *or* the kid to the homicides. We're lucky we have the kid on the car theft, although how long we can keep him locked up, I don't know."

"Suppose Hayes has the mom's Glock, and the Walther isn't the murder weapon, what is?"

She didn't know that, either.

"The Bushnell family has hired Gregory Thomason," Debra Bergman said when Jessie was seated in her small Santa Monica courthouse office. "He's very good, and very expensive. I almost worked for him when I started out."

Until a year and a half ago, Jessie knew, the pretty, brown-haired, brown-eyed, thirty-two-year-old deputy district attorney had been a criminal defense attorney. *Our gain*, Jessie thought. The D.D.A. had a quick intelligence, and from Jessie's limited experience (one case four months ago) and from what she'd heard from other detectives, she was an extremely effective prosecutor.

And now she'd asked Jessie to come in and report on the Bushnell triple homicide—the D.A. was impatient and wanted to know why there had been no arrest.

"I'm not surprised," Jessie said. "I'm sure Ethan's aunt reported to her brother that Ethan was apprehended. Meissner must have called Celeste Bushnell. She's devoted to Ethan. She probably feels guilty, too." Jessie gave a brief summary of the boy's history.

Debra sighed. "God, what a mess. You wonder why some people have kids. You'll be interested to know that the boy won't talk to the attorney. He won't say why."

"Pride, maybe. He was rejected by the Bushnells, so now he doesn't want their money or their help."

"The court will assign a public defender. In the meantime, the family is posting the thirty thousand dollars bail today. I don't suppose he'll turn *that* down."

"I doubt it." All that chasing, and for what? "The suspect is a flight risk. He tried fleeing to Israel, then to Mexico. I apprehended him just before he crossed into Tijuana."

"His record is clean, Detective."

"Jessie."

"Only if you call me Debra." She smiled. "Anyway, no priors, and we're talking about a car theft, not a homicide. The judge will knock it down to a misdemeanor, 108.51."

Driving without permission of the owner. Jessie nodded.

"Probably give him a slap on the hand, call it time served. Or drop the charges altogether—Thomason's talking to the cook."

"Rabbi Klingerman's doing, no doubt," Jessie said glumly, although that wasn't really fair—the cook had her car back, undamaged. Why would she waste her time testifying in court? And she'd obviously liked Ethan.

"Who's Klingerman?" Debra wrote down the name.

Jessie explained about the Big Bear seminary and its founder. "He believes Ethan is innocent. He tried stonewalling me, didn't want me to talk to Ethan." She felt renewed anger as she repeated the frustrating exchange. "I pointed out that if he was wrong, Ethan could be a danger to others. That shook him up, and he said he'd talk to Ethan. But by then Ethan was long gone."

Debra was frowning. "I doubt that Judaic law advocates helping a murderer remain free and a danger to others. I'll ask my dad. He's a rabbi, and he knows the entire Talmud by heart."

"Really?" That was a surprise. "What denomination?"

"Orthodox." Debra looked at her curiously. "My whole family is Orthodox. Why?"

"Sorry." Jessie blushed. "I don't mean to sound nosy. I'm taking classes at Ohr Torah, on Pico. With Ezra Nathanson?"

"I don't think I've heard of him. I've definitely heard of the school. So you're studying Judaism?"

Jessie smiled. "It's a long story."

"I'd like to hear it. Maybe we could get together for lunch. Or you could come for a Shabbat meal. Where do you live?"

Ezra would be pleased—he was always telling her to expand her social circle. "West L.A. How about you?"

"On Citrus, just west of Hancock Park. I guess that would be too long a walk. So lunch it is."

Jessie drove on the Sabbath, but maybe Debra wouldn't feel comfortable about that. "Dinner's okay, too."

"Let's make it lunch. I've been married a year and a half, and my husband's still in the honeymoon stage. Not that I'm complaining." Debra laughed.

"Sounds nice," Jessie said with a twinge of envy.

"Anyway, as far as Jewish law goes, in a civil case, if both parties are Jewish, they're supposed to resolve the issue in a Jewish *bet din*, or court of law, rather than in an American court. But if a Jew is subpoenaed by an American court, he has to testify. It's called *dina de'malchusa dinah*. The law of the land you're in has to be obeyed."

"I'll tell Klingerman." Jessie smiled. "By the way, the only reaction I got from Ethan was when I mentioned the rabbi's name. He wanted me to tell Klingerman he was sorry for disappointing him. I told Ethan he was entitled to make a phone call, but he didn't want to do it."

"Interesting." Debra wrote that down. "The D.A. wants an arrest in the Bushnell case, Jessie. He's getting tons of calls a day. You can still talk to Ethan alone, since he's declined to seek counsel. Maybe you can convince Klingerman to get the boy to talk. The problem is, whatever the boy tells Klingerman is privileged."

"The rabbi's already been to see Ethan this morning." Jessie would have paid to be able to listen in on that conversation. "Ethan didn't call him—in fact, he has yet to make a phone call. His father probably called the rabbi."

"How does the boy strike you?"

"He seems dazed. Then again, it's as though he's two people." She described his wildly divergent interests and reputations. "Talk to his English instructor, and he'll tell you Ethan is a terrific, sensitive kid. Talk to some of the others, including his biological aunt and Celeste Bushnell's brother, and they'll tell you he's trouble."

"You're not sure he did the murders, are you?" Debra sounded unhappy.

Jessie hesitated. "To be honest, no. Okay, here's what makes me think he did. He had motive—he was furious with Bushnell for breaking up his romance with Bushnell's daughter. Add to that a drug and alcohol problem. He had opportunity. He tried to flee the country twice, and he stole a car to escape the police."

"What about means?"

Jessie expelled a breath. "We thought we had the murder weapon, but Ballistics says no." She told Debra about Meissner's Walther, then about Sally Hayes's Glock. "Ethan may have the Glock. But if Kevin Hayes has it, Ethan used another gun. In any case, we don't have it."

Debra was watching her, assessing. "But that's not what's bothering you."

"Guns aren't hard to come by, unfortunately. But without a gun with Ethan's prints on it that Ballistics identifies as the murder weapon, we don't have any physical evidence tying the boy to the murders. No identifiable fingerprints at the crime scene. No bloodstained clothing. No shoes that can fit the prints at the crime scene. So I'm not sure." Jessie paused. "Meissner's dad had motive, too. He *hated* Ronnie Bushnell—for having a long-term affair with his late wife who killed herself, for stealing his kid, for rejecting him and driving him out of the house."

"The affair happened ten years ago, right? Why strike now?"

"That's my partner's argument." Jessie nodded. "The affair was ten years ago, but now, when his kid is rejected, the feeling of being wronged all comes back to him. Meissner has a drinking problem, too, and a temper."

Debra grimaced. "Nice family. But the boy did try to flee. Twice, you said."

"Maybe he's scared." Jessie felt again an uncomfortable tug of sympathy for the runaway. "Or maybe the father put him up to it to deflect suspicion from himself, or because the boy knows something that would incriminate the dad."

"Any other suspects?"

"Celeste Bushnell. Meissner's sister doesn't know whether she was aware of her husband's affair with Lucy. What if she was?"

"Again, that was ten years ago," Debra pointed out.

"Maybe she just found out. Suppose Meissner told her *now*, because he's angry that they threw out his son. But Celeste has an alibi. She was shopping with her daughter when Bushnell and the others were killed."

"Have you considered the daughter?"

"Because her father was keeping her from her true love?" Jessie nodded. "As much as anyone else. She seems devastated by his death, but who knows? There's a nurse, too, that Bushnell fired two weeks ago. I think she was having an affair with him. She may be pregnant. I haven't been able to talk to her yet."

"The doctor was some player," Debra said. "Maybe they all killed him. *Murder on the Orient Express*."

Jessie smiled. "In my flights of fancy, I even wondered if the housekeeper did it. She's fiercely loyal to Celeste. What if she found out Bushnell was cheating on her? But she wouldn't have made an appointment for a Clifford Bronte." Jessie explained about the name. "Of course, someone else could have made the appointment and decided not to show."

"So basically, you have nothing that I can take to a jury.

My boss won't be happy." Debra tapped her pen on a legal notepad. "What's your hunch?"

Jessie considered for a moment. "The boy."

Debra nodded. "You need a confession."

"He won't talk."

"Work on him. I'll ask the judge for a bail enhancement. He'll laugh me out of the courtroom, but maybe it'll buy us some time."

Jessie checked her watch. Nine-thirty. "So I have till noon."

"If you're lucky. You have physical evidence connecting him to the stolen car?"

"His fingerprints are on the door and steering wheel and on the note he left. He wrote, 'I'm sorry.'" She'd sent copies of the car theft reports to a judge through the court clerk's office and was waiting for the judge to sign the Probable Cause Declaration.

"Too bad he wasn't more specific. If I know Thomason, he'll claim Ethan was traumatized by the murder of his foster father and took the car because he was desperate to be with his foster mother."

Jessie rolled her eyes. "It's like the definition of *chutzpah*. A boy who kills both parents and pleads for mercy because he's an orphan."

37

IN PERSON BARBARA Martin's hair was a richer auburn than in the photo Jessie had seen. She was tall and needle thin in red Capri pants and a white turtleneck sweater.

"I was away for a few days and was shocked when I heard about the murders on the news. It's so awful," she said in a low, sad voice. "I feel so bad for the families." She was sitting stiffly on the slipcovered sofa across from Phil and Jessie, who were seated on two armless chairs, and she held her curled fists tightly on her lap like pistons. "I just played my messages, and I was going to phone you as soon as I finished unpacking."

Thanks to Melinda Kramer, they'd been informed of the nurse's return. Jessie had been on the way to Pacific Station to have another go at Ethan Meissner when Phil had paged her with the news.

"When was the last time you saw Dr. Bushnell?" Phil asked.

The nurse frowned. "I don't remember exactly. Why?"

"It's routine, ma'am. We're talking to anyone who knew the doctor or either of the two staff people who were killed. We've interviewed the bookkeeper and the nurse who replaced you. I understand that you were fired and that you filed a workmen's comp suit against Dr. Bushnell."

She flushed. "Then you know I haven't been in the office in over two weeks."

"A number of patients think you're a terrific nurse," Jessie said. "They were surprised you were fired. You must have been, too."

"My attorney instructed me not to comment on that." She shifted on her seat.

"You must have been angry," Jessie said. "I would have been."

"I wasn't thrilled," she said dryly. "I'm sure I'll find something else, and I'm collecting unemployment, but it's a hassle, going on interviews, starting over."

Phil said, "We have a witness who heard you wish Dr. Bushnell ill, Ms. Martin. In fact, you wished him dead."

She gripped the edge of the sofa cushion. "Who told you that, Suzanne?" she asked with a flash of anger. Then she sighed. "Yes, I was angry. Yes, I was upset." She turned to Jessie. "I said things I didn't mean in the heat of the moment. It's *ridiculous* to think I had anything to do with the murders."

"Who do you think killed him?" Jessie asked in a conversational tone.

"I don't know. I've been thinking about it nonstop. Dr. Bushnell was a wonderful doctor, and Marianna and Nicole were so sweet." Her forehead was furrowed in concentration. "There was this patient, Carla Luchins? She was calling the office ten times a day, demanding a redo on her nose. Other than that, I can't think of anyone."

Suzanne Ord hadn't come up with any other dissatisfied patients, either. "What about his wife?"

The nurse stared at Jessie. "His wife?"

"Did she know you were having an affair with her husband?"

Color had tinted her cheeks almost the same shade as her hair. "I don't know what you're talking about."

"We have a witness who saw you kissing him. He was upset and told you to stop. We know all about it, Barbara," Jessie said not unkindly. "I don't think it'll be hard to find

other witnesses who saw you together with him. Maybe in
your apartment, maybe at a hotel."

The nurse licked her lips and avoided Jessie's eyes.

"Did Celeste Bushnell know?" Jessie asked again.

Barbara shook her head. "At least, I don't think so. Do
you have to tell her?" she asked anxiously.

"Why did you leave town on Monday?" Phil asked.

"I needed a break. I was drained from everything."

"Everything meaning what?"

She waved her hand. "Being fired, dealing with attorneys.
I had to get away."

"You were having an affair with Dr. Bushnell, and then he
fired you. And you just happened to leave town a few hours
after he's murdered? You expect us to believe that? Where
were you on Monday at four o'clock?"

"I had an appointment."

"With whom?"

Her face was contorted in pain. "I didn't kill Ronnie. I
swear I didn't! Can't you leave me alone? Please!" She
began to cry and buried her face in her hands.

Jessie signaled to Phil to leave her alone. He rose from the
sofa and walked into the dining room.

She moved to the sofa, next to the nurse, and waited until
she'd calmed down. She put her arm around the woman's
shaking shoulders. "You loved him, didn't you?" she said
quietly. "You still loved him, even after he fired you."

The nurse nodded. Tears streamed down her face.

"What happened, Barbara? Why did he let you go?"

She bowed her head.

"Barbara, you can talk to me here, just you and me, or
my partner will take you in for questioning. He may even
detain you." Jessie looked pointedly at Phil's back. "He
can do that, and I won't be able to stop him. He wants answers, Barbara." She paused. "Where were you on Monday
at four? Tell me, and I'll tell him and get him off your
back."

The nurse glanced angrily in Phil's direction, then back at Jessie. "I had a doctor's appointment."

"Which doctor?"

She didn't answer.

"Was it an obstetrician?"

Her head whipped up. "No! What are you talking about?" she demanded indignantly, but the panic in her eyes gave her away.

"Barbara, if you have an alibi, that's great, but you have to be specific, and we'll have to verify it. Even if you don't tell us, we can find out. We can subpoena *all* your doctors' records," she lied. "And then the media may find out, and all of this will become public. Is that what you want? Do you want your parents to hear about your private life on the six o'clock news?"

"I didn't kill him! Don't you understand? I *loved* him! He loved *me*!"

"If he loved you, why did he fire you?"

"He didn't fire me. We had an argument and I quit. Then we made up, but Ronnie thought it was risky for us to continue seeing each other if I worked for him. He was afraid Suzanne would find out. She's nosy, and she has a big mouth."

But the bookkeeper wasn't as perceptive as Jessie had thought. She'd obviously missed something big. "So why did he tell everyone he fired you?"

Barbara hesitated. "Ronnie wanted me to have money, but he couldn't take it out of his accounts, because his wife would find out. Ronnie saw a TV show where this company needed to pay off an employee, but they didn't have the money, so they had him sue them, and the insurance company paid. Ronnie said we could do the same thing."

"Why would you need money, Barbara? Because you're pregnant with his child? That's it, isn't it?"

She shook her head and started to cry again.

Not what she'd expected. Jessie thought for a moment, then nodded. "But you *thought* you were?"

"I miscarried a week ago," she whispered mournfully. "I went for a checkup on Monday, to make sure everything was okay. That was at four. You can check with the doctor. He'll tell you I was there. He said I was fine, but I didn't *feel* fine. I felt so depressed, so guilty. I don't think I'll ever get over it."

"I had a miscarriage, too, Barbara. I understand how you feel." She had felt depressed, too, and guilty. Whenever she saw a pregnant woman, whenever she was with Helen, she mourned the loss and wondered whether she'd ever carry life again.

"And then, when I got home, I heard about Ronnie." Barbara's face twisted. "I couldn't bear it! I had to get away. I didn't even know where I was going, just away."

"When was the last time you saw him?"

"A few days before, when I had the miscarriage. He came to the hospital to see me." Her mouth quivered. "I didn't want to talk to him. I *blamed* him." She was crying quietly.

"Why?" Jessie asked softly. "Why did you blame him, Barbara?" she repeated when the nurse didn't answer.

"He wanted me . . . to have an . . . abortion. I wanted . . . to keep . . . the baby." She was crying harder, gulping between words. "He said—" She sniffed and tried to compose herself. "He said he didn't want to go through this again, that an abortion was the best thing for me, for us. We argued about it, and I wouldn't give in. That was the day I quit, the day I was so mad at him! But God punished me anyway, and now he's *gone*, and I blamed him, and then he died! I don't have any part of him!" Her body was wracked with sobs.

Jessie rubbed the woman's back absentmindedly, thinking furiously. "Barbara, what did Dr. Bushnell mean when he said he didn't want to go through this again. Go through *what* again?" But she already knew. She had one of those moments of clarity, and suddenly everything made sense.

The nurse sniffed again and wiped her nose with the back of her hand. "I guess he meant raising another child. I told him I'd raise the baby on my own. He got upset. He said that I was naive, that there would be problems, there always were. That once the baby came, I'd want him to be there, and if he wasn't, I'd be depressed. He said he wasn't going to leave his wife, and he wasn't going to have anything to do with the baby, and he wasn't going to feel guilty about it." She was crying again, softly. "He was so mean, and I hated him. And now he's dead."

38

"LET ME TELL you a story," Jessie began. It was 10:40, and she was sitting in the interrogation room across the small table from Ethan Meissner, who was wearing a black velvet yarmulke Klingerman had brought him. She'd inserted a fresh tape into the recorder and, after consultation with Debra Bergman, who was at this minute requesting a bail enhancement, had again advised the teenager of his rights.

"Once upon a time there was a little boy, and he lived with his mother and his father. The mother was sad most of the time, but he didn't know why. And the father was angry, because the mother was sad and unhappy."

His face was expressionless, but his eyes flickered, and she sensed he was listening intently.

"One day, when the mother was very, very sad and the father wasn't home, the little boy wanted to play at his friend's house. The mother asked him to stay, but he said please, so she let him go. When he came home, he called her name, but she didn't answer. So he went into her bedroom, and he saw that she had killed herself, with a gun."

The teenager winced, as though recoiling from the sound of the gunshot. She felt no satisfaction.

"The father blamed the son for leaving the mother, and the little boy went to live with a man who was not his father and a woman who was not his mother and a girl who was not his sister. They loved him and took care of him the way his father and mother never could. They told him he was like their son, and he believed them. He worked very hard to make them proud of him, and he avoided his real father, because it brought up so many bad memories, and because he wanted badly to be happy, to be part of a healthy, loving family."

A twitch in the boy's lips showed her she'd struck a chord. She'd heard from the jail personnel that Celeste had visited with Ethan. Gideon Meissner had arrived right after. He'd been furious when told that inmates were allowed only one visitor per day, aside from attorneys or clergy.

"The boy grew up into an intelligent, hardworking, sensitive young man," Jessie continued. "He excelled in school and sports and music, and his new family proved their love and treated him like a son. And all was well. And it came to pass that he fell in love with the beautiful girl who was not his sister. And she loved him, too. But the girl's father was displeased, and he told the young man that this could not be."

Ethan glared at her and averted his eyes.

"Now the young man was confused, because he had believed in the love of this man who was like a father. He became hurt and angry, and he started drinking alcohol and doing drugs to make the man sorry. But he still loved the girl, and the girl loved him. And the girl's father discovered that they were still seeing each other. He was furious with the boy! He yelled at him, and the boy left the house, vowing never to return. The girl was heartbroken, but she had to listen to her father. And the girl's mother was heartbroken, too, because she loved this young man as if he were her own son, but she had to listen to her husband."

Ethan was staring at her now, fascinated. She thought she detected a small, unconscious nod of his head.

"The boy went to his real father, because he had nowhere else to go. The father wanted to send him far away to a school where he could find peace. So the boy listened, and he began feeling better about himself, and he stopped drinking alcohol and doing drugs. But he felt sad about the girl, because he hadn't even said good-bye, and he needed to explain why he couldn't see her anymore."

Ethan was clenching his fists and unclenching them. "I want to go back to my cell."

"The story isn't finished, Ethan. So the boy returned to the house to see the girl. And he loved her one last time, and she loved him. But the father came home and found them together."

"I don't have to listen to this." His lips trembling, he placed his hands over his ears.

"And the man told his daughter to stay in her room, and he took the boy downstairs to his office. And he told the boy what he had not told him before."

Ethan's brown eyes were filled with anguish, and she remembered what the Korean housekeeper had said, that the boy had looked like a person who knew he was going to die.

"He told him why he could never, ever be with the girl again. Years ago he had loved the boy's mother, and the mother had loved him, and from that illicit love had come the boy. And so the girl whom the boy loved was his real sister. And that could never be."

He started to cry. His whole body was convulsed, and tears were streaming down his face. He covered his face with a large hand.

"The boy didn't believe him," Jessie continued over the boy's sobs. "So he went to the man whom he had known to be his father all these years and demanded the truth. The father was shocked. And he was furious. He told the boy that he had suspected that the girl's father and the boy's mother had loved each other, but he had never suspected this."

Jessie sat quietly for a moment. "That's as far as my story goes, Ethan. I need you to tell me the rest. Will you do that?"

"There's nothing else to know," he mumbled through his hand. "You know everything."

"I don't know what happened after that, Ethan. But you do. Did Celeste find out that Ronald was your father?"

"No!" He dropped his hand and revealed a face blotched with tears and drained of color. "She doesn't know, and Adrienne doesn't know. Leave them alone!"

Jessie wasn't sure if she believed him. "Did you go to Dr. Bushnell's office that afternoon? Or did Gideon go?"

"Gideon has nothing to do with this!" the teenager exclaimed quickly. "No one has anything to do with this except me. Not Gideon, or Celeste, or Adrienne. I'm the one who sinned." He slammed his fist into his chest. "No one can help me now except God."

Jessie felt a thrill of excitement. "Did you kill Dr. Bushnell and the others, Ethan?"

"I wanted to die, but Rabbi Klingerman said that's a sin, too," he said in an urgent tone, as though he were seeking absolution. "He said it's not my fault, because I didn't know. But it doesn't change what happened. I'm a *mamzer*, a bastard."

"It's Ronald Bushnell's fault, isn't it, Ethan? He did that to you. And then he didn't tell you the truth, so you allowed yourself to fall in love with Adrienne. With your sister. Did you sleep with her?"

"Yes." The word emerged as a strangled hiss, as if he were choking on it.

"Because he didn't tell you the truth. I feel so bad for you, Ethan. You must have been devastated."

"Do you know what the punishment is for what I did?" he said in a mournful voice. "It's in the Torah. I looked it up. It's called *karet*. You're cut off from the Jewish people forever, for eternity. Not just your body, but your soul. Rabbi Klingerman says in my case that's not so, because Celeste isn't Jewish. So it's not really incest. But he's just saying that. Maybe I won't be punished, because I didn't know, but in God's eyes I'm lost."

"Because Ronald Bushnell didn't tell you. You must have blamed him in your heart."

The boy nodded.

"You must have wanted to punish him for what he did."

He was crying again, soundlessly.

"Did you kill him, Ethan?" Jessie repeated softly. "Did you kill Dr. Bushnell and the others?"

He stopped crying but didn't answer. She listened to the hum of the machine recording the silence.

"If I tell you what happened, what will happen to me?" he asked after a moment.

Her heart pounded. "I don't know. I can't make any promises, but the district attorney will take everything into consideration." It was unlikely the D.A. would ask for the death penalty for an eighteen-year-old suspect.

"I want to talk to Rabbi Klingerman. Is he still here?"

"I'll check."

"I almost killed myself, that day at the cliff. Rabbi Klingerman says it's a sin. He says I should use my life for good, that I have a chance to do *teshuva* for my sins. Penance. I'm ready to do that."

❖ 39 ❖

THIS TIME PHIL was in the room with her. Jessie identified herself for the tape and indicated the date and time. Then she had Ethan state his full name. Again, she advised him of his rights, and had him state clearly that he waived his right to legal counsel.

Ethan seemed strangely calm, and she wondered what the rabbi had said to him. She'd seen Klingerman exiting the visitors' room, after she'd returned from conferring with Debra Bergman. His shoulders had been bowed with weariness, his eyes troubled. They had greeted each other with a stiff awkwardness. She hadn't said "I told you so," and he hadn't apologized.

"Eitán wants to confess," he told Jessie. "But only if he's assured that the district attorney won't go for the death penalty."

"I just spoke to the deputy district attorney. They're willing to take the death penalty off the table. But it has to be a real confession. The D.A. wants details."

"I'll tell Eitán. He needs a lawyer, Detective Drake. I don't think he knows what he's doing."

"He's refused to meet with the lawyer Mrs. Bushnell hired. The court will appoint a public defender." She had also asked Manny Freiberg to evaluate the boy. She'd worked with the department psychologist several times and trusted his judgment.

"By then it may be too late," Klingerman said.

"Let's start with Sunday," Jessie told Ethan now. "When Dr. Bushnell found you with Adrienne in her room."

His face turned pink. "It's like you said. We were . . . doing stuff. He waited outside the room while I put on my clothes, then took me to his office. I told him I was sorry we'd gone behind his back, but Adrienne and I loved each other and wanted to get married as soon as we could. He said that was impossible. He begged me not to see her again. I refused. He threatened to cut us both off. I said we'd make it on our own. That's when he told me he was my father, that he'd had an affair with my mother." He was in control now, his rendition of the story flat and without emotion. Probably the only way he could tell it.

"Where was Adrienne?"

"Upstairs, in her room. She was crying."

"Go on."

"I didn't believe him. I thought he was making it up so that I'd stop seeing Adrienne. But he swore it was the truth. He said he was sorry. He said he'd make it up to me, that he'd call his lawyer in the morning and have him change his will so I would get half of everything, like a son. He wanted me to promise that I wouldn't tell anyone the truth. Not Gideon, not Adrienne, not Celeste."

Ethan ran his hand across his mouth. "I told him I didn't want his money, but he said it was only fair. I was his son, and he loved me. He said he was going to call Adrienne down, and he wanted me to tell her we were through, but not why. So I waited while he got her, and I told her something. I don't remember what I said, but she was crying. Then I left. I couldn't think straight. I couldn't look at him. I thought I was going to be physically sick. I thought I was going to hurt him. I—" He stopped and bent his head.

"What did you do then?" Jessie prompted.

Ethan looked up. "I went to Kevin Hayes's house. I wanted to punch him, to *pulverize* him." He clenched his fists. "I told myself if Kevin hadn't ratted to Dr. Bushnell about me and Adrienne, none of this would be happening. He followed us one time to a hotel." The teenager flushed. "He was waiting when we came out. He said if I didn't write his term papers and essays for him and help him study for tests, he'd tell Ronnie. I didn't care, but Adrienne freaked. So I said okay, I'd help him. But he kept *needling* me and Adrienne, wanting to know details about the sex. I told him the deal was off. He must've gone to Ronnie, 'cause the next night was when we had the big fight and I left the house."

Phil nodded at Jessie, and she was flushed with pleasure. She'd been right about that.

"I hated Kevin, really *hated* him for what he did," Ethan said. "Deep down, though, I knew it wasn't his fault. I guess I needed to hit someone, and I couldn't hit Ronnie. Anyway, Kevin wasn't home. I don't know what I would have done if he'd been there." He frowned.

"What did you do then, Ethan?"

"I went to my father's apartment, but he wasn't home, either. I walked around for hours, I don't know where. When I came back he was there. He was angry, because I was supposed to be in the seminary. I asked him if it was true my mother and Dr. Bushnell had been lovers. He turned purple, and he grabbed me by my collar and told me to shut my filthy mouth. So I told him what Ronnie had said, that I was his son. Gideon got real quiet. He said it wasn't true. He said Ronnie was making it up to keep me and Adrienne apart. But I could tell he didn't believe what he was saying. I could see him watching me, trying to figure out if I looked like Ronnie.

"I hadn't touched alcohol since I was in the seminary, but I drank a whole bottle of my dad's stuff and went to sleep. I dreamed I heard Celeste talking to me, crying, saying she was sorry. I woke up around two in the afternoon with a terrible headache. Gideon wasn't there. I felt hung over and scared and disgusted with myself. When I thought about who I was, and what I'd done with Adrienne, I couldn't bear to be alive. I didn't want to think. I wanted to kill myself. So I drank some more. At some point I decided to go to Ronnie's office." He rubbed the edge of the table.

"Did you want to kill him, Ethan?" Jessie asked quietly. The answer could make a huge difference: murder one—premeditated—or murder two.

"No. I was going to kill myself, right in front of him. I wanted to punish him, to make him suffer like I was suffering. Like he'd made my mother suffer. I took the Metro to the city, then a bus to the office. By the time I got there my head was pounding and pounding, and I was angrier and angrier." Ethan stopped. "So I killed him," he said softly. Tears welled in his eyes. "And the others. I'm sorry for what I did. I wish I could undo it, but I can't. I wish I could undo everything."

"Where is Kevin Hayes, Ethan?"

He frowned. "I don't know. You asked me that last night, right? I couldn't figure out why. I haven't seen Kevin in weeks. The last time was the day before I had that fight with Ronnie."

"Did you take his mother's gun?"

He looked surprised. "The Glock?" He shook his head. "Kevin showed it to me a couple of times, trying to impress me. I took one of my dad's guns. I was going to kill myself in my dad's apartment, then I decided to do it at Ronnie's."

"Your father has more than one gun?" she asked causally. That would explain why Ballistics hadn't made a match between the gun Jessie had found in the vacant apartment and the bullets recovered from the victims.

"He has two. A Walther and a Smith & Wesson. He's had them as long as I can remember." Ethan hesitated. "My mother used the Smith & Wesson to kill herself. I don't know why my father kept it, after that. I took it out sometimes when he wasn't around. The therapist asked me why, but I don't know. That Monday I was glad he kept it. I wanted to use it—the same one my mom used. It seemed right."

Croton had said Lucy had used one of her husband's guns, Jessie suddenly recalled. Phil would have picked up on it, but she'd been too busy showing off for the English teacher. Her earlier self-satisfaction was gone. She was chagrined at not having paid closer attention to Croton, or to Hedda Gabler, who had used one of her husband's pistols to shoot herself. Jessie had read that only last night.

"What time did you get to the office, Ethan?"

"A little after four."

"How did you know Dr. Bushnell would be there?"

"He's always there that time of the day. That's his schedule. He usually stays pretty late."

Jessie exchanged a quick look with Phil. "You didn't make an appointment?"

The teenager narrowed his eyes in concentration. "Maybe. Like I said, I was pretty gone most of the day. I could have called the office. Maybe I called." He nodded.

"Whom did you kill first?"

He frowned. "Marianna, I think. Then Ronnie and the nurse. But I don't know who died first. I was pretty drunk, so it's hard to remember everything."

"Why did you kill Marianna and the nurse, Ethan? You weren't angry at them."

"I don't know why. I was just so angry, angry at everybody. Ronnie, and Gideon, and Kevin, and my mother. I couldn't think clearly. And my head hurt so much. I thought Marianna was going to stop me from going in to see Ronnie. I feel terrible about her little boy," he said softly.

"Tell us about the wounds, Ethan."

He frowned again. "I don't remember much. The room was spinning and my head was pounding. I just kept shooting until there were no more bullets, and then I put in another round and kept shooting. When I was out of bullets, I left and took a bus back to my father's apartment. I changed my clothes, because there was blood on them. When my father came home, I asked him to drive me back up to the seminary."

"You didn't tell him what you'd done?"

"No."

"What time did you get back to your father's apartment?"

"I don't know exactly. It was dark outside. Probably around five-thirty or six. Something like that."

"How did you get back?"

"A bus. And then the Metro."

"Where was Dr. Bushnell when you shot him?"

"Where in his office, you mean?" He hesitated. "I can't remember."

"The nurse?"

He shook his head again. "I'm sorry."

Jessie suppressed a sigh. "What did you do with the gun, Ethan?"

"I wrapped it up in a bag with the clothes I was wearing, because there was blood on them. I took pants and a shirt from my dad's closet. When he drove me back up to the seminary, I pretended to be carsick, so he stopped the car. I got out and threw the gun and clothes over the cliff."

"Would you be able to show us where?"

He shook his head. "It was night, and there are so many spots where we could have stopped."

"Does the name Clifford Bronte mean anything to you?"

The boy flushed. "That was a private joke, between me and Adrienne. It was the name we used whenever we went to a hotel. Mr. and Mrs. Clifford Bronte. It's from *Wuthering Heights*. It's about this guy who's adopted and falls in love with the father's daughter."

Jessie nodded. "Who else knew about Clifford Bronte?"

He thought for a moment. "Celeste. She found love letters I wrote to Adrienne. I signed them Clifford Bronte. I was fooling around." The color in his face had deepened. "She must've told Gideon, because he asked me about it. She promised she wouldn't tell Ronnie."

"What about the housekeeper? Did she know, too?" Jessie asked, just to be thorough.

"Kim? Kim knows everything." A half smile flickered across his sad face.

Jessie showed him the lyrics she'd found. "Can you tell me about this, Ethan? What were you thinking when you wrote those lyrics?"

He read them silently, as if he'd never seen them before. "Where did you find this?"

"Behind a drawer in your desk." The lyrics might prove premeditation, although Thomason would argue to have them excluded, since Jessie hadn't had a search warrant when she'd found them. She would explain that she'd been looking for information that would help her find Ethan, not for incriminating evidence. The lawyers would fight it out, and the judge would rule.

Ethan said, "I was angry at Ronnie, because he didn't want me to see Adrienne. I was angry with Kevin, with everybody. It was the alcohol, too, and the drugs."

She took back the paper. "The district attorney is going to want more details, Ethan. You're going to have to think harder."

"I can't tell you what I can't remember. I remember taking the gun, and being in the office. I remember seeing the blood on my clothes."

Jessie sighed. "Okay. Let's go over it again, Ethan. . . ."

❖ 40 ❖

"HE'S PROTECTING SOMEONE," Jessie told Rabbi Klingerman.
"But you probably know that."

The rabbi nodded. "That's my feeling, yes."

He looked uncomfortable, and she couldn't blame him.
Sitting in the interrogation room wasn't great, but the other
choice was one of the narrow benches, complete with dan-
gling handcuffs, where suspects were usually kept before
being booked. She wished they were on her home turf, at her
desk in West L.A.

"Did he tell you whom he's protecting?" she asked.

"Everything we talked about is privileged."

"He asked to see you before he confessed. Can you tell
me what you talked about, if it's not incriminating?"

"I don't feel comfortable sharing anything Eitán said."

"But you're *comfortable* having him go to jail for the rest
of his life for something he didn't do?" Not that it would
happen. Even the most inept defense attorney would have
the confession tossed as an obvious fake.

"No. Are you *comfortable* accepting a confession that you
know is fake?"

Fair enough. "Did Ethan *tell* you he was giving a false
confession? Help me *help* him, rabbi."

Klingerman didn't answer immediately. "He asked me a
halachic question," he finally said. "A question of Jewish
law. He wanted to know whether it was permissible to con-

fess to a crime if the punishment was death. He wanted to know if that was the equivalent of committing suicide."

Interesting, Jessie thought. Was that why he'd insisted on an answer from the D.A. before he confessed? "What did you tell him?"

"I told him yes. I begged him to reconsider and talk to an attorney."

Jessie nodded. "Because you don't think he should be executed for killing these three people, even if he did it. No witnesses, no warning."

He looked at her steadily. "Correct."

"He's tormented about his incestuous relationship with his sister. He said he'll be cut off from the Jewish people for eternity. If what he did isn't incest, and if he's not to blame, why is he blaming himself?"

The rabbi sighed. "Guilt isn't rational, Detective. He feels tainted because of the biological incest, because he's the product of an adulterous union, which is prohibited by the Torah. A *mamzer*—a bastard. The combination is overwhelming. I think he blames himself because he wants to punish himself. It doesn't have to make sense."

He blamed himself for his mother's death, too, Jessie thought. "What's the practical law in Ethan's case?"

"According to Torah law, it's not incest, because Adrienne's mother isn't Jewish. I explained that to Eitán, but he doesn't seem to believe me. According to rabbinic law, however, he and Adrienne can't marry. And as a *mamzer*, he can only marry another *mamzer* or a convert. The same applies to his children and grandchildren."

"A tough punishment, considering it wasn't his choice to *be* a mamzer. How is that fair?"

"It isn't fair to the individual, but it's essential to the holiness of a nation, to its survival. The law is intended as a strong deterrent to the person about to engage in forbidden sexual practice. People may sin and suffer the consequences of those sins, but most parents don't want their children to suffer because of the parents' sins. And when the Messiah comes, *mamzerim* will be purified."

"That doesn't help Ethan now, does it? He really *is* cut off. Pretty ironic, wouldn't you say? Four weeks ago Ethan wasn't interested in Judaism at all. Then he comes to you, and you help him find himself, help him find the Torah, because it's going to save him, give his life meaning. And now the Torah tells him he doesn't belong, that his life is meaningless after all. He would have been better off not knowing the law, don't you think? At least he wouldn't feel so despondent, so cut off."

"He doesn't *have* to be cut off," Klingerman said earnestly. "I explained that there are girls he can marry—Jewish girls, fine girls. Girls who have the same background, or who have converted to Judaism."

"But he didn't buy it, did he?" She didn't need the rabbi's answer. "No wonder he doesn't mind taking the rap for a crime he didn't commit. What difference does it make? Either way, he figures he's in a prison with a life term."

Debra Bergman pulled over a legal pad. "Okay. Tell me the problem."

"He's vague about all the details," Jessie said. "He can't tell us where he disposed of the weapon and bloodstained clothes. Everything he told us, he could have read about in the newspaper or heard on the radio. The time, the place, the victims. He can't tell us the placement of the victims when he shot them or where on their bodies he shot them, or how many times. He didn't mention the contact wound to Bushnell's head—that surprised me. His mother killed herself with a shot to the temple." Jessie had checked with Croton.

"Reliving the tragedy?" Debra asked.

"If his mother killed herself because she was in love with Bushnell . . ." Jessie shrugged. "My sense—and my partner agrees—is that he's being as vague as possible because he doesn't want to contradict any of the forensic evidence. He's covering up with a story about being drunk. The only thing he told us that we didn't know before is about the money Bushnell offered him. Bushnell's attorney confirmed that Bushnell phoned him early Monday morning and instructed him to change his will so that Ethan would get half of his estate." Too late now—Bushnell had died before he could sign the amended will.

Debra chewed on her upper lip. "It's possible that Ethan *was* drunk, isn't it? He has a history of drinking, like his father."

"It's possible. He said he just showed up at Bushnell's because he knew he'd be there. When I asked if he'd made an appointment, he backtracked and said maybe he had. He didn't *remember*." Jessie made a face. "*Someone* made an appointment using the name Clifford Bronte. Celeste could have made it. Gideon Meissner could have. Adrienne could have, too. Ditto for the housekeeper, although I can't see her doing it." Jessie repeated what Ethan had told her about the name.

"Ethan could have made the appointment. Maybe he really *didn't* remember."

"You're desperate to pin this on him."

Debra shook her head. "Just trying to see the whole picture. Why would he confess to something he didn't do?"

"He's despondent. He doesn't care if he lives or dies—he said as much. The only reason he didn't kill himself is because Rabbi Klingerman told him it's a terrible sin, and he should use his life to do penance."

"So who's he protecting?"

"Could be Gideon. Ethan must feel more guilty than ever about his father—or the man he *thought* was his father. Gideon has a temper. He has a drinking problem. All these years the suspicion that his wife had an affair with Bushnell was eating at him. Now he knows it's true, and he knows they've been making a fool of him all this time. And the wife killed herself—depressed because of Bushnell. It's time to pay."

"Okay." Debra nodded. "But why would he kill the receptionist and nurse?"

"To cover up Bushnell's murder. He has two guns. He uses one for the murders and dumps it somewhere—maybe over a cliff, the way Ethan said. And he hides the other one. He knows Ballistics isn't going to show a match, so he's not really worried. And he tries to get the kid out of the country."

"A plausible theory," the prosecutor agreed. "But you don't have proof. Does he have an alibi?"

Jessie shook her head. "He says he was showing a vacant apartment to a couple. They didn't leave their name."

"Naturally." She smiled.

Jessie smiled, too. "There's also Celeste Bushnell. She was devoted to Ethan, always took his side. She's the one who insisted he come live with them, according to her brother. Maybe Ethan suspects that she did it and wants to repay her kindness. Plus he's got to feel guilty that his mom was cheating with Celeste's husband."

"What do you think?" Debra asked.

Jessie considered. "She's a wreck. Maybe it's her husband's murder. Maybe it's guilt because Ethan's in jail for something she did. She doesn't strike me as all that stable."

"Did she know about the incest?"

"Ethan says no. But what if she found out that night? Can you imagine how she felt—this boy that she'd loved and raised like a son was her husband's illegitimate child? Was sleeping with her daughter?" Jessie sighed. "I could see her flipping out, wanting revenge. That would explain why Bushnell was shot in the groin. Poetic justice."

Debra grimaced. "Why kill him in the office?"

"She doesn't want to involve Adrienne. That's why she kills the others, too. To draw suspicion away from herself. When I was there that first night, the daughter mentioned a patient who'd been harassing Bushnell. Celeste seemed reluctant to believe it. Maybe she didn't want to look too eager. The daughter, on the other hand, was *very* eager to pin it on this patient." Too eager? Jessie wondered.

"You said the mother has an alibi."

Jessie nodded. "The daughter. They were shopping together after school. Maybe the daughter's lying to protect the mom, or to protect herself. I checked my notes before I came here. Celeste was unclear at first about when she phoned her husband that day. She said she was confused, couldn't think straight. The daughter piped up and said they were together. At the time I didn't think anything of it. And the next day when I was talking to the daughter, the mom came in. I had the feeling she was nervous about what the daughter was telling me. But then Celeste told me about Ethan and his fight with Bushnell, so I thought that's what made her nervous." Hindsight, Jessie knew, was often infinitely clearer. "If Celeste *is* the killer, or if she thinks Adrienne is, that would explain why she was so eager to get Ethan out of the country."

"What reason did she give you?"

"She was afraid he'd kill himself if he was locked up."

"She could be telling the truth." Debra thought for a moment. "Or maybe she wanted him away so that the incest wouldn't come to light. Her daughter would have found out. And it would have been all over the media. That would have ruined the daughter's life, and Ethan's. So she was protecting the daughter, and Ethan. Separating them by a continent, hoping they'd lead separate lives."

It made sense, Jessie thought. "I wonder if the daughter knows about the incest. Celeste visited with Ethan at the jail today, before I spoke to him. Maybe she asked him not to say anything about it. Or maybe," she said, thinking aloud, "maybe they figured that with a confession, there would be no trial. No media. And they could keep everything under wraps."

Debra tapped her pencil on her pad. "Let's do this. Check out Gideon Meissner and Celeste Bushnell. Talk to the girl, see if you can break the alibi she gave her mom."

"Okay."

"In the meantime, go back and tell Ethan the deal is off. Murder one, capital crime."

Jessie frowned. "I gave him my word."

"Tell him it's out of your hands. His confession wasn't convincing, and the D.A. changed his mind. Three people are brutally shot—the public is demanding justice. Which is true," she added.

"And if he doesn't open up? Like I said, he doesn't seem to care whether he lives or dies."

"That's today. In a day or so, he may change his mind. And if word gets out that we're going for the death penalty, maybe the killer will feel forced to talk."

"No one's talked so far."

"No one knows he's confessed. Talk to Ethan."

"*Lie* to him, you mean."

Debra looked at her appraisingly. "It's important that he believes you, Jessie. Can you lie convincingly?"

"Sure." Jessie stood and picked up her purse. "I do it all the time."

❖ 41 ❖

THE HOUSEKEEPER WAS in the kitchen. Jessie spoke to her for a few minutes, then went looking for Celeste but found the brother instead, in the family room.

Celeste was sleeping, he told Jessie.

"She was a wreck when she came back from seeing Ethan at the jail. She was so distraught she couldn't talk. She took Valium and went straight to bed. To tell you the truth, I'm extremely concerned about her." He frowned at Jessie, as if she were responsible.

"Where's Adrienne?"

"In her room. She's been crying nonstop since the arrest. This has devastated the family. I'm supposed to go to Washington right after the funeral on Sunday, but to tell you the truth, I'm afraid to leave them alone."

"What about your parents?"

"Just two more people for Celeste to worry about. I think she's near the breaking point. I really do."

Jessie nodded. "I'd like to talk to Adrienne. Can you ask her to come downstairs?"

The brother expelled an impatient breath. "Is this *really* necessary? She's had enough for one day."

She wondered if he knew about the incest. "I really do have to talk to her. I'll wait in Dr. Bushnell's office, if that's all right."

Privacy, and a door she could close. She didn't want anyone overhearing. She walked to the office and chose to sit in Bushnell's large leather armchair behind the handsome rosewood desk. More authority.

Adrienne appeared in the doorway a few minutes later. "My uncle said you wanted to talk to me."

"Come in, Adrienne." Jessie pointed to the love seat to the right of the desk.

"I've told you all I know. I don't know what more you want."

"I have a few more questions." She made her voice pleasant but firm. "Please shut the door behind you."

Adrienne approached hesitantly and sat on the sofa. She placed her folded hands on her lap.

"I'm sure you're upset about Ethan," Jessie said. "We know you were in love with him."

The girl's eyes welled with tears. "I *do* love him. I'll always love him. I know he didn't kill my father."

"Your father didn't approve of the relationship. Why?"

"He was worried. He said if Ethan and I broke up, there would be hurt feelings. But I knew that wouldn't happen, because we love each other."

"Ethan told us he was here on Sunday. He told us your father found the two of you in bed. What did your father tell you after Ethan left?"

The girl's face turned crimson. "He said I could never see Ethan again. That Ethan understood, and I had to also."

"Did he say why?"

"The same thing he told me last time. He made me come down and have Ethan tell me it was over. Ethan was upset. When he left, I ran after him, but he didn't want to talk. I called him at his father's apartment later, but no one answered. I called him from school on Monday, too."

If the girl knew the truth, she was a terrific actress, Jessie thought. "Was your mother home?"

"No. She came home later. She was out with friends. I think she went to a movie."

That corroborated what Celeste had said. Although mother and daughter could have coordinated their stories.

"Ethan confessed, Adrienne. He admitted he killed your father and the others." She felt terrible, constantly referring to Marianna Velasquez and Nicole Hobart as "the others"—as though their deaths were less significant.

The girl stared at her, open-mouthed. "I don't believe you. You're trying to trick me."

Jessie shook her head. "It's the truth. But there are a few things we have to clear up. You mentioned that Ethan was friendly with some people. Big M and Torro. You made those up, right? Them and the girl?"

She flushed. "I didn't want you to know about us. I was afraid you'd suspect Ethan."

"I see." Jessie nodded. "So when you said you were shopping with your mom, you said that to protect *her*?"

"I *was* shopping with her."

Jessie fixed her with a stern look. "Adrienne, a murder investigation is very serious. You could go to jail for lying to the police. Do you understand that?"

"It's the truth." She moved her hands to her knees.

"I talked with your housekeeper a few minutes ago. She says on Monday afternoon, between four and five, there was only one car in the driveway." The housekeeper had been sullen and uncooperative until Jessie had threatened to take her to the station. "Why you make trouble for this family?" she'd demanded.

"Kim is wrong," Adrienne said. "Anyway, how would she know that?"

"She was watering the plants in the front, and she remembers clearly seeing only one car. The Expedition. That was right before she left for the evening." Jessie paused to let that sink in. "So if you were with your mother, Adrienne, who had the other car?"

She was rubbing her hands up and down her knees.

"We can check with all the stores your mother says the

two of you went to. I'm sure we'll find enough people to tell us that you weren't with your mother."

"Why can't you leave us alone?" the girl demanded in an anguished whisper.

Almost exactly what the housekeeper had asked. "I need the truth, Adrienne. The fact that you weren't with your mother doesn't mean your mother did anything wrong. Ethan confessed, so we know she didn't have anything to do with the murders. But we have to clear this up, for the record. Why did you say you were with her when you weren't?"

"I don't know." She was rocking back and forth on the sofa. "My mom was crying and upset, and I could see she wasn't thinking clearly. I was scared you'd think she was lying, because she wasn't answering the questions so quickly. So I said I was with her, because I knew she didn't kill my father. She loved him!"

"Did you see her when you came home from school?"

The girl nodded. "She was lying down, in her room. She didn't feel well."

"Do you know why?"

She hesitated. "I heard my parents arguing Sunday night in their bedroom. I think it was about Ethan. I guess she was still upset about it."

"You didn't hear what they said?"

Adrienne shook her head. "My mom was crying when she came out of the room. She said Ethan wasn't going to be living with us anymore. She wanted to know what happened that afternoon, when Ethan was here. I told her I didn't know."

"So on Monday, when you came home from school, your mom was in her room. Then what?"

The girl hesitated. "My mom left. I did, too, a little later. I went to the Beverly Center."

"What time was that?"

She thought for a moment. "Around three-thirty. I came back about an hour or so later."

Giving Celeste plenty of time to drive to her husband's Century City office, Jessie realized. "Was your mother home when you returned?"

Again, the girl hesitated. "She came home a little later. She said she was shopping. Then we went to dinner."

"Did she have any bags with her when she came home, Adrienne?"

"No. I guess she didn't find anything she liked. That doesn't mean she was lying," Adrienne added defensively. "I didn't find anything, either."

But that didn't mean Mom was telling the truth.

❖ 42 ❖

CELESTE WAS OUT cold in the king-size bed under the comforter, snoring lightly, her hand shielding her closed eyes from the pale slivers of light coming through the plantation shutters. A vial of prescription pills lay on the nightstand, next to a crystal glass and a carafe filled with water and the framed photo from the Maui vacation. Jessie left a note, asking Celeste to phone her, and left.

She wondered how Phil was doing. With the assistance of two uniformed officers, he was showing copies of Gideon Meissner's photo, obtained from his driver's license, as well as Celeste's, to the parking staff and guards at the building where Bushnell had his offices, to all the occupants of the other offices on the twenty-fourth floor. A thankless job, and Jessie was relieved that it wasn't hers.

She was entering the Pacific Station lobby as Manny Freiberg was leaving. The thin, wiry psychologist was walking so fast that he almost bumped into her.

"I should cite you for speeding," she said. "Thanks, Manny."

"You owe me. Shabbos is in an hour and a half, and I promised Aliza I'd pick up some things at the market."

She hadn't realized it was so late, hadn't thought about the Sabbath since the early morning, when she'd gone to the kosher markets on Pico before work and bought challah and wine, a rotisserie chicken and some kugels. Ezra was probably getting ready. She'd been so rushed that she hadn't had time to think about him all day.

"So what's your assessment?" she asked.

"Walk with me to my car, and I'll give you a five-minute sketch."

They crossed Sepulveda. "Basically, I can't tell you much," he said.

"So why am I walking with you?"

"It's good exercise. The kid is seriously traumatized, Jessie, but you know that. He seems disconnected, not aware of the severity of his situation. Is that real or an act? I don't know. I'm a psychologist, not a mind reader."

"His mentor says the boy has found meaning in Judaism."

Manny nodded. "Could be. His life has been so screwed up, he's probably drawn to anything with order and regulations."

"I can see that." The order and rules appealed to her, too. But that was only part of it.

"You wash your hands a certain number of times on rising," Manny said. "You wind the phylacteries a certain number of times in a specific pattern. You recite specific prayers by a certain time. You recite other prayers for specific foods. You put on your right shoe first, then your left."

She raised a brow. "Do you?"

"As a matter of fact, yes. The point is, it gives him structure and a sense that someone's watching over him, 'cause it sure as hell hasn't been his family."

"God, you mean."

"God the protector, God the forgiver, God the father. The boy hasn't been doing too well in the dad department. Oedipus had it easy in comparison."

"God isn't much of a comfort, either. According to the Torah, Ethan's a *mamzer*. He told me he's lost in God's eyes."

"But the boy is praying, searching. He's not shutting the

door. That's a healthy sign. This is me," Manny said, stopping in front of a red Mustang.

She whistled. "Pretty snazzy."

"Anticipating my premidlife crisis." He brushed a leaf off the hood and leaned against the driver's door.

"What did he tell you?"

"That he did it and he's sorry."

"Did he?"

"I don't know." He pushed his glasses up on his nose. "Everything about this boy's background screams danger. I read the notes you faxed me. He's a textbook case. An alcoholic father with a temper. A depressed mother who commits suicide. I noticed he was separated from the mom for two months at birth."

"She had postpartum depression."

"Whatever the reason, it could have caused attachment disorder. Meaning, he may not have been able to develop the normal attachment to his mother or father, so he has a hard time attaching to anyone. Add to that the alcoholic father, the depressed mother, the suicide, the abandonment, all before the age of eight. The fact that this kid led a normal, productive life till now is amazing."

"His life was much better with the Bushnells."

"Easier, yes. More luxurious, yes."

"More stable, too. Well, as far as I know. My family looks perfect from the outside."

Manny nodded. " 'Stable' is good."

"Plus he got along great with the foster sister, and Mrs. Bushnell doted on him."

"And the doctor was demanding and authoritarian. Mixed parental messages are bad for any child, but especially for someone with this kid's history."

"I guess that's why there's never been an execution of a *ben sorer u'moreh*—it's hard to find parents who speak with the same voice."

Manny cocked his head. "Heavy stuff for beginning Judaism. You're studying that in one of your classes?"

"Private lessons," she said, blushing.

"Oh, yeah?" He looked pleased.

"You were saying?"

"Mind my own business, huh?" He laughed. "Where was I? Oh, yeah. A kid like this can grow up without connecting to people, without feeling remorse for anything he does, without a sense of right and wrong."

"Why?"

"Kids are born with a natural empathy, Jessie, but if they live in homes filled with conflict, and if they rarely feel a mother's love, they become less empathetic. A kid whose parents are permissive basically learns that anything goes, that there's no need for self-control. He may also feel that the parent is permissive because he or she doesn't really give a damn. A kid whose parents are autocratic gets the message that mom and dad are imposing the control, so he doesn't have to develop his *own* sense of control."

"What about Ethan?"

"The dad yells, the mom's basically not there for him. The kid's empathy may be impaired. The Bushnells are a mix, so he hasn't learned self-control from either of them. But that's the textbook, Jessie. Kids aren't textbooks, and this kid seemed to be doing well until recently, right?"

"Very well. Straight A student. Got along with his peers, though somewhat of a loner. Things went downhill when Bushnell broke up the romance with the daughter."

"Who is really his *sister*. Jeez!" Manny sighed. "So the kid can maintain a relationship. That's a good sign."

"His English teacher thinks he's great. His other teachers don't."

"Hey, on that basis you could lock up half the population, including yours truly. I almost flunked out of high school.

On the other hand," he said, serious now, "Ethan could be presenting a different face to different people. Depending on what he wants."

"Don't we all do that, Manny?"

"To a degree." He nodded.

She hesitated. "You talked about growing up in a home without a mother's love, how that can affect a child's empathy."

"And you're thinking about yourself, and your mother, and the abuse," Manny said gently. "So you see? By the textbook, Jessie, you should have been cold and manipulative, and here you are, oozing empathy."

" 'Cause I'm hoping you'll let me drive your Mustang." She smiled.

"You wish. I haven't even let Aliza touch it." Manny laughed. "So you got his confession, I take it?"

She sighed. "For what it's worth." She repeated what she'd told Debra Bergman. "I think he's protecting someone."

"Who?"

"Could be his dad, but I'm leaning toward the foster mother. She knew about the incest, and she lied about her alibi. If it's her, I'm hoping guilt will make her fess up. But why would Ethan be willing to sit in prison for the rest of his life for something he didn't do?"

"Talk about empathy, huh?" Manny considered. "A, right now he thinks he doesn't have much of a future anyway. He's a *mamzer*. He believes his choices are limited. B, he feels guilty 'cause he's centrally involved—if he hadn't been born, if he hadn't fallen in love with the girl and slept with her, et cetera. C, he wished Bushnell dead, so in his mind and heart he's guilty anyway. And don't forget, he's still lugging around the guilt over his mom's suicide."

"We're putting the death penalty back on the table to shake him up."

Manny shook his head. "The kid I saw just now? If he's faking, he's smart enough to know you're bluffing. If he's for real, he's somewhere else."

"So if he's for real, he'd go to death row to protect someone?"

"He'd be a martyr, wouldn't he? A hell of an atonement for all the guilt he's been carrying around his whole life."

❖ 43 ❖

ETHAN LISTENED QUIETLY when Jessie relayed Debra's message. He seemed ethereal in his acceptance, and she was disappointed. She'd hoped for an emotional reaction—anger, fear—but after talking with Manny, she wasn't surprised.

"The district attorney feels you're not telling us everything," she told him. "Maybe if you're more forthcoming. . . . I can't promise anything, though."

"I've told you everything I know. If this is God's will, I can't do anything about it."

She wondered if he was in denial, or whether he'd tapped into a more spiritual world that offered peace of mind and salvation for the soul, if not the body. From the jail personnel she knew he'd been praying all morning, rocking back and forth in front of his cot while holding the prayer book Klingerman had brought. Klingerman had brought him kosher food, too, but Ethan had barely touched it.

She drove to West L.A. and parked in the police lot. Gideon Meissner was in the lobby, sitting on one of the attached orange chairs. He jumped up and accosted Jessie the minute he saw her.

"Why can't I see my son?" he demanded angrily. "What is this, Iran?"

The volunteer behind the reception desk stared at him.

"Let's talk upstairs, Mr. Meissner," Jessie said.

She led him up the staircase to the second-floor detectives' room and her desk. Phil was still out. Simms and Boyd were out, too. She pulled over Phil's chair and motioned to Meissner to sit down.

"You can see Ethan in the morning," she told him. "I'm sorry, but those are the rules. I didn't make them," she added. "He confessed to the murders, you know."

Meissner glared at her. "Because you tortured him! Celeste hired a lawyer for him. Why isn't he there?"

"Ethan doesn't want to be represented by Mr. Thomason. That's his right. He's waived his right to see an attorney."

"He's an idiot! He doesn't know what he's doing!"

"The court will appoint a public defender, but if I were you, I'd encourage him to retain Mr. Thomason. The district attorney is going for the death penalty."

Meissner's face looked like putty. "My God," he said quietly. "My God." He dragged his hand across his mouth and chin, pulling the skin.

"Ethan told us the truth, Mr. Meissner. That your wife and Dr. Bushnell had an affair, that Ethan is their son."

"Ronnie said this because he did not want Eitán involved with Adrienne." Meissner spoke without conviction, like someone who hopes that repeating something often enough will make it true.

"We can run blood tests to prove paternity."

The man crumpled in front of her eyes. His shoulders slumped, his face seemed to dissolve. He covered his eyes with his hands and groaned.

"I can understand how you feel," Jessie said quietly.

He shook his head. "No one can know. *No one*. To live a lie all these years. To think that Lucy and Ronnie . . . But in my heart Eitán is still my son. No matter what happened."

"Celeste says you called her when you found out," she lied.

"I called Ronnie first, to tell him I know what a monster he is!" Meissner's face darkened with anger. "I woke them up. I heard him tell Celeste I was a patient with an emergency. He took the phone into another room. Coward! He *begged* me not to tell her. This was between us, he said. Why did she have to know? You're right, I told him. This is between us. In the morning, after he went to the office, I called her. I told her what Ronnie told Eitán, I told her everything. She did not believe me. 'Ask your husband,' I told her. 'Go, ask.' She hung up on me. An hour later she came to the apartment. She wanted to know about Lucy and Ronnie, did I think it was true. She was crying, hysterical. She tried to talk to Eitán, but he was sleeping, drunk. She said she wasn't leaving until she talked to him, and I had an appointment, so I left her there."

So Ethan hadn't been dreaming about Celeste's being there, talking to him. "Did you go to see Dr. Bushnell?"

"I *almost* went. But I did not trust myself. I knew if I saw him, I would kill him. Not with a gun—with my hands. I should have gone," he said, his voice filled with sorrow. "I should have killed him. Better me, than Eitán."

Phil returned a short while later. "No luck," he said. He sat down heavily on his chair. "What about you?"

"Celeste Bushnell knew about the incest, and she has no alibi." Jessie reported the details.

"Aren't *you* proud of yourself. Now what?"

"I told Ethan the D.A.'s going for the death penalty, but he didn't react." She repeated what Manny had told her.

Phil nodded. "Maybe another night in jail will help."

"I hope so. By the way, Mr. Pervez called. He wants to know if we found out anything about the nephew."

Phil rolled his eyes. "Give me a break."

"Why don't you ask him to come to the station with the son, make up something. While they're here, I'll go talk to the wife. Maybe she'll tell me something if she's alone."

"I was figuring on going home. I'm still not a hundred percent."

"When are you?" she teased. "Your call."

Sighing, he picked up the phone. She went to the rest room and found him smiling when she returned.

"They'll be here in a half hour," Phil said. "I told them I wanted them to look at some mug shots of a suspicious person seen near their nephew's apartment."

"You rascal, you."

She typed up her notes of the day's events and left the station. The drive to the Pervez house was short. She checked to make sure the Chevy she'd seen in the driveway the other day wasn't there, and rang the bell.

The woman looked startled to see her. "My husband and son went to the police station," she told Jessie.

"I wanted to talk to you, Mrs. Pervez. May I come in?" Without waiting for an answer, Jessie pushed the door open, entered the living room, and sat on the sofa.

Mrs. Pervez remained standing at the door. "My husband and son will be back soon. It is better if you come then."

"You seemed upset the other day, Mrs. Pervez. I had the feeling you couldn't talk in front of your family."

She shook her head rapidly. "No, this is not true. Please, will you come later?"

The woman's nervousness was contagious. "You're a mother, Mrs. Pervez. Don't you want to find the person who killed your daughter? Don't you care?"

Her dark eyes flashed. "Of course, I care! I do not sleep at night. I cry. Of course, I care!"

"Then sit down, Mrs. Pervez," Jessie said gently. "Talk to me."

The woman hesitated. She shut the door and sat next to Jessie. "What is it you want to know?"

"We think Jamal killed Lily," Jessie said. "We think he was in love with your daughter and wanted to run away with her. That's why he took the money from the bank. But Lily didn't want to go with him."

Mrs. Pervez shook her head. "When Jamal came here, Lily helped him with his English. He and Lily are friends and cousins, nothing more. This is *truth*." Her voice rang with sincerity.

So much for that theory. "Do you think your nephew killed Lily?"

"No. My husband says no. My son, too." She darted a glance at the door.

"Are you afraid of someone, Mrs. Pervez? Do you think whoever killed your daughter will harm your family if you tell the police?"

"I don't know who killed Lily." She was clenching her hands tightly together.

"We can protect your family."

"I don't know who killed Lily."

Like a broken record. "Why did your nephew take ten thousand dollars out of the bank? Was he being blackmailed?"

"For business reasons, I think. Computers."

She was parroting the husband. Something was definitely wrong here. "Why did your daughter go to your nephew's apartment that day?"

Mrs. Pervez stood. "Please, can you come back when my husband and son are here, okay?"

Gently, Jessie pulled the woman back down and took her hand. "Tell me what's wrong, Mrs. Pervez."

She glanced at the door again. "My husband is a good man. But if he comes home, and finds me talking to you, he will not be happy."

"Why not? Is he afraid you'll tell me something? Is he afraid that whoever killed Lily will hurt your family?"

The woman had a trapped look. "In our culture, it is the man who talks."

"Mrs. Pervez, your daughter was brutally killed. She was stabbed over and over and over." From her purse she withdrew an envelope with crime scene photos of the butchered girl. "This is what happened to your daughter, Mrs. Pervez. This is Lily."

The woman gagged and covered her mouth. She turned her head and began weeping.

"Lily isn't at rest, Mrs. Pervez. Her body is torn and her soul is crying out, just as she cried out when she was being stabbed. Over and over again."

The mother was clutching her stomach and moaning.

"She is crying for justice, Mrs. Pervez. Her soul can't rest until that happens. She needs her mother's help."

"I found money in my son's closet," the woman said in a strangled voice. "Thousands of dollars. And Jamal's credit card and wallet. I did not tell my husband I found it."

Jessie felt a tightening up her spine. "Your nephew's money."

She nodded. "A few weeks ago I heard my husband on the phone with Jamal. He asked to borrow ten thousand dollars for a short time."

"Did you ask your husband why he needed the money?"

"I asked. He told me this is not my business. Then Lily was killed, at Jamal's apartment. And then I found the money in my son's room."

Jessie wondered whether the mother had searched, already suspecting the truth. "Your son killed Lily? Or did your husband do it? Or did they do it together?"

She bowed her head. "I do not know."

Probably the son, Jessie decided. "Your son went to get the money and killed your nephew." She frowned, confused. "But why did he have to kill Jamal for the money? And why did he kill Lily? Because she happened to be there?"

"In our culture, a girl does not have men friends. A girl gets married. Lily knows this. She is a good girl, but she spends too much time at her cousin's apartment. Even though they are just friends."

Jessie stared at her, shaken. "And your husband and son didn't approve," she said quietly. They'd had it all wrong, all upside down.

"I tell them Lily is a good girl, but they are worried what people will think. My husband asked me a few times to talk to Lily. I tried. *Believe* me, I tried! She says, 'This is America.' "

"Your son killed his sister because he suspected she had done something improper?"

"For the honor of the family," the woman whispered.

An honor killing. Jessie had heard the term, had read about the Muslim practice, which a new generation of Muslims, including the wife of the king of Jordan, were now condemning. She was chilled to the bone. "And the money?"

"I do not know."

A red herring to make it look as though Jamal had planned his escape before the murder, Jessie decided. Like the credit card purchases intended to make it seem as though Jamal were alive.

"What will happen to me now?" the woman asked. "To my family?"

❖ 44 ❖

EZRA HAD LEFT a bouquet of yellow roses at the front door. "To help the Prom Queen welcome the Shabbos queen," he'd written on the note.

He'd left a message on her machine, too: "I know you're swamped. I miss you. Talk to you after Shabbos."

She missed him, too.

She placed the roses in a round glass vase and set them on top of the white cloth-covered table, then showered and washed her hair. She'd missed candlelighting by hours.

After calming down Mrs. Pervez, she'd phoned Phil from the car and apprised him of the situation. He sent the Pervez father and brother back home. An hour later, with a telephonic warrant in hand, he and Jessie and two uniformed policemen showed up at the house. To protect the mother, they began with the living room and dining room and master bedroom. A search of the son's room revealed the money (Jessie counted nine thousand fifty), Jamal Pervez's credit card and driver's license, and an antique ring and necklace that the mother identified as Lily's. The father and brother were now in custody.

Jessie had warmed the food and was about to light the Sabbath candles—better late than never, she told herself—when her father arrived.

"I'm not interrupting, am I?" he asked after he kissed her. "Your mother and I just had dinner at Helen's, and I wanted to stop by." He followed her into the breakfast room.

"I've been meaning to call, but it's been a crazy day. So you and Mom are talking?"

He nodded. "I came to thank you, Jessie. You were right. I shouldn't have kept this from her, or from Helen."

Relief washed over her. "How'd they take it?"

"Upset, concerned. But they're not falling apart. Your mother called Mark and demanded to hear all the details. I think she's going to scare the Parkinson's into submission." He smiled.

Jessie smiled, too. "If anyone can do it, Mom can."

He looked at the table, and she saw what he was seeing: the two porcelain white-and-blue candlesticks Ezra had given her seven months ago; a bottle of wine; a silver cup; a white square of cloth, embroidered with Hebrew letters and flowers, that covered the challahs.

"Were you about to have dinner?" he asked.

"I'm going to light Sabbath candles first."

She felt shy, as though she were a child showing off a newly learned feat. She lit the candles, waved her hands around them three times, covered her eyes and recited the blessing. Good Shabbos, she said silently to the candles.

"What does the waving mean?" her father asked.

"I'm welcoming the Sabbath queen and tranquility into my home." She thought about Ethan Meissner, welcoming the Sabbath queen into his jail cell, about Nicole Hobart's parents, who had arrived today to take their daughter's body back to Chicago. She wondered how Alex Velasquez was doing, and Mrs. Pervez, whose first name she didn't even know.

"A nice idea. This gives you pleasure, I see."

"Very much." She'd never discussed her interest in Judaism with her father, and though she was nervous, she decided to take the opening. "Does it bother you?"

"I've never been a particularly religious man. I love the holidays, of course—Christmas, Easter. But it's the traditions I enjoy, and the getting together with family."

Not really an answer. "Do you believe in God, Daddy?"

"Yes. I can't say He's a presence in my life. Is He a presence in yours?"

"I'd like Him to be."

He nodded. "Your mother's concerned about where this is going. I hope it won't cause problems, Jessie."

"In other words, don't upset Mom. Why am I not surprised?"

He shook his head. "That's not what I said. I think it's fine that you're exploring your mother's heritage. It's fascinating and filled with rich traditions."

"As long as everything stays theoretical, right? Well, I can't promise that. I'm attracted to Judaism because it's allowing me to reclaim my past, to find out what I lost. And I've found something spiritually satisfying that I've never felt before. This is *important* to me, Dad."

"Family is important, too, Jessie. I hope you remember that. There's nothing spiritual about causing a rift in a family."

"I don't want that, either, Dad. But I have to see where this goes."

"No matter who gets hurt?"

"You mean Mom."

"And Helen. But yes, I'm worried about your mother. She's been through a lot, Jessie. She—"

"You know, Dad, I'm a *little* tired of hearing that. It doesn't excuse everything."

He frowned. "What do you mean?"

"Never mind."

"You alluded to something last night, too, Jessie. If you have something to say, say it."

"Okay." She took a breath. "My whole childhood and adolescence, you made us worry about not making Mom upset. You protected her, but you never worried about us."

His lips were pinched. "That's not true. I know there were problems, but every family has problems. Your mother was more nervous than most, but she had good reason. She was terribly damaged in the war. You know that now."

"She hit us, Dad."

"She may have spanked you. Years ago parents *spanked* their children. Things were different then."

"She abused us."

He shook his head. "That's ridiculous."

"She abused us and you knew it and you did nothing about it. *Nothing*." She was breathing hard and felt as though a stone had been lifted off her chest.

"There was no abuse, Jessie. I never saw any abuse."

"You didn't *want* to. She cut up our clothes, Dad. She twisted our arms. She dislocated my shoulder. She beat me and Helen with a belt until we were bleeding."

His lips trembled. "You and Helen were tomboys. You fell. You had scratches. You had accidents."

"How many accidents are normal, Dad? Mom told you that, and you wanted to believe it, so you did. But you knew. You *knew*, Dad. Why did you let her do it?" It was an effort to keep from screaming.

Her father sighed. "Jessie, if things happened that I didn't know about, I'm sorry. What else can I say?"

She took a deep breath. "I want you to say, 'Jessie, I knew your mother was abusing you, and I didn't stop it.' "

"I'm not going to say what isn't true."

"Ask Helen."

"I don't have to ask Helen. Isn't it enough that I'm saying I'm sorry?"

"No, it's not enough."

"It's enough if you want it to be, Jessie. If I made mistakes, I'm sorry. I can't undo the past."

"Then at least acknowledge it honestly, Dad."

They stared at each other for a long moment.

"Well, good night, Jessie. So much for the tranquility of your Sabbath candles."

She flinched.

"I'm sorry," he said quietly. "That was cruel. I love you, Jessie. I'd like to get past this. I hope you do, too."

So now it would be her fault if they had no relationship. Well, she supposed that was true. It was her choice. She could accept what he had to offer, and try to have a relationship, or she could insist on a truth that he would probably never give.

She walked him to the door. He bent down and she let him kiss her cheek.

In the breakfast room she picked up her prayer book.

"Come, my beloved, to greet the bride," she murmured, "the Sabbath presence let us welcome. . . ."

The ringing of the phone woke her. Still dark outside. She opened one eye and looked at the green liquid crystal numbers on her clock radio. Six o'clock. She'd hoped to sleep late today.

She groped for the receiver and brought it to her ear. "Hello?"

"It's Phil. I just got a call from the station."

She covered her mouth to stifle a yawn. "Ethan's ready to talk?"

"It's Celeste Bushnell, Jessie. She's dead."

❖ 45 ❖

A BLACK-AND-WHITE and the coroner's van were parked in the driveway, looking decidedly out of place next to the Beemer and the Expedition and the Range Rover.

Déjà vu, Jessie thought, getting out of her Honda and walking along the flagstone path. But instead of Celeste Bushnell, a rookie policeman she didn't know by name opened the door and gave her a rundown of what he knew.

The girl had found her mother. Her bedroom was next to the dead woman's bedroom, and she'd heard the shot. She'd phoned 911, then her uncle. The housekeeper had heard a noise and come upstairs to see what had happened. Minutes later the ambulance siren had awakened the grandparents, who had been sleeping in a downstairs guest bedroom.

Jessie gloved her hands and slipped booties over her shoes, then went upstairs. Celeste was on her back in the king-size bed, her arms at her side. Blood from a small blackened hole at her left temple had trailed down her face and neck onto the pale blue silk nightgown and expensive lace-trimmed white bed linens. Someone—either Futaki, who was busy writing notes, or his assistant—had bagged her hands to preserve evidence of gunshot residue.

History repeating itself. Jessie shook her shoulders to dispel the sadness and futility that seemed to settle on her as soon as she'd stepped into the room.

Futaki grunted in response to her hello. "Where's Okum?"

"On the way from Thousand Oaks. He should be here soon. What do you have?"

"Just the one shot. A contact wound to the temple."

"Does the angle seem right for a suicide?"

"If she's left-handed. I found GSR on her left hand, so it would seem that she is. There's nothing to indicate foul play. Apparently, she took tranquilizers before she killed herself, and she left you a note on her nightstand."

Jessie glanced at the nightstand. "For me?"

"Is there another Detective Drake?"

Wiseass. She walked to the nightstand. The vial of pills she'd seen yesterday lay on its side. She picked it up. Empty. The water glass was a third full. She glanced at the faces in the photo, still smiling though two of the people were now dead, and one was in jail. Next to the photo was a cream-colored envelope addressed to Jessie.

Holding the envelope by one corner, she flicked open the flap and carefully drew out a card embossed with the initials CBR. Celeste and Ronald Bushnell. Proper even in her last desperate act.

" 'By now you know everything,' " Jessie read aloud. " 'My guilt and pain are too great to bear. I'm sorry.' "

She slipped the card back into the envelope. "The brother was worried about her," she told the medical examiner. "He thought she was near the breaking point."

"Then it would seem that she broke," Futaki said.

"Where's the weapon?" Jessie asked the young redheaded policeman who was in the room.

"Over there." He pointed to a long dresser across from the bed. "The girl said she put it there."

"Did she say why she touched it?"

"She said it was on the floor at the side of the bed, and she automatically picked it up before she knew what it was."

An SID photographer had placed a numbered plastic tag

next to the gun. A Smith & Wesson nine millimeter. Meissner's other gun—it had to be. Celeste had been in Gideon's apartment the day of the murder. Gideon had left her there alone when she'd insisted on staying to talk to Ethan. She must have taken it then.

"Aside from the girl and the housekeeper, was anyone else in the room before you got here?" she asked the officer.

"No. The uncle from Pasadena got here after we did. The grandparents stayed downstairs."

"What time did you get the call?"

"Nine-one-one contacted us at four-thirty-seven."

All of the movable evidence had been tagged and numbered. Jessie placed the gun, envelope, vial and lid, water glass, and carafe in separate evidence bags, which she dated and signed after identifying the contents.

Phil arrived. She talked with him for a few minutes, filling him in, then went downstairs.

The family was in the den. Celeste's gray-haired parents were sitting at one end of a large sectional black leather sofa. Adrienne was at the opposite end, looking like a little girl in red pajamas with a candy cane print. Her uncle was holding her hand and talking to her in an undertone, but she was staring into space with red-rimmed eyes dulled by crying and didn't seem to hear what he was saying. Kim was there, too, next to Celeste's parents. The housekeeper looked as if she'd aged ten years overnight.

Jessie approached Adrienne and crouched in front of her. "I know this is a horrible time to have to answer questions, Adrienne, but you understand that we have to ask. I'm probably going to repeat some of the questions the police officer asked you."

The girl's nod was almost unnoticeable.

"She's in shock," the uncle said. "Can't this wait?"

"I'm afraid not. Let's go into the breakfast room, Adrienne."

"Can't we do it here?"

"It's better if we talk privately."

"Why?" the uncle demanded. "We all know that my sister took her life. You can ask your questions here."

"Until we know for certain what happened, Mr. Hepley, we have to treat this like any other investigation."

"Adrienne, you don't have to go if you don't want to."

Jessie sighed. "Mr. Hepley, you're making this more complicated than it has to be. I just want to clarify the details."

"You want to grill her, the way you grilled my sister. You can talk to Adrienne here, with her family around her, or you can talk to her with a lawyer."

Shit. "Is that what you want, Adrienne?"

The girl looked at her uncle, then at Jessie, and nodded. "I want to stay here."

Jessie sat down next to the girl. "Tell me what happened, Adrienne."

"I was sleeping, and something that sounded like a truck backfiring woke me up. I don't know why I was scared, but I was, so I went into my parents' bedroom."

"Was anyone else up?"

"No, just me. The lights were out, and I called my mom's name. She didn't answer, but I thought she was sleeping very hard, because she took tranquilizers yesterday."

"She is taking too many pills," the housekeeper interrupted. "She is very-very upset when she come home from seeing E-tan. Crying all the day."

"Not now, Kim," Celeste's father said.

"This is why I wanted to talk to Adrienne alone, Mr. Hepley," Jessie said, annoyed. "Go on," she prompted Adrienne.

"I went over to her bed, and I saw—" The girl stopped. "I saw her. I saw—" She started crying and covered her mouth with her hand.

Her uncle put his arm around her and gave Jessie an angry look.

"What time did you hear the shot?" Jessie asked.

"I don't know. I didn't check my watch."

"It is four hours and thirty-one minutes," Kim volunteered. "I look at clock."

"Did you turn on the lights?" Jessie asked.

Adrienne shook her head. "I didn't want to see."

"I turn on lights," Kim said.

Jessie silenced the housekeeper with a frown. "What did you do then, Adrienne?"

"I checked my mom's wrist for a pulse. I didn't think there was one, but I phoned nine-one-one. Then I phoned my uncle."

"You phoned from your mother's room?"

She nodded.

"Then what?"

"Kim came upstairs. She heard the shot. I didn't know how to tell my grandparents, and I didn't want to leave my mom alone, so Kim said she would do it. But by then the paramedics came, and my grandparents were up."

The housekeeper was nodding. "Eight o'clock, in the night, I bring her some food, but she no want to eat." She turned to the parents. "I tried very-very much to make her eat." She started crying.

"We know, Kim." The man sighed and patted the housekeeper's hand. "We know you did your best."

"What did you do then, Adrienne?" Jessie asked.

"Nothing."

"She wash hands in Missy Celeste's bathroom," the housekeeper said. "When I come in."

"Right, I forgot." Adrienne nodded. "I had blood on my hand, from the gun. I couldn't stand it." She shuddered.

"Why did you touch the gun, Adrienne?"

"I almost stepped on it in the dark. I picked it up without thinking. I'm sorry. I guess I shouldn't have done that."

"How did you pick it up? Where did you hold it?"

"I don't remember."

"Try to re-create it in your mind, Adrienne." Jessie waited.

The girl pressed her lips together, thinking. "I think it was by the long part."

"The barrel?"

Adrienne nodded.

"Do you know where your mother got the gun?"

The girl shook her head.

"Did any of you see Mrs. Bushnell after eight o'clock?" Jessie asked, glancing at the family.

"I went in to say good night," Adrienne said. "I think it was around ten o'clock. She was sleeping, so I didn't want to bother her."

"The police found a note on your mother's nightstand. Was it there when you saw her at ten o'clock?"

"I don't think so. I didn't notice."

The brother hadn't seen Celeste since early Friday afternoon. He'd been on the phone with the coroner's office and the mortuary, making the funeral arrangements, and had driven home to Pasadena. Celeste's parents had eaten a quiet dinner that Kim had prepared and gone to bed early. At her mother's insistence, Celeste had come downstairs to join them, but after a few spoonfuls of soup had returned to her room. She had kissed them good night.

"What was in the note?" Andrew Hepley asked. "You said there was a note."

"I can't tell you at this time." If Thomason heard about the note, and it's confessional tone, he would spring Ethan in ten minutes. And Jessie still wasn't sure . . . "How many tranquilizers were in the vial on her nightstand?"

"It was a refill for thirty tablets," the brother said. "I just picked it up for her yesterday morning. She took two before you came yesterday, and probably a couple more in the afternoon."

So his fingerprints were on the vial. "Did anyone else touch the vial?" Jessie looked around the room.

"I don't understand," Celeste's father said impatiently. "Celeste took her life. What's the difference who touched the vial?"

"It's just police procedure, Dad," Andrew said wearily. "They have to ask these questions."

"Doesn't make sense. None of this makes sense to me."

"I touched it," Adrienne said. "My mom was so tired in the afternoon. She asked me to give her two pills. I poured some water in the glass and gave her that, too."

Jessie turned to the housekeeper. "What about you? Did you touch the vial?"

The woman shook her head. "New pills, no. Water glass and ca-rafe, yes."

"Adrienne, was your mother left-handed or right-handed?"

"Left. I'm right-handed. So was my dad."

"Are we *done* yet?" Andrew Hepley demanded.

"Just a few more questions. Looking back, Adrienne, did your mother say anything during the day that would indicate she was thinking of killing herself?"

"She was hardly talking. When she came back from seeing Ethan at the jail, she looked awful, liked she'd seen a ghost. I asked her what Ethan had said. She just shook her head. She took my face with both hands and looked into my eyes. She said it was going to be all right. Then she went to her room to lie down."

"She was despondent, more so after she heard that Ethan confessed." Andrew sighed. "I was an idiot to tell her. I should have stayed here last night. I shouldn't have left her alone." He squeezed his niece's hand.

Overwhelming guilt, Jessie thought.

"Actually, she seemed a little calmer during dinner," Celeste's mother said. It was the first time she'd spoken. "I thought so, at least. Didn't you, Walter?"

Her husband shrugged.

"She is calm from pills," the housekeeper said with an angry intensity. "Too *many* pills. I say this all the time. She worry about too many things. About Dr. Bushnell. About E-tan. About Adri Anne." She glanced disapprovingly at the girl. "Too many problems, so she need too many pills."

Adrienne flushed. Sobbing, she jumped up and ran out of the room.

"That's enough, Kim!" The uncle glared at the housekeeper and hurried after his niece.

Phil appeared in the doorway a moment later. "Talk to you a minute?" he said to Jessie.

She left the room and followed him up the stairs. "Find something?" she asked when they were out of earshot of the family.

"One of the officers did."

He took her to a hall closet across from Celeste's bedroom. The contents of the shelves lay on the floor: sweaters, purses, shoes, blankets, pillows.

"These were toward the back." Phil picked up a white court shoe. "Somebody tried to clean them, but look here." He pointed to minute specks of a rust-colored substance on the tongue and laces, on the stitching, and along the edge where the rubber sole met the white leather upper.

"And here." Turning the shoe over, he pointed to flecks in the grooves. He put down the shoe and picked up its mate. "Same with this one."

They were Celeste's, Adrienne said when she was shown the shoes.

The housekeeper confirmed the fact. "Missy Celeste just buy them. Why you ask?"

❖ 46 ❖

FUTAKI FINALLY LEFT with the body. Uniformed officers were still searching the rest of the enormous house and grounds, and SID techs would be dusting for fingerprints and bagging evidence for some time. Jessie and Phil had rolled fingerprints—Adrienne's, her uncle's, grandparents', and the housekeeper's.

"For purposes of elimination," the two detectives explained.

But there would be no news until Monday. Saturday was a day of rest for Ballistics and lab technicians, if not for Jessie, who still had miles to go, if not promises to keep. Forget about Shabbat services or lunch at Dafna's, a standing invitation. She would call Ezra's sister after sundown and explain.

She drove to Pacific Station and was pleased to hear that Ethan had eaten dinner and cereal this morning. He was in the middle of his prayers now. She waited in the interrogation room that was becoming like a second home while he finished.

He looked the same—calm, disinterested, as though this were happening to someone else.

"How are you doing, Ethan?" she asked when he was seated across from her.

"It's my Sabbath. I'm trying to focus on what the day means."

She nodded. On the drive here, she'd been trying to figure

out the best way to tell him that the woman who had mothered him for the past ten years had killed herself. Just like his birth mother.

"I have some very sad news, Ethan. Mrs. Bushnell is dead. I'm sorry."

He stared at her—eyes wide, lips parted. "Dead?"

"Apparently she killed herself." He didn't ask how, and she wasn't about to volunteer the information. "I know you spoke with her yesterday. Can you tell me what you talked about?"

He didn't answer. She wasn't certain he'd heard her, so she repeated the question. "It might help Adrienne, Ethan. She's devastated, as you are. Anything you could tell her might ease her pain, and her family's." *I am such an information whore,* she thought.

"Is it true? That she's dead, I mean?"

Jessie nodded. He was crying silently, tears streaming out of his eyes as though they were leaky faucets.

"What did you talk about, Ethan?"

"She wanted me to talk to the attorney she hired. She begged me to let him help me."

"Why didn't you?"

"Sometimes no one can help you. Sometimes you have to do it alone."

"Did Celeste say anything else?"

"She asked me if I was eating, if I was sleeping." He wiped his eyes. "Who's with Adrienne?"

"Her uncle, and her grandparents."

"Can you tell her I'm sorry about Celeste?"

"I can do that. Do you have any idea why Celeste killed herself, Ethan?"

He sighed. "She must have been in terrible pain."

"Is there anything else you want to tell me?"

He was silent for the longest time, and she sensed that he was struggling with something.

"I'm going to say *tehilim* for her soul," he finally said.

"Psalms," he explained. "For Adrienne, too. Rabbi Klinger-man says God always listens to *tehilim*. It doesn't matter if you say them in English or Hebrew. He still listens."

"I'm sure He does."

"Was it with a gun?" he asked suddenly.

"Yes, it was."

"Did she . . . was it in the head?"

"Yes. I'm sorry."

He nodded sagely, as if he'd already known the answer.

"I feel like Alice in Wonderland," Jessie told Phil. They were both back at West L.A. station, deserted now except for a few detectives from Burglary as unlucky as they were to be here on a weekend. "Nothing is what it seems."

"You don't think Celeste killed herself?"

"Everything says she did. She's left-handed. Futaki found GSR on her left hand. The shot to the temple conforms to a wound that would have been self-inflicted by a left-handed person. She wrote a note. Her shoes have what is probably dried blood on them."

"I'm sold. Why aren't you?" He looked at her with interest.

"Why did she kill herself, Phil?"

"She was depressed, like the brother said, especially after she heard that the kid confessed."

"Because she thought he was protecting her. But if that's so, why didn't Ethan admit the truth when I told him Celeste was dead? He had no reason to protect her."

Phil frowned. "So she *didn't* kill herself?"

"She took over twenty tranquilizers, Phil. Maybe to get up the nerve to do the ugly deed—or beautiful, if you're Hedda Gabler." Jessie explained the reference. "Or maybe someone fed her the pills. When she's unconscious, this person simulates a suicide. Puts the gun in her left hand, places it against her temple, shoots. There's GSR on Celeste's left hand, and everything's kosher."

"This someone being the daughter?"

Jessie nodded. "She knew the mom was left-handed. She had opportunity. And motive."

"Which is?"

"To make Celeste look guilty and protect herself. She knows the mom suspects that she killed daddy. She's afraid Celeste will crack under police questioning, which she's sure is going to happen because I'm there all the time, asking questions. See, Celeste didn't need an alibi when she said she was out shopping around the time Bushnell was murdered. Why would she? So when the daughter jumped in and said she was with the mom, Celeste must have wondered why. And then Ethan's in jail, and he won't accept help from an attorney, even though she begs him. Why?"

Phil pulled at his mustache. "So Ethan isn't protecting Celeste."

"Right. But everything suggests he's protecting *someone*. I don't think it's Gideon. No proof—just a feeling in my bones."

"Arthritis." He smiled. "So he's protecting Adrienne. True love runs straight to death row."

"He knows that won't happen. He won't accept help from Thomason because he doesn't want to tell Thomason the truth. But Celeste knows, or suspects. And she's caught in the middle here—the foster son she loves is in jail, probably going to prison for the murders her daughter committed."

"No way out. So maybe Celeste *did* kill herself, Jessie. A mother's love, and all that."

A desperate love, if that's what had happened. "Maybe she did. She takes the rap for the daughter and frees the son. The autopsy and blood tests will tell us."

"Too bad you didn't check the daughter for GSR."

"She washed her hands. But I got her long-sleeved pajama tops." Jessie smiled, pleased.

"Wipe the bird feathers from your mouth." Phil swiveled back and forth for a while, his arms behind his head. "Two problems: One, the housekeeper identified the shoes we found as Celeste's, not Adrienne's. Two, if Ethan's protecting Adrienne, and Celeste's dead, why doesn't he say Celeste did it? He's out, Adrienne's safe."

Jessie looked at him. "Damn you, Phil." She pressed her hands against her temples.

Phil went for a cup of coffee.

She started writing up her notes but couldn't concentrate because she was brooding about Phil's questions. She doodled on her notepad.

"Try this," she said to him when he returned. "He doesn't say it's Celeste, because she's been like his mom, and he loves her. He can't besmirch her name, not even for Adrienne."

"Be*smirch*?" He crinkled his face. "Who're you trying to impress? The English teacher isn't here."

"Well?" she demanded impatiently.

He nodded. "I could buy it. But what about the shoes, Miss S.A.T.?"

❖ 47 ❖

SHE STOPPED AT a retirement facility to visit Hilda Reinhart, the widowed Holocaust survivor she'd befriended four months ago. Hilda adored romance novels but had difficulty reading because of cataracts not ready to be removed. Jessie read to her from the newest Nora Roberts, then went with her for a walk.

The weather forecasters had predicted rain, but the sky was blue except for an occasional cloud. Hilda was bundled up as if she were braced for the North Pole, her lined cheeks pink from blusher and the crisp air. Hooking her thin arm in Jessie's, she walked slowly but with an erect carriage (she was proud that she didn't need a walker or a cane), and in her pronounced European accent, brought Jessie up-to-date on the goings-on of the facility's residents.

"So, what about you, Jesse James?" she asked after they'd circled the block once. "You look sad. You're missing the reporter?"

"Actually, I'm seeing someone else. Very nice. My Judaic studies teacher."

"A rabbi?"

"No. But he's very religious."

"So this is why you're sad! He's so *frum* he won't kiss you until you're married? Maybe it's not so good you're reading romance books to me." Hilda smiled impishly.

Jessie laughed, but the woman had a point. "It's not that.

I have a lot on my mind. The case I'm investigating. Personal stuff, too." The Bushnells, the Meissners, the Pervezes—her mind was crowded with dysfunctional families, with the lies and secrets and tortured relationships that destroyed them. Shadows of sin. Her problems with her own family paled in comparison.

"The case I can't help you with—Miss Marple I'm not." Hilda frowned. "You're having problems with your mother again?"

"My father." It was amazing, how easily she could confide in this eighty-six-year-old woman she barely knew. She told her about the Parkinson's, about the quarrel.

Hilda tssked. "Every day they're finding new medicines, Jessie." She patted her arm. "About the other thing—you want to be angry, or you want to go on?"

"Sometimes I want to be angry. Now I'm almost sorry I confronted him. For years I had this fantasy that I would tell him how I felt, and he would cry and admit the truth and say he's sorry."

"And now, no more fantasy." Hilda sighed. "An egg is cracked, Jesse James. The yolk spills out. You can't put it back, you can't fix the crack."

"So what do you do?"

"Or you throw it out, and waste a good egg. A shame, no? Or, you make an omelette."

Jessie smiled. "An omelette?"

"Or scrambled. It's a figment of speech."

"*Figure* of speech." She loved Hilda's quaint malapropisms and fractured idioms. "You're a very wise woman, Hilda." She stopped and pecked her cheek, inhaling the powdery, rose-scented perfume.

"If not at my age, then when? Bring the rabbi, I'll check him out."

The sky turned dark and brooding, and by the time she came home it was raining. Ten minutes later the sky was blue again, the sun bright. A mercurial day. She did fifteen minutes of stretches to unwind, ate a late lunch of cold leftovers from her Sabbath night dinner, and resisted the pint of vanilla Häagen-Dazs ice cream in the freezer. Funny, how religion worked where her will power failed.

She had missed her morning prayers and the spiritual balm they offered. She read them anyway, though the designated time had passed, and curled up with her afghan on the den couch to study the Torah portion of the week: *Lech Lecha*.

"Go for yourself. . . ." God instructed Abraham to leave his land, his birthplace, and his father to practice the monotheism in which he believed. No wonder Ezra had called Abraham a lonely man of faith. She tried to imagine leaving her city and friends and family and couldn't imagine how Abraham had done it—and he'd been seventy-five at the time, Jessie read in the commentaries. As conflicted as she was about her feelings toward her parents, she didn't want to separate from them. She would have to make it work.

When she heard knocking at the front door, she knew it was Ezra—he wouldn't ring the bell on the Sabbath.

"I loved the flowers," she told him when he was inside. She hung his raincoat in the guest closet and thought how handsome he looked in a navy suit and white shirt. "How long did it take you to walk here?"

"About forty minutes. Not bad."

"What if I wasn't home?"

"But you are." He smiled.

In the kitchen she fixed a paper plate with cookies she'd bought at the kosher bakery yesterday morning and another with fruit, conscious that none of her dishes or glassware or serving utensils were kosher.

"The cookies are pareve," she told him. Nondairy. They took both plates and a bottle of soda and two paper cups into the den.

Ezra made a blessing and ate a cookie. "I figured since

you didn't make it to Dafna's and I didn't hear from you yesterday, you must have been really busy."

"It's been insane. Ethan confessed. He found out the day before the murders that Adrienne is his sister. And Celeste is dead, probably suicide." She gave him a summary of the days' events and what she'd learned, careful to omit details intrinsic to the investigation.

"So much tragedy for one family." Ezra sighed. "That poor kid."

"Rabbi Klingerman says since Adrienne's mother isn't Jewish, according to the Torah Ethan didn't commit incest. But I don't think that's much comfort to Ethan."

"Not much. And now he's lost a second mother." Ezra was silent a moment. "It's weird, you know. I was telling you about the *ben sorer u'moreh*? The Torah section before that deals with a man who during war captures a *yefat to'ar*—a beautiful woman—and weds her. The commentaries say the man knows this union is wrong. Ultimately he comes to resent and hate the wife, as well as the child they have. But the child is entitled to his full inheritance."

Jessie frowned. "I don't get it. What's your point?"

"The commentaries ask why those two sections are connected. And they answer that this child, the product of this union that should never have been—"

"Is the *ben sorer u'moreh*," Jessie interrupted. She shuddered. "Creepy."

"Not exactly the same situation Ethan had with Bushnell."

"It's pretty damn close. Lucy Meissner wasn't a captive in a literal sense, but I suppose she was emotionally captured by Bushnell. Their union was inappropriate, and the son they conceived definitely had problems."

"But is he a *ben sorer u'moreh*? Or is he a kid trying to protect the girl he loves?"

Troubled, Tim Croton had said, but not trouble.

When the Sabbath was over, and three stars appeared in the onyx sky, Ezra recited the evening prayers. In the kitchen

Jessie opened a jar of allspice and another of cloves. She held high a tall braided candle whose wicks joined to form one large flame while Ezra, a paper cup of kosher wine in his hand, performed the havdalah ceremony that separated the Sabbath from the rest of the week.

Though she didn't observe the Sabbath strictly, she liked the idea of this separation between the holy and the secular, between the tranquility of the day and the accelerated pace of the rest of the week (this morning, though, there hadn't been all that much tranquility). She'd bought the candle a month ago and had performed the havdalah herself every week since then, but there was something special about sharing this ritual with Ezra.

She drove him to his apartment, then returned home and changed into an ice blue cashmere sweater she'd bought on sale at Nordstrom's and a short black lycra-blend skirt that had a nice swish to it. He picked her up an hour later. They walked along the Third Street Promenade, and although she would have liked to be like the other couples, most of whom were holding hands and exchanging an occasional kiss, she was all right, at least for now. They drove to a kosher restaurant on Pico that lived up to Ezra's promise of having sinfully delicious desserts. She devoured a huge slice of cheesecake and finished his lemon tart.

Altogether, a very fine evening.

She slept late and woke up refreshed. After her morning prayers and some gardening, she drove to Helen's. The housekeeper answered the door. They had all gone to Santa Barbara for the day.

She felt like a little girl who hadn't been invited to a party the whole class was attending. The lonely woman of faith, she thought, thinking about the week's Torah portion, though her separation from her family wasn't really about faith, and it wasn't really clear who had left whom.

❖ **48** ❖

IN SOME WAYS police work was like fishing, Jessie thought. You cast several lines into the water, and then you waited. Sometimes you got a nibble but came up empty. Sometimes, a piece of old tire or seaweed. Still, you waited. Sometimes you'd land a small fish—not enough to make you happy, but a sign that there were bigger fish in the area. So you'd wait again, because sometimes you reeled in the big one, and sometimes he got away.

Jessie had liked fishing the few times she'd gone with her dad and Helen. But she'd never liked the waiting.

Monday morning, Phil drove to Oxnard. He returned two hours later with the grocery clerk's tentative identification of Lily Pervez's brother as the man who had tried to use Jamal Pervez's credit card. Lily's father and brother had been heatedly protesting their innocence through their attorneys, and police had as yet not found Jamal Pervez's body, but Phil was confident that with the clerk's identification, he would be able to break either the father's or the brother's story.

Jessie had gone downtown and observed the autopsy Futaki had been pressured to perform on Celeste Bushnell by the D.A.'s office. Not a fun morning for Jessie, but the medical examiner had ruled the head wound as the cause of death. Toxicology results were pending.

"Based on the mostly undigested tablets in the victim's stomach," Futaki had told her, "and the fact that digestion and absorption cease at death so that the stomach, blood, and urine contents and drug concentrations are relatively frozen, not much time elapsed between the ingestion of the tablets and the gunshot. Probably about thirty minutes. So the victim could easily have been awake enough to self-inflict the wound."

Tests of Adrienne's pajama tops had detected no GSR.

Latent Prints had lifted multiple prints from the Smith & Wesson. Several of the prints on the gun handle and one on the trigger matched those of the dead woman.

So it looked like suicide.

Latents had yet to identify the other prints they'd lifted. The ones on the barrel, Jessie assumed, would match with Adrienne Bushnell's prints, since the girl had picked up the weapon by the barrel. There was another print, not Celeste Bushnell's, on the trigger. A line cast in the water, and Jessie wondered what it would bring in.

She talked that over with Phil. That plus the news, reported from Thomason via Debra Bergman, that the seminary cook had dropped all car theft charges against Ethan. So the teenager was freed of one charge, and Jessie wondered how, in all fairness, she could detain him on the Bushnell murders when his confession was so inadequate. He'd been arraigned this morning at the Santa Monica courthouse, Debra had told her. Bail had been denied, and he'd been transferred downtown to the county jail.

Jessie phoned Ballistics: they had received the Smith & Wesson from Latents and promised to have results by the end of the day or the next morning, at the latest. Latents promised the same about prints on the note Celeste had left and the athletic shoe. The mate was in the lab, where samples of the stains, already determined to be blood, were being compared to blood from Ronald Bushnell, Nicole Hobart, and Marianna Velasquez.

A few more lines in the water.

A lot more waiting.

*   *   *

She phoned Sally Hayes and learned that the missing teen had returned home last night.

"I was just about to call you," the attorney-mother said. "We're *so* relieved."

"It would have been nice to be informed right away, Mrs. Hayes." Jessie knew she sounded annoyed, but didn't care. "We have police all over the city looking for him." Typical, she thought. People always called in with emergencies or complaints, rarely with thank-yous.

"It was after ten, Detective, and I didn't want to bother you." No apology there. "He was afraid the police bugged my phone and my ex's, and word would get out, and then Ethan would find him. That's why he didn't call home. That's why he took my gun. I told you there was a reason."

So all was well in the land of Hayes, until the next time. The kid would probably get a raise in his allowance. "My partner and I would like to speak to him."

"Kevin's exhausted. He's had a frightful few days."

At least he's alive, Jessie felt like saying. "We'll be over in twenty minutes. Please make sure Kevin's there and awake." She hung up before the woman could argue.

The brown-haired teenager sat on the sofa in the family room, nervously tapping his feet on the floor. He'd been in a motel on Beverly Boulevard near Fairfax that had cheap weekly rates, he told Jessie and Phil. It was within walking distance of a market and a cheap-tickets movie theater where he'd spent the hours waiting for Ethan to be arrested.

"I heard about the murders on TV Monday night, and it scared the shit out of me. I knew Ethan hated the guy, and he was pissed at me."

"Kevin, watch your mouth," the mother warned.

"Fine." He rolled his eyes.

"Why was Ethan angry at you?"

" 'Cause I told Bushnell that Ethan and his precious daughter were doing it."

"You ratted him out because he stopped helping you with your schoolwork, right?" Phil said.

"Ethan and I had a deal, and he broke it." The boy shrugged. "I warned him I'd tell Bushnell, but I guess he didn't believe me." He sounded pleased with himself.

"This isn't how your father and I raised you," the mother said.

"What about Adrienne?" Jessie asked. "Did she hate her father, too?"

Kevin snorted. "Why should she? He let her do whatever she wanted. She's a spoiled bitch."

"Kevin!"

"It's not like you don't talk like that," he retorted. "I hear you on the phone. You say lots worse."

The woman turned crimson and glared at her son.

"Funny, I heard you liked Adrienne, Kevin," Phil said.

"She's hot, but she's a bitch. And Ethan was whipped."

"In what way?"

"If she wanted to party late, he'd stay out late. If she wanted a reefer, he'd get her one. And he'd end up taking the blame with her old man. Word is she drove her mom's car into a pole, and Ethan said he was driving."

What else had Ethan taken the blame for? "But she loves Ethan, right?" Jessie asked.

"She says she does, and she acts like it. But she likes nice things, and I don't think she'd go without for him, you know? If her dad told her to say good-bye or he'd cut her off, she'd slam the door so fast the guy would get whiplash. I think Ethan knows it, too. But hey, it doesn't matter anymore. He's going down for the murders, right?"

At the county jail, Ethan, dressed in the orange jail uniform, bristled when Jessie asked him about the accident.

"No way. Who told you that?"

"One of Adrienne's friends," she lied. "Why did you take the blame, Ethan?"

"What's the difference? No one was hurt."

"But why did you do it?"

He concentrated on rubbing a scratch on the table. "He dad was on her case lately," he finally said. "She was scare of what he'd do if he found out."

"Dr. Bushnell must have been extremely upset with you.

"He grounded me, but it was no big deal. It would've bee worse for Adrienne. She'd had a few drinks, and she wa worried about losing her license and having it on her record I wasn't drinking that night."

"This wasn't the first time she was in trouble with he dad, was it?"

"I don't understand what this has to do with anything."

"What do you think he would have done if he'd found out?

"She was fine with her dad. Can I go now, please?"

Jessie met Klingerman as she was leaving.

"I heard that Mrs. Bushnell killed herself," the rabbi said "Did she leave a note?"

"I can't comment on that, Rabbi."

"How can you let this happen?" he demanded. "You an I both know Eitán didn't commit the murders."

"Get him to tell the complete truth, Rabbi Klingerman. I he'll listen to anyone, it's you."

"I'm trying. I'm going to talk to his public defender."

"And tell him what?"

The rabbi hesitated. "The other day, when I told you wha he asked me about the *halacha* about confessing to crime? wasn't completely honest, because I felt uncomfortable vio lating his confidence."

"What did you leave out?"

"Eitán asked me whether a person could confess to crime he didn't commit knowing that the penalty wa death."

Jessie stared at him. "He said that?"

Klingerman nodded. "I know he'll be angry, but I can' keep this to myself any longer."

*   *   *

Late Monday the blood test results came in: the levels of the tranquilizer were low, indicating that the victim could definitely have been awake enough to pull the trigger. Ballistics informed Jessie that the bullets that had killed Bushnell, Hobart, and Velasquez had come from the Smith & Wesson used to end Celeste Bushnell's life.

A little fish, because Jessie had already assumed as much. But she wasn't about to throw it back into the water.

The prints on the barrel belonged to Adrienne Bushnell. No surprise there, either, or in the fact that Ethan's prints had been found on the handle and trigger. He'd told Jessie he'd handled the gun several times when he was at Gideon's. The surprise was that Latents had found Adrienne's prints on the handle, too, as well as on the trigger.

And on the envelope and note Celeste had allegedly left (the dead woman's prints were on both, too).

And on the tongue and laces and tops of Celeste's athletic shoes, shoes stained with Ronald Bushnell's blood. Shoes that matched perfectly with the prints left at the crime scene.

"Celeste mentioned that very first night that she and Adrienne had the same shoe size," Jessie told Phil.

He nodded. "If the shoe fits. . . ."

Sometimes, she thought, fishing could be damn exciting.

❖ 49 ❖

"I JUST SPOKE with Ms. Bergman in the D.A.s office," Gregory Thomason said. "Celeste Bushnell's death is clearly a suicide, so I don't know why you've detained Adrienne."

He was sitting next to the girl in the interrogation room at West L.A., across the table from Jessie and Phil. The attorney was shorter than Jessie had expected, and rounder, with a cherubic face and bifocals and a halo of snowy hair. Andrew Hepley had phoned him when Jessie and Phil had arrived at the house to take Adrienne in for questioning, and had warned his niece not to say a word unless the attorney was present.

Phil said, "We need to ask Adrienne some questions pertaining to the murders of her father and Ms. Hobart and Ms. Velasquez."

"I've told you everything I know!" The teenager's face was flushed, her eyelids puffy and red from crying.

"You admitted to Detective Drake that you lied to give your mother an alibi. Why did you do that, Adrienne?"

They'd decided that Phil would conduct the questioning because he was a male, and in Adrienne's eyes, probably more like the authority figure her father had been.

"Just a minute." Thomason frowned. "You have a confession from Ethan Meissner. Are you now saying that you believe *Mrs. Bushnell* committed the murders?"

"We're trying to establish the facts, Mr. Thomason. Your client said she was shopping with her mother at the time of the murders. She later admitted that wasn't so."

"All right. Then you've established that Mrs. Bushnell didn't have an alibi. I assume the note she left contained a confession of sorts. But again, why is Adrienne here?"

"There are a few details we'd like to clear up."

"Such as?"

"Adrienne's fingerprints are on the gun Mrs. Bushnell used to kill herself."

His smile was condescending. "Of *course*, they are. Adrienne picked up the gun after she almost stepped on it. She told you so yesterday when you asked her."

"She said she picked it up by the barrel. Her prints are there, and they're also on the handle and trigger."

Thomason's face showed no expression. "Adrienne, do you remember what you told the detective?"

"I think I said I picked up the gun by the handle. I was very upset, and I couldn't really remember. I told the detective that." She gave Jessie a hurt, betrayed look.

"Why would your prints be on the trigger, Adrienne?" Phil asked.

"Don't answer that, Adrienne," the attorney cautioned. "Where is this leading, Detective?"

"The weapon Mrs. Bushnell used was the same weapon that killed Dr. Bushnell and his staff."

Adrienne licked her lips.

Thomason tapped a short finger against his lip. "This is *not* about Mrs. Bushnell. You suspect that Adrienne committed the murders?"

"We're tying up loose ends."

The attorney grunted. "You're trying to ambush a seventeen-year-old girl who just lost both of her parents. I'd like to speak to my client alone for a few minutes."

Phil stood. "No problem."

Jessie left the room with him. Ten minutes later Thoma-

son informed them that Adrienne was ready, and they re
turned to the interrogation room.

The attorney looked unhappy. "I've advised Adrienne tha
it's not in her best interests to answer anything at this tim
Against my recommendation, she wants to answer you
questions."

Covering his butt, Jessie thought.

"I have nothing to hide," the girl said with quiet intensit
"I didn't *do* anything."

"Good. Then we should be able to clear all this up." Ph
nodded. "Adrienne, how did your fingerprints get onto th
handle and trigger of the gun?" he asked pleasantly.

"I touched it when I was at Gideon's apartment."

"When was that?"

"A while ago, before Ethan went away. Gideon was ou
of town for a week, so Ethan and I went to the apartment
be together. Ethan had a key." Her pale cream complexio
had turned pink. "We were talking about his mom, and h
asked me if I wanted to see the gun she used to kill hersel
It was creepy, but I said okay. I knew he wanted to show
to me."

Very creepy, Jessie thought. Very sad.

"Where was it?" Phil asked.

"In Gideon's room, underneath some shirts. There wer
two guns. Ethan picked one up and showed me the safet
was on. He held the gun to his head. That's how his mo
did it."

Too much pain, Jessie thought. She didn't look at Phil.

"I asked him if I could hold it. He gave it to me, and I p
my finger against the trigger, like I was going to shoo
That's why my fingerprints are on it."

Phil gazed at her without speaking for a moment. The gi
shifted on her seat.

"Why would you do that, Adrienne?"

She shrugged. "Just to see what it felt like. But it made m
nervous, so I gave it back to him."

Phil narrowed his eyes. "You didn't mention on Sunday that this was Gideon's gun, Adrienne."

"I didn't know, for sure. All guns look alike to me. But if my prints are on the trigger, then it has to be Gideon's gun," she said doggedly. "It's the only one I ever held."

A plausible explanation. Jessie was watching the girl but couldn't read her.

"Can you recall what day you were there?" Phil asked.

"We were there a couple of times, so it's hard to remember. We went after school. My mom was with clients, and my dad was at the office."

When the cat's away, Jessie thought. Amazing how little parents knew about their kids' activities.

"Did any of the neighbors see you?" Phil asked.

"I don't think so. Well, *I* didn't see anyone, so I don't think anyone saw us."

"So how did the gun get into the house?"

She frowned. "I don't know. I guess my mom took it from Gideon's."

"Why would she do that, Adrienne?"

"I don't know. I guess—" She broke off. "I don't know."

"Did she show it to you?"

"No. I didn't know it was there."

"Do you think she killed your father, Adrienne?" he asked quietly. "Is that why you lied, to give her an alibi?"

She nodded. Her lips were quivering.

"Why would she kill your father, Adrienne?"

"I don't know!" she whispered. "She was acting weird at dinner. She started crying out of nowhere. She scared me. I guess that's why she killed herself, because she was sorry."

"Did you read the note, Adrienne?"

She hesitated, and her eyes narrowed into slits. "Yes."

A wise admission, Jessie thought. She probably realized she'd left her fingerprints on the envelope and card.

"Why did you read it?" Phil asked.

"I wanted to understand. I needed to *know*."

"Needed to know what?"

"Why she did it," the girl said in a low voice. "Why she killed my dad."

"If you thought your mother killed your dad, Adrienne, why did you let Ethan take the blame?"

"I didn't know what to *do*. She's my *mother*!"

"So you don't think Ethan killed your father?"

"No." She shook her head.

"Your prints were on your mother's shoes, Adrienne. How is that?"

"Adrienne, don't answer," Thomason cautioned.

"I can explain that," she told the attorney. She faced Phil. "The tread on my court shoes was gone, so I threw them out and borrowed my mom's. We wear the same size. Nine and a half."

"But your mother's prints weren't on the shoes."

"They were new. I guess she hadn't worn them yet."

"You took them even though they were brand-new?"

Adrienne shrugged. "My mom didn't mind. It was just a pair of shoes."

"How do you explain the blood?"

She blinked rapidly. "What blood?"

"Adrienne!" Thomason frowned and put his hand on her arm. He would have liked to clamp his hand on the girl's mouth instead, Jessie guessed.

"Our lab technicians identified your father's blood on both shoes," Phil asked. "The shoes match the prints left at the crime scene."

"Adrienne, do *not* say a thing," the attorney warned.

Phil said, "If your mom didn't wear the shoes, Adrienne, and you borrowed them, and your dad's blood is on them. . . . You can see why we have a problem here."

"I don't understand."

Thomason was glaring at the girl. "Adrienne, I *insist* that you follow my instructions. That's why your uncle retained my services. Trust me."

"My mom must have used the shoes."

The attorney pursed his lips.

"Her prints aren't on them, Adrienne," Phil said.

"I didn't kill my father!" She gripped the edge of the table. "I *loved* him! Why would I kill him?"

"Because the good times were over, Adrienne. Daddy was sending you away to boarding school."

"That's a lie!"

"We have a witness who will testify that your father had talked about it before."

Barbara Martin. Jessie had phoned her and learned that Bushnell had complained to her bitterly about the trouble he was having with Adrienne. He'd had enough, he told his lover. He was clamping down, taking away her credit cards, setting a strict curfew. And in January, she would be going away to school—away from Ethan.

"So what? He didn't mean it. My dad was upset that day, okay? He was mad because he found me with Ethan. But I knew he'd get over it. He always did." She was angry now and had dropped her little girl voice and posture.

"Adrienne, *shut up*!" Thomason's face was dangerously red.

"You didn't mention any of this before. You lied to Detective Drake and to me, over and over."

"I was scared! I knew you'd misunderstand. My dad loved me. He would *never* have sent me away."

"He asked the headmaster at your school to recommend several boarding schools," Phil said. "He phoned the schools and he had them mail applications. They arrived on Friday. He made appointments to meet with the headmasters."

"No." She shook her head.

"He canceled your credit cards. We checked. He told you he'd had it with the drinking and the drugs and the late nights, Adrienne. We know he talked to you Monday morning from his office. You were begging him to give you another chance. He said, 'I've made up my mind. I should have done this a long time ago.' " Phil leaned toward her. "Sound familiar, Adrienne?"

She looked shocked but quickly gained her composure. "He didn't mean it. I knew he didn't mean it."

Thomason looked like a lifeguard helpless to save a thrashing swimmer about to drown.

"This time he did. He was cutting you off, and you were angry," Phil said. "And he was having his lawyer change his will so Ethan would get half his estate. Did he tell you he'd give Ethan *all* of it if you didn't shape up?"

"No!" She glared at him with venom. "Anyway, I don't care about the money. I love Ethan. He loves me. We wanted to get married."

"Why would your mother kill your father, Adrienne? She had no motive. Why'd you read the note, unless you were worried she was telling us who *really* killed all those people? She killed herself because of you, Adrienne. Because she knew what you'd done."

"She hated him!" the girl yelled, lunging forward. "She was *screaming* at him on the phone! I *heard* her!"

"When was that?"

She leaned back and panted, exhausted by her outburst. "When I came home from school. She was in her room. I picked up the phone and I heard them."

"What did she say?"

"She wished he was dead. She said she knew everything—that he'd lied to her all these years, that Ethan—" Her face was screwed up in anger. "That Ethan was his *son*."

"So she took Gideon's gun and went to your father's office and killed him."

Adrienne nodded.

"But her prints aren't on the shoes, Adrienne. Yours are," Phil said softly. "Why would you hide the shoes in the hall closet if you weren't worried about them?"

"I didn't hide them," she said, her tone sullen and defiant. "I don't know how they got there."

"When you found out Ethan was your brother, that ended the romance, right?"

She didn't answer.

"So maybe you weren't thrilled about your dad giving him half the money. Maybe you wanted Ethan out of the picture."

She wouldn't meet his eyes. "No, that's not true."

"Ethan knows about your mother. He's retracting his confession."

She looked at him warily.

"He admitted he's been protecting you. He said *you* did it, Adrienne."

"For God's sake, Adrienne, don't answer," Thomason warned.

She froze. "You're lying. You're trying to trick me."

Phil shook his head. "He says he can't lie anymore. He's found faith in God, Adrienne, and that faith won't let him lie, not even for you."

"Ethan wouldn't say that."

"Wouldn't say what? The truth?"

"He loves me. You're making this up."

"He's tired of taking the blame, Adrienne. He said so."

"Ethan loves me."

Like a mantra, Jessie thought.

"You committed incest because your father hid the truth. Is that why you killed him, or because you didn't want to share the money with your brother? Or was it both, Adrienne? I don't blame you for being disgusted, for being angry with your father."

"I didn't *do* it." Her eyes darted from side to side. "*He* did. Ethan."

"*Ethan* killed your dad?"

She nodded vehemently. "He had the same reason. Why would he confess if he didn't do it?"

"He confessed to protect you, Adrienne. Your father called the lawyer. Your father was going to give Ethan half his estate. Why would Ethan kill him, Adrienne?"

She didn't answer.

"I thought you said your mother did it."

"I guess I was wrong."

"But what about the shoes, Adrienne?" Phil said. "What about those shoes?"

THE DRIVE TO Big Bear seemed less frightening this time, maybe because she'd done it so recently. Jessie listened to Tony Bennett, then a little Barbra, then ABBA's "Dancing Queen," which made her think of Ezra and smile. They had dinner plans tonight, as soon as she returned from the seminary. To celebrate the end of the case, he'd said, and she was certainly ready to do that.

Adrienne had been arraigned on Wednesday morning in an adult court, a result of Proposition 21. State law prevented the district attorney from going for the death penalty, even though citizens were demanding harsh sentences for violent crimes, no matter what the age of the perpetrator. The girl was now in county jail, awaiting her trial, which was months away. And Ethan was back at Etz Chayim, immersed, Klingerman had reported, in study and prayer.

Ethan had never confirmed Adrienne's guilt or his suspicion. He'd listened quietly when Jessie told him that Adrienne had been arrested, had insisted that there must be some mistake. He'd been heartbroken when Adrienne had refused to talk to him. Thomason's instructions, Jessie wondered, or her anger at his supposed betrayal? She felt a little guilty about planting that seed, but she had learned long ago that the ethics of homicide investigation didn't always bear close examination, that the end very often *did* justify the means, as long as those means were legally, if not morally, defensible. It was hard not to feel proud about having accomplished her goal. At the same time, she felt sullied by the process. Klingerman, she was certain, would not applaud her manipulations and lies or Adrienne's indictment. Two witnesses and a warning, he would say.

The local media gave the arrest almost hourly coverage when the news broke, and even the national stations picked it up. There were the usual questions: Were there warning signs? What is happening to our teen population? Where will the violence end? And as usual, there were opinions presented on news shows by psychologists who were dragged from anonymity into the limelight and would be forgotten just as quickly until the next tragedy.

You could try to analyze Adrienne Bushnell, Jessie thought: a spoiled, wealthy girl accustomed to getting her way; a girl raised by an authoritarian father and a permissive mother, both of whom were clueless as to what was going on in their daughter's life until it was too late. Drinking, drugs. And if you wanted to talk psychology, you could ponder the fact that like Ethan, Adrienne had been separated at birth from her mother. Had that caused attachment disorder?

Or was she simply a wayward daughter raised by two parents who didn't have similar voices?

Klingerman wasn't around, and she was relieved. She wasn't in the mood for I-told-you-so's. The tall boy who had answered the door on her first visit informed her that Ethan was in his room.

He was sitting at his desk, reading, and stood up when she entered. His face was still pale but not as gaunt, and she sensed a peacefulness that had been missing the other times she'd seen him.

"Rabbi Klingerman told me you were coming." He sounded curious.

She opened her purse and handed him an envelope. "Gideon just found this. He thought you'd want to have it.

It's from Celeste. She must have left it that Monday when she came to see you."

He stared at the envelope, then took it and sat down on his bed. Opening the flap, he pulled out a folded piece of stationery and read to himself. He looked up.

"She says no matter what happened, she'll always love me, and I'll always be her son," he said in a thick voice. "That I shouldn't despair, that God doesn't blame me." He offered the letter to Jessie.

She shook her head. "Celeste meant that for your eyes only." Two days ago, she would have combed it for details, for clues. Two days ago she would have had the handwriting compared with a known sample of the alleged author to verify its authenticity. She'd done that with the suicide note— Celeste had written it.

He slid the letter back into the envelope and placed it on his desk. "You came all the way up here to bring this to me? Gideon could have mailed it."

"It's a good opportunity for me. I have to overcome my fear of driving these mountains. It's a little ridiculous." She smiled. "Actually, the assistant district attorney needs to talk to you. Today I'm just the chauffer."

He tensed. "I don't want to testify against Adrienne."

"I'm afraid you don't have a choice," she said gently. "You're a material witness, Ethan. I suppose you can arrange with the van driver to pick you up later today."

"I guess I'll stay overnight with Gideon. The funerals are tomorrow."

Both funerals. Andrew Hepley had postponed Ronald's funeral until Celeste could be buried, too. Jessie had forgotten. And the deceaseds' daughter was in jail.

She waited while he stuffed toiletries and a change of clothing into his backpack and slipped a suit into a short black plastic garment bag.

"Ready."

In the car she switched on the radio to fill the silence, but he started talking. His plans were unclear, he told her. For now, he was content staying in the seminary, although maybe someday he'd go to college. And there was music. Music was his passion.

"Like Gideon," Jessie said.

"Like Gideon." He sighed. "It's going to be awkward, being around him. I don't know what I am to him anymore."

"His son. That's what he told me."

"But I'm a reminder that my mom cheated on him."

She hugged the right side of the road, searching ahead for oncoming traffic.

"Rabbi Klingerman said when the time comes, he's going to find the right girl for me," Ethan said. "I think he's saying that so I won't feel hopeless."

Jessie debated, then said, "I've been thinking about that. You look an awful lot like Gideon, you know. Your hair, your eyes, your build. What if Ronnie was wrong?"

The teenager stared at her. "How could he be wrong? You mean he lied?" He sounded shaken.

"Maybe he thought he was telling the truth. Suppose your mom wanted Ronnie to leave Celeste, but he refused. Maybe she lied and told him she was pregnant with his child to force his hand. I doubt that Ronnie demanded a paternity test."

The teenager was silent for a moment. "But when Ronnie didn't leave Celeste, why didn't my mother tell him the truth?"

"That would have been hard, to admit that kind of lie. Then your mom became more and more depressed. When she planned to take her life, she wanted to insure you'd be taken care of. She knew Gideon wasn't capable of raising a child by himself. Maybe she hoped Ronnie would feel responsible and adopt you."

"I know you're trying to make me feel better, Detective Drake. But the fact is, I'm a *mamzer*."

"Maybe not. It's worth checking into, Ethan. We have

samples of Ronnie's blood. It's easy to do a paternity test. The lawyers will probably insist on one anyway before they settle the estate."

He didn't answer.

"I've upset you," she said, chagrined. "I'm sorry. I was just trying to help."

"No, that's okay. I know you mean well. I don't know if I want to put myself through that, get my hopes up, just to find out I'm back where I started." He shook his head. "I think I'll leave it alone. Ronnie was sure."

She nodded. "Okay."

She noticed a sprinkling of drops on the windshield. A moment later it was pouring, and she shut the Honda's electric windows. Just as suddenly the thunderstorm passed.

"There's a rainbow," she said.

"What?"

She pointed to her right.

Ethan looked out the window. "Rabbi Klingerman said there's a blessing you're supposed to say. God's warning us that He could have destroyed the world."

She wasn't surprised that the teenager saw the negative. "True. But He's also affirming His promise to save us. Life is filled with dualities like that, Ethan."

"I guess you're right."

He sounded distracted and was probably brooding about what she'd said. She wished she hadn't spoken.

"Will I have to face her? Adrienne, I mean?"

He looked so sad, she wished she could give him a hug. "In court, during the trial." She smiled at him reassuringly. "And then it'll be over."

"I don't think it'll *ever* be over. I've had nightmares about my mom's suicide since I was a kid. The last few days I've been dreaming about Ronnie and Celeste, too. I guess it's 'cause they all died the same way. I keep seeing the bullet wounds in their heads." He shuddered and hugged his arms.

"You might want to go for therapy, Ethan."

He nodded.

She decided to leave him to his thoughts. She didn't immediately absorb what he'd said. Seconds later she did, and her heart pounded. She clutched the steering wheel.

How had he known about Bushnell's head wound?

She looked straight ahead and hoped her face didn't betray her shock. She had unconsciously moved toward the center of the road and didn't see the car coming toward her until it was practically right on top of her, the driver honking furiously. She moved sharply to the right.

Out of the corner of her eye she saw that he was watching her—brown eyes fathomless, without expression, face frozen.

He knew he'd slipped up.

Her gun was in her purse, on the floor at her feet.

"My ears are popping. Want some gum?" she asked in what she prayed was a casual voice. She reached for her purse, but in one swift movement he had picked it up and taken out her Beretta.

He sat back, out of her reach, and aimed the gun at her. "I can't believe how dumb that was," he said quietly. "That's what happens when you think you're safe. You drop your guard. And you distracted me." He sounded angry with himself, with her.

"What are you doing, Ethan? That's not funny."

"We both know I just blew it. So I've got to figure out what to do next. Keep both hands on the wheel!" he warned when she moved her right hand.

"Put down the gun, Ethan. Now."

"I'd never be able to explain a gunshot wound," he said with a frightening calm, as though he were trying to prove a geometry theorem. "But I'm not going to jail for the rest of my life. I'd rather be dead."

"We can get you help, Ethan. We can—"

"Don't bullshit me." He cocked his head. "I really had you going, didn't I? You felt sorry for me—you and your partner and that shrink you sent. And Rabbi Klingerman. He was *begging* me not to confess." He allowed himself a half smile.

Her hands were clammy and her heart was racing. "Why did you go to the seminary in the first place?" Get him talking, keep him calm.

"Gideon insisted. He said it was the best place for me to detox, but I think he wanted to make Ronnie and Celeste sweat. I did, too." He scowled, as if remembering his grievances. "And it was kind of fun, playing the game. Easy, too. You give them what they want. I learned that a long time ago. You smile or sigh or cry. You open up to them. You tell them how much you appreciate everything they're doing, and they believe you."

If she could keep him talking, if she could reach the flat highway and think straight. . . . "But you weren't playing the game all the time. Your grades were falling. Most of your teachers said you were headed for trouble."

"That was the drugs and the booze. Dumb." He nodded. "I lost control. But I was so *pissed* with Ronnie. Nothing I did was good enough for him, nothing."

She forced herself to ignore the gun and concentrate on the oncoming cars and the sharp curves that loomed, one after the other, causing havoc to her stomach and nerves.

"Mr. Croton thinks you're special. He really likes you, Ethan. He cares about you."

"Because I was his AP star student. I made him look good. I told him my sad little story so he'd feel all warm inside for trying to help me, and in return he wrote me a great recommendation and was always on my side. Croton's okay, though." The teenager looked thoughtful. "He won't think I'm so special if he knows I killed three people."

There was so much cynicism, so much defensiveness. She sensed that Croton *had* touched a chord.

Another curve. She slowed and did what seemed like a 180-degree turn until she finally straightened the car. "Do you want to tell me what happened, Ethan?"

"Turn the car around," he suddenly ordered.

She could see the beginning of another curve about fifteen car lengths ahead. "I can't do that, Ethan. I'll kill both of us."

"Turn it around *now*, dammit!" With a sharp movement, he twisted the wheel with his left hand and moved his foot onto the accelerator.

She fought him, but he was incredibly strong. The Honda veered left. For one terrifying moment she thought the car would go off the cliff, but she stopped fighting him and spun the wheel to the left until the car was facing uphill.

Slamming on the brakes, she brought the Honda to a screeching halt.

❖ 51 ❖

THE GUN AT her temple was cold. She was shaking uncontrollably and refused to imagine the nothingness that lay a few feet away beneath the blue sky.

A car was coming down the road.

"Keep your hands on the wheel and don't say a word." Ethan pressed the gun tight against her head.

The car was coming closer. See the gun! Jessie demanded silently, but the driver passed without slowing.

"Pop the hood latch," he ordered.

The nausea in her throat was rising, compounded by the stench of burning rubber. She found it an effort to speak. "Put the gun down, Ethan, and we'll work something out."

"Pop the hood. If someone stops, you'll say the radiator overheated and we're just waiting till it cools down. If you do anything else, I'll shoot you, and then I'll shoot the other driver." He pressed the barrel against her head. "Do it."

The flat look in his eyes convinced her. She released the hood. Anything to buy time. Maybe another car would see her and stop.

"Let me tell you a story," he said somberly. "Once upon a time there was a boy who had the shittiest parents in the world. A loser drunk father and a self-absorbed mother who didn't give a shit about anyone but herself, especially her kid, so she sprayed her brains all over the bedroom and let her little boy find her."

He was mocking her, feeling superior. That was good, she told herself. Superior was better than desperate. People who were desperate often did desperate things.

"The boy went to live with another family. The dad was a moron and a control freak, Goddammit, you'll do as I *say*, Ethan!" he hissed. "And the mom was clueless," he continued in a soft voice, "and didn't even know that the boy and the daughter, a rich bitch princess who made him cover up for her all the time, were doing it on the parents' five-hundred-dollar sheets. And it was good, detective, very good, and the boy figured he was finally safe.

"But the dad said, Whoa! No way are you going to get my little princess. And guess what? You've been doing your *sister*, sucker. So disappear and don't bother me, and I'll pay you off. But the boy figured it wasn't enough. No *way* was it enough, after everything they'd done to him and his mom, after the dad made him feel like he had to be *grateful*, when all the time it was coming to him. So he popped the dad in the head, and in the balls, too. That was for his mom. And that felt good, very good." He took a deep breath. "That's basically the story, Detective. I think you know how it ends. How's that for details? Last time you said I didn't have enough details."

His voice was flinty with anger, but beneath it she heard the pain. If she weren't so terrified, she might have felt sorry for him. "How did you get Dr. Bushnell's blood on the shoes?"

Another car passed them and continued down the mountain. She supposed it wasn't unusual to see vehicles pulled over to the side of the road, but she felt choked with helplessness and frustration. She wanted to scream.

"Ronnie keeps a box of latex gloves in the house," Ethan said. "Adrienne and I used them for water balloons when we were kids. I put on a pair and took the shoes from Adrienne's closet. I have a small foot, so I knew they'd fit. When I came back, I put the shoes in a hall closet. I dropped the gun off, too. Kim's off Mondays from five on, so I knew Celeste and Adrienne would be out. Monday night is family night out. Celeste's idea of togetherness." He sneered.

"How did you know no one would see you when you picked up the shoes?"

"Just one car in the driveway. Adrienne was in school, Celeste had appointments. I heard her whisper that just before she left Gideon's. I knew she wouldn't cancel. She's got fabric swatches for brains. And Kim walks to the market the same time every day. For *fresh* fruit and veg-e-ta-ble. Nothing stale for fam-i-ly." He mimicked the housekeeper's accent and pronunciation.

"So you *wanted* Adrienne to be blamed."

He shrugged. "I didn't much care. Why should I? No one cares about anyone. I knew that eventually the police would search the house. I didn't mind waiting."

He sounded totally detached. No empathy, Manny had said. "I thought you loved Adrienne, Ethan, and she loved you. How can you let her go to prison for what you did?"

"Love is crap. My mom said she loved me, and look what happened. My dad, too. Adrienne was grossed out by the incest thing. I told her when she ran after me, begging me not to leave her. She looked at me like I was scum. She tried to cover up, but I knew she'd want me out of her life, and she'd convince Ronnie to cut me out. That's been my whole life—people screwing me. I decided I wasn't going to let it happen again. That money is *coming* to me. I'm the firstborn son." His face was mottled with anger.

"And Celeste? How did you get her to use the gun?"

She heard the sound of a car engine laboring up the road. A moment later the driver was honking at them, and she saw his impatient face as he passed the Honda.

"Let's get this over with." With his left hand, Ethan groped for the seat belt button and released her straps.

"If you shoot me, they'll know it was you," she said, her tone reasonable. "People at the seminary saw you leave with me. My partner will find you. He's relentless." She refused to believe that she was going to die here, that she would never again see Ezra, or Phil. Or her sister or mother or father, with whom she still hadn't talked since Friday night. Or Helen's baby. "Put down the gun, Ethan. We'll work something out."

"You're going to have an accident. A tragic fall. I'll cry and tell them how you tried to save us. I'm a terrific crier. Real convincing, but you know that. Open your door."

Her heart hammered in her chest. "I guess you're going to have to shoot me. They'll know you did it."

"You're going to get out of the car," he said, his tone cold. "And you're going to stumble off the edge of the cliff, because you were a little disoriented."

With a sudden move, he slammed her face into the steering wheel. She cried out at the pain. Grabbing a fistful of hair, he yanked her head back and slammed it into the wheel again. Lights flashed in front of her eyes, then waves of blackness, and she thought she was going to pass out.

"Get out," he ordered a moment later.

His voice came from her left. Moaning, she lifted her throbbing head slowly and saw through blurred eyes that he had walked around and opened the driver's door. The hood was all the way up.

"I'm dizzy." She touched her face gingerly and felt a huge bump on her forehead and something moist where the skin had broken. A sharp pain radiated from her nose, and she wondered if it was broken. She licked her upper lip and tasted blood.

Shifting the gun to his left hand, he grabbed her upper arm and pulled her out of the car. Her legs buckled. He yanked her straight and dug his fingers into her arm.

"Simon says put your hands on top of your head, Detective."

She obeyed. He stood behind her, the gun at the back of her head. They were a foot away from the edge of the cliff. The sun was too bright and hurt her eyes. She was dizzy and nauseated and scared to death. She welcomed the brisk wind on her face and inhaled deeply, hoping to clear her head. She tried to imagine the clear sheet of glass, but like last time, it didn't really help. She wondered if Jerry Light would be the one to find her broken body.

"Tell me about Celeste," she said. "About the gun. I'm just curious." She was stalling, praying that a car would come, any car. Up or down.

"I was hoping she'd use it." His breath was warm on her neck and made her shiver. "That day she visited me at the jail, I told her Adrienne and I had done the murders together, that I'd hidden evidence where she'd never find it that would lead the police to Adrienne, not me. I told her Adrienne had put the gun behind her doll collection. The only way to save Adrienne, I said, was if Celeste killed herself and confessed. Use the gun, I told her. That's how it all started, when my mom killed herself because of you."

She wondered if he believed what he was saying. "Celeste was always so good to you, Ethan. She always protected you." She considered moving her hands down swiftly, but he would pull the trigger. She knew that.

"This was really her fault, you know. I told her that. I told her she was a fat cow who couldn't keep her husband happy. I told her that's why Ronnie turned to my mom, why they had me, why my mom killed herself. I told her it was her fault that Adrienne and I committed incest, her fault that we killed Ronnie and the others. All her fault. She was crying hysterically because she knew it was true."

"Ethan—"

"Here's the deal," he said crisply. "You can jump, or I can push you. I want to be fair."

Her chest tightened, and she couldn't breathe. "The police will know."

"They may suspect, but they can't *know*. Simon says, take one step forward." He prodded her forward with the gun.

Her feet were inches from the edge of the cliff.

"Do you feel the pull, Detective Drake?" he said softly. "You asked me that, remember?"

She felt the pull. She looked down at the hard, unforgiving rocks. This wasn't how she wanted to die, her body broken into little pieces. She would rather be shot.

In one swift motion that rattled her head and made her scream with silent pain, she dropped suddenly to her knees and whirled around as the bullet flew invisibly and soundlessly into the air where her head had been a second ago.

•Surprise was on her side. She knocked him to the ground and chopped at his wrist until his fingers opened like claws in a quarter-a-game machine and released the prize. Her gun.

Her breath was ragged, her forehead was pulsing madly. She thought she would lose consciousness at any moment. She held the Beretta in both hands. "Stand up, Ethan."

He lay there on the ground, not moving.

"Get up." Her handcuffs were in her purse, in the car.

Slowly he rolled over and rose to his feet.

"Move to the car," she ordered.

He took a step backward. "You'll have to come get me. I know you're afraid of heights, but if you want to take me, that's what you'll have to do."

"Ethan, don't be crazy."

He moved back another step. He rocked on his toes and spread his arms, like a diver about to do a backward flip into a pool.

"Ethan!"

Another step, and now his heels were off the ground. Suddenly he lost his balance. His arms were flailing, and she could see the panic in his eyes. Even as his mouth opened to scream, she rushed forward and tried to grab his arm but found herself clutching air.

She sank to the ground and retched. His scream still rang in her ears and she wasn't sure she heard the thud of his body as it hit the hard mountain stone.

❖ 52 ❖

THERE WAS A blessing for everything, Jessie learned.

Ezra accompanied her to the synagogue on Thursday morning, where she stood in the women's section, behind the latticework *mechitza*, and recited *birchat ha'gomel*. A prayer of thanks to God for having saved her from a perilous situation, "for having bestowed every goodness upon me," she intoned.

She couldn't remember how long she had lain on the ground, her cheek against the moist earth. Whatever impetus had given her the courage to come so close to the edge had forsaken her, and she was too terrified to move. At some point she'd pulled herself onto all fours and crawled backward, very carefully, toward the road.

She'd phoned the Big Bear sheriff's department first, then Phil, then Ezra, and had sat in her car for what had seemed an eternity until help arrived in the form of Jerry Light and company. After making certain she didn't need emergency medical treatment, he listened somberly while she told him what had happened. She was grateful that he'd let her get by with pointing to the spot where Ethan had been standing when he'd fallen. When Light walked to the cliff's edge and crouched down, she turned her head aside.

While another officer followed in her Honda, she went with Light in his car to Lake Arrowhead, where a doctor examined her pupils for signs of concussion and she answered a sheriff's deputy's questions about Ethan's fatal fall and what had led to it. She had a fierce headache and felt as though chips of cranial bone were rattling around inside her skull. Every part of her face hurt. It was purpled and bloodied and swollen, especially her forehead and eyes. She barely recognized herself in the rest room mirror.

Clamping together her bruised, puffy lips, she tried not to wince as the doctor swabbed her forehead, chin, and nose (not broken, but badly bruised, he judged) and applied an antibiotic ointment. He gave her Tylenol with codeine and a tetanus shot and five stitches just below her left eyebrow. She was damn lucky, he told her, that she hadn't shattered the bones above both eyes, or worse.

She already knew that. She wondered whether they'd need a helicopter to retrieve the body or whether hikers would use rappelling gear.

She wanted badly to go home. When she mentioned that she could probably drive back to L.A., the doctor talked about hidden concussions and possible light-headedness, and Light said, no way. It had been a dumb idea, really, because even without the codeine, she was sleepy and wanted to lie down. She did that on a bed in one of the examining rooms, after she finished answering the deputy's questions, while she waited for Phil, who had insisted on coming to get her though Jerry Light had offered to drive her home.

What seemed like minutes but was actually almost three hours later, she heard someone calling her name. She opened her eyes, and for a moment thought she was dreaming.

"Hey." She smiled wanly and winced at the pull on her lips and cheeks.

Ezra's eyes were filled with anguish, and he looked as though he were about to cry. "You're in pain."

"It looks worse than it is." She sat up too quickly and felt the blood rush to her head. "Where's Phil?"

"Talking shop with one of the officers. Are you sure you're well enough to sit in a car for three hours?"

"Try and stop me."

She stood up shakily and almost fell. He caught her and hugged her tight. "Thank God you're okay," he whispered.

She rested her sore cheek gingerly on his chest and shut her eyes. She wanted to stay in his arms forever, but a moment later he released her and took an awkward step backward. She supposed she would have to feast on the memory of that embrace for some time. "I look like an eggplant."

"I like eggplants."

Her eyes filled with tears. She was lucky to have him in her life, lucky to be alive. In her mind's eye she saw herself standing at the edge of the cliff, saw the boy's arms flailing before he disappeared, like a bird unable to take flight. "I tried to catch him."

He nodded.

"He totally fooled me, Ezra."

"He fooled everyone. Don't blame yourself, Jessie."

It was hard not to. She cringed at the smug certainty with which she'd pursued Adrienne. Now the girl was orphaned. Jessie wondered whether she could have prevented Celeste's death, though she wasn't sure how. Maybe not. Maybe everything had been set in motion long ago, when Lucy Meissner and Ronnie Bushnell had taken that first, ill-fated step.

"It's eerie the way he died," she said. "Stoned to death—almost like the *ben sorer u'moreh*, except that no one executed him. He did it to himself."

"Maybe not."

She thought about that, and the fact that Adrienne Bushnell could have spent the rest of her life in prison.

Maybe she was seeking absolution.

From the synagogue she drove to Forest Lawn Mortuary and listened to a minister eulogize Ronald and Celeste Bushnell. Adrienne had been released late yesterday afternoon, and she was in the front pew with her uncle and grandparents and housekeeper. After the service Jessie debated walking over to pay her respects and offer apologies, but she decided her presence wouldn't be appreciated. She would stop at the Bushnell house in a day or so, though she wasn't sure what she'd say.

She wondered where Adrienne would live. Probably with her uncle. At least she had family. Jessie had talked with Alex Velasquez's great-aunt two days ago. The woman had still made no decision about keeping the boy permanently.

Forest Lawn wasn't far from Meissner's apartment. Orit Yardeni opened the door. She looked startled when she saw Jessie's face, but her surprise quickly turned into displeasure, and she stepped aside wordlessly to allow Jessie to enter.

Gideon was on the sofa, next to Klingerman. Both men looked ravaged, but while Gideon's face was darkened because he hadn't shaved in days, Rabbi Klingerman's beard appeared grayer than Jessie remembered, and the lines around his blue eyes more deeply etched. The rabbi flinched when he saw her face. Meissner seemed not to notice.

She sat on the ottoman. "I'm terribly sorry about Ethan, Mr. Meissner."

Meissner nodded. "Your partner was here yesterday. He told me. Did Eitán say something? Did he explain?"

She had debated while driving here how she would answer that question if asked. She shook her head. "He was a very unhappy young man, Mr. Meissner."

Meissner stood abruptly and left the room. His sister went after him.

"The father's going to sit shiva," Klingerman told Jessie. "To him, Eitán will always be his son."

The man had picked up the mantle of fatherhood too late, Jessie thought. Too late for himself, too late for Ethan.

"You're thinking I'm a fool," the rabbi said. "You're thinking I'm naive."

She could tell him Ethan had goaded Celeste into killing herself, but what would be the point? She had been fooled, too. She shook her head. "I'm thinking there are no answers, Rabbi."

"He had a spark," Klingerman insisted. "Everybody does. If he had stayed with us, I could have reached him."

At the station she received an awkward but sincere "Glad you're okay" from Simms and a careful hug from Ed Boyd. He'd settled on a pair of onyx and silver earrings for his girl-friend, he told Jessie. Sheryl loved them.

Phil hummed the opening of the wedding march. Simms sang the first line of "Working on a Chain Gang" and laughed when Boyd punched his arm.

Even Espes was solicitous in his gruff way. "You look like shit, Drake," he told her in his office, after she'd reported what had happened. "Take a day off."

She considering driving down to La Jolla to make peace with her father, but her parents would be horrified if they saw her battered face, and Frances would demand again that she quit her job and urge her to have that little bump re-moved from her nose, now that it had been bruised.

Even if she'd contemplated taking up Espes on his offer, she had too much work to do. Writing up her notes of what happened took a while. Then she and Phil interrogated the Pervezes, *père et fils*, in the presence of their respective at-torneys. Yesterday, Phil had told her when he'd driven up to Lake Arrowhead with Ezra, Mr. Pervez had disclosed the hiding place of his nephew's body—a shallow grave his son had dug in the yard of an abandoned property.

Early in the afternoon Espes handed them a new case: four children had burned to death at their home. The suspect was the mother, who had survived the fire. Neighbors had heard her threaten her ex-husband, the children's father, be-cause he'd left her.

"Something else you should know, Drake," the lieutenant told her when she stood to leave his office. He looked somber. "I just got word that Raymond Brock is out."

She stared at him stupidly. "Out? The judge gave him life without parole."

"It's Rampart. The witness who testified against him admitted he'd been bought in another case by one of the officers under investigation. So Brock's attorney got the D.A. to throw out the testimony against Brock, too. I thought you should know," he repeated.

Brock had threatened to kill her. She was shaken by the news of his release but told herself convicts were released all the time and rarely carried out their threats. It would be dumb of Brock to make a move against her. Still . . .

At her desk she phoned her father's office. "How are you feeling?" she asked when he was on the line.

"Steady as a rock. Is everything okay?"

She could hear the anxiety in his voice. "Everything's fine. I just called to say hi. I love you, Dad." Hilda was right. Better an omelette than no egg at all.

"I love you, too, sweetheart." His voice was husky. "I'm glad you called. So tell me what's going on. . . ."

If her face healed reasonably by Sunday, she would drive down to La Jolla, she decided after she hung up the phone. If not, it was less than two weeks to Thanksgiving, when they would all be together. Frances, Arthur, Helen, Neil, Matthew, and herself. Not Ezra—not this year, anyway.

She didn't delude herself. Hers wasn't an easy family, and there would be problems. But she thought about the photo on Ronnie Bushnell's office credenza, about Alex Velasquez, about Mrs. Pervez mourning a murdered daughter and nephew and the husband and son who had killed them, about Gideon Meissner sitting shiva for a son he wasn't sure was his. And she thanked God for many things.

For her life, and her family, for having bestowed every goodness upon her. For the warning of the rainbow, and the promise.